THE STOLEN PRINCE
OF CLOUDBURST

To Michael and Jane
For excellence in friendship

This is an Arthur A. Levine book
Published by Levine Querido

LEVINE QUERIDO

www.levinequerido.com • info@levinequerido.com

Levine Querido is distributed by Chronicle Books

Originally published by Allen & Unwin as
The Stolen Prince of Cloudburst
in September 2020

Library of Congress Control Number: 2020912347
ISBN: 978-1-64614-076-3

Printed and bound in China

MIX
Paper from
responsible sources
FSC™ C144853

Published March 2021

First Printing

The STOLEN PRINCE *of* CLOUDBURST

by

JACLYN MORIARTY

LQ

LEVINE QUERIDO

MONTCLAIR · AMSTERDAM · NEW YORK

PART

1

THE STOLEN PRINCE OF CLOUDBURST

A Narrative Account

by

ESTHER METTLESTONE-STARANISE,
GRADE 6

1

LONG AGO, FAR away, on a damp and sniffly day—

This happened.

A little prince, not yet two years old, played upon the shore.

"Hoopla!" said his nanny, and the boy leapt over a frothy wave. Nanny and boy giggled.

"Hoopla!" the nanny repeated, and again the tiny boy leapt. He wore a little romper suit and his name—*Alejandro*—was embroidered on the collar. His little feet were bare, for the nanny had removed his shoes.

If you are wondering where the shoes were, well, I think they were probably just off to the side somewhere, on the sand.

"Again!" said little Alejandro.

"Hoopla!" the nanny obliged.

The child leapt.

This could have gone on for hours, days—maybe even years! Well, perhaps not years, they'd have gotten hungry—but the nanny's gentleman friend happened to stroll by along the boardwalk. He spotted the pair on the beach.

"Ahoy there!" called the gentleman friend.

The nanny straightened, raised her hand to wave, and that was all the time it took.

A Water Sprite burst from the waves and stole the child.

The nanny saw him. She felt a *whoosh*, a splash, turned at once and saw. The gentleman friend up on the boardwalk, he saw too.

The Water Sprite had broad shoulders. He gathered Alejandro into his arms, leapt into the waves, and swam away. "Right before my eyes!" said the nanny. "I chased him! Into the waves, I dove! Ruined my good pinafore! But the Water Sprite—and darling Alejandro—were gone!"

By the way, all this happened in the town of Spindrift, in the Kingdom of Storms, about ten years ago. Ordinarily, the Royal Family of Storms live in the city of Cloudburst, but they were on holiday by the sea.

Everyone searched the sea for the prince, even the lighthouse keeper: his lighthouse beam swept back and forth like a duster on the sideboard.

King Jakob and Queen Anita were distraught. Well, of course they were.

(They were the little boy's parents, if you haven't figured that out.)

They were also bewildered.

"Why should a Water Sprite steal a child?" they asked each other, over and over. "Water Sprites don't steal children!"

Meanwhile, the Water Sprite was asking himself the same question.

His name was Caprito, and he had swum far out to sea, little Alejandro babbling beneath his arm, and then paused, treading water. Carefully, he'd placed the little prince on an ocean lily.

Then he had swum down to his home beneath the sea, and—

"What have I *done*?" he asked himself. "Why did I steal a child?"

For it was true that Water Sprites *do not* steal children. Not ordinarily, they don't.

The Water Sprite swam directly to his own king, King Khalid, and confessed.

"You stole a child?" cried King Khalid. "Well, give him back at once!"

"I can't," replied Caprito. "I placed him on an ocean lily."

(Ocean lilies, in case you don't know, are just like the water lilies you see on ponds, only bigger and stronger. They spread themselves over the surface of the ocean like floating picnic blankets.) (That was a helpful aside.)

"Then fetch him back from the ocean lily!" ordered King Khalid, exasperated. "At once!"

Caprito thought that was genius, and he streaked through the water to the place where the ocean lily had been.

But it was gone.

And so was the child.

Caprito returned to his king. *"Gone,"* he said.

The Water Sprite king was very upset. He got stuck on the issue of *why* Caprito had stolen the child in the first place.

"Why would you *do* such a thing?" the king complained.

"I cannot say," Caprito replied.

"Yes, you can," the king snapped. "Say!"

But Caprito sadly shook his head. "I cannot say," he said, "because I do not know."

Eventually, King Khalid summonsed a shore's-edge meeting with King Jakob and Queen Anita. Caprito confessed all.

It was a heated meeting, as you can imagine.

Everybody asked the Water Sprite why he had done this: King Jakob, Queen Anita, constables, guards, the nanny, the nanny's gentleman friend. But Caprito's answer was always the same:

"I cannot say."

And then, more quietly: "I cannot say because I *do not know.*"

Caprito wept and apologized, begging forgiveness.

The king and queen did not much feel like forgiving him.

However, they did not throw him in a dungeon or declare war on the Water Sprite Kingdom, for they believed his regret and confusion.

While many thought the prince must have fallen from the ocean lily into the sea and drowned, others said that the lily could have floated across the Kingdoms and Empires, washing ashore in a distant land.

And so the search for little Alejandro continued, year after year, and King Jakob and Queen Anita grew ever sadder, sorrier, thinner, and older. Sometimes they sat side by side on the beach, staring at the waves, taking turns with the spyglass, looking for their lost little prince.

2

MEANWHILE, WHAT OF the little prince?

This is what.

He floated about on the ocean lily awhile. Perhaps he fell asleep? I do not know. I was not there. What I do know is this: the currents carried the ocean lily a fair distance, but it did not wash up on a shore.

Instead, pirates spied the child and scooped him aboard their ship. They did not know he was a prince, of course, or they'd surely have demanded a mountain of gold for his return. They're all about mountains of gold, pirates.

All they knew was that his name was Alejandro, for that was embroidered on his collar.

The pirates thought him as cute as a baby otter, gave him a parrot to play with, and let him splash about with dolphins now and then.

As Alejandro grew older, however, they began teaching him

things: how to fight with a sword, for instance, or to shoot with a bow and arrow, and how to load and fire a musketoon.

He excelled at these, and the pirates cheered and congratulated themselves on their forethought in fishing him out of the waves.

But then?

When he was eleven years old?

Well, they sat him down and told him that now he must become a pirate.

"And what must I do as a pirate?" Alejandro inquired.

"You must steal gold and treasure from other ships!" one pirate exclaimed, very excited to tell him. (They loved their work.)

"Use the sword, the arrow, and the musketoon to kill any who try to stop you!" a second cried.

"Set the ships alight and watch them sink!" all the other pirates bellowed.

Alejandro was eleven, as I said, and very shocked to find out that *this* was how his pirate friends spent their days. How they "earned a crust," as they put it. (They'd kept him belowdecks while they pirated up until now.)

He had a golden heart and did not *want* to steal, destroy, and kill!

The pirates were furious.

"Not angry so much as disappointed," one of them said, which hurt Alejandro's feelings, but then the others said, "Not *angry*? Why, I'm angry enough to rip apart a shark with my bare teeth! I'm furious! Livid!"

They *were* also very disappointed. "All the *work* we put into bringing him up!" they complained. "This is how he repays us?" And they squabbled about who had been too soft, so that he was raised to be *nice*. A milksop.

They began to beat him then, and to inflict punishments upon him, trying to make up for years of kindness. Trying to un-milksop him.

"We will make a pirate of you yet!" they swore.

Poor Alejandro. He was very unhappy.

He used his wits and cunning, and he escaped from the pirate ship!

They recaptured him.

He escaped again!

Upon the shore, he made friends with a girl his own age named Bronte Mettlestone, who was an adventurer. She invited him to live, *happily ever after*, with her family in faraway Gainsleigh.

3

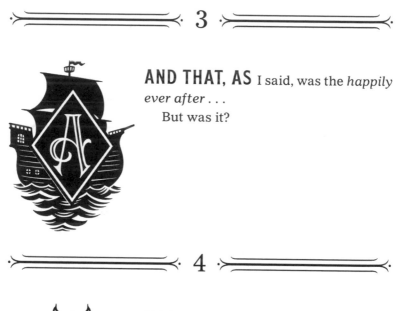

AND THAT, AS I said, was the *happily ever after . . .*

But was it?

4

NO!

We are forgetting the parents!

One night, Alejandro dreamed that his long-lost parents were sad.

The dream told him to have an adventure to find out who those parents were. (He'd forgotten.)

The story of this adventure is too long to put here, especially as it's nearly midnight and my candle is almost completely burnt down—and the other girls in the dormitory are snoring beneath their feather quilts.

So I will only say this: he *did* find his parents!

And he returned home to Cloudburst in the Kingdom of Storms to be reunited with King Jakob and Queen Anita! As we speak, they are planning an enormous party to officially welcome him.

5

AND *THAT* IS the end of the story.

(One last thing. Guess what? The girl in the story named Bronte Mettlestone? The adventurer?

She's my cousin!!!

My sisters and I have even *met* Alejandro, the Stolen Prince of Cloudburst!!!

It's true that we only met him for a short and busy time two years ago, so he might not remember us. But I remember him.)

THE END

Esther, yes, I have read much of this story, or its basic facts, anyway, in the newspapers. You have not made them more interesting here. Worse, you have tried to put yourself in the story. You might be related to some of these interesting people, but that does not make you interesting.
Do not put yourself in stories where you do not belong.

Do not tell fibs. You are very far indeed from Cloudburst, and highly unlikely ever to so much as glimpse the Stolen Prince.

Also, do not begin sentences with the word "And" or "But." Do not break your sentences and paragraphs into pieces; it makes your tale very disjointed. Do not boast by saying that your asides are "helpful"—that is not becoming.

I see that you stayed up past midnight to do your homework. Dreadful behavior. DEMERIT. As this is your third demerit, please attend detention on Friday evening as punishment.

Finally, you began this story with the words "Long ago, far away, on a damp and sniffly day." Please write out the following, 100 times:

A DAY CANNOT BE "SNIFFLY."

C—

PART

2

CHAPTER 1

A DAY *CAN* be sniffly, you know. My father told me it could.

He had a cold last summer. Father, I mean. He had a cold and sniffles the day I overheard the telephone conversation.

I was in the kitchen at home, underneath the table with a glass of lemonade. (That's why I was underneath the table—the lemonade. It was meant for Mother's work colleagues, *not for you girls, I do not want to see you drink a drop of that!* So I was very kindly hiding, to save Mother from seeing me drink a whole glassful of drops.)

I was also reading *Dragon Detective: The Shadow in the Wind*, a new novel by my favorite author in all the Kingdoms and Empires, G. A. Thunderstrike. It was 9:42 A.M., and I was happy.

When the telephone rang, I quickly pulled my legs in and curled them underneath me. I held myself still and waited.

Father's footsteps approached. Slower, more considering, than Mother's.

I relaxed. If Father caught me drinking lemonade under the table, he'd only murmur, "Lemonade! Nice one! Where is it?" and pour himself a glass too, keeping an eye out for Mother.

Father's slippers shuffled by the table. He blew his nose. It made a sound like a panicking cow. He picked up the phone.

"Morning," he said, a bit croaky.

The sound of a distant voice.

"Gordon!" exclaimed Father, his voice gathering strength. "How's the summer treating you?"

Gordon is one of Father's research assistants. Father teaches history at Clybourne University, although mostly he doesn't teach at all, he travels about collecting information and stories for his books. His research assistants do the teaching.

More chittering from Gordon's distant voice.

"Steady on," Father said.

More chittering.

"But if you—"

Chitter, chitter.

Father laughed. "Well, that sounds just like Jonathan J. Lanyard, of course, but—"

The volume of the chittering rose. I still couldn't make out the actual words.

Father blew his nose again. "Sorry," he said, "did I hear you say—?"

Chitter.

Chitter.

. . .

Chitter.

Father had been silent so long that I peeked out from under the table to check he hadn't fallen asleep.

He was leaning up against the kitchen sink, holding the telephone to his ear. In his other hand he held his handkerchief, and he was twisting this between his fingers. His cheeks and nose were bright pink from his cold, and his eyes seemed a strange mix of amused and irritated.

And then a curious thing happened.

He straightened up.

He pressed the telephone closer to his ear.

He crushed the handkerchief and shoved it into the pocket of his robe.

"Gordon," he said, interrupting a rush of chitter. "Gordon, listen. This is important. The water around this orange patch you keep on about—is it a constant temperature or does it vary?"

Chitter.

Father listened.

Right before my eyes, the pink in his cheeks and nose faded. His whole face turned the grayish white of a late winter storm.

"Right," he said. "I'll be there tonight." He hung up the telephone.

He stood very still, facing the kitchen tap, for a long moment. Then, abruptly, he swung around, crouched down, and looked at me under the table.

"Hello, Father," I said.

"Esther," he replied steadily. "How long have you been there?"

"Not long."

"The whole time, then."

I nodded.

"And how much of that did you hear?"

"Not a word."

"So, everything, then." He studied me a moment. "Do me a favor?"

"Sure!"

"Forget what you just overheard?"

"Well, I'll try," I said doubtfully. "But you know, if you ask somebody to forget something, they're more likely to *remember* it?"

Father nodded. "A fair point. Just don't repeat it to anyone, then," he said. "It's probably nothing, but—still, keep it to yourself, Esther. Promise?"

I promised. There didn't seem much in what I'd overheard to make an interesting tale anyway—just *chitter, chitter* and so on—so it was an easy promise to make.

Father glanced with interest at my lemonade and I guessed that he was about to say, "Nice one! Where is it?" but then his face paled again, and he straightened up and hurried from the room.

There was a squabble with Mother then, something to do with Father being "very foolish indeed! Dangerous beyond words! Don't even think about leaving this house! And you, with a *cold*!"

And so on.

Meanwhile, Mother's work colleagues were filing into the house ready to have meetings. These colleagues listened avidly to the argument between my parents, while pretending to be busy drinking lemonade.

That afternoon, we saw Father off in the coach.

My sisters and I chased it as far as we could up the road, waving madly, while Father craned his neck to wave back. Mother stood perfectly still.

CHAPTER 2

TWO WEEKS LATER, we returned to the coach station, this time so that my sisters and I could journey back to Katherine Valley Boarding School.

"Off you go then," Mother called, as the sun, shining like a diamond, lit up the buttons of her coat and the buckles on her satchel.

Imogen, Astrid, and I were in the back of the coach, our suitcases propped between our knees. Mother stood outside the coach. She had already made us recite how you recognize each of the major Shadow Mages, pretended not to hear us when we reminded her that there are never Shadow Mages in the mountains, given each of us a small tin of chocolate fudge, insisted that we win any competition we entered at school, waved twice, and that was enough farewelling for her, I suppose, because she banged on the side and called through the open window: "Off you go then!"

We stared at her. Honestly, there was not much off-you-going we could do. That was up to the driver, surely, and he was outside, chatting with some pals, eating a pastry, and offering water to the horses.

Passengers in the other seats were also staring at our mother with puzzled expressions.

"Off you go then," Mother repeated, "funny things," and she banged the side of the coach three times: *thwack, thwack, THWACK!*

The third *thwack* was so hard that it flung Mother herself back a step, and she stumbled, tripped, and landed on her bottom on the cobblestones.

Imogen, Astrid, and I hopped up from our seats and pressed our noses to the windows.

"Are you all right, Mother?" Astrid called.

Mother sat perfectly still, trying to appear as though tripping onto her bottom was exactly what she'd planned. But then she noticed that her satchel had landed upside down, with papers spilling out of it, and she gave up appearing nonchalant. She sprang to her feet and hurried to collect the papers—just as a gust of wind blew across the square and scattered them.

"Do you need any help?" I shouted.

"Hush, Imogen," Mother snapped. "Or who is that? Astrid?"

"It's me," I said. "Esther. The middle daughter."

But the wind was sending papers skittering this way and that, and Mother was busy chasing them. An envelope flew across the cobblestones and landed just by the coach wheel.

"There's one here!" I yelled.

At that moment, the driver crumpled his paper bag, shook his pals' hands, and climbed up to his seat.

"All aboard!" he boomed.

"You'd better hurry and grab this letter, Mother, before it gets run over!" I called.

Mother zipped forward and snatched up the envelope. As she did so, I caught a glimpse of block letters on its front:

ESTHER METTLESTONE-STARANISE
DIME HOUSE, FURRIER LANE,
BLUE CHALET VILLAGE

"But that's *me*!" I cried. "*I'm* Esther Mettlestone-Staranise!"

Mother frowned at the letter. She gave a startled gasp, rummaged through her satchel, and drew out a small stack of additional envelopes.

"Here you go," she called, reaching up to the window and handing the stack through. "I saved these as a goodbye surprise for you."

"Away then!" boomed the coach driver, jiggling the reins.

Clip-clop, clip-clop, said the horses' hooves.

Mother stood back, satchel beneath her arm, and clasped her hands.

CHAPTER 3

MY SISTERS AND I settled back into our seats. All three of us looked at the stack of letters in my hands.

"She didn't plan to give them to you as a goodbye surprise," Imogen, my older sister, murmured.

"She forgot she had them," Astrid, my younger sister, agreed. "I bet she's been collecting them from the post office all summer, putting them into her satchel, and forgetting them."

"Who are they from?" Imogen asked. "Georgia and Hsiang?"

Georgia and Hsiang are my best friends at boarding school. I flicked through the envelopes. Four were from Georgia, five from Hsiang.

All summer long I'd been writing to my friends, wondering why they didn't reply. At one point, I'd sent them both postcards that said: *HELLO???*

I'd begun to worry that I'd offended them somehow, yet they'd been replying to me all along.

Well, soon I would arrive at boarding school, where I'd see my friends and hear their stories in person.

I tucked the envelopes into my suitcase and set them to the far side of my mind.

CHAPTER 4

ON THE FIRST day back at school, Principal Hortense always holds morning tea in the gardens.

It was already a quarter past ten when we arrived, and we hurried through the school. Other just-arrived girls were running along too, everybody looking shiny and sunny, the way people do after the summer break, and everybody calling, "Hello! Love the new haircut!" to each other. Things like that.

We hurried past the trophy cabinet and there were the gold medals my sisters and I had won in the Kingdom and Empires Poker Competition. (Our mother taught us poker before we learned to read.)

"When's the competition this year?" Astrid asked.

"Last two weeks of this term," I said. "We get to start our holiday early." We all grinned.

But actually I love my school. I hope that's not strange. There are things I *don't* like about it, of course, such as schoolwork and homework, rules and getting in trouble for breaking rules, which I do, fairly often—but let's say your heart has a *core*, like an apple core; well, right there amongst the seeds and chewy bits, I love my school.

So at this point, as we ran panting into the gardens, I felt like a kite that was sailing in a clear blue sky.

CHAPTER 5

 **I COULDN'T SEE** my best friends, Hsiang and Georgia, anywhere in the gardens, so I settled into a shady spot under the mulberry tree with a group of other Grade 6 girls. We ate orange-and-poppy-seed cake and chatted about our summers.

Meanwhile, something strange seemed to be happening.

It was like this. Look at these words:

The new teacher is an Ogre.

Now imagine that those words keep brushing up against you, as if a ghostly cat is wandering the garden, brushing its fur against bare legs, and then moving on.

That's what it was like.

The first time it happened, I said, "Did I just hear that? There's a new teacher this year? And it's an *Ogre*?"

The others giggled, as if I'd made a joke. They often laugh at me, even when I'm being serious.

But the words kept drifting by with the breeze.

After a while, the others stopped chatting about their holidays and began to ask: "Did somebody say there's a new teacher who's an *Ogre*?"

"It's *not* true," scoffed Katya Burla. "They'd *never* hire an Ogre. An Ogre wouldn't even fit through a classroom door!" (She's very scoffy, Katya.)

Hetty Rattlestone was nodding. "Our Aunt Cynthia saw an Ogre once. She said his arms and legs were like logs of firewood. He wanted to hire a rowboat, but the man said that his boats were too small for Ogres, sorry—so what did the Ogre do? He grabbed a rowboat, dragged it into the lake, hopped aboard—and it sank. Then the Ogre swam ashore and demanded his money back. Even though he'd never paid."

"Is Aunt Cynthia one of your *royal* relatives?" Zoe Fawnwell interjected.

Zoe is best friends with Hetty Rattlestone and her twin sister, Tatty. As far as I can tell, her main job as best friend is to remind everyone that the twins happen to have some royal relatives.

Hetty ignored Zoe's question, so Aunt Cynthia must not be a royal.

"Ogres have violent tempers," Tatty Rattlestone said. "Our mother was at a restaurant once when an Ogre who'd been wading in a swamp came tramping in, leaving mud and slime everywhere. The waiter asked him very politely to wipe his feet please, so the Ogre picked up the waiter and threw him through a window."

We were quiet, picturing the flying waiter and shattered glass.

"Ogres only live in three different regions," Katya put in. As well as being scoffy, she's excellent at geography. And at all the other school subjects. "The three regions are far from here." She ticked them off on her fingers. "Horseshoe Island off the coast of the Kingdom of Storms. The Fangaral Crescents. And Fox Valley in the Empire of Broken Leaves."

"So if the new teacher is from one of those places, we'll know they're an Ogre," Zoe Fawnwell breathed.

"We'd know anyway just by *looking* at them," Hetty said sharply.

DONG! DING! DONG!

That was the sound of a bell being struck.

Principal Hortense was standing very tall in the arbor, striking the bell and beaming around at us. Which meant she was about to speak.

We all turned as one to hear.

CHAPTER 6

"GIRLS! WHAT A *delight* to see you back again!" Principal Hortense gave a general wave and then began offering special little waves to individual girls. Her hand became like an excited butterfly jumping from flower to flower. Finally, the butterfly grew tired and settled down.

"Such a delight!" she continued. "Why, I was just saying to Mustafa yesterday, I said: *Mustafa, the place is too quiet.* And do you know what Mustafa replied?"

We all looked at Mustafa, the gardener. His cheeks bulged with cake. When he noticed us staring, he began to chew very quickly. I saw him swallow.

Principal Hortense continued. "He said: *Too quiet? No. Not really.*"

Everyone laughed. Mustafa relaxed and took another bite of cake. He is famous for finding us students annoying. He'd prefer to take care of the grounds in peace.

"I trust you've caught up on your summer stories by now, girls—" Principal Hortense began.

"No. Not really," a Grade 8 girl joked. Or not-joked, because we'd hardly *begun* to catch up. I hadn't even *seen* Georgia and Hsiang yet.

Principal Hortense chortled. "Well, classes don't start until tomorrow, so plenty of time! At any rate . . ."

Then she made her Welcome Back speech.

"There are thirteen weeks in this term," she said. "Wait now, is it thirteen or twenty-five?" She consulted with the closest teacher, who said it was definitely thirteen. "Shame. Twenty-five sounds fun. And then two weeks of holidays?"

"Yes," everyone agreed.

I won't tell you everything she said, mainly because I don't know. I always drift off when teachers talk. They say many pointless things.

"As usual, I will take girls to town for afternoon tea on their birthdays. You will work *very* hard, and you will *all* behave with respect and . . ."

Do you see what I mean? Pointless.

I did tune in when she said: "Bad news! Matron is away this year! She's traveling the Northern Climes! But good news! We have a new nurse! Nurse Sydelle!"

It *was* bad news that Matron was away. She's part-Faery, takes care of us when we're ill, and bakes treats. I wouldn't know whether this Nurse Sydelle was "good news" or not until I'd met her.

Eventually Principal Hortense listed our teachers, starting at the top—Grade 8—and working her way down.

My sister Imogen's teacher (Grade 7) turned out to be Mr. Dar-Healey. He's a lively man who does tumbles in the air whenever a child gives a correct answer.

Principal Hortense skipped over Grade 6 and went straight to Grade 5.

Strange, I thought. *She's forgotten how to count.* But it was backward counting, so maybe she found that trickier.

My sister Astrid's teacher (Grade 4) turned out to be Ms. Saji. Gentle Ms. Saji only joined the school last year.

When Principal Hortense reached the Kindergarten teacher and stopped, Hetty Rattlestone sang out: "You've forgotten Grade Six!"

"Observant, Hetty!" Principal Hortense twinkled. "But *wrong*! I did not *forget* Grade 6, I *saved* it on purpose! It's the most exciting news! Are you ready?"

We agreed that we were ready.

"Professor Jonston has retired! So we have a *new teacher at Katherine Valley Boarding School!*"

I was suddenly anxious. The ghost cat was slinking around my legs now, twirling between my ankles.

Principal Hortense grinned so hugely you could see where her teeth grew from her gums. "A teacher from *far, far* away!"

The ghost cat froze.

"Her name is Mrs. Pollock! She's arriving tomorrow! And she's from—now just a moment, what was the place called? Cattlefork? Donkeyslipper? Guess-what-Isles? No. It's . . ."

A pause. "What?" various girls called.

"That's right. She's from Horseshoe Island off the coast of the Kingdom of Storms!"

The ghost cat leapt into the air and sank its claws into my throat.

CHAPTER 7

THERE WASN'T *REALLY* any ghost cat, to be clear. That's just what it felt like.

After that, I began to feel pale and important, as if I'd just been diagnosed with a rare and serious illness. The other girls in my grade felt similarly, I think, and we gave each other wild-eyed glances. *Our teacher is an Ogre!*

Whispers and murmurs flew between us. "She *must* be an Ogre!" "We don't know for *sure*?" "But she comes from Horse-shoe Island!" "Does nobody else live there except Ogres?" "Nobody."

"It's all right," Hetty and Tatty announced after a quick twin conference. "We're going to the office to send an urgent message to our mother. She'll never allow us to have an Ogre for a teacher. She'll call on some of our *relatives* to help too."

"You mean your *royal* relatives?" Zoe Fawnwell put in obligingly.

"Oh, yes," the twins said, as if they'd forgotten for a moment. "Them."

* * *

That evening, we were in the dormitories, unpacking our suitcases.

My dormitory this year had six residents, including me (obviously) along with

> * Katya Burla (as well as being scoffy and good at geog-
> raphy and all other subjects, Katya has wild curls,

loves the color purple, and coaches the junior chess team),

* Dot Pecorino (a tiny, shy girl),

* Hetty Rattlestone,

* Tatty Rattlestone (the twins—you remember them), and

* a new girl, who had not yet arrived.

The new girl's bed was to the right of mine. A tartan suitcase sat on it, with a label that said:

Autumn Hillside

New girls are rare at Katherine Valley, and I felt shimmery reading that label.

Autumn Hillside. A name like a whisper or a song.

Or like the side of a hill in the autumn, I suppose.

I was very keen to make friends with this new girl. If I couldn't have a name like Autumn's, at least I could be friends with her. I felt panicky that the Rattlestones would get in first, and I kept looking over my shoulder as I unpacked to check that Autumn wasn't standing awkwardly in the doorway. The moment I saw her I'd pounce. "Oh, hello," I would say, "you must be the new girl! Welcome!"

Or something more interesting than that.

Hetty and Tatty were unpacking very noisily. They were in a rage about the fact that their best friend, Zoe Fawnwell, was not in our dorm.

"It's all right, we already *know* you've got lots of royal relatives," I muttered.

Katya giggled. Dot blinked.

(The twins also annoy me because their name sounds like ours. Rattlestone. Mettlestone. See? Imogen says *their* name rattles around like a bunch of old stones in a suitcase, whereas *ours* is solid, like the gateway to a castle. Which helps.)

We would all have to sign a petition, the twins were insisting, demanding that Zoe join our dorm.

"If we're going to petition for Zoe to join, we should petition for Hsiang and Georgia too," I pointed out.

The twins, who were placing their silk dresses onto hangers in one of the wardrobes, both turned around and burst out laughing. "Why would we do that? Hsiang and Georgia aren't *our* friends."

Now, there are two wardrobes in each dorm and each is split up into three sections. One section per girl. But as the twins laughed alongside the open wardrobe door, it became clear to the rest of us that they'd been using all three segments of that wardrobe.

"Oh, hey," Katya said. "You're accidentally using the whole thing."

"Not an accident," Hetty said, suddenly serious.

"We *always* use three sections," Tatty explained.

"You see, Mother says that twins need *more* than double what a single child needs."

"That's the loopiest thing I ever heard," Katya scoffed. (Sometimes I like it when Katya scoffs.)

"We *always* do this," Hetty said soothingly, as if to settle a group of fretful toddlers. She continued hanging dresses in the third segment.

"Yes, every year," Tatty agreed. "Nobody's ever had a problem with it before. Usually Zoe just keeps her clothes in her suitcase, but that's because she's a true friend."

Hetty sighed. "Which is why it's so unfair that we're without Zoe. Imagine if we also had to give up our wardrobe space? Two of you will have to share. Perhaps Dot Pecorino could share with the new girl? What's the new girl's name?"

"Autumn Hillside," said a voice.

And there she was, standing in the doorway: the new girl.

CHAPTER 8

I'D MISSED MY chance to pounce.

I mean, I still could have pounced, but everyone was staring and it would have looked obvious.

Autumn Hillside was slender, tall, and had beautiful hair. Dark as night it was, and hanging loose and free like laundry on the line, all the way to her waist. Her eyes were like crescent moons.

(I don't mean they were up in the sky, I just mean her eyes were shaped like fine curves.)

These eyes were gazing around the dormitory, from the polished oak floorboards to the rugs to the bookcase to the corkboard where we pin up sketches and photographs.

She seemed very calm, standing there gazing at the furniture while five girls stared.

"Where are our manners?" Hetty cried suddenly, scuttling forward and shaking the new girl's hand. "Welcome! Autumn, did you say? What a *fascinating* name! My name is Hetty, and this is my twin, Tatty. Rather less exotic, I'm afraid. Come in, Autumn! Do you see that bed there? It's yours!"

"Have a bounce on it," Tatty recommended. "They're lovely and bouncy."

So.

It seemed the twins had pounced. I'd been a fool to worry about looking obvious.

But Autumn, after shaking the twins' hands politely, remained standing in the doorway gazing around. She smiled at me.

She smiled at me! I was very happy.

At last she stepped into the room.

"I keep hearing about an Ogre teacher," she said. "The word *Ogre* seems to be floating down corridors."

"Like a cat brushing up against your legs," I suggested.

"Like *what*?" scoffed Katya.

Dot Pecorino gave me a baffled look.

"Don't worry about her," Tatty Rattlestone said. "That's just Esther. She's a bit strange. When everyone else runs *inside* to avoid a thunderstorm, Esther runs *outside*."

"Without even an umbrella," Hetty added. "She does it all the time."

But Autumn was nodding at me. "Yes," she said. "It's exactly like a cat."

The twins frowned briefly, then seemed to decide Autumn was joking and punched her arm in a friendly way.

"The thing is," Tatty explained, "we think our teacher this year is an Ogre."

"Because she comes from Horseshoe Island," Hetty put in. "And only Ogres live there."

The new girl looked toward a window. "Anyone want to help me tie some sheets together so we can escape?"

Everybody laughed.

Oh, I loved her.

Autumn Hillside.

So funny and sensible.

I would make friends with her. Hsiang, Georgia, Autumn, and I would become a gang of four. What would our gang do? Maybe tour the Kingdoms and Empires playing music? (Georgia is musically gifted, and I'm sure I could learn an instrument if I put my mind to it.) Or playing sports? (Hsiang is an excellent cricketer, and I can—well, I can keep score okay when I concentrate.)

Better: have adventures! I've always wanted one of those—an adventure.

Anyway, plenty of time to decide. I tuned back into the conversation.

"I mean, an Ogre is a *Shadow Mage*," Hetty was saying. "It should be illegal for a school to employ a Shadow Mage!"

I shook my head. "Ogres are not Shadow Mages," I said. "They're not magical, they're just huge and bad-tempered. And they have—"

"Esther is obsessed with magic," Tatty interrupted, shaking her head as if I was a tiresome child with a stamp collection. "It's magic, magic, magic with her, Autumn. And she wants to be a Spellbinder so badly she spends most of her time hoping her toenails will turn blue!"

"You do?" Autumn asked me, interested.

"Not *most* of my time," I said, annoyed. Although, actually, it was a lot of the time. "But listen, the reason people get confused about Ogres is that they have a long history of *helping* Shadow Mages. So they've picked up a few shadow powers."

Our new teacher, an Ogre, could have shadow powers. A thread of fear wound slowly through the room.

"It's all right." Tatty looped an arm through Autumn's. "Our mother is sure to enlist the help of our . . . relatives."

She and Hetty looked around the room significantly, but nobody jumped in to inform Autumn that these were *royal* relatives. The twins sighed.

"Let's go now," Tatty said, "and see if Mother's replied."

"Oh, yes." Hetty took Autumn's other arm. "Let's."

Katya and Dot followed, but I decided to stay. I wanted to check the other Grade 6 dorms for Georgia and Hsiang.

CHAPTER 9

THE FIRST DORMITORY I checked was empty. They must have finished unpacking already.

The second had its own new girl.

We almost never get new people so it was remarkable to have two in one grade. I could only catch glimpses of her from the doorway, because the others had crowded around her. She was sitting cross-legged on a bed, holding an open box of chocolates. Hands kept reaching into the box. She must have told them to help themselves.

She had short, shaggy hair, very bright eyes, and a nose like a snail shell.

(I don't mean her nose was brown and would crunch if you stepped on it. Or that it had a slug-like creature living in it. Just, her nose was a cute little round shape.)

This new girl was talking and the others seemed transfixed.

I decided I'd make friends with her too: a challenge, as she was already popular, what with the chocolates, the transfixing, and the nose.

Around then, I heard slow footsteps climbing the staircase. It was Hetty, Tatty, Katya, and Dot, and I could tell by their mournful pace that they hadn't had any luck.

"Nothing from Mother yet," Hetty told me.

Tatty began thudding her forehead against the corridor wall. The twins can be very dramatic.

Thud, thud, thud, thud.

"Where's Autumn?" I asked, remembering her suddenly. I'd

have to be careful not to forget her when she became a best friend.

"Oh, the garden or something," Hetty said, listlessly.

"Wanted to explore on her own," Tatty added, irritably.

Well, that was something. They'd lost control of Autumn.

"What's going on in there?" Katya asked, peering into the open doorway of the dorm.

"Another new girl," I said.

"*Another* one?" cried Hetty. "Why didn't you say?"

Hetty and Tatty flew into the room to join the crowd.

CHAPTER 10

HSIANG AND GEORGIA were not at Games-by-the-Pond that afternoon. Nor were they at the Welcome Back Banquet that night.

We have to sit with our grades for meals, so I didn't see my sisters again until the recreation room that night.

Monday evenings, we practice poker. There's a small table by the window where we play.

As she dealt the cards, Imogen said: "Looks like you've got an Ogre for your teacher, Esther!"

"Yes!" Astrid exclaimed.

They both beamed.

Beamed.

Not worried. Not sorry for me. But *beaming.*

"Nothing *to* worry about," Imogen declared. "If this Mrs. Pollock is mean to you, just come find me and I'll take care of her."

She's such a confident person, Imogen, you sometimes forget that she's a thirteen-year-old girl and would not be able to "take care of" an Ogre. It's true that she has reached level 16 in kickboxing classes, which is three levels higher than her kickboxing master himself. (Mother taught us all the basics of kickboxing and Imogen decided to enroll in summer classes.) But Imogen is not the size of a small mountain. She's not an undercover assassin.

"An *Ogre!*" Astrid repeated, eyes shining like polished silver. "I mean, you already write brilliant stories, Esther, and you'll have great new subject matter."

"You'll be able to write a book," Imogen agreed, "called *My Teacher, the Ogre.*"

I fanned out my cards, thinking that, whatever Mrs.-Pollock-the-Ogre was like, Georgia, Hsiang, and I would face her together. Then I flicked a card with my fingernail and remembered that Georgia and Hsiang were still not back.

"They must both be having an extra-long holiday somewhere," Imogen suggested.

"Have you opened their letters yet?" Astrid asked. "They probably explain their lateness in their letters."

Which is why, that night, when we were all in bed and reading by lamplight, I opened Hsiang's and Georgia's letters.

Now, you might have already guessed this. I don't know why I didn't. The two new girls should have been a clue.

Actually, I think that in a way I *did* guess, I just didn't want to believe it. Uneasiness had been swarming around my shoulders all day, but I'd put that down to news of the Ogre.

I won't tell you everything my friends' letters said, just the important part.

Here it is.

They'd left the school.

Georgia's letters said she'd transferred to a music conservatory, to focus on her flute. (Playing it, I mean. Not sitting and staring at it.)

Hsiang's letters announced she was going to a sports academy, where she'd won a cricket scholarship.

They both said they were very sorry to be leaving, and that they would miss me.

I felt as if I'd pulled out a drawer, really *wrenched* it, in a rush to find socks, say, and it had toppled all the way out and crashed to the floor, hitting my toes. There should be a little hinge or catch to prevent that happening, shouldn't there?

I think there usually *is* one in a chest of drawers, actually.

But not in life.

CHAPTER 11

I HAD THE dream for the first time that night.

You don't know what I mean when I say "the dream," do you? That's only because I haven't told you yet. Don't worry, I'm telling you now.

It's just a short dream.

Father always wants to know about our dreams. "And then what?" he says excitedly. "No! What are the chances? Okay, brilliant, and then what?" As if it really happened. And he seems disappointed when the dream ends, or when you can't explain what happened next. Dreams just fade into other, unrelated dreams sometimes, don't they? It's nobody's fault.

Father especially likes it when he himself features in the dream. He chuckles, very pleased about whatever "dream Father" has said or done. "*Did* he now?" he says. "Well, *he* sounds a clever chap."

Mother listens to our dreams in a distressed sort of way and then halfway through says, "Wait a minute, is this a *dream*? Oh, you funny thing, don't go telling me *dreams*!" And then she hurries off to put away the laundry.

Anyhow, if you're the sort of person who hurries away with the laundry when someone starts telling you a dream, don't worry. This one, as I said, is very short.

All that happens is this.

I'm lying on my back on a rug, looking up at a cloudy sky. It begins to rain.

That's it.

I'm lying on a rug. It starts to rain. I wake up.

You are probably wondering why I'm even telling you about this dream.

It's because I dreamed it maybe 250 times in the last year.

And because every time I woke from the dream, I felt as if an elephant was standing on my chest, splintering my bones.

CHAPTER 12

THAT FIRST NIGHT, I screamed.

Only, the elephant had crushed all the voice out of my voice box, so the scream was a tiny *ee!*—like the sound Elves make when they're annoyed.

"*Ee!*" I said, and I leapt up in bed, clutching at the sheets. As if the sheets were going to be any help. (They weren't.)

I felt like a person with wild eyes and disheveled hair.

I looked around for Imogen or Astrid, but of course my sisters weren't there, and I looked for Georgia or Hsiang, and of course *they* weren't there.

The other girls were dark shadows sleeping.

I needed to wake somebody. But who? Quickly, I ran through the options.

The Rattlestone twins—waking them would be like waking a pair of silky kittens. They'd sulk, purr at each other, admire themselves in the mirror, and go back to sleep.

Autumn Hillside—still a stranger. I felt too shy to wake her.

Dot Pecorino—so tiny and quiet I hardly knew who she was. Which made her a stranger too.

Katya—ha, imagine how loudly she'd scoff if I woke her and said: "Katya, I just dreamed that it rained."

In the end, I didn't wake anybody.

I got out of bed and staggered to the door.

That embarrassed me, the staggering. I knew I was all right, really, and that it was just a dream, and not even a scary one. Even if you disliked rain, you still wouldn't call that a nightmare. And here's the strange thing: I *love* rain!

I crept out into the corridor.

There is always one lamp burning in case you need to go to the bathroom, but I walked in the opposite direction. A long, narrow window overlooks the gardens at the back of the building.

Moonlight swayed mistily across the lawns. It shimmered in the pond and glanced against the windows of the Old Schoolhouse, a huge building at the back of the gardens. It was shut up years ago and has been empty ever since. There's never anybody in it.

Except for now.

I blinked.

A light had just flashed in one of the windows. Next, a shadow flitted.

I pressed my forehead to the glass and peered more closely.

There it went again—passing the next window. A pinprick of light, like a candle flame, followed by a shadow.

Flit. Flit (candle flame). *Whoosh* (shadow).

Ghosts.

My heart lit up like fireworks.

Maybe I had an Ogre for a teacher, and maybe my best friends had left the school, and maybe I'd just had a strange dream about rain—*but there were ghosts in the Old Schoolhouse.*

I smiled and returned to bed, very happy.

CHAPTER 13

EXCEPT THAT THERE *weren't* any ghosts in the Old Schoolhouse.

I found this out the next morning.

At breakfast, all of us Grade 6 girls were very solemn about our first day of classes with Mrs. Pollock, the Ogre. Some people were full of gloomy predictions, saying things like, "If I don't make it through the day, please make sure the ceramic cow I got for my birthday goes to my brother. *Not* my sister. She broke my locket."

Others tried to be positive. Autumn Hillside said, "Maybe she won't be so bad?"

The twins, seated either side of her, studied her.

"Yes," Hetty said. "Good attitude."

"I mean," Tatty added. "She's not a Shadow Mage. She's not a *Whisperer*."

Autumn Hillside stirred a cube of sugar into her tea and nodded. "Yes, she's not a Whisperer."

Then Principal Hortense stood up and said: "Girls! I forgot to mention something important yesterday! You know the Old Schoolhouse out the back?"

We all nodded. A thrilling chill ran down my spine. She was going to tell us that it was haunted! And command us to stay away!

I wouldn't. I'd have adventures with ghosts.

"Well," she continued, "it was refurbished over the summer and is now a convention center. Please respect the privacy of people staying there, and for goodness' sake, do not go throwing balls through the windows! Apart from the expense of replacing the glass, you'll give the people there a dreadful fright!"

Ha ha ha, everyone laughed.

"What's a convention center?" I called, without even raising my hand. This is because I was annoyed that it wasn't ghosts. Also I didn't find her comment about throwing balls through windows funny. Nobody smashes a window *on purpose.* At least, the windows I've smashed in my time at Katherine Valley have all been complete accidents.

As soon as Principal Hortense started explaining what a convention center was, I lost interest. I remembered that I already knew—it's just a place where grown-ups hold meetings.

Principal Hortense was *still* going on, trying to define what a convention is, what a center is, and *you put them together and you get*—I don't know. I wasn't listening. Suddenly, I had a thought.

"Have the people already arrived?" I called.

Maybe the people weren't due for another week? Maybe the lights I'd seen *were* ghosts? Disturbed by the refurbishment? And when the people arrived, they'd get a dreadful fright, not from a ball through the window but from ghosts in the corridors.

"Esther Mettlestone-Staranise!" Principal Hortense exclaimed, shaking her head. She stirred her tea vigorously. "Yes, there are accountants there now. That aside, you've given me a shock, Esther," she said. (Easily shocked, she is.) "That's *two* questions asked without raising your hand! What sort of impression can you be making on our new teacher? For I noticed Mrs. Pollock slipping in the back door of the dining hall a moment ago and she's been standing there all this time! Mrs. Pollock! Do come up to the teachers' table!"

I turned around, and there she was, staring straight at me.

Our new teacher.

Mrs. Pollock.

CHAPTER 14

MRS. POLLOCK WAS SHORT.

Short as a sheep.

Ha. No. Not that short. But as short as a ten-year-old child, anyway.

Curly, gray hair. Glasses with square frames. Wrinkly face. Scrawny little body with knobbly elbows and shoulders. Blue cardigan.

And she was staring at me.

The whole dining hall was silent. It was her. At first, we'd all frozen—spoons hovering, hands stopped just short of the croissants—then slowly, slowly we had turned to stare.

"Esther, is it?" Mrs. Pollock said. Her voice was much stronger than her little scrawniness suggested. "Esther Mettlestone-Staranise? Is that the name I heard Principal Hortense use?"

I only stared. To speak would have been impossible.

The light sparked off the lenses of her glasses so I could not see her eyes.

"Well, is it? Is your name Esther?"

I carried on staring. Rabbits do the same thing if you catch them with your lamplight. Freeze in place. I was being a rabbit. Embarrassing. But nothing I could do.

"Good gracious, do you not know your *name*, child?"

A long pause.

Then the strangest thing happened.

Mrs. Pollock pulled a silly face.

Mouth stretched down, lips pouting. The kind of face a child pulls to annoy a parent who is trying to photograph them.

"Do we not know our *names* at this school?" she demanded, and she twisted her face from that silly expression to another, and then another—the way you do to make a baby giggle. "Is it just Esther who's lost her name, or have you *all* misplaced them? The same way I misplaced my bobbled woolen gloves last spring? Loved those gloves, just *loved* them!"

And she grinned.

Everyone burst out laughing.

"Morning, everybody!" Mrs. Pollock shouted, making her way between the tables, slapping people's hands as she passed— like an athlete greeting a crowd after winning a game. "Morning! Morning! So happy to be here! Can't wait to meet my Grade Six class! Honestly, *cannot* wait!"

When she reached the teachers' table, Mr. Dar-Healey hopped up and pulled back a chair for her. She sat at the table, gave us all one more comical face—we burst out laughing again—and said, "Carry on eating! Don't mind me!"

CHAPTER 15

FOR THE REMAINDER of breakfast, words went zooming around the dining hall, only this time they weren't like a cat, they were like a flock of noisy birds.

Every bird was chirping, "She's *tiny*! She *can't* be an *Ogre*! Ogres are huge!"

And: "She's *nice*! Mrs. Pollock is *nice*!" and "She's *funny*! Mrs. Pollock is *funny*!"

Also: "It was just a rumor! Don't listen to rumors! There must be *other* people who live on Horseshoe Island beside Ogres!"

The excitement made us giggle and squawk, spill drinks and grab each other's forearms. It made us eat our cereal and toast, our poached eggs, our bacon and our beans, with great appetite.

"Girls!" Principal Hortense cried, standing up suddenly. A piece of toast fell from her mouth to her table. "Oh, I forgot I was eating," she added, surprised. She brushed herself down.

"Everyone! Attention! We have welcomed our new teacher, but we must also welcome *two new girls*!"

People began to quiet, watching her with interest.

"Both have joined Grade Six!" Principal Hortense declared. "Can you stand up for us, new girls?" A scraping of chairs at our table and we gazed at our new girls proudly. "Everyone! Welcome, Autumn Hillside and Pelagia Blue!"

Pelagia! A mysterious name, just as good as Autumn's. I wondered if new girls were only allowed at the school this year if they had unusual names.

Autumn held herself very still, her shoulders back, expression grave, dark hair glowing in the morning light. Pelagia beamed around, crinkling her little snail-shell nose.

"What else have I forgotten?" Principal Hortense asked, suddenly serious and staring hard at the new girls.

Both girls blinked and stared back.

"I'm not sure," Pelagia ventured.

"I know!" The principal was excited again. "One final announcement, everyone! Sit down, Autumn and Pelagia! I should have told you all yesterday! Turns out, there have been some sightings of Shadow Mages in our— Oh my goodness, the new girls might not know what Shadow Mages *are*!" Principal Hortense's mouth opened in an O at this idea. "They might not even know how *magic* works hereabouts! They could be from the Northern Climes! Are you from the Northern Climes, girls?"

Both Autumn and Pelagia shook their heads and murmured, "No," but Principal Hortense carried on. "Right, we have to tell you how magic works here in the Southern Climes. It's quite different. Who can tell our new girls the three types of magic user?"

I remembered to raise my hand.

"Yes, Esther?"

"True Mages, Spellbinders, and Shadow Mages."

"Correct! And what do True Mages do?"

"They practice bright magic," I explained. "Spells for things like healing, love, kindness, poetry, wealth, music—"

"Yes, yes, thank you, Esther. Examples of True Mages? Somebody else?"

Several hands flew up.

"Faeries, Crystal Faeries, Elves," a Grade 5 girl said.

I could have added more, but Principal Hortense was moving on.

"Number two is Spellbinders!" she cried. "Do you know what Spellbinders are, new girls?"

Autumn and Pelagia both nodded firmly. Pelagia even called, "Yes," and started to explain Spellbinding, but Principal

Hortense was pointing at Hetty Rattlestone, whose hand was flapping around like a pigeon.

"Spellbinders are regular people who happen to be born with the gift of Spellbinding," Hetty declared. "You know you have the gift if your toenails turn blue. Spellbinders are good because they can bind the wicked magic of Shadow Mages. Esther *wishes* she could be—"

Principal Hortense leapt in. "And finally, Shadow Mages! They practice shadow magic, of course. Now, usually they stay *far* from the mountains around here, but this is what I have to tell you. A warning. Shadow Mages have been spotted around our neighborhood."

Eyes widened. Mouths fell open. *Shadow Mages around here?* Impossible!

Principal Hortense nodded. "Impossible, yes, I'd have thought so too. Still, I've been told they're *migrating* lately. Something to do with a river overflowing its banks somewhere? Anyhow, let's tell the new girls some examples of Shadow Mages!"

Before anybody could reply, Principal Hortense herself began to list Shadow Mages in a ringing voice: "Radish Gnomes! They have long claws, which can rip you apart. Sterling Silver Foxes! They'll steal your laughter, which is profoundly painful and can kill you. Ghouls! Most terrifying of all, and will crush your very soul with a little finger. Witches! Oh, they'll break every bone in your body for a laugh. Odd sense of humor, those Witches. Plenty more Shadow Mages, of course, so do keep an eye out. But don't worry! We'll be fine!"

And she sat back down amidst a stricken, wide-eyed silence.

"Did I do that wrong?" she asked the teacher beside her.

Along the table, little Mrs. Pollock replied loudly: "That depends. Was your intention to scare the wits out of them, possibly causing fainting fits? If so, you were *perfect*."

"I was?" Principal Hortense replied, pleased. Then her face fell. "Oh."

There were giggles.

Mrs. Pollock herself stood up then. "Girls!" she said. "I come from far away myself, but I hear you have *many* True Mages living in the mountains around here! Now, what do Shadow Mages *think* of True Mages?"

"They hate them!" several girls called.

Mrs. Pollock nodded. "Shadow Mages might have been spotted wandering around the mountains, sure," she told us. "I honestly don't think they'll stay."

Then she squeezed her nostrils shut, flapped at the air, and spoke in a high-pitched, squeaky voice: "Shadow Mages find True Mages to be *very stinky*!"

And she grinned.

There was a great burst of laughter, and little Mrs. Pollock sprinted up and down between the tables once again, slapping everyone's palm with her own. She even did the same at the teachers' table.

We drank the last of our juice, pushed back our chairs, scraped off our plates, and set off to class.

"Good luck with Mrs. Pollock!" Imogen joked, when I passed her at the doorway. I laughed.

When I waved at Astrid though, she was frowning.

"What's wrong?" I called.

She looked startled.

"Oh, nothing," she said. "Just—I forgot my pencils."

Which was an odd thing to say, because the teachers always hand out our supplies on the first day of class. But Astrid had gone before I could remind her. She's always been a bit scatty.

CHAPTER 16

THE FIRST THING that Mrs. Pollock did was hop up on her desk. We all stared. There she stood, hands on hips, gazing up at the ceiling fan.

"So *this*," she said, "is what it's like to be tall."

She clambered back down and sat on the edge of the desk, swinging her legs. "Why do you all look so confused?" she cried. "I just wanted to know! I'm tiny!"

Everyone giggled.

"Of course," Mrs. Pollock said. "This one here *already* knows." She pointed to Durba, the tallest girl in the class—she's almost as tall as my father. "What's your name? No, don't tell me, let me guess. Is it *Giraffe? Telegraph Pole?* Am I getting warm?"

Again, everyone giggled.

"It's Durba." Durba smiled.

"Strange," Mrs. Pollock said. "I'd have sworn it was Tree. Shall we change your name to Tree?"

Durba shook her head, chuckling.

"Suit yourself." Mrs. Pollock shrugged. She hopped off the desk and scampered over to Durba. "How about something like this?" she said. She gestured for Durba to raise her right palm, slapped this with her own palm, spun in place, clapped her hands above her head—and waited, expectantly.

Durba stared.

We all did.

"It's a greeting!" Mrs. Pollock told us. "A personalized greet-ing! Only Durba's supposed to do what I just did too. You must all invent one just for *you*! That's how I'll say hello and good-bye and 'how are you?' each day."

We spent until morning tea working on our "greetings" and practicing these with Mrs. Pollock. Each person's was different although they all included slapping our palms together at some point, which made a satisfying *thwack* sound. There were clicking fingers, pirouettes, fist bumps, and wiggling fingers. Mine included swinging hips and a lip-popping sound.

It was the best first morning back at school I'd ever had.

After morning tea, we lined up to go back into the classroom and Mrs. Pollock remembered every single one of our personalized greetings.

"About me," she said. "I was a teacher for many years, then I retired *here* . . ." She grabbed chalk and drew five circles on the board.

"The Candle Islands. I lived on this one." She tapped at the smallest circle. "Horseshoe Island. Shaped a bit like a horsesh—hmm."

She rubbed out the circle and redrew it in a horseshoe shape. "That's better. Not much there. An inn. A few cottages. And living in caves carved out by the sea? A colony of Ogres. So, it turns out, Durba-the-giraffe, I *have* seen people taller than you before! *Much, much* taller!"

We all laughed, entranced.

"These Candle Islands are about a two-hour boat ride from the Kingdom of Storms." She drew a rough sketch of the coastline. "And my job was to ferry tourists across from the town of Spindrift. Fresh air. Sun on my face. Loved it. But do you know what I love more?"

We waited in suspense.

"Teaching! Teaching kids like you! Missed it too much, didn't I? So here I am back again!"

She erased her drawings and wrote this:

A LETTER.

As the chalk scratched along, she spoke aloud. "Your turn," she said and turned to grin at us. "Write me a letter of introduction. Tell me what your name is. Tell me if you're *happy* with your name! Or do you think it's a crappy name?" Everyone laughed in shock. She'd used the word *crappy*! She carried on as if nothing had happened. "And tell me—"

ALL ABOUT YOU.

Where you are from?

Your family.

Your friends.

Your hobbies/talents.

A secret!

She replaced the chalk, dusted off her hands, and handed out papers and pencils.

"Well, then," she said, suddenly annoyed. "What are you waiting for? Don't you think it's time I got to know you? Begin!"

CHAPTER 17

Dear Mrs. Pollock,

I'm delighted to meet you.

My name is Esther Mettlestone-Staranise. I suppose I'm happy with my name, but it's the only one I've ever had. If you'd like to call me something else, please do.

Maybe <u>Peppermint Teaspoon-Radishbone</u>?

Or <u>Ohmygoodness Lollipop-the-bus-to-Mathematicsclassislate</u>?

Where am I from? Thank you for asking. I'm from Blue Chalet Village, which is two hours east of here by coach. It's a tiny village, nestled amidst the dramatic landscape of the Tinderbox Alps.

Nights, when I'm home, I gaze through my bedroom window at the moonlit peak of Mount Opal. Dragons often swoop by, crossing its silhouette—silent, graceful—and I wish I could be swooping along with them.

In winter, my village decks itself out in starbursts and paper lanterns for the Festival of Snow. It's magical, even if chilly.

In spring, it rains and I walk the streets and laneways, water streaming down my shoulders and dripping into my shoes. The mountainside grows colorful with wildflowers and Father strides about pointing out their names. Astrid gathers bouquets to bring home for Mother, which Mother throws away, as she's allergic.

In summer, my sisters and I climb the sycamores, swim in the lake, and buy iced melon treats in the village square.

My family? Well, my father is Nigel Staranise, a professor of history (modern and classical) at Clybourne University and the author of over twenty-five popular history texts. Father is funny, kind, and easy to beat at word games. you'd think he'd be great at those, as an author, but when it's his turn, he's always lost in thought—and when you tug at his sleeve, he apologizes and says, "Right, whose turn is it?" By which time, his two-minute time slot is over.

Then he sighs: "Oh, well, better luck next time, me."

My mother is Nancy Mettlestone, and she is very professional but I'm honestly not sure what her profession is. I know she met Father at university, where they were both studying history, and that her current job has to do with committees and homemade lemonade. She is fairly friendly except when we do sports without "putting our whole heart into it" or break the refrigerator door. (I was only swinging on it gently.)

I have two sisters: Imogen and Astrid. Imogen can be bossy and Astrid can be scatty, but it's not like I don't have any faults of my own.

For example, I often run out into the school grounds when it rains. I like to take my shoes and stockings off and squelch in mud or wade in the pond. Once

I wore a watering can on my head for a week. Another time, I collected several cups of rainwater and kept them under my bed (until a ball rolled under, knocked them over, and ruined a carpet).

My friends? Well, my best friends are Hsiang and Georgia, but they've left the school.

My hobbies/talents? My favorite things in the world are

    *reading books (favorite author is G. A. Thunderstrike)

    *writing stories (all-time favorite thing)

    *playing poker

Poker is a card game with a lot of pretending. You pretend you have great cards when they're actually crappy, and same in reverse. A big part of winning is knowing when other people are lying.

Imogen and I are good at this, and Astrid is the best. She's so good that the local paper did a story on her last year.

IS THIS CHILD A MIND READER? was the headline. Mother's the only person who can beat Astrid.

We've won the K&E Junior Title the last four years in a row, and I'm especially excited about this year's competition because it will be held in Gainsleigh. My cousin Bronte, who is a great adventurer, lives there and we'll get to visit her.

The final thing you asked for is a secret!

Hmm.

Okay, I've got one.

In my family, there are <u>Spellbinders</u>! You're never supposed to reveal Spellbinders' identities, so I can't tell you their names, sorry. But it makes me feel special knowing there's Spellbinding in my blood. <u>Maybe</u> I could be one???

Looking forward to your reply!

Warmest wishes,

Esther

CHAPTER 18

MR. DAR-HEALEY MADE AN
announcement at dinner that night.

You might remember that
Mr. Dar-Healey is Imogen's teacher?
Don't worry if you've forgotten. I told
you quite a few chapters ago.

Anyhow, Mr. Dar-Healey got up from the teachers' table
and began to dance.

Two steps forward, two back, swinging his hips.

When other teachers want your attention they clap their
hands once and say, "Girls?" Mr. Dar-Healey is different.

By the time he'd danced awhile, everyone was looking at
him and giggling. He's youngish, Mr. Dar-Healey, but his forehead is very high. (That's the polite way of saying he's already
going bald, Father says.) He has warm brown skin and his eyes
are as bright as sunshine on a pond.

"Welcome back, everybody! You'll recall from Principal
Hortense's welcome speech that *I'm* in charge of Wednesday
Afternoon this year!"

Everybody nodded. Well, I only half-nodded. Not having listened to most of Principal Hortense's speech, I did not recall
this at all.

Still, I was interested to learn it now. Wednesday afternoons, we do "activities." These are chosen by one teacher and
often take place in town. (*Town* just means Pillar Box Town,
the picturesque town set on a lake that's a ten-minute walk
down the road from our school.)

Mr. Dar-Healey smiled his wide smile and asked: "Who
here can swim? Raise your hand if you can."

About half of the girls raised their hands, including my sisters and me.

"And of those who *can* swim, who could swim, let's say, across the Turquoise Lake?"

That's the lake in town.

Everybody laughed and put their hand down. Turquoise Lake is huge—its far side is a hazy, distant blur. Imogen enters swimming tournaments every summer, but even she couldn't make it across that lake.

Mr. Dar-Healey squinted, pretending to look for raised hands. "Well, starting tomorrow, the Wednesday activity will be swimming classes!"

Everyone made the face you make when you're not sure how you feel about that. You sort of pull your lips down and tilt your chin up. Would swimming lessons be fun? Not as boring as Etiquette at Afternoon Tea anyway, which had been Principal Hortense's choice for Wednesday activity last year.

"There are beautiful new bathing facilities in town," Mr. Dar-Healey told us, encouragingly. "A pool all enclosed in glass. You can look at the mountains as you swim!" Then he spun in place and did a backflip.

"Oh, *my*!" That was Mrs. Pollock exclaiming. The other teachers are used to Mr. Dar-Healey's flips, and they had carried on slicing up their lamb chops and sipping their wine. Mrs. Pollock, however, fanned her face and said, "Mr. Dar-*Healey*!" Then, boldly: "Will you teach me that trick?"

Everyone laughed again. Mrs. Pollock is very old.

But she pulled an outraged face and said, "What's so funny? Why shouldn't *I* be able to tumble in the air?" We just laughed more loudly until Mrs. Pollock cried out: "Is there a hyena loose in here? I'm sure I hear a hyena!"

Now we *shouted* with laughter. A girl in Imogen's grade, Lee Kim, has this shrill laugh that you can always hear over the top of everyone else—and it does sound like a hyena. We are accustomed to Lee's laugh, and usually take no notice of it.

"Show yourself, hyena!" Mrs. Pollock bellowed.

By now, we were *all* screaming like hyenas—Lee Kim loudest

of all. I could see her across the dining hall, trying to smother her mouth with her palms.

At this point, Mr. Dar-Healey boomed: "Any time you want a backflip lesson, Mrs. Pollock, just say the word. All right, everyone, back to your delicious chops before they get cold."

He sat back down beside Mrs. Pollock, and over the last of the fading laughter, I heard him say: "I mean that, by the way. No reason you shouldn't learn a backflip if you like."

Mrs. Pollock flicked his shoulder and shook her head.

CHAPTER 19

IN THE RECREATION room after dinner, I saw my sisters chatting in the corner about Astrid's pajamas. These had
apparently been packed in Imogen's bag
by accident.

Once they'd sorted out the pajama
issue, they asked me about Mrs. Pollock, and I described the
day. "She's hilarious," I said. "We love her." Then I added
generously: "Still, you both got good teachers too. You're so
lucky to have Mr. Dar-Healey, Imogen. He does tumbles in
the air."

Astrid nodded. "True," she agreed. "It's a shame he's so sad."

Imogen and I both frowned at her.

"What do you mean?" Imogen demanded. "He's always smiling! And dancing! And singing. He sings all the time in class.
Gets a bit annoying, to be honest. But he's happy!"

Astrid shrugged. "Something is making him terribly sad."

Then one of Astrid's friends grabbed her by the elbow and
pulled her over to join a board game, and one of Imogen's
friends shouted for her to come share cake with them.

I went to the corner table and wrote letters to Georgia and
Hsiang. I told them all about Mrs. Pollock; how we had thought
she was an Ogre, only she'd turned out to be lovely; how we
each exchanged personalized greetings with her; and were
going to do swimming as our Wednesday activity.

Then, in both letters, I wrote:

It's only the first day of classes yet so much has happened! And you are NOT HERE for it to happen to! Listen, remember how I used to tell you two over and over to stop practicing your flute and your cricket? Because I KNEW something like this might happen one day. But you took no notice, did you?

And now it has happened.

I meant that to be humorous rather than angry and worried it might not come across that way. I tried to fix it by writing *CONGRATULATIONS* inside circles of stars in both letters.

By this time, the bell was ringing for us to go to the dormitories. I crept downstairs to the mailroom instead to post the letters. This was against the rules, but I wanted Georgia and Hsiang to hear from me as soon as possible.

CHAPTER 20

THE MAILROOM WAS dark, but moonlight spilled through the windows, so I could make out the familiar shapes.

The wall lined with pigeonholes.

The slot for posting letters.

And, against the far wall, the coat closet from which, if you climbed inside and pressed your ear to the back, you could listen to conversations taking place in the principal's office next door.

I don't know if anybody else knows that.

I discovered it the first year I came to the school, when I was playing hide and seek with Georgia and Hsiang one Sunday afternoon. The closet had seemed a perfect spot to hide. The coats hanging inside were soft and warm, and I'd snuggled into them. Then I'd worried about accidentally knocking the wooden hangers, making them *clunk* together and alerting Georgia (who was seeking) that I was inside. It was too risky, I'd decided, and I'd been about to hop back out when I heard Principal Hortense's voice.

"I've lost my tea!" she'd exclaimed.

A long quiet.

Then, "Oh, no, I haven't. It's right here on my desk."

That was all I'd heard that first time. Except for slurping, which I suppose was her drinking the tea.

The night when I crept into the mailroom to post my letters, I did not climb into the closet with the *intention* of listening to a conversation.

I would never do that!

Or hardly ever anyway. Or, I mean, not *constantly*.

It was late, so I didn't even expect Principal Hortense to be in her office. I only hopped into the closet because I suddenly wanted the coziness of soft, warm coats.

But the moment I did, I heard voices. Just a faint murmur, so I pressed my ear to the back of the closet.

"Well, *they* are taking it seriously anyway," said Principal Hortense's voice.

Who? I thought. *And what are they taking seriously?* The trouble with eavesdropping is you can't ask important questions.

"It'll be nothing," a man's voice declared—I couldn't place it. "I mean, are they havin' a lend of us?"

Oh, now I knew. It was Mustafa, the gardener. He sounded annoyed. "Shadow Mages roaming the mountains?" he complained. "They never come around these parts! Much too pretty for them. Lakes and glaciers, blue skies and whatnot. And that Mrs. Pollock is right about the True Mages. Village of Crystal Faeries not an hour's ride from here! Can't stand that, can they, the Shadow Mages?"

A rapping sounded now.

That gave me a fright. I thought someone was knocking on the closet door. Then I realized it was Principal Hortense knocking on her desk. "It's right here in the letter," she said. "They're worried enough to do *this*."

Do what? I thought.

Slurping sounds. Tea drinking, I suppose.

"An undercover Spellbinder," Principal Hortense exclaimed. "I can't believe it! A student! *I* don't even know which one she is! Grade Six, I believe."

Grade 6? That was my year!

"A Grade Six girl!" Mustafa cried, sounding suddenly angry. "That's too young! How's she supposed to protect the school, little scrap of a thing?"

"They're not *all* little scraps, the Grade Six girls," Principal Hortense mused. "Have you seen Durba? She's really shot up over the summer. And those Rattlestone twins are very . . . *forceful* personalities."

"Not the point," grumbled Mustafa.

"I know," Principal Hortense agreed, pacifyingly. "Still, apparently they've started training younger Spellbinders. Even Carabella-the-Great has provisionally allowed it."

More muffled grumbling from Mustafa, then: "*I always thought it wore them out if they tried to spellbind too young.*" I'd heard that too.

"The letter says this girl will create a Spellbinding ring around our school, but she'll have to reinforce it daily. Too young to make a permanent one. Also, she's not strong enough to spellbind any Shadow Mages who *do* get in."

"If they're so worried, why don't they send a *proper* Spellbinder to guard the school? Put in a permanent Spellbinding?"

"Well, that's it, isn't it?" Principal Hortense declared. "They *can't* be that worried."

After that, Mustafa said that it was time to "call it a night," and Principal Hortense said, "Oh, look at the time!"

And then there were the shuffling, groaning sounds of grown-ups getting out of chairs. Their footsteps passed the mailroom and disappeared toward the back of the school.

I waited for the faint thud of the back door closing. Then I opened the coat closet, sat on the moonlit floor, and trembled.

A girl in my grade was a Spellbinder.

It must be one of the new girls, of course. Autumn or Pelagia.

Autumn with her shiny hair or Pelagia with her box of chocolates and scrunchy nose. Which one?

I took off my slippers.

I stared at my toenails.

As usual, they stayed their regular color.

I am not special. I'm just an ordinary girl.

I sent fierce messages to my toenails: *Prove me wrong! Change color! You can do it!*

Nothing happened.

I must have fallen asleep because I woke suddenly, still on the floor.

Checked again. Toenails were still their regular, regular, not-blue color.

Crept back to the dorm.

CHAPTER 21

WE WALKED INTO town in pairs for our first swimming lesson. The sky was cloudy and birds sat high on wires and branches.

I was paired with Autumn Hillside. As she kicked at pebbles, I kept glancing at her, wondering if she was the Spellbinder. I also wondered what conversation I could start. I sensed that she was trying to think of something to say too, although maybe she was just concentrating on pebbles. She had braided her long hair, probably to keep it tidy while she swam, and I'd just decided that this would be my topic—"I can never braid my hair without bits coming loose, what's your trick?"—when a voice sounded behind us.

"And there were *seven* Whisperers?" it exclaimed.

Autumn and I both turned our heads.

Not far behind us, Hetty Rattlestone was walking alongside Pelagia.

"Yes," Pelagia agreed. "Seven Whisperers. And no way out of the bowling alley."

"*Pelagia!*" cried Hetty. "You must have been *terrified!*"

Autumn and I carried on walking, but I knew we were both listening.

"Pretty scared, yes," Pelagia agreed. "I was crouched in one of the racks with the bowling shoes."

"How old did you say you were?"

"Five."

"FIVE!" Hetty shrieked. "HIDING IN A BOWLING ALLEY WITH SEVEN WHISPERERS!"

Whisperers are people from the Whispering Kingdom. They used to kidnap children from all over the Kingdoms and Empires and were once more terrifying than all the other Shadow Mages combined.

And *seven* Whisperers had gone to a bowling alley to kidnap Pelagia?

She *must* be the Spellbinder in our grade, I realized in a rush. That was the only way she could have escaped from seven Whisperers. She must have spellbound them! At five years old!

Hmm. If so, how would she explain her escape to Hetty without giving away her identity?

I was riveted. What would she say next?

No idea.

Because, at that point, Pelagia lowered her voice. *Murmur, murmur,* she said, and "WHAT?" or "NO!" cried Hetty. Not helpful. Only frustrating.

Eventually I gave up trying to hear and told Autumn I liked her braid. She touched her hair, pleased, and said, "Thanks."

"How do you get it so neat?" I asked.

"I don't know," she replied.

That was it. Not what I'd call great conversation.

We arrived at the swimming pool.

CHAPTER 22

WHEN I SWIM, a peculiar thing happens.

I start off well. I use *good strong arms*! (When my mother taught us to swim, she'd shout, "Come on! You're faster than that! Let's see good strong arms!")

I kick my legs, face pressed into the water, turn to the side to breathe—

And then—

I notice the bubbles.

You know when you slap your hand on the water as you swim? And teeny bubbles form, a trail of them? Well, you're probably a sensible swimmer who just gets on with the swimming.

But here is what I do.

I try to swim through the bubbles. They're so soft and tickly!

I swim a stroke, then twist myself around into the bubbles, sort of curling back *into* the stroke, then I swim another stroke and twist myself back into *those* bubbles. And so on.

It sure does slow you down, this method. ("What *are* you doing?" Mother used to bellow when she was teaching us. I could never really explain it.)

We all had to swim a lap at the pool, while swimming teachers watched and assessed us. You were allowed a kickboard if you couldn't swim that far, and I suppose they assessed how well those girls kicked. One teacher stood at the end of each lane with a clipboard, while the head swim teacher, Raelene, strolled up and down the side, getting an overview. Once you'd had your turn, you sat up on the bench seats to watch.

Raelene was a large, muscular woman, wearing a bathing

suit with a frill around it. Her eyes were a bit squinty, I think because her swimming cap was dragging on her forehead.

When it was my turn, everyone was waiting to see if I would do as well as my sister Imogen. She'd been the best so far, you see—very fast and strong. The whole place had cheered for her. "Excellent form," I heard Raelene say. I was proud.

I started swimming. Raelene bellowed, "What are you *doing*?" just as Mother used to do, and when I came up for air, the whole place was laughing.

I tried switching to backstroke halfway down to stop myself being distracted by teeny bubbles, but, well—remember Mr. Dar-Healey saying that the pool was in a glass building? It was. So when I turned onto my back, there were the snow-capped mountains soaring into the blue sky! Right above the glass!

I stopped swimming altogether and trod water, gazing up. Everyone laughed at me more loudly. Then I tried to carry on, still backstroke, only the glass reflected the water's move-ment, shadows rippling and fluttering up there—

All in all, it took about half an hour to reach the end of the pool and by the time I got there, the teacher who was meant to assess me was leaning against the back wall chewing gum.

As I approached the bench seats, a group of older girls chanted, "Go, Esther! Go, Esther!" as a joke. I grinned at them even though my heart was beating in a fluttery, embarrassed way. Mr. Dar-Healey called for me to come sit by him. I thought he might scold me for wasting time in the pool, but when I reached him, all he said was "It's beautiful, isn't it? This structure?"

I sat beside him, my towel around me, and we had a good chat about the meaning of beauty. Mr. Dar-Healey thought beauty is snowcapped mountains and I said yes, mountains are lovely, but beauty is a deluge of rain.

As we chatted, Pelagia stepped up to swim her lap.

We thought that Imogen had been speedy.

You should have seen Pelagia.

Mr. Dar-Healey stopped speaking halfway through a sen-tence. Lines sprang up all over his forehead. "Good *grief*," he muttered, and he leaned so far forward I thought he might topple over.

It was like this.

Have you ever skipped a pebble across a pond? And done it properly so it goes *spring! spring! spring!* over the water?

That's how Pelagia seemed to swim.

She *can't* have been swimming like that, of course—her arms and legs must have carried her along, as usual. But honestly, it was like *zip!* And there she was. Up the other end.

The swim teachers all swarmed together. I felt a bit sorry for the other girls swimming valiantly onward, unaware they'd been forgotten.

The teachers must have asked Pelagia to swim back in the other direction, please, because she bobbed about in the water looking up at them, then spun around and did it again.

Zzzzzip! Up to the other end.

"She didn't come up for air!" Mr. Dar-Healey murmured. "Who is that, Esther? That's the new girl in your grade, isn't it?"

"Yes," I replied. "Pelagia."

Mr. Dar-Healey shook his head slowly as Pelagia skimmed back up the pool. It seemed as if she was about to commence a *fourth* lap, when—

CRACK!

A pattern of fine lines, like rivers on a map, appeared on the surface of the glass wall facing us.

Then the entire wall exploded into pieces.

CHAPTER 23

STRANGELY, AT FIRST it was beautiful.

Like a surprise of bright confetti. A waterfall bursting from the sky. A jangling of musical light.

Then the chaos started.

We get hailstorms at home, and you sit in the kitchen listening to the clattering and rattling outside. This was like a thousand hailstorms in your head.

Most of us had finished our laps and were sitting on the benches, safely across the pool from the shattering glass, but some girls had been waiting to swim their laps, some were in the pool—

And three tiny girls, about six years old, had been walking along the opposite side, heading toward the change rooms.

These three crouched, arms wrapped around their heads as shards, fragments, *sheets* of glass rained on them.

Everyone else swarmed back toward the benches, to safety.

The glass stopped falling.

The three little girls remained frozen.

Knee-deep in a river of glinting silver.

There was a powerful silence. Next, the eerie sound of the wind outside—now that the wall had vanished—and the sudden trill of a bird's song.

Many girls started screaming then, or burst into sobs.

This was not helpful. I mean, I understood it—we'd just had a terrible shock. But it wasn't helpful to the three little girls over there.

One of these girls was shaking her head slowly, side to side, trying to shake glass fragments from her hair. Lines of bright red appeared on her arms and legs. She had been cut and was bleeding.

The second girl brushed glass from her own shoulders. She was also bleeding.

The third remained perfectly still. A shard of glass had pierced her thigh. She stared at it.

"EVERYONE, STAY PERFECTLY STILL," Mr. Dar-Healey boomed over the screams. I'd forgotten he was beside me. He rose now, his face a grayish color.

He leapt down the steps of the benches—I could see he was shaking, his whole body trembling—and it made his leaps awkward. He skirted around the pool, skidding on the wet tiles. Raelene, the head swim teacher, seemed to blink back into herself, and she also rushed over. But both paused at the carpet of glass and began to tread carefully through it toward the girls.

Through the blankness where the glass wall had been, the blue of the sky and green of the town park were visible. A group of townsfolk, about ten or twelve adults, were running across the park toward us—worried expressions, voices calling to each other.

"Did you see that?"

"The wall's come down! The swimming pool wall!"

"Is everyone all right in there?"

Just as Mr. Dar-Healey reached the little girl with the shard in her thigh, she plucked it out herself. At once, bright red blood streamed down her leg. Mr. Dar-Healey caught her up in his arms, turned to Raelene, and lunged for the towel over her shoulder. He bound this around the little girl's leg, around and around, speaking to her gently all the while. You could see her eyes staring up at him, and you could hear the crunch of the glass under his feet.

This is when I noticed that Katya from my dormitory was skidding toward the other two little girls. I remembered that they were both on her junior chess team.

I looked around for my sisters and caught Imogen's worried

glance a few benches away. Astrid shuffled up to sit beside me. She'd been in the pool when it happened and had scrambled out without a towel. She was shivering, her lips a violet color, and I wrapped her in my towel, pulling her close to me to warm her up.

The townsfolk crossing the park were closer but had slowed to a more cautious pace. Glass had splashed out in both directions, scattering in the grass outside, so they were carefully picking and weaving amongst the glints.

"Is one of you a doctor?" Mr. Dar-Healey called to them. He took a step in their direction, the little girl still in his arms. "Can someone get her to the hospital?"

At which point, a voice behind me screamed, "NO!"

CHAPTER 24

IT WAS AUTUMN Hillside.

She had leapt up onto a bench and was gesticulating wildly. Her long braid flew about behind her.

"NO!" she screamed. "MR. DAR-HEALEY! GET AWAY! GET THE GIRLS AWAY!"

Everyone turned and stared at her. People muttered things like "Lost her marbles." Mr. Dar-Healey's brow crinkled and he took another careful step toward the approaching towns-folk, the little girl still in his arms. Blood was already seeping through the towel around her leg.

But Autumn hadn't finished. "RUN!" she bawled.

I wondered if I should go and gently sit her back down again. "It's *already* happened," I would say. "The glass wall has *come down*. It's *too late to run*." Things like that.

"*HURRY!*" Autumn bellowed. "*GET AWAY!*"

Many people sighed. Some covered their ears with their hands.

It was as if she was a few moments back in time—as if she was living her life the way I swam, turning back into the bubbles of the stroke before.

"Autumn?" I called. Yes, I decided, it probably was my job to calm her. After all, I'd walked here with her. She was in my dormitory. And most important, I'd decided to be her friend— you have to take your friends as they are, even if they turn out a bit odd.

Two people outside had almost reached Mr. Dar-Healey, and both held out their arms for the little girl. The woman wore jangling bracelets and a sundress printed with daisies. The elderly man was in a suit and tie.

Autumn ignored me, only shrieking more loudly. And then, most astonishing of all, she began to laugh.

A shrieking, hammering laugh.

The two people outside paused and looked across at her. Their arms dropped. Mr. Dar-Healey spun around.

"Hey!" he called.

Autumn carried on laughing.

"Hey, what are you doing?"

She ignored him.

He turned back to the townsfolk—frowns creased their foreheads. The other townsfolk outside had also paused, a little distance away.

Mr. Dar-Healey looked down at the girl in his arms—and then, quite suddenly, his head snapped up.

He cleared his throat.

"Ho!" he said, "Ho!" He paused. "Ha!" he said. "HA HA HA HA HO HO HO!"

And he was laughing too.

The woman in the daisy dress stepped back. The elderly man pressed his fists to his ears.

Autumn breathed in, then cackled again.

I looked from Autumn to Mr. Dar-Healey to the townsfolk outside.

The townsfolk winced. They pressed forward a step and stopped. Sunlight dazzled against the broken glass and sprang from the jewelry of the townsfolk: bangles, necklaces, anklets—

And with an ice-cold surge through my veins, I understood.

These were not townsfolk at all.

CHAPTER 25

THEY WERE STERLING Silver Foxes.
Like regular people but with tiny dif-
ferences: Ears slightly pointed. Plenty of
jewelry.

And if one gets close to you?

Your only chance is to laugh.

When you've had a shock—such as when a great glass wall
crashes down and a gang of Sterling Silver Foxes approaches—
it's difficult to laugh.

At first, I couldn't do it. I stood up on the bench, gave it a
shot, and barked like a strangled walrus.

But other girls had also understood and were trying to
laugh. More and more stood and laughed. Over amongst the
glass, Raelene let loose a high-pitched giggle.

That was good because it was funny in itself. Surprising.
She seemed too large and strong to giggle. My little sister, Astrid,
burst into chuckles that sounded real, and I found myself joining her.

As you probably already know, laughter is more contagious
than the common cold—its sound lights a spark in your chest.
It's like a feather at your chin.

Soon the entire place was *roaring*—hooting, guffawing, and
chortling.

The elderly Sterling Silver Fox in the suit scowled. So did
the one in the daisy-print dress. Both took several steps
back. The others behind them tried to push forward instead,
and one—huge man, very muscular, fists to his pointy ears—
crossed right into the building. He trod amongst the glass in a
fearless way.

But Mr. Dar-Healey backed cautiously away calling "Ho! Ho!" and Raelene intensified her shrill giggle. Each time the big guy took his fists from his ears, ready to work his shadow magic, he grimaced and shoved them back again.

The rest of us bellowed with laughter. Lee Kim, who has the hyena laugh, threw her whole body into it.

The big guy took his fists away again, right as Katya, still shielding her chess team girls, let forth a magnificent scoffing howl, as if she found him *ridiculous*. At the same time, Lee Kim's laugh became a shriek, like something clawing at the air.

The big guy quit. He shot Katya and Lee Kim ugly looks and retreated. Once he was on the grass, he began to jog and then run.

They all ran.

All the Sterling Silver Foxes fleeing from the sound, then pausing, turning, and watching us from a safe distance across the park . . .

We carried on laughing.

Mr. Dar-Healey and Raelene gathered the little girls and hurried, stumbling, back through the glass, around the pool, and up through the pool's entryway. As he left, Mr. Dar-Healey lifted one hand high in the air, then higher still, meaning we should keep it up—keep up the laughing.

In all my life, I've never laughed so hard, so loud, or so long.

It was the strangest thing, because laughter billows a sort of joy in you even as it hurts your belly and makes tears run down your face, and you feel reckless with it, but also sometimes you feel alarmed, when you can't get ahold of the laughter, and here we were, all of us, shouting and shouting, *screaming* out our laughter in absolute, mind-numbing terror.

CHAPTER 26

EVENTUALLY, SPELLBINDERS arrived in their hooded black cloaks, bound the shadow magic, and rounded up the Sterling Silver Foxes.

It still took some time before we felt safe enough to stop laughing, and by then other teachers had arrived to lead us back to school.

Principal Hortense addressed us during dinner. First, she was silent, just sort of gazing down at her own hands, which were pressed against her chest. We all waited.

At last she looked up and started to cry. She does this sometimes. Stands at the front sobbing. The first time it happened I was a bit horrified, to be honest, but now I'm used to it. Most of us are—we just sigh quietly.

(However, I noticed Mrs. Pollock half-choked on a mouthful of food and had to be slapped on the back. She wasn't used to it.)

Eventually, Principal Hortense wiped her eyes with a handkerchief and smiled tearily. "What a day you've had," she murmured. "What a day."

Then she led us all in stretching exercises. We had to hop up from our seats, reach toward the ceiling, and touch our toes.

"To ease the tension," she said, "of your very trying day."

She told us that the three little girls who'd been hit by falling glass were back from the hospital already and recovering in the infirmary. "All patched up," she said. "A few bruises, a few stitches here and there.

"It seems," Principal Hortense continued, "that the gang of Sterling Silver Foxes were from a settlement of Shadow Mages in the Ranciford Empire—two Kingdoms away from us."

They'd used their shadow magic to crack the glass, she said, and it could have been a catastrophe if it was not for the quick thinking of—

She paused.

Some of the older girls started a drumroll, banging their palms on the table.

I smiled over at Autumn—everyone was grinning in her direction—but she had ducked her head down, to hide behind her long hair.

More and more people joined in with the drumroll, until *all* of us were thwapping our hands on the tables and the sound built and built—

"AUTUMN HILLSIDE!" cried Principal Hortense.

We erupted into applause.

Autumn tipped her hair to the side for a second so we could see her face and she smiled shyly. This made everyone cheer more loudly. She hid again.

"A mind like lightning," Principal Hortense continued. "Somehow, Autumn recognized that the strangers approaching were Sterling Silver Foxes! It would not have occurred to *me,* had I been here! But Autumn knew, *and* used the only defense we have: laughter! Mr. Dar-Healey was *full* of praise for her actions!"

Mr. Dar-Healey nodded. "Still am."

Principal Hortense went on a bit about how the rest of us had also been brave, joining the laughter, so that the girls could be taken to hospital and the Sterling Silver Foxes repelled and captured.

I think that's the gist of what she said. I got bored around there.

At last, we were allowed to eat our dinner.

I know this might seem strange to you, but it wasn't until I was up to the apple crumble that I realized: *Autumn must be the Spellbinder!*

Not Pelagia at all.

That was how she'd recognized the Sterling Silver Foxes. Of course, she hadn't been able to spellbind them herself— Principal Hortense had said that the Spellbinder in our school wouldn't be strong enough to do that—but she'd figured out how to save us anyway.

And she was saving us right now by keeping a Spellbinding around the school, which, it turned out, was much more important than Principal Hortense and Mustafa had imagined. There *were* Shadow Mages in the mountains.

* * *

Later, we were given extra time in the recreation rooms as well as a treat of hot chocolate and waffles with ice cream to "calm our nerves."

Ordinarily, we might have made a joke or two, but I noticed that nobody—not a single girl in the school, I mean—laughed that night. It took a few days before we remembered how to do that again.

CHAPTER 27

EACH MORNING I went to Mrs. Pollock's classroom excited to see what she would write in reply to our letters. I imagined how I might reply to her reply. I could tell her about the time Imogen found a duckling wandering in our vegetable patch. And how we took it for walks in the hills and it would quack angrily whenever a dragon flew over but quickly hide in one of our pockets if the dragon flew too low.

But days went by, and nothing.

I also hadn't received replies from Georgia and Hsiang, and this time I couldn't blame my mother. We passed the mailroom on the way to breakfast every day and always checked the boxes. Mine, so far, had been empty.

Mrs. Pollock carried on teaching us regular classwork, somehow making her lessons entertaining. She was so unexpected!

For example, we did the history of the Whispering Wars by acting it out. First, she divided us into groups. Some people were Whisperers, some Shadow Mages, some Spellbinders, and some "regular people." I was disappointed to be a regular person.

Next, Mrs. Pollock had the Whisperers say, "We live in the Whispering Kingdom! We can Whisper thoughts into people's heads!"

"Oh, yes?" Mrs. Pollock inquired. "Let's see!"

Each Whisperer had to choose a "regular person" and whisper, whisper, whisper into her ear. *I want cake*, they whispered. *I'm tired. I feel like dancing.*

"Now what could you do about these Whispers?" Mrs. Pollock asked us regular people.

We shouted back at the Whisperers: "I *don't* want cake! I'm *not* tired! I don't *want* to dance!"

Mrs. Pollock swung back to the Whisperers.

"So what did you do, Whisperers?"

The Whisperers acted out digging. "We found threads of shadow magic in an old mine," they said. They pretended to weave threads together and place these around their wrists. "We used them to weave shadow bands."

"What happened to your whispers when you did that?" Mrs. Pollock asked.

Then the Whisperers had to whisper to us regular people again: *I want cake, I'm tired, I feel like dancing.*

Only this time, instead of shouting back, we had to clutch at our foreheads and wail as if in agony. (Pelagia was good at that, shrieking so wildly Mrs. Pollock had to tell her to hush in case she disturbed Grade 3 next door.) The Whisperers carried on whispering: *I want cake, I'm tired, I feel like dancing!* And us regular people pretended to eat cake, sleep on the classroom floor, or dance, all while looking very sad.

"So your whispers became *superpowerful* when you wore shadow bands?" Mrs. Pollock checked.

Gleefully, the Whisperers cried, "Yes!"

"Then what did you do?" she asked.

"Stole children from across the Kingdoms and Empires to help us dig out *more* shadow thread! For *more* shadow bands!" they replied and began running about, taking us regular people prisoner. We had to pretend to be children digging in mines.

"What else?" Mrs. Pollock demanded.

"We joined with the Shadow Mages!" the Whisperers replied. They linked arms with the girls playing Shadow Mages. "And set out to take over *all of the Kingdoms and Empires!*"

We acted out various battles.

"Oh no! Who can defeat the Whisperers and Shadow Mages?" Mrs. Pollock cried.

That was the cue for the Spellbinders to march in and wave their hands about, as if weaving Spellbindings in the air.

"We are defeating Whisperers and Shadow Mages!" they cried. "We are creating a Spellbinding ring all around the Whispering Kingdom!"

"Which of you is the greatest Spellbinder of all time?" Mrs. Pollock asked.

Hetty Rattlestone replied: "I am! I am Carabella-the-Great!"

(Most of us were pretty annoyed that Hetty had been cast as Carabella-the-Great. Well, I was annoyed, anyway.) (By the way, I know a secret about Carabella-the-Great.)

The Spellbinders, led by "Carabella," marched around and around the group of Whisperers, who huddled together, looking crestfallen.

The Spellbinders cheered in triumph.

"And that was the end of the Whispering Wars!" Mrs. Pollock crowed. "The entire Whispering Kingdom was locked away inside a powerful Spellbinding! Nobody could get out! But what kept happening for years *after* the Whispering Wars had ended?"

"Some of us Whisperers escaped!" the Whisperers replied. A few demonstrated by pushing through the Spellbinders. "And kept stealing children!"

Most of us shuddered a little. Although the Whispering Wars had ended before we were born, we'd all grown up being warned by our parents of the dangers of escaped Whisperers. You could recognize a Whisperer because they grew their hair down to their ankles. I used to have nightmares about getting tangled in a Whisperer's hair.

"So Carabella-the-Great *strengthened* the Spellbinding!" Mrs. Pollock exclaimed, and Hetty proudly demonstrated this, marching around the Whisperers, weaving at the air. "So they could never escape again! And *that* is the end of our tale!"

We all bowed.

Only, that was not the end of our lesson. Because once we'd completed acting it out, we had to act it out again. And again. And again. Each time, we did it faster than the time before. Faster and faster we got. By the time we reached the ninth retelling, we could hardly make out anybody's words we were babbling so fast, and we were gasping for air, dizzy, and laughing hysterically. Autumn accidentally ran into a table at one point, fleeing a Whisperer, and bruised her shin quite badly.

It was fun.

Eventually, when we'd collapsed back into our desks, too worn out to do it again, Katya raised her hand.

"We didn't do the last bit, Mrs. Pollock," she said.

"The last bit?"

"The Whisperers were set free two years ago," she reminded us all. "It turned out that their king had *forced* them to wear the shadow bands. They tore off their shadow bands, the Spellbinding was broken, and now they're free. And back to being regular Whisperers with gentle Whispers."

"My cousin Bronte Mettlestone helped to set them free," I called, "by defeating the Whispering king. My sisters and I saw it. We'd been chained up by pirates at the time, so we weren't much use, but Bronte was a proper adventurer."

Mrs. Pollock winked at me—I wasn't sure why—then nodded at Katya. "Quite so," she said. "However, that wasn't a part of the history of the Whispering Wars, so we didn't include it."

"Hmm," said Katya. "If we define—"

But Mrs. Pollock was pointing at Zoe Fawnwell, whose hand was raised. "What should we do if we see a Whisperer?" Zoe asked.

Hetty and Tatty both gasped. "We *wouldn't*," they said. "The Whispering Kingdom is far away!"

"Nothing." Mrs. Pollock shrugged. "They're safe now." Then she touched her own wrist softly. "Although . . . you might keep your eye out for shadow bands. *Just* in case they decide to wear them again. You never know . . ."

A chill ran through the room.

Then Mrs. Pollock ran around the classroom doing our greetings as fast as she could and crying, "Congratulations! Great performances! Super history lesson!" and we all laughed again.

* * *

Sometimes, Mrs. Pollock would call a girl to the front of the room while the rest of us were working. They would sit at her desk and have conversations in low, serious voices. I could never make out what they were saying, but these conversations always ended with Mrs. Pollock grinning and doing the personalized greeting. The girl would return to her desk with a grave expression on her face.

"What did you talk about?" I asked Dot Pecorino after she had one such conversation.

Dot shook her head. "She's very nice," she murmured, blushing. She always blushes when she speaks. The shyness does that.

CHAPTER 28

ONE DAY, MRS. POLLOCK arrived wearing a bright pink wig of wild, curly hair.

"What?" she said, when we giggled. "What's so funny?"

Then she pointed to Katya's hair and cried: "Hey, same wild curls! We match! Only, you're going to have to dye yours pink!"

Everyone laughed, and Katya smiled. But the following day, Katya came to class with her hair knotted up tightly into buns. As if she'd locked her hair away. It looked wrong like that, I thought, and seemed to miss the joke.

Another day, Mrs. Pollock brought in a shoebox filled with caterpillars she'd collected from the gardens. She handed around the box and told everyone to take one out and eat it.

"*Eat it?*" I gasped.

Mrs. Pollock frowned. "Go on then. Pass the box along. Everyone take one."

A lot of girls squealed or squeaked, some refused to take one, but most sat with a caterpillar on their palm, looking at it.

"Now imagine how gooey and delicious it's going to be," Mrs. Pollock said. "What do you think it's going to taste like?"

Most of us were laughing, but Dot Pecorino began to cry.

"What's to cry about?" Mrs. Pollock demanded. "Yummy caterpillar! Eat up! Go on! Yum!"

Dot Pecorino buried her head in her arms.

"Oh, come now!" Mrs. Pollock said. "Have you lost your sense of humor, Dot? Is it with my lost bobbled woolen gloves?"

Dot looked up from her arms and smiled. Her cheeks were pink and her eyes red. "We don't have to eat them?"

"Of course not! Here. Put them back in the box. These are insects, girls, and that's our topic for today."

"A caterpillar isn't technically an insect," Katya pointed out. "It will *become* an insect when it's a butterfly or moth. At the moment, it's at the larval phase and is in the order Lepidoptera." She's very smart, Katya.

"Oh, all right. *Bugs,*" Mrs. Pollock complained. "If you want to get persnickety on me!"

Everyone giggled again.

So, as I said, it was always fun in Mrs. Pollock's class.

* * *

At last, on the Monday of the fourth week of term, Mrs. Pollock handed back our letters.

She hadn't replied to them. She'd graded them.

I could see little comments and grades on other people's letters as she passed them around. That shocked me because I hadn't imagined it as schoolwork. I'd thought it was a getting-to-know-you exercise.

Also, so far, we'd not done any tests or even had work corrected. I'd almost forgotten that this was what happened at school.

Now, I don't know how to say this without sounding like I'm showing off, but I think it's important to know this: I usually get A+ for writing work.

Which is why, once I'd got over the surprise, I was secretly happy that Mrs. Pollock had graded the letters. I like getting A+. It makes me happy.

Mrs. Pollock put my letter down on my desk. There was my handwriting (a bit messy):

Dear Mrs. Pollock,

I had written (you might remember)

I'm delighted to meet you.

I turned over the pages until I got to the end.
Here is what Mrs. Pollock had written.

Esther, most of your description of your hometown is obviously taken from a book or encyclopedia. Please only use your own words in future assignments.

By Grade 6 you should know that the word "crappy" is unacceptable. Shocking. DEMERIT. This is your first demerit. THREE demerits mean a Friday night detention.

You seem surprised that your father is good at word games. However, if he is an author, it makes sense that he'd be good at word games. Please try to use logic and reason.

You say that you sometimes "run outside," wade in the pond, collect cups of water, and put watering cans on your head? This sort of behavior will NOT be tolerated in my class.

Finally, you say that a member of your family is a Spellbinder. By Grade 6, you should know that it is DANGEROUS and FOOLISH to reveal the identity of Spellbinders. These people MUST remain anonymous if they are to do their work against Shadow Mages effectively. Please use common sense.

C—

CHAPTER 29

FUNNY!

That's what I thought at first. I mean, a *strange* sort of funny, but still.

When Mrs. Pollock said that I'd stolen the description of my village, she must have meant it was so well written that it must be from a book!

The part about the word "crappy" was definitely a joke, because the only reason I'd *used* the word was that *she'd* said it to us that day. "Or do you think it's a crappy name?" she'd asked.

The "demerit" must have been a joke too. I'd got lots of demerits before. Georgia, Hsiang, and I used to get them all the time: "We have demerits coming out of our *ears*!" Georgia used to say, proudly. But demerits had never had anything to do with "detention"—I wasn't even sure what a detention *was*. They used to just build up, the demerits, and then, at the end of the year, my report card would say "107 demerits."

"One hundred and seven demerits!" Mother would exclaim, frowning at my report.

And I would say, "Oh, that's a tally for the whole school."

Father would snort and Mother would ask, "What's funny?" and Father would say, "Nothing, nothing. Well *done* on your writing grade, Esther!"

Speaking of Father, my letter to Mrs. Pollock had *not* said that he was *good* at word games. It had said the opposite—that he always drifted off and forgot to have his turn.

And I didn't plan to wear a watering can on my head again! I'd done that when I was nine! I'd only included it in the letter to make her laugh!

And the Spellbinder part.

I *know* you aren't supposed to reveal a Spellbinder's identity—I'd *said* that. But I hadn't given away a *name.* I have a huge family! My mother has ten sisters, which means I have ten aunts! And my father has three brothers. Cousins? Thousands! (Practically.) And what about second cousins? It could have been anyone!

Also, Mrs. Pollock *had* asked for a secret. You can't ask for a secret and then, when a person obeys and tells you one, scold them for it. She must have been being humorous.

Hilarious! I chuckled to myself.

However, then I looked around and saw that most people had A or B on their papers. I caught glimpses of comments that Mrs. Pollock had written. *Excellent!* or *Most entertaining!*

Why was she only being "funny" with me?

Hetty Rattlestone, who sat behind me, leaned forward to look over my shoulder. I heard a little gasp. She sat back and whispered to Tatty, beside her: "Esther got a C minus."

Next thing, it was whispering and gasping its way all around the class. "Esther got a C minus!" "No way!" "Esther got a C minus!"

The whispers were very loud. Mrs. Pollock must have heard.

I watched her closely, waiting for a little grin, a dimple, a wink.

But her face remained perfectly blank.

CHAPTER 30

AT POKER TRAINING with my sisters that night, I took the letter along, ready to show them.

"Mrs. Pollock is *wonderful*," I would say, "so I don't understand this comment."

My sisters would have an explanation.

However, they were both talking when I arrived, their words layering and bumping like messily shuffled cards. It turned out that Mr. Dar-Healey had asked Imogen to compete in a swimming tournament. Events would be held in various Kingdoms and Empires. Mrs. Pollock had apparently told Mr. Dar-Healey about the tournament, knowing he was interested in swimming.

"Which was thoughtful of her," Imogen added. "Do you still like her, Esther?"

"I like her a *lot*," I said, "only—" I hesitated, suddenly embarrassed that my complaint was about a bad mark. They might tease me. I changed the subject instead. "When's the swimming tournament?"

"In three weeks. And we'll be away for two. We have to bring schoolwork. Oh, and that new girl in your class? Pelagia? Mr. Dar-Healey asked her to compete too. He wants us to train every afternoon at Nicholas Valley—since the local pool is still being rebuilt. So I'm going to be really busy."

"Me too!" Astrid said. And she told us that she'd been asked by the local mayor to work as his assistant on occasional afternoons.

We both laughed, but she seemed to be serious.

"Assistant to the mayor!" I blinked. "You're ten years old."

"I know!" She giggled. "The mayor read that article about me. Remember the one that said I was a mind reader? He wants me to start coming to top-secret meetings with him and tell him which people are lying."

"Top secret?" I started. "But you'll—"

Astrid giggled again.

"He says I'll sit behind a glass wall and look at their faces while they speak, without hearing them. Then I have to speak into his earpiece and let him know if they're lying."

"Will you be able to tell?" I asked.

"Of course." She shrugged modestly. She's very matter-of-fact about her talent.

"Deal, Astrid," Imogen said. "I've got homework."

And we took out our coin purses and began to play.

CHAPTER 31

THAT NIGHT, I had the dream again.

Don't worry. I'm not going to tell you every time I had it. As I mentioned, it's been at least 250 times, so this story would become dull and repetitive if I did. You'd fall asleep yourself.

But this time, the second time, was important.

First of all, I saw more details. Remember how the dream starts with me lying on a rug? This time I noticed that the rug was blue. With a smear of strawberry jam.

And you know how I look up at a cloudy sky? This time, I turned my head slightly and saw big bushy trees, and the outline of a huge rock. The rock was shaped like a turtle standing on its side and poking its head out of its shell.

As usual in the dream, it began to rain—and I woke up.

Also as usual, I felt a crushing weight on my chest. I seemed to be breaking into thousands of pieces, like a glass vase crashing to the floor in slow motion.

I slipped out of bed, tiptoed out of the dormitory, slunk down the corridor, opened the window, climbed out onto the ledge, clambered up the drainpipe, and squeezed through a slightly ajar window into the school attic.

CHAPTER 32

I'VE DONE THIS before, by the way.

Also, I've checked the School Rule Handbook and there's not a single rule that says: *Girls must not climb out of the window and up the drainpipe to the attic.*

Not one.

I suppose teachers would say, "Come on, Esther, you know perfectly well that you shouldn't be climbing out of windows."

Or maybe: "For goodness' sake, use your common sense!"

Still. It's honestly not one of the rules.

Nobody knows I do it.

Well, Hsiang and Georgia know, of course. I told them about it the first time I did it—I think we were in Grade 4—and they were *hugely* proud of me. They thought I should get an Award for Very Courageous Exploring at the end-of-year assembly. But that would mean confessing I'd done it. Not worth it.

Georgia and Hsiang were keen to sneak into the attic with me, and we used to make plans to have secret feasts up there— we even gathered provisions while on trips into town, and packed baskets full of crackers and cheese, jam doughnuts, and chocolate cake. But each time, when it came to it, when we crept down the corridor in the night and opened the window— Hsiang and Georgia couldn't do it.

It was the height.

"I mean, I'm not *afraid* of heights, of course," Hsiang explained. "It's just—this window ledge is very narrow, and that drainpipe looks kind of slippery, and if you slipped and *fell,* well—"

"You'd die," Georgia confirmed.

Which was true, I suppose, as the attic was four stories up.

So we used to sneak to a recreation room instead, and have the midnight feast there, by candlelight.

I never think about falling when I climb up to the attic, I just—well, I just climb up.

It's not a dusty, cobwebbed attic, by the way. It's a huge, neat space, running the length of the building. School records are lined up in filing cases.

At the far end, there's a trapdoor with a ladder. That's the usual way to get in and out of the attic. But it goes down into the utility room, which is locked at night, so that's no use.

You might be wondering why I like to climb into this attic.

Here's a clue: evenly spaced along the skirting boards, are vents.

These vents run into rooms below: recreation rooms, teachers' offices, and the teachers' lounge.

Lights out for students is 8:30 P.M., but teachers stay up chatting as late as they like.

Imagine the things that you can hear.

CHAPTER 33

THERE'S NO SCHOOL rule against eavesdropping either.

Ha, imagine my father's face if he ever reads this.

"*Esther,*" he would sigh. My name would blend with his sigh.

My parents are always telling me I need to stop listening in to adults' conversations. It's *very rude,* and *an invasion of privacy,* and *one day, I'll find my ears burning!*

(Unlikely. Unless I'm eavesdropping on flames in a fireplace.) (They just mean I'll overhear someone saying something nasty about me.)

I'm trying to stop.

Father says, "You can quit this habit! Perhaps replace it with another? Tried smoking a pipe?" (He's only joking—pipes are not good for your health.)

Mother says, "Oh for goodness' sake, are you behind the couch again, Esther? Get out at once."

So I've promised I'll stop. And I'm proud to say, on this particular night, I only listened in to *one short conversation.*

The conversation happened in the teachers' lounge. You can always tell when Principal Hortense has retired to her cottage for the night, because the teachers sound completely different. When she's there, their voices are polite, friendly, and evenly pitched. Every now and then all the teachers laugh in a gentle, *ho ho!* way, as if being conducted.

But when the principal's gone, the teachers' voices become quick and high-pitched. Splutters of laughter rise up and crash against shouts. It's as if the conductor has walked out, leaving the orchestra to smash instruments about.

As the night goes on, the teachers' voices stretch out, becoming low and slow, with relaxed pauses in between. You can't actually see anything through the vent, but you can imagine the teachers lazing about on the couches. Thinking their teacherly thoughts.

There's also more swearing when Principal Hortense isn't there.

Anyhow, this night, the teachers were at the relaxed-slow-voices stage, and I knew Principal Hortense wasn't there.

"She seems like a lot of fun," someone said. It was an older man's voice—I thought maybe Dr. Lanwish, the Grade 8 teacher. His next words were buried behind crunching, so then I knew it *was* Dr. Lanwish. He always walks around with an open packet of crisps, reaching for handfuls, even as he's speaking. Bits of mashed-up crisp visible in his mouth.

Who seems like a lot of fun? I wondered.

"Yes, Daisy Pollock is a hoot." That was Ms. Saji, Astrid's teacher, speaking. I almost called, "Thank you!" through the vent. Obviously I didn't. But I was pleased with her for answering my question.

They were discussing Mrs. Pollock. And now I knew her first name was Daisy, and that she wasn't there tonight. Plenty of teachers go to bed early. To cope with us, they need to be well rested.

"Funny," Ms. Saji said next. "I heard a rumor before she arrived that she was an Ogre!"

There were chuckles. "She's *so* tiny!" several voices murmured.

There was a pause. Liquid being poured into a glass—*glug, glug, glug*—and somebody said, "Cheers."

"Where did the rumor start?" somebody asked.

"Well, she's from Horseshoe Island, apparently," said a clipped voice. "And it's mostly Ogres who live there, you see." That was Ms. Ubud, the school secretary. She sits behind the counter in the admin offices and scowls distrustfully when you speak to her, even if you're saying something innocent like "Mr. Brown says the stationery closet is out of paper clips."

"Horseshoe Island? Where's that?" somebody asked.

"It's one of the Candle Islands," Mr. Dar-Healey replied—I recognized his voice, but it sounded odd. Formal. Like someone giving a speech. "A cluster of small islands off the coast of the Kingdom of Storms—about equidistant from Spindrift in Storms and the Whispering Kingdom. It's well known for its Ogre population."

"Imagine if Hortense had hired an Ogre!" Dr. Lanwish exclaimed.

"I wouldn't put it past her," somebody added drily.

They all laughed and a few voices said, "That Hortense."

"Ogres aren't Shadow Mages though, are they?" Ms. Saji asked.

"No, just very large people," Mr. Dar-Healey said, using the same careful tone. "But centuries ago, they used to help Shadow Mages with their shadow mines. Apparently, the contact with so much shadow thread affected them, gave them shadow powers. Strengthened their handshake, I believe."

A splutter of laughter. "Strengthened it! They're so big, their regular handshake could surely crush a person's hand as it is!"

A number of teachers agreed.

"Anybody been to Horseshoe Island?" Ms. Saji asked.

The sound of somebody clearing his throat. "Yes," Mr. Dar-Healey said.

"I have. I was at the Candle Islands on vacation about ten years ago. I don't recall seeing the Ogres on Horseshoe Island, but I don't recall much of that trip, to be honest. It was—" His voice fell away. A scraping sound, a muttered "So sorry, excuse me," footsteps, and a door closing.

There was a pause.

"What did I say wrong?" Ms. Saji wondered.

Dr. Lanwish spoke up. "You only started here last year, didn't you? So you probably don't know. Toby Dar-Healey used to have a little girl named Paige. His wife had died not long after Paige was born, and then, when she was two years old, he took her to the Candle Islands for a vacation. She disappeared while playing in the shallows. She must have drowned."

"Oh," murmured Ms. Saji softly.

Another long pause.

After a while, there were sounds that might have been people slicing cheese, putting it on crackers, and eating them.

Voices rose and faded.

I climbed out of the attic, back down the drainpipe, reached my toes for the window ledge, hopped back inside, crept along the corridor, and went back to bed.

No wonder he'd chosen swimming lessons as our Wednesday activity, I realized. His only little girl had drowned.

Astrid had been right. Mr. Dar-Healey did have a sadness deep within him.

CHAPTER 34

THE NEXT DAY, I dressed sleepily and was late to breakfast. Most people were already in the dining hall while I was still drifting by the school's entryway.

So I was the only person who saw a flash of lightning cross the window.

Thunderstorm! I thought, pleased.

Right then, the door opened, revealing a clear blue sky. No thunderclouds.

Pelagia slipped in. She didn't see me. Her eyes were bright, her hair was wet, and there was a towel over her shoulder. She sprinted toward the staircase.

Had Imogen and Pelagia's swimming training started already? But Imogen had said they would be *afternoon* sessions. And when I arrived in the dining hall, I saw Imogen at the Grade 7 table and Mr. Dar-Healey sitting with the teachers.

Strange.

I was pouring milk into my cereal when Mr. Dar-Healey stood up, twirled, and made another announcement.

"I think you're ready for a new Wednesday afternoon activity while they rebuild the pool. It's going to be"—he jiggled his hips side to side—"dance classes!"

Not surprising. We smiled.

"Classes will take place here in the school gymnasium," Mr. Dar-Healey continued, "and the boys of Nicholas Valley Boarding School will be joining us. First class is tomorrow."

Boys from Nicholas Valley! We couldn't believe it!

"Not boys!" Mrs. Pollock yelped, and she leapt up and hid under the teachers' table. There was a nervous pause, then she emerged again, grinning, and we all laughed.

CHAPTER 35

IN CLASS THE following day, something *completely astonishing* happened.

Mrs. Pollock was whistling a tune. (That's not the astonishing bit.)

She was wearing linen trousers and a blouse, and she strolled between the desks, thumbs hooked into belt loops, whistling. Very snazzy for an old person.

We were shading a map of the Kingdoms and Empires using a code. Yellow for farming regions, red for urban centers, pink for Faery territory, gray for Shadow Realms, and so on. We were allowed to chat quietly as we worked, and it was very relaxing.

Mostly, we chatted about the fact that our first dance class would take place that afternoon, with boys from Nicholas Valley Boarding School attending.

"Two of our cousins go to Nicholas Valley," Tatty Rattlestone said, nudging her twin. "Don't they, Hetty? The older one, Sam, is all right, but Simon is awful! He plays the *cello*!"

There was a pause. I caught Autumn's eye and she tilted her head in a humorous, puzzled way. I giggled.

"Oh, are those the sons of your Aunt Tiana?" Zoe Fawnwell piped up. "And isn't your Aunt Tiana the Queen of the Cascade Kingdom?"

"Aunt Tiana?" Tatty murmured. "Now, *is* she a queen? Or is that Great-Aunt Tiona? I'm trying to remember . . . Hetty?"

Of course she knew the answer.

Hetty spoke loudly. "Yes, that's right. Aunt Tiana *is* the queen of the Cascade Kingdom. Great-Aunt *Tiona* is Queen of the Unruly Straits, I think. Might be wrong. I get all the royals in my family *so* mixed up."

Both Hetty and Tatty shifted their chairs a little toward Zoe.

"Still," Hetty admitted after a moment. "Our cousins at Nicholas Valley are not actually the sons of Aunt Tiana. Their parents are Uncle Dave and Aunt Jan."

"Ah well," a few people said.

Then Autumn spoke up. "What's wrong with playing cello?" she asked. "I love the cello."

Tatty looked startled. She shifted her chair back toward Autumn. "Oh, me *too*," she said. "*Adore* it."

"Beautiful instrument," Hetty agreed.

"All I meant about my cousin Simon was that playing the cello . . ." Tatty paused.

"Makes him proud of himself," Hetty offered.

"Exactly."

"That must be annoying," Autumn agreed, and both Tatty and Hetty beamed.

Zoe Fawnwell sighed quietly.

"I know a boy at Nicholas Valley," Pelagia put in now. "He's from my hometown. I once rescued him from a swamp turtle. Remind me to tell you the story. Clive's his name."

Other girls contributed stories of Nicholas Valley boys they knew, or boys their relatives knew, or boys they'd seen at coach stops.

I glanced across at Katya. Her twin brother, Stefan, is at Nicholas Valley, and I thought she'd mention him. But she carried on shading her map, her face solemn. Now and then her forehead creased and she pressed it with her fingertips, as if shading had given her a headache.

I myself was coloring in the area around the Kingdom of Storms. It's the most dangerous Shadow Realm of them all—generally known as the region of Wicked and Nefarious Kingdoms—and I was riffling for my sharpener when Mrs. Pollock stopped whistling.

"Oh!" she said. "Almost forgot!"

We looked up at her expectantly. You never knew what zany thing she might say.

"There are two new girls in your class this year!"

Disappointing. Not zany. We already *knew* there were new girls.

"You see, you are *all* new to me," Mrs. Pollock explained, "so I forgot that two were new to *you*. Does that make sense?"

Sure. Plenty of sense.

"These girls should introduce themselves! Tell stories about themselves! Share *who* they are!"

At once, Pelagia straightened. Her heels bounced. Even though I hadn't spoken to her directly, it was clear to me that Pelagia enjoyed telling stories. She was always surrounded by mesmerized girls. I was excited to hear her introduction.

Pelagia stood. Took a step toward the front.

"Autumn Hillside!" Mrs. Pollock cried, eyes skating right over Pelagia. "Come on up!"

Pelagia dropped back into her seat. Her cheeks turned candy pink and I felt sorry for her.

But then I glanced at Autumn.

If Pelagia's cheeks were candy pink, Autumn's were ice-cream white.

She had picked up a colored pencil and was rolling it rapidly between her palms. Her hands trembled.

"Come along then!" Mrs. Pollock coaxed. "We already know you're a hero! You saved everyone from Sterling Silver Foxes! But there must be more to you than that! Hop up and tell us! Brothers? Sisters? Hobbies? Talents?"

At this point, Autumn caught my eye.

And her expression reminded me of the summer there had been a wild thunderstorm in my village. *Lightning!Thunder! Lightning!Thunder!* Or maybe more like: *lightning—*

THUNDER!!!

Really loud thunder, I mean.

I had taken cover in our local cake shop—I'm happy to be out in rain, but I know lightning can be dangerous—when I caught sight of a pair of deep brown eyes underneath a shelf. It was the owner's puppy.

Help me! the puppy's eyes had said. *I have never been so frightened! Help!*

That's exactly what Autumn's expression said.

I wanted to rescue her.

"Maybe," I suggested, "*Pelagia* could tell us about herself instead?"

Pelagia's shoulders jumped, pleased.

Autumn's shoulders relaxed and she smiled. "Yes. Good idea."

But Mrs. Pollock raised her eyebrows. "Don't you *want* to hear from Autumn, Esther?" she said. "Are you *afraid* of her? Anybody else here frightened of Autumn?"

There was laughter. "I'm not—" I began. "I just—"

"You *do* want to hear from Autumn? Or you don't? You're making my head spin, Esther! Wait, *is* it actually spinning? Anybody see anything odd about my head?" She twisted her neck this way and that.

Again, the class laughed.

I gave up. "Of course I'd like to hear from Autumn," I said. "I just thought maybe she'd prefer—"

"Okay, Autumn!" Mrs. Pollock interrupted. "Good news! Esther has made a decision! News alert! Esther has *made a decision*! She wants to hear from Autumn! Let's go, Autumn! Quick!"

Autumn walked to the front, took a deep breath, and started speaking.

I have no idea what she said. She spoke at the speed of a runaway carriage.

Mrs. Pollock sat on her own desk, swinging her legs and pulling humorous faces.

"What?" she kept saying. "Um, excuse me, *what*?"

Everyone giggled.

I did catch that Autumn had a cat named Polly (or maybe

Holly). She usually lived with her father (a teacher or preacher) and mother (plumber or drummer) in Nina Bay (or maybe Gina Hay?).

I think her hobbies included fishing and darts, but it might also have been knitting and arts.

At last, Autumn smiled. "And that's it!" she said. "Great to meet you all!"

She stepped toward her desk.

"Well, hold up," Mrs. Pollock said. "Hold on there, Autumn."

CHAPTER 36

AUTUMN'S EYES PANICKED like that puppy in the storm again.

"You haven't told the *full* story yet, have you?" Mrs. Pollock grinned.

"The full story?"

"You said you were living in Nina Bay for the past two years, yes?"

Autumn blinked.

Had she said that? I'd only heard her say she *lived* in Nina Bay (or Gina Hay)—I must have missed the two years bit.

"What about *before* then?" Mrs. Pollock prompted.

Autumn widened her eyes at Mrs. Pollock. She seemed amazed.

"You want me to tell them . . . ?" she began. Her voice drifted away like leaves in the wind.

"Tell them *all* about yourself, Autumn!"

No, I thought.

Surely Autumn hadn't told Mrs. Pollock the secret that she was a Spellbinder?

Surely Mrs. Pollock wasn't telling Autumn to give away her identity as a Spellbinder?

Surely Autumn wouldn't do it?

There was a long, long pause.

Autumn gazed at Mrs. Pollock, and Mrs. Pollock, who had stopped swinging her legs, gazed right back.

Then Autumn gave a little shrug, turned to the class, and spoke: "The Whispering Kingdom," she said. "That's where I lived before. I grew up there. I'm a Whisperer."

CHAPTER 37

"OH *MY*," MRS. POLLOCK said. "You decided to tell them *that*, did you, Autumn? I thought that was a *secret*!"

Autumn frowned. "But you just said that I should . . ."

"Oh, I see! No, I just meant you lived in Vanquishing Cove for six months before moving to Nina Bay!"

Autumn was trying to get hold of her breathing. It was like an overflowing shopping bag.

"Calm down!" Mrs. Pollock said. "You sound like you've run a race! Don't worry! Everybody will treat you the same! Won't you, girls? Help Autumn fit in? Despite her difference?"

We all nodded. Our mouths were open in wide circles, but you can nod and have a wide-open mouth at the same time. (Try it.)

Autumn did not appear reassured. In fact, her face was crumpling.

"Never mind, Autumn!" Mrs. Pollock said. "You can't take it back now! It's out!"

It certainly was.

Autumn Hillside was a Whisperer.

CHAPTER 38

ONE, TWO, THREE.

One, two, three.

One, two . . . three.

One, two . . .

"Hold up, hold up."

That's what our dance class was like.

Mr. Dar-Healey was our instructor, along with a teacher from Nicholas Valley Boarding School named Ms. Potty. She was dressed in a startlingly colorful smock that appeared to have been splashed with paints by a toddler. This was maybe to distract us from her name.

When we first arrived in the gymnasium, we were all so caught up in the news about Autumn Hillside that we hardly even noticed the boys waiting for us to be their dance partners. I do remember thinking, *Oh, there are some boys.* And then thinking: *Tall ones, small ones, and middle-size ones.* But mostly, as I said, we were distracted.

Girls from my grade were busy murmuring to girls in other grades about Autumn and then, as we mingled with the boys from Nicholas Valley, saying hello to those we knew. I'd walked in with Katya, and she introduced me to her brother, Stefan, even though we'd already met. He and I had both represented our schools in the district speech competition the year before, and Katya had come along to watch. We'd even had milk shakes afterward.

"Remember?" I prompted Katya. "You asked for caramel mixed with strawberry and Stefan and I laughed, but the man in the shop said that was beautifully innovative and well done.

Stefan and I were jealous so we asked for banana mixed with pineapple and he said that was just plain silly?"

Katya rubbed her eyes with her fists, murmuring that they were itchy.

I shrugged at Stefan and he shrugged back, and we might have gone on shrugging, except that, as I've mentioned, the place was buzzing with news about a Whisperer.

The Whisperer herself, Autumn Hillside, was hovering near the coat hooks at the back of the room, pretending not to hear.

She must have heard.

Words were flying around the room like— Oh, I need a new way to describe words flying between people. Why is that always happening in my story?

Okay, got it. This time the words flew around like a Satin Sugar Glider flitting between plum trees on the Isle of Curtain Falls. (I haven't actually seen this but Father described it to me after he'd been there on a research trip.)

Here were the sorts of words that were flying:

"There's a *Whisperer* at Katherine Valley Girls!"

"In Grade Six!"

"It's that one—the one with the long hair!"

"*SHHH!* She's looking at you!"

"She'll *Whisper* you! Stop staring!"

Giggle, giggle.

"Why did they let her in into the school?"

"Maybe they didn't know!"

"Well, of *course* she has long hair! All Whisperers have long hair! How did nobody *realize* she was a Whisperer?"

"I thought Whisperers had hair all the way their ankles or something? Hers is just to her waist, which is what I had until my mother got tired of brushing it and made me cut it off."

"Still!"

"Didn't I say there was something strange about Autumn? I saw her in the dining hall the other day and I thought, *She's too quiet.*"

"You did too! You said that!"

"They should expel her. It's dangerous."

"How do we know she's not Whispering us *right now*?"

Muttering and hissing. Boys and girls babbling away. I didn't say anything, I was still bewildered. I mean, I *liked* Autumn, as you know.

But I didn't want her to be a Whisperer.

Stefan and I rocked on our heels listening to all of this.

Then Stefan said, "Isn't Autumn Hillside the girl who saved you lot from Sterling Silver Foxes at the swimming pool?"

I nodded. "Yes."

He bit his lip in a thoughtful way.

Everybody else seemed to have forgotten Autumn's heroism.

Anyhow, the Sugar Gliders flitted about for a few minutes (that's my metaphor for the chattering, remember), and then Mr. Dar-Healey, who was standing on the stage, clapped his hands and did a backflip.

Now, here was an interesting difference between Katherine Valley girls and Nicholas Valley boys.

Whenever Mr. Dar-Healey does a backflip at my school we all stop what we're doing at once and look at him, smiling. But the *boys* whistled, *whooped*, or clapped—then, instantly, turned around and began telling each other loud stories about people they knew who could do *double* backflips, or circuses they'd been to, or acrobatic shows. Also, many started trying to do backflips themselves. Two of them could do quite good ones.

Mr. Dar-Healey looked a bit alarmed up on the stage.

The teacher from Nicholas Valley in the colorful dress, Ms. Potty, screamed, *"STOP THAT RIGHT NOW! LISTEN! RIGHT NOW!"* in a furious voice that must have hurt her throat, and the boys finally, reluctantly, slowed down and looked in her direction, some of them rubbing their heads where they'd hit them on the floor.

Mr. Dar-Healey raised his eyebrows and made a little speech about how excited he was to be teaching us to dance. Already he'd lost the attention of the Nicholas Valley boys again. They were making jokes, knocking into each other, and a few even wrestled. Laughing and grinning, as if it was great fun being smashed against the floor.

Ms. Potty shrieked again, they settled down, and the dance class began.

* * *

I don't really need to say any more about that dance class.

We were matched up with partners about the same height as us. Stefan was matched with Dot Pecorino, and I noticed him chatting and asking her questions, to which she smiled in a terrified way, without speaking. Stefan did not seem to mind. I ended up with a boy named Arlo, who picked his nose absent-mindedly. When I stared, he took his finger from his nose, looked at it in surprise, and grinned at me as if something hilarious had just happened.

He then reached out to take my hands for the dance.

I held on to his wrists.

Ms. Potty switched on the gramophone, Mr. Dar-Healey explained the steps, and the class went exactly like I said:

One, two, three.

One, two, three.

One, two . . . three.

One, two . . .

"Hold up, hold up."

One, two, three.

One, two, three.

One—

"Hold up! Let's try that again."

And so on.

CHAPTER 39

AUTUMN DISAPPEARED AFTER the dance class, missed dinner altogether, and was already asleep when we came into the dormitory later.

Her black hair was a deep shadow across her pillow. Other nights I had admired that shadow and wished my hair could be glossy like that, but this night a shudder zigzagged from my chest to my toes.

There was a *Whisperer* in the bed next to mine.

Even though Father was always telling us there was nothing to fear from Whisperers, I was afraid. (As a matter of fact, my cousin Bronte, the adventurer, who I've mentioned, happens to be half-Whisperer. But she's also half-Spellbinder, so I always think the second cancels out the first.)

Autumn, on the other hand, was a full Whisperer, who grew up in the Whispering Kingdom. I wanted to be kind. I knew that Whisperers are actually good people who'd got caught up in a war because of their king. And I knew they were only powerful if they wore shadow bands. But I had grown up terrified of Whisperers, and my sisters and I had watched Bronte battle with the ferocious Whispering king. These things had got lodged into my chest. After all, it had only been two years since Whisperers were freed from their Spellbinding.

I kept trying to check Autumn's wrists for a shadow band—the other girls were doing the same—but one of her arms was tucked under her pillow as she slept. I curled myself onto the far side of my bed from her.

In the morning, though, I was sprawled out as usual. Autumn's bed was empty, neatly made. The rest of us got up, used the washrooms, and dressed, glancing often at the empty bed and at the door. Nobody mentioned her: she could have reappeared any moment. We walked down to breakfast together.

There is always a stack of the *Katherine Valley Times* at the entry to the dining hall at breakfast. I think the idea is that we read the news while we eat our toast. Nobody does that, except for the senior girls, who occasionally take one to show they are "mature" now. However, they get bored quickly and drop them. Mostly, we just glance at the headlines.

That day, when we glanced, we saw this headline:

WHISPERERS STEALING OUR JOBS

Then, a subheading:

Moves to ban Whisperers from taking any employment outside the Whispering Kingdom

I read the first line.

"These people have *not* earned the right to live amongst us," said Anti-Whisperer League President Carmen Roadhouse, "let alone steal our jobs! My husband still cannot walk, since—"

I didn't see the next bit as there were people behind me, shuffling me forward, hungry. Probably Carmen's husband had been injured in the Whispering Wars and Carmen didn't see why we should forgive Whisperers now.

Glances were exchanged between girls as we continued to the table. We'd seen plenty of headlines about Whisperers before and had never taken much notice.

Now everything was different.

There was a Whisperer at our school.

The article was talking about *Autumn*.

Of course, she was too young to be getting a job anyway, but one day she'd want one, wouldn't she? What if she wanted to work at, I don't know, the swimming pool in town? She could warn people of approaching Sterling Silver Foxes. That was a talent of hers. Would Carmen Roadhouse, President of the Anti-Whisperer League, shout at her to go get a job in the

Whispering Kingdom? What if they didn't *have* swimming pools there?

Autumn had mentioned her parents' jobs in her introductory speech. Maybe they'd lose those jobs now?

Then how could they pay the school fees here?

Would Autumn have to leave?

I have to admit, even though I liked her, I was a bit relieved at that idea. It's true I like an adventure, but constant danger from the girl who sleeps in the bed next to mine seemed too much.

On the other hand, maybe she and her family would starve! I didn't want her to starve.

Autumn herself was already eating her breakfast of scrambled eggs—not starving for the moment anyway—when the rest of us reached the Grade 6 table. Tatty and Hetty made a show of taking the seats either side of Autumn and saying, "Good *morning*, Autumn! You're up early!"

The rest of us were strangely polite, speaking softly so that the sounds of chairs scraping and cutlery clanging were extra noticeable. As if the chairs and cutlery were scolding us.

We could see girls at other tables craning their necks to stare at Autumn. It was not relaxing.

Then Pelagia spoke up. Usually she was busy telling long, riveting stories, and making me wish I could get a seat near her. I *still* hadn't heard one of her stories. Mrs. Pollock had forgotten to get her to introduce herself after Autumn's talk.

Today, though, as I mentioned, Pelagia spoke up.

"Autumn?" she said. "Can I ask about your hair?"

Autumn blinked once, then said very cautiously: "Yes?"

"It's just that I thought Whisperers had hair all the way to their ankles?" Pelagia said. Her voice was friendly and curious, as if she was asking about homework or a pet back home.

Autumn's face relaxed a little.

"Oh, that's only adult Whisperers. We all grow our hair gradually, so most twelve-year-olds like me have only reached waist length."

"And is it true that the long hair is what makes you Whisper?" Pelagia inquired.

Somebody gasped softly. I don't know who it was, but I knew what they meant. It was one thing to ask about Autumn's hair, but now Pelagia was referring to *Whispering*!

Just mentioning this might give Autumn the idea to start Whispering us!

"It's complicated," Autumn replied. "Long hair isn't essential to Whispering. Of course, only adults can Whisper anyway— you don't get Whispering power until you're around sixteen— but our hair is tangled up with our sensitivity, and—"

"Tangled up." Zoe Fawnwell giggled.

Autumn gave Zoe a polite nod.

"Wait," Zoe said, her giggles changing to a sly smile. "So the reason you knew those people were Sterling Silver Foxes was because of your *hair*. It makes you *sensitive*?"

"Oh yeah," some others said. "She *sensed* their evil!"

Everyone was nudging each other.

I chimed in then. The others seemed to be missing the point. "You *can't* Whisper?" I checked. "Not for a few years?"

Autumn shook her head. "I can't."

We all gazed at her. All seventeen Grade 6 girls, gazing quietly at the eighteenth.

"Also," Autumn continued, "the scary Whispers—the ones used during the Whispering Wars?—were from shadow bands. Wristbands made from shadow thread. Nobody wears them anymore." She held up her arms to show us her bare wrists. "All we can do is Whisper little ideas into your head that are very easy for you to shake away. The only other talent some Whisperers have is that they can hear Whispers from the future. So they know what's going to happen. My parents can do that." She looked wistful for a moment and then carried on. "But we consider it impolite to Whisper people, so I'd never do it even if I could."

I looked down the table at Pelagia, whose eyes were bright.

If Autumn was a full Whisperer, she was almost certainly not the Spellbinder (I realized), and it was back to being Pelagia. A Spellbinder would not be afraid of Whisperers. *That's* why she'd been brave enough to ask questions.

But everyone else was growing brave now too.

"What was it like for you," Hetty inquired, "in the Whispering Wars?"

Autumn turned to her. "I was born after the wars had finished," she replied. "I'm the same age as you."

Tatty flicked a dismissive hand at that. "Yes, but the Whispering Kingdom was trapped behind a Spellbinding *after* the war, right up until two years ago! So it's *like* the war carried on for *you*!"

Autumn picked up her fork.

"What was it like living behind a Spellbinding?" Hetty tried.

Autumn shrugged. "It's how I grew up. I didn't know anything different."

"But you were *trapped*!" Hetty persisted. "You must feel so *free* now! Isn't it wonderful that we've set you free?"

Autumn scratched the back of her neck and returned to eating her eggs.

CHAPTER 40

AFTER THAT, I had the dream four nights in a row, sometimes more than once a night.

You remember the dream? I'm lying on a blanket. The blanket is blue with a stain of strawberry jam. I can see bushy trees, and a rock shaped like a turtle.

It begins to rain. I wake up.

I got pretty sick of the dream that week.

I mean, it's not exactly filled with plot twists, is it?

More to the point, every time I had it, I'd wake up gasping for air, absolutely terrified, with the sensation of a boulder on my chest.

A couple of times when it happened, I flung back my bed-clothes and hurried down the corridor, planning to climb out of the window and up into the attic again. But when I looked out, lights always seemed to be darting around behind the windows of the Old Schoolhouse.

If it had been *ghosts,* as I'd once hoped, that would have been all right. I could have scrambled up the drainpipe to the attic and the *ghosts* would have ignored me, getting on with being ghostly.

But those were regular accountants—or town planners or dentists; it changed all the time—attending a regular convention over there, not ghosts at all, and at any moment, one of them might look through a window and catch a glimpse of me climbing. You can't trust adults (especially accountants) not to go worrying about you falling to your death.

So I did not climb.

Eventually I stopped getting out of bed and running down the corridor at all. There was no point.

The fourth night, Sunday night, when I woke from the dream and was gasping for air, a small voice murmured, "Are you all right?"

That gave me a fright.

It turned out to be Katya, who is three beds along from me.

"Bad dream," I said.

I waited for her to ask what the dream was about and prepared for how loudly she would scoff. But there was a long quiet in the dark room.

"I can't sleep," Katya whispered eventually. "My ankles and knees are hurting."

I sat up in bed.

"What did you do to them?"

"Nothing," she replied. "I think it's growing pains. My brother gets them all the time."

"Do you want me to get the nurse for you?"

I heard a rustling. I think it was Katya shaking her head. "No," she said. "The only thing that helps my brother is when our father massages his legs. I don't want the nurse to do that for me."

I knew what she meant. Nurse Sydelle sits in her little office, which is just before the bathroom, reading books. If you look in at her on your way to the bathroom, she purses her lips and raises her eyebrows as if she finds everything about you somehow *unlikely*, and not at all pleasing to the eye.

After a few more moments, Katya said, "I wish Matron was here."

Again, I knew what she meant. Matron is kind and chats about her husband in a way that makes you giggle. Her healing is always excellent.

"I wish she'd come back," Katya whispered. "I'll try sleeping now. Good night, Esther."

"Good night, Katya."

The dream had faded. I turned over and closed my eyes.

Then I opened them again: I couldn't remember the last time I'd heard Katya scoffing.

"Katya?" I whispered.

"Yes?"

"Is everything all right with you?"

More quiet and then, in a very small voice, Katya said: "Everything is fine."

CHAPTER 41

I THOUGHT OF this incident the next day when we had a mathematics test.

The test was quite tricky and I was only halfway down the first page (there were three pages altogether) when I noticed Katya placing her pencil onto her desk and closing the paper.

This was not surprising. She's the smartest girl in our class, as I think I've mentioned several times, and finishes tests long before anybody else.

I worked out the next sum.

$$
\begin{array}{r}
7,564+ \\
339 \\
4,982 \\
\hline
12,885 \\
\hline
\end{array}
$$

I checked it. It was correct.

Katya raised her hand.

"Yes, Katya?" Mrs. Pollock asked in a loud whisper. Some of us giggled. Mrs. Pollock had stood up and was slinking toward Katya's desk, her head darting around as if she was an undercover spy or an octopus. It was funny.

Katya spoke softly, trying not to disturb the class. "I only wondered if there might be a worksheet I could do? Or a supplemental test?"

Other teachers used to offer Katya extra work, or tests from higher grades. Katya would always say, "Yes, please!" excitedly. This made the rest of us raise our eyebrows, although not seriously. We were used to Katya.

But Mrs. Pollock had never offered her any extra work.

Now she was staring at Katya. Abruptly, she threw her arms into the air and gasped.

We all stopped working on our tests and looked over.

"More work?" Mrs. Pollock cried. "Let me get this straight, you want *extra* mathematics! *More difficult* mathematics?"

Katya nodded slowly.

"Are you a *real* child?" Mrs. Pollock breathed. "Girls? Is she a robot? Oh, I know! You're an undercover Shadow Mage, *disguised* as a child! You've just given yourself away, Shadow Mage! No *child* would ever ask for extra work!"

Mrs. Pollock scuttled to the front and crouched behind her own desk. "Come on, everybody! Over here! Take cover!"

Everybody laughed hilariously. A few girls hopped up and ran to join her, and Mrs. Pollock beckoned them excitedly. "Get down! Get down!" she shouted.

Eventually, she rose again. "Oh, my old knees. Go on, girls, scoot back and carry on with the tests. And Katya? Did you *mean* that? Tell me it was just a joke!"

Katya pressed her fingertips to her forehead.

"Never mind, Mrs. Pollock," she said. "It was just a joke." She put her chin in her hand, elbow on the desk, and, while the rest of us finished our tests, she stared toward the window.

No wonder she's become so quiet, I thought. *She loves schoolwork: the more challenging, the better. Regular schoolwork for Katya is like doing 1 + 1 for us.*

She's bored.

And maybe she's worried, I thought next, *that too much easy work will flatten out her brain.*

CHAPTER 42

ONE OTHER CURIOUS thing happened to do with that mathematics test.

When we got it back that afternoon—Mrs. Pollock must have graded it at lunchtime—my grade was C–.

I sighed.

It's true that math is not my best subject, but usually I get at least a B. I supposed I'd made more mistakes than usual.

As I looked sadly at the test, my eyes happened to land on a question. You might remember this one, as I included it in the previous chapter.

$$
\begin{array}{r}
7{,}564\,+ \\
339 \\
4{,}982 \\
\hline
12{,}885 \\
\hline
\end{array}
$$

It was the sum I'd just finished and checked when the episode between Mrs. Pollock and Katya took place. I'd accidentally checked it *again* after that episode, and had been annoyed with myself for wasting time double-checking.

Yet here it was, marked with a big red X.

It was wrong?

Well, does my answer look wrong to you?

Go ahead and check it if you like.

Or don't worry about checking it if you prefer not to do

extra mathematics. Just trust me. It *was NOT* wrong. I checked it again five or six times.

"Mrs. Pollock?" I said, raising my hand. But the bell was ringing for afternoon tea, and Mrs. Pollock was busy performing her greetings with everyone.

* * *

At dinner that night, Principal Hortense leapt up to make an announcement.

"A fundraising weekend!" she exclaimed. "In Week Eight! Parents invited! On the Friday evening? A twilight picnic with our local Elves! Music, lanterns, cakes!"

Everyone clapped. We love our local Elves. We love music and lanterns. Especially, we love cakes.

"On the Saturday," Principal Hortense continued, "an art show! Each grade will create a masterpiece to be auctioned! Parents will visit your classrooms!"

We all clapped again, but that was just automatic. Who cared about art shows and classroom visits?

"*Why* do we want to raise funds?" Principal Hortense asked. Girls began calling suggestions ("to get ice cream machines for our dorms!" "a school pony!"), and she talked over them. "For the fishing village of Bobsleigh!"

Here, her face, which had been glowing with joy, withered into dismay. You have to be speedy to keep up with Principal Hortense's moods. "Many of you will know Taba Ringston?" she asked, still dismayed. "Wave, Taba?"

A shy wave from Taba, a girl in Grade 3.

"Taba is *from* Bobsleigh," Principal Hortense continued. "Recently, the currents around Bobsleigh have changed dramatically so there are no longer any fish! Catastrophic for Bobsleigh! Anybody guess why?"

I raised my hand.

"Yes, Esther?"

"Because it's a fishing village."

"Well done! We are raising money for Bobsleigh *because*

they have no fish. Anybody with a relative who's an artist? Ask them to donate a painting to be auctioned too! Do it! Tell them that the people of Bobsleigh have no fish! Carry on with dinner, girls. Eat up your string beans."

CHAPTER 43

AS IT WAS Monday, I went to the recreation room for poker practice after dinner.

My sisters were late, so I sat at our table, looking around the room.

On a nearby couch, the Rattlestone twins sat either side of Autumn Hillside, with Zoe Fawnwell and a few others cross-legged on the carpet. They were all eating cake.

I studied Autumn's face.

At first, it had seemed as if Pelagia had saved her.

By asking questions, Pelagia had made it seem as if Autumn was not a terrifying monster but a regular person with a fascinating background, like the circus. And if she could ask Autumn questions, anyone could!

So everyone did.

For the last few days, they had asked Autumn questions and she had answered them politely.

But just the day before, I'd noticed the teeniest crinkle at the top of Autumn's nose. A group of girls had been quizzing her. She'd quickly smoothed the crinkle away and answered.

And now, as I watched, I saw her give a tiny sigh. But she hid the sigh and answered the latest question.

My sisters arrived, and Imogen started chatting about her swimming tournament, which was coming up in less than two weeks.

"Mr. Dar-Healey says he'll bring treats for the road," she told us, "and board games for when Pelagia needs a break from telling stories."

We laughed. "She tells a *lot* of stories," Imogen added. "They're riveting. She's had so many adventures, Mr. Dar-Healey says there can't have been a single moment in her life when she wasn't in extreme peril."

Again, we laughed.

"Mr. Dar-Healey is so funny," Astrid said, "even though he's sad."

Imogen started to disagree, but I spoke quickly and softly, telling them what I'd overheard from the attic.

"So you're right, Astrid," I said. "He *is* sad. He just hides it well."

Astrid picked up her cards, nodding solemnly, but Imogen dropped hers, sat back, and raised her chin. This means she's angry. She's always furious when somebody she loves has been hurt and she can't help.

"I'm going away too," Astrid announced, to distract her. "Same day as you, Imogen. The mayor has been happy with my work at local meetings, and now he's asked me to come to a convention in Clybourne. It's for two weeks but Principal Hortense says it's okay because I can bring schoolwork and because '*attending government meetings will be thrillingly educational.*'"

"You'll both be back in time for the fundraising weekend?" I checked.

They'd return just in time, apparently. Astrid mentioned how sad our father would be to miss the fundraiser weekend— he loves school functions, but he was still away on his mysterious mission and hadn't even been able to write to us or telephone as he usually did—and Imogen said that Mother would be too busy working.

Then all three of us remembered at once that one of Mother's many sisters—Aunt Emma—is actually an artist. I volunteered to write to her and ask if she could spare a painting for the people of Bobsleigh, who no longer had any fish.

"Let's play now," Imogen suggested, reaching for her cards.

"Wait," I said. "Can you check this for me?"

I'd brought my mathematics test along and handed it to Imogen.

"Your answer is correct," she said, before turning the page and finding three more correct answers with cross marks.

"Show it to Mrs. Pollock tomorrow," Imogen advised. "She must have rushed grading it and I'm sure—"

"And *this* is called chocolate cake!" a high-pitched voice declared.

All three of us looked across the room.

"Chocolate cake," Tatty was repeating, pointing to her plate. "Did you have that in the Whispering Kingdom, Autumn?"

"Yes," Autumn agreed. "We had cake."

"But *chocolate* cake?" Tatty persisted.

"Yes," Autumn said. "We had chocolate cake."

"Oh, this is milk," Hetty said next. "Was there any *milk* in the Whispering Kingdom?"

My sisters and I raised eyebrows at each other.

After a pause, Autumn replied calmly: "We had milk in the Whispering Kingdom."

More and more questions were asked about objects available in the Whispering Kingdom.

Forks. Spoons. Bowls. Carpet. Chairs. (I'm not joking. Zoe asked if they had chairs.)

Each time, Autumn smiled, nodded, and said, "Yes. Yes, we did."

Eventually, somebody asked about peaches.

"Well," Autumn replied. "Well, no, we didn't have peaches. No peach trees. I remember my mother reading a story to me when I was seven or eight, and it mentioned peaches. I asked her what they were."

At this, the girls grew noisy with enthusiasm.

"*What?* No peaches!"

"Oh, you poor thing! Imagine living without peaches!"

"What was it *like* when you tried your first *peach*? You must have been *so* excited!"

Autumn smiled. "Delicious," she said. "Juicy."

The twins hugged her.

"How wonderful!" they said. "Lucky you! Getting to try a peach!"

My sisters and I rolled our eyes at each other.

"What did you do during the Whispering Wars?" Zoe asked.

"Nothing," Autumn said patiently. "I wasn't born yet when they ended. As I've mentioned before. I'm twelve."

Hetty's voice became thoughtful: "Are *ages* different in the Whispering Kingdom, though?"

"What do you mean?"

"You know, is *time* the same?"

"Time," Autumn said, still patient, "is exactly the same in the Whispering Kingdom."

Hetty and Tatty both winced, disappointed. "I suppose so," they said.

"Well, what did your parents do in the Whispering Wars?" Zoe tried. "Did they help kidnap children from other Kingdoms? Shoot people?"

Autumn blinked.

"Oh, *Zoe*," Hetty cried. "Don't remind her! She must feel *so* guilty about the wars! Are you all right, Autumn?"

Autumn's chin was slightly raised. "Yes," she replied. "I'm all right. My parents were actually—"

"Because I mean, it's true that your people stole children," Tatty said. "And invaded practically everywhere. *And* joined forces with Shadow Mages. You probably cry yourself to sleep about it! And it's true that—"

This was when Imogen loudly cleared her throat. "Autumn?" she called. "Want a game of poker with us?"

"Poker?" Autumn inquired, looking over. Her voice trembled slightly. "I don't know it."

"It's a card game. Come on, we'll teach you."

I was only imagining this of course, but to me it seemed as if the others had been steadily shelling nuts all over Autumn's lap, and that now, as she stood and smoothed down her skirt, stepping over to join us, the nutshells slid to the floor.

She learned the game of poker very quickly, and we told her she should join us anytime.

CHAPTER 44

THE NEXT DAY, while our class sat quietly filling in the answers to a comprehension exercise, I approached Mrs. Pollock.

"Mrs. Pollock?" I said. "May I ask about this?"

I placed my mathematics exam on her desk and pointed to the first incorrectly marked sum.

Mrs. Pollock was wearing her glasses with the square frames. She leaned forward, toward my test. She leaned so far forward that her nose touched the paper. Her fingers began tracing the numbers. She looked up at me. Her glasses glinted.

"What *is* this?" she said, voice loud enough that people in the class glanced up. "What *is* this?" Even louder. "Esther! I want to help you! I want to answer your questions about—about *this*!" She picked up my math exam and shook it so that the papers rustled. "But!" And she put it back down again. "But I do not—I *cannot* understand!"

"It's only that there were a couple of questions—" I began.

"Yes, yes," she interrupted. "Questions. Quite. Just a moment. I'm sure it will come to me." Again, she pressed her face so close to the test that her nose, and now her glasses, hit the desk with little thuds.

The whole class was watching now, some giggling.

"It's my—" I tried, but Mrs. Pollock waved at me.

"Hush!" she cried. "Hush! I think I—It's beginning to . . ."

And then, with a great *whoosh* of breath, she flung her hands up and beamed. "I've got it! I *understand*! This is *mathematics*, Esther! No *wonder* I was baffled! We are doing a *comprehension* exercise! *Words,* Esther! We are doing *words* today! And this is— Now, what are these things in mathematics called again? These squiggly little things?" She scratched her head.

"NUMBERS!" half the class shouted.

"Precisely." Mrs. Pollock fanned herself with my math exam. "Well, you've given me quite a fright, Esther, but I will survive. Here, personalized greeting? Yours is a fun one! Right. Go and sit down and carry on with your comprehension now."

She opened her drawer and placed my paper inside.

I gave up. I sat down.

Maybe she would look at my mathematics paper later and give it back, apologizing for her mistakes?

She didn't. I've never seen it since.

CHAPTER 45

LATER THAT DAY, Mrs. Pollock told us we had to prepare a three-minute speech on a topic of our choice.

"Whatever you feel *passionate* about!" she exclaimed. "Look to your heart! What makes it sing? Research that!"

We do these speeches each year, by the way. Classes vote for their favorite, and the winner goes to the interdistrict speech competition. I'd won favorite the previous two years and was secretly hoping to win again.

(Not that I win at the interdistrict level—the other speakers leave me flummoxed, they're so good—just because it's a fun day out from school.)

The thing I feel passionate about is magic, so I chose that. We had to get our topic approved and Mrs. Pollock nodded. "Magic. Perfect. That's your passion?"

I mean, specifically, my passion is that I wish I was a Spellbinder, but I didn't say that. I just agreed. "Yes," I said, and she put a tick by my name.

"I wish I was a Spellbinder" would not be long enough for a speech anyway. Even if I added, "I *really* wish it." I had to think of something more to say about magic, and so, during study hour, I went to our school library to find new ideas.

The librarian's name is Carlos and you never know when he'll have a beard. One day it's there, thick and bushy, the next, it's just his chin, fresh and new, blinking around at the world.

That afternoon, Carlos was crouched behind the circulation desk, peeling the tape from a cardboard box.

"Not long until the new G. A. Thunderstrike," he sang out as I walked by.

That's a skill of Carlos's. He always knows who's passing his desk. He says every student has a distinctive footfall.

He also knows every student's favorite author, even if they haven't got one. ("Ah, but this author will become your favorite," he says. "You just haven't read them yet.")

I stopped and looked over the counter.

"Yes, I know," I said. "I've got it in my calendar."

Carlos glanced up. He had a beard that day, but just a prickly one, not yet thick and bushy.

"Want a recommendation while you wait?" he asked.

"Not today," I replied. "Researching."

"Topic?"

"Magic."

"Big topic." Carlos whistled. "Fifth shelf on your right, between the seven nineties and the eight twenties."

"Thanks, Carlos."

I ran my hands along the spines of books in the 100s and 200s as I passed and paused at the 290s. It's a section called "classical mythology." In the time before magic, over a thousand years ago, people used to make up stories and share them— around the fireplace, I suppose. A lot of the stories are about "nature" choosing regular people and making them into "Fiends" or "Weavers" with special powers.

For a moment, I considered writing a speech about one of the famous Fiends or Weavers from the stories. Lady Susan Hart Van Metre, maybe. She was the majestic Fiend of the Dazzling Canyon. Or Professor Nicole Yule, an exquisite Forest Weaver, who ate apricots while saving lives.

But I decided to move on to the magic section instead: I wanted *facts*, not made-up stories. Plus, I wanted magic. I felt very sorry for the people in the time before magic. No wonder they had to invent Fiends and Weavers. They must have been bored and sorrowful.

In the magic section, I spent some time pulling out thick

textbooks and flimsy volumes, then putting them back. *A Comprehensive Survey of the History of Magic* had teeny print, and no pictures. *The Dung Radish Gnome* seemed promising—I'd never heard of Dung Radish Gnomes—but then I found a pamphlet tucked in the back.

Update from Author

Sorry, readers! Thought I'd uncovered a new species of Radish Gnome, but turns out the fellow in the shop was referring to those "DARN Radish Gnomes down Eanback Street." Not those "Dung Radish Gnomes." Wasted a year of my life researching ordinary Radish Gnomes, didn't I?

I found a book called *Crystal Faeries: Everything You Wanted to Know but Were Too Afraid to Ask*. Strange title. Who would be afraid to ask about Crystal Faeries? They're pretty nice, as far as I know.

Although Crystal Faeries are rare throughout the Kingdoms and Empires, we have plenty in the mountains around my school. That's a big reason why Shadow Mages don't usually come here—Crystal Faeries make them nauseated.

They might make a good topic for a speech, I decided—but when I opened the book, it was full of misty illustrations of Crystal Faeries smiling wisely and playing their xylophones. Only a few words were printed on each page and all they said was how *beautiful* Crystal Faeries are, and how much more powerful their magic is than that of regular Faeries, and what excellent dental hygiene they have, compared to regular Faeries. The book advised any regular Faeries who felt envious of Crystal Faeries to seek help.

I sighed and put it back. I missed our school Matron—she's part regular Faery, but her teeth have always seemed fine to me. If Matron was here, I'd have taken this book to her. First, she would have had a good belly laugh, then she'd have torn the pages to pieces, muttering, "*Beautiful*, are they? *Powerful*, are they?

Haven't met my great-grandma, have you? More power in her little fingernail than a hundred *Crystal* Faeries." That kind of thing.

After that, she'd have felt guilty about ruining one of Carlos's library books and she'd have taped it back together again.

Well, Shadow Mages were more exciting than True Mages anyway. I pulled out a stack of thin, blue books called the Astonishing series. One was *The Astonishing Truth about Radish Gnomes*, the next *The Astonishing Truth about Fire Sirens*, and so on, through all the major Shadow Mage groups.

Perfect, I thought.

I took the stack to a table and sat down to take notes.

The Favorite Foods of Witches, I wrote, as one heading. Then: *Common Phobias of the Radish Gnome.*

I grinned to myself, and then—

A strange rush of darkness crossed my vision.

Shadow Mages are not funny, I thought.

The faces of the Sterling Silver Foxes sauntering toward the shattered glass.

Principal Hortense's voice: "Shadow Mages have been spotted around our neighborhood."

Everybody said that the Sterling Silver Fox attack was a "one-off" and that nothing like that would *ever* happen again. What if they were wrong?

It was all right, I reminded myself. Pelagia, the undercover Spellbinder, had created a ring of protection around our school and was reinforcing it each night.

I wrote another heading:

Allergies Often Suffered by Sirens.

CHAPTER 46

I SPOKE TO Pelagia for the very first time that day.

Do you find it strange that I hadn't spoken to her yet?

Me too.

Only eighteen people in my grade, and we eat meals together and have classes, sports, games, study hours, dance lessons, arguments, teeth brushing, chores, and recreation together. You'd think I'd have at least asked if she'd pass me the gravy.

Of course, it was difficult to get Pelagia's attention because others were always gathered around her, waiting for her next story, and she was busy doing swimming training with my sister and Mr. Dar-Healey.

But it was more than that. One night, I'd been walking to my dormitory to fetch my slippers and had seen her emerging from *her* dormitory, carrying a cardigan.

I could easily have called out, "Oh, hi, Pelagia. Were you cold too? I'll walk back to the recreation room with you." (Or something like that.)

Easily!

And we could have chatted our way back down the stairs.

But I didn't do that. I ducked into my dorm and by the time I'd found my slippers, she was gone.

It was the Spellbinding thing, you see.

Even when there'd only been a *chance* she was the Spellbinder, it had meant something, and now I knew Autumn was a Whisperer, so it was definitely Pelagia—

Well, it just made her seem too important and too . . . *busy?* . . . to want to speak to me. It made me shy.

At Free Time that afternoon, I was wandering in the gardens behind the school. A few other girls sat in the shade of trees reading or chatting.

I walked to the pond, sat down, pulled off my shoes and stockings, and splashed my bare feet in the water.

This is not actually allowed. However, I do it all the time. Sometimes I even wade around the edges, or slip into the pond up to my waist. It's at the back of the gardens, so you usually don't get caught.

It's quite close to the Old Schoolhouse, though. I swirled my feet, making the water lilies shift and bump into each other, and gazed up at that building.

The sun reflected off the windows, dazzling them, so I couldn't tell if any accountants—or surgeons or electricians or vets—were watching me, making plans to report me to my school principal.

That's when a voice spoke.

"Hello, Esther," said the voice.

And there she was, standing behind me: Pelagia. Still had her cute little snail-shell nose. (Well, of course she did, what would she have done with it?)

"Hello," I replied, but Pelagia was kicking off her own shoes, pulling off her stockings, and sitting beside me.

Splash went her feet in the pond.

"Aaaah," she said.

I smiled.

We sat quietly, listening to distant murmurs of girls' voices, the *snip-snip* of Mustafa trimming a bush somewhere, birds singing their fragments. They get caught on one bit of a song, birds, and don't move it along.

Pelagia began kicking her legs back and forth in the water. It became quite splashy: sparkles of water flying everywhere.

It reminded me of how she'd *zipped* from one end of the pool to the other like a skipping stone at the swimming pool that day.

"Have you always been such a good swimmer?" I asked.

Pelagia kicked her legs a few more times then stopped.

"I don't know," she said. "I just . . . swim."

Funny.

It reminded me of people asking Autumn what it was like to be a Whisperer and her saying, "I don't know. I just *am* a Whisperer."

For the first time, it occurred to me how strange it was that our two new girls were opposites.

In the Whispering Wars, the Whisperers had used shadow magic to attack, and Spellbinders had bound that shadow magic to defeat them.

Autumn was a Whisperer; Pelagia was a Spellbinder.

Whisperers and Spellbinders. Opposites.

Enemies.

Autumn and Pelagia should hate each other. As far as I could see, they did not. They didn't pay much attention to each other, but when they did, they were polite. In fact, Pelagia's questions to Autumn had *helped* people relax about Autumn.

Maybe I was missing something.

"I'm not that good a swimmer," Pelagia added. "Just average."

"Well," I said, "if you think that was average, you must come from a land of swimming superstars. Where *do* you come from, Pelagia? Mrs. Pollock never got you to introduce yourself."

Pelagia shrugged.

"That's okay," she said. "I don't mind."

Another long quiet. She hadn't answered my question and I wasn't sure if she'd forgotten or didn't want to—maybe she just couldn't believe I didn't know already, as she was always telling stories. It seemed a bit pestery to ask again. I reached for a stick in the grass instead and used it to stir the water. Lily pads floated serenely by.

Pelagia was much quieter than I expected. Rather than sharing dramatic stories with me, she was humming a little tune.

"Is everything all right with you?" I asked.

I thought she'd say, "What do you mean?" but instead she sighed.

"I'm fine," she said. "It's just that there's too much . . ."

She stopped.

"Homework?" I suggested.

"*Responsibility,*" she whispered.

At least, I think that's what she whispered. It was a whisper softer than feathers.

"Responsibility?" I checked, but she shook her head. In the water, the weeds swayed slowly.

Of course, I thought.

Imagine how much responsibility there is being the undercover Spellbinder. Keeping students and teachers safe from any wandering Shadow Mages. Training for a swimming tournament must be exhausting enough, without—

That same strange rush of darkness from the library plunged again, like a black waterfall, before my vision.

"Pelagia," I said, blinking, blinking. "The swimming tournament. You'll be away for two weeks."

Who would protect the school then?

Pelagia took a deep breath, and I turned to her—

But all she said was "Look," and she pointed out an Elf that was riding on a frog, leaping through the reeds. We both watched until the Elf disappeared.

In the water, a school of tiny fish darted by.

Pelagia hummed again, the same tune.

CHAPTER 47

SPEAKING OF FISH, everyone seemed to be painting them.

Every grade had to produce a "masterpiece" for the art show, you see, and *many* grades were doing fish.

Either fish paintings or fish made from foil stuck to ocean-blue backgrounds.

I worried that the paintings might hurt the feelings of the Bobsleigh fishing village. It was like we were showing off: "Look at all the fish *we've* got! And you don't have *any!*"

The others told me that was silly. For one thing, the Bobsleighans would never see our artwork, just the money we made from it. For another, our fish were not edible.

"You're overthinking it, Esther," Katya advised.

For a few days, Mrs. Pollock told us she "didn't have a clue" what our masterpiece would be. She was very funny like that, often shrugging and saying, "How should *I* know?" when someone asked her a question or replying with their personalized greeting.

People would make suggestions and she would pull her clown faces until everybody laughed, then change the subject.

Until one day, when we were learning about Plants and How They Grow. Mrs. Pollock had just explained sunlight and its job (don't really remember what, sorry) when suddenly she stopped, flung a piece of chalk against the wall, and shouted, "The weather!"

We stared.

"Our masterpiece will be the best!" she crowed. "Because we will paint"—and here, she hurried to a window, wrenched it open, stuck out her head, and shouted—"*you*! We will paint *you*, weather!"

Basically, we had to choose our favorite kind of weather and paint it. Then we'd glue our pictures onto—Mrs. Pollock waved a hand vaguely—"a tree or something."

We giggled.

"Maybe a big piece of corkboard," Hetty Rattlestone suggested.

"Yes. Genius. A piece of corkboard." Mrs. Pollock nodded.

Everyone in the class painted a blue sky and a big yellow sun.

Except me. My favorite weather is rain. So I painted that.

A pale gray background and lots of little black dots.

It looked very boring, to be honest.

But then Autumn suggested I crowd the bottom of the painting with colorful umbrellas. Once I'd done that, I was almost dizzied by the beauty. The splashes of umbrella color against the gray made it magical! I'm not very good at art, and this was definitely the best painting I'd ever done.

"That was good advice about the umbrellas," I told Autumn.

Autumn smiled. "Thanks," she said. "You did a good job." Then she ducked her head back down, hiding behind her hair again.

CHAPTER 48

THE FIRST IN the class to present a personal interest project was Katya.

"I feel passionate about the cycle of life," she announced. Her voice made the words into a series of dull, gray thuds. She yawned.

"All water was once gas," she continued. "When temperatures dropped, it condensed into rain. Rain fell into the great basins and troughs on the surface of the Kingdoms and Empires and formed oceans and lakes. The oceans and lakes . . ."

I don't know what she said next. Everyone settled down to think their own thoughts.

Next was Hetty Rattlestone.

"The thing that I feel most passionate about," she began, "is . . ."

Long pause.

Hetty looked around at us, her eyes dancing.

"My family tree!" she cried.

Oh, worth the wait, then. (Ha ha.)

She then spent fifteen minutes outlining her family tree.

Here is a sample:

"And then there's Great-Aunt Pickled Possum, who *happens* to be Queen of Smileypop, and *her* daughter, of course, is Cousin Tilly Billy-Buttocks, who, by the way, is Vice-Regent of the Empire of Plum Jam."

(I'm making up the names as I forget the real ones. But this was basically how it went.)

The only interesting thing about this speech was how much Mrs. Pollock loved it. I stopped watching Hetty altogether and stared at Mrs. Pollock instead. She was sitting on her chair, elbows on her knees, chin in her hands, and her eyes glittered like the ocean on a sunny day. At each new name that Hetty mentioned, Mrs. Pollock nodded vigorously.

At last it was over.

"Any questions?" Hetty asked us.

Not even Zoe Fawnwell could bring herself to ask one.

Mrs. Pollock applauded loudly.

"Fascinating!" she said. "Great job, Hetty. You made your project so much more interesting by bringing *yourself* into it. You shared your remarkable connections to such important people!"

There was a pause.

I waited for Mrs. Pollock to make a joke—I think we were all waiting—but she only beamed, scribbled something down, and called for the next person to present.

Tatty Rattlestone spoke next. At least she didn't pause for "suspense," but Tatty's speech was on her favorite fashion magazines.

I fell asleep halfway through.

When I woke up, Mrs. Pollock was saying: "It's our resident giraffe's turn! Or do you prefer to be called by your original name of Durba?"

"I don't mind," Durba said. "Whichever you like." She's a good sport, Durba.

"I suppose your passion will be something rather *high*," Mrs. Pollock suggested next, "like a mountain, say, or the sky?"

"No," Durba replied. "My topic is the Children of Spindrift."

Everyone straightened up, pleased. We'd all grown up playing games where we pretended to be the Children of Spindrift. Back in the time of the Whispering Wars, you see, a group of brave children from Spindrift had helped to win the war. Although we knew the story well, we were always happy to hear it again.

But Mrs. Pollock gasped.

"Oh *Durba*," she said, "is that quite the thing?"

Durba is not one of those tall people who hunches, embarrassed by her height. She generally stands straight and proud. However, at this point, she sank a little. Her face was both worried and confused.

"Because we have a *Whisperer* in the class!" Mrs. Pollock stage-whispered. "You'll remind everybody!"

Of course, the story of the Children of Spindrift *is* connected to the Whispering Kingdom. Until Mrs. Pollock spoke up though, I'd completely forgotten that Autumn herself was a Whisperer. Or, at least, I'd set it aside: she was just Autumn again, a girl with a beautiful name.

I think most of the class had done the same, actually. We'd all smiled at Durba when she announced her topic, but the moment Mrs. Pollock reminded us, we swiveled to look at Autumn instead.

Autumn kept her face blank. (Her new poker-playing skills might have helped?)

"Ask *Autumn* if your topic troubles her, Durba?" Mrs. Pollock urged, still in her loud whisper.

Durba looked stricken. "Sorry, Autumn," she said. "Is it okay with you if . . . ?"

"Of course," Autumn said quickly. "Talk about whatever you like."

"Oh my goodness," Mrs. Pollock exclaimed suddenly. "Autumn probably doesn't even know what we're talking about! Autumn? Do you *know* who the Children of Spindrift are?"

Autumn's blank expression collapsed slightly. She had hoped to hide this, I realized. "No," she admitted. "I mean, I suppose the Children of Spindrift are . . . children who . . . live in the town of Spindrift?"

Giggles.

But Mrs. Pollock's face was serious. "Makes sense that you wouldn't know," she murmured. "Everywhere else, of course, the Spindrift Children are heroes, whereas in the Whispering Kingdom, they'd be the *opposite*. And people might prefer to . . . *forget* them!" She laughed suddenly and turned to Durba.

"Go ahead!" she said. "It's about time Autumn learned about the Children of Spindrift! Fill in the gaps in her education!"

And she leaned back, ready to listen.

It was very awkward then. Durba appeared wretched. Every word seemed like a poisoned dart, directed at Autumn. People kept glancing at Autumn, to see her reaction, and Autumn tried to nod along, interested.

At last it was over. "Any questions?" Durba asked.

I raised my hand.

"Did you know," I said, "that one of the Children of Spindrift grew up to be my favorite author? The orphan girl named Glim became the best-selling author G. A. Thunderstrike."

Durba smiled. "Oh, really? I didn't—" But Mrs. Pollock interrupted.

"Oh, *very* nice, Esther!" she cried. "Pointing out a gap in Durba's speech! Want to show her up, do you?"

She grinned, wide-eyed, and everyone laughed.

"No, no," I said. "I didn't mean to point out a *gap*. I just—"

"Just wanted her to know she'd missed important information? Like what happened to the Spindrift Children when they grew up? Tell us about the others, Esther."

I stared at her, miserable. I didn't want to show up Durba any more than I had.

"Oh, you want Durba to answer?" Mrs. Pollock said. "Good point. Durba?"

Durba blushed. "I'm not sure I . . ."

"Esther?" Mrs. Pollock interrupted. "Can you help? Durba doesn't know."

I spoke in a quick mumble: "As well as becoming an author, Glim was the first ambassador to the dragons; Honey Bee, Finlay, and Hamish became acclaimed athletes; the twins became doctors; and Victor works in the back room of a bank."

Mrs. Pollock turned to Durba. "There you go, Durba. Bits you missed in your speech. *Bits you missed*—what's another word for that?" Mrs. Pollock snapped her fingers. "Gaps! Yes! You were pointing out *gaps*, Esther!"

My head was tangled. Mentioning Glim hadn't been a

criticism—I'd just thought Durba might be interested! Also, I'd wanted to change the subject, to shift it away from the Whispering Wars, for Autumn's sake.

But maybe I *had* embarrassed Durba?

How could I explain myself?

Faces had turned to me, smirking. Durba was rocking on her feet, looking very worried now—probably thinking that she *should* have included what had happened to the Spindrift children when they grew up.

"I don't think—" I began, and stopped. "I mean, I was only—See, Durba's speech was not *about* what— It was *great*— And I really—"

Again, I stopped.

"Oh my stars, Esther, I hope you remember how to finish sentences when it's *your* turn to speak! Actually, let's find out now! Sit down, Durba! Your turn, Esther!" And Mrs. Pollock waved me up to the front.

CHAPTER 49

SO THAT WAS not a great start.

Standing at the front, I took a few moments to gather my thoughts. I opened my mouth to begin and then closed it again. Did that a second time.

"Are you one of the fish that have swum away from Bobsleigh?" Mrs. Pollock inquired.

Everyone giggled.

I took a deep breath.

Most people use index cards to do presentations, but I like to memorize mine. I get too confused otherwise—you look around to make eye contact with the audience, then back down at your index cards. How do you find your spot? So I practice my speeches every time I have a bath. I have a lot of baths, so I get a lot of practice.

Come on, I told myself. *Remember the tub!*

I pictured the curve of the tap over the bath and heard the sound of water rushing, and my own voice rehearsing.

At last it came back.

"The thing that makes my heart sing," I began, "is *magic*."

I paused. I try to include pauses in my speeches. Short ones.

"In fact," I said, "magic makes my heart sing, dance, and turn cartwheels. I myself am not very good at cartwheels."

I turned a cartwheel.

See, I also try to do unexpected things in my speeches, to give the audience a surprise. That gave them a surprise. Mrs. Pollock gasped. We don't usually turn cartwheels in class.

It also made the class laugh because my cartwheels really are very bad. Legs crooked and clattering back down.

"But my *heart*," I said, standing up again, "is great at cartwheels. I think, anyway. Don't know for sure, I've never actually *seen* my heart."

The class laughed again. Things were going well.

"As you know," I said, "magic began when people discovered magical thread buried deep in the ground and began to mine for it, weaving it into spells. Different-colored thread was used by the three different kinds of mages. Eventually, of course, mages only needed to *imagine* thread to weave spells."

I won't tell you the entire speech. I tried to make it entertaining, listing unexpected habits, allergies, and sporting preferences of various Shadow Mages.

Now and then Mrs. Pollock made popping sounds with her lips, which was distracting, but most girls smiled or nodded along. I like to include personal stories, to make it interesting.

For example: "Now, I live in a very safe neighborhood—the mountain village of Blue Chalet—and when I'm not at home, I'm perfectly safe here at Katherine Valley. As you know, you have to do an interview to get into this school and you'd never pass that if you were a Shadow Mage."

(Everybody laughed softly.)

"They wouldn't interview you in the first place, actually," I added.

(They smiled. That's nice, but I prefer it when they laugh.)

"The point is, in my entire life, I have almost *never* seen a Shadow Mage. I've only had two encounters."

(Everyone brightened, excited to hear my encounters.)

"The first was when I was nine. I saw a Witch at one of Father's university's Family Open Days. She was sitting on a picnic blanket and eating a boiled egg."

Everyone's eyes widened.

"Then my father said, 'No, that's just Professor Karshoroff, she has unfortunate taste in fashion and is often mistaken for a Witch.'"

The class laughed.

"So maybe I shouldn't call that an encounter," I admitted. "And the second . . ."

Another pause.

"Well, you all know this one . . .

"Sterling Silver Foxes caused the wall of the new swimming pool to shatter, and then pretended to offer help. *None* of us realized that they were Sterling Silver Foxes.

"None except for the brave Autumn Hillside!"

(Everyone glanced at Autumn, and she looked shy but, I *think*, also pleased.)

"What would have happened if Autumn had *not* recognized them in time?"

I paused again, for suspense. Then I whispered: *"They'd have stolen our laughter."*

"Eh?" said Mrs. Pollock.

That was a bit annoying of her. I was whispering loudly enough for the class to hear—it was for dramatic effect. Also, she knew perfectly well that Sterling Silver Foxes steal laughter. Everyone knows. But now people were giggling at Mrs. Pollock instead of at my speech.

I waited for them to calm down.

"They are strange, the Sterling Silver Foxes," I continued. "Our laughter causes them *agony*, but stealing it brings them power. Their shadow magic is energized by stolen laughter.

"What would it mean for *you* if you had your laughter stolen?"

I looked around at different faces, so people would feel like I was speaking to them personally. Some looked back at me very intensely, which was good.

"First, your skin would turn a pale blue color.

"Second, you would get terrible headaches.

"Third, your bones would ache, and you would itch.

"Fourth, you would feel sad and tired most of the time.

"Fifth, you would not be able to laugh *ever again*."

Once more, I looked around the room, meeting people's eyes. Katya had turned to look out the window, so I chose somebody else's eyes to meet.

I lowered my voice for the next part.

"And sixth," I said. *"You might die."*

Gasps.

"Of course," I said, "if you get to a Faery treatment center quickly enough, you'll probably survive. But the treatment is painful, cannot return your laughter, and if you *don't* get it in time . . ."

The room was silent.

Then Mrs. Pollock popped her lips again, which broke the tension and caused more giggles.

"It is therefore very lucky," I said fervently, "that Autumn saved us from those Sterling Silver Foxes."

Everyone nodded vigorously.

After that, I told a bloodcurdling story about a Shadow Mage attack, and finished by lightening the mood with a story about an Elf who accidentally turned himself into a clothes peg.

There were a couple of questions, and then I said, "Thank you for listening," and everyone clapped loudly.

Mrs. Pollock said, "Thank you, Esther," and beckoned me over for a congratulatory personalized greeting.

I sat back down.

CHAPTER 50

DOT PECORINO DID her speech next, but I could not hear it.

I think it was about cats. I do remember her making a little *mew* sound.

Dot is so shy. She trembled throughout the speech, ducking her head so that she was mostly speaking to her shoulder.

"What?" Mrs. Pollock kept asking. "It's like a teeny mouse talking!"

Everyone giggled.

"Is your shoulder more interested in your words than we are, Dot?" Mrs. Pollock wondered.

Again, the class laughed.

Dot straightened up.

"Still can't hear you!" Mrs. Pollock crowed. "Is it my old lady hearing? Should I stand *closer*?" She sidled up beside Dot and placed her ear by Dot's mouth.

Dot stopped.

"Nope." Mrs. Pollock slid away. "No difference. Carry on, Dot. We'll take wild guesses."

I looked around. Some girls smiled at me, and some mouthed, "Good speech." Durba gave me a thumbs-up.

Katya was still staring out the window.

Strange. She usually focuses on speeches, even ones you can't hear. Even if only to scoff at whatever the person is saying.

The part of my speech about Sterling Silver Foxes had gone well, I decided. Everyone had stared at me, wide-eyed.

Everybody except Katya.

I glanced over at her again. Still gazing toward the window.

Maybe she wanted some fresh air?

She did look quite pale, actually. You could see the veins on her face, purple lines against drastically white skin. Her skin is usually a soft brown color, but now it was so white it was almost—

I felt as if a great clump of snow had fallen onto my head.

Blue.

So white it was almost blue.

An image crept into my mind: Katya running around the swimming pool, toward the broken glass, toward the approaching Sterling Silver Foxes, wanting to help the little girls in her chess team.

Ice-cold rivulets swarmed down my neck.

So white it was almost blue. Now that I studied her, Katya's skin did have the faintest blue tinge to it.

First, your skin would turn a pale blue color.

But it must be the light! If her skin had turned blue, other people would have noticed!

Second, you would get terrible headaches.

Another memory: Katya pressing her fingertips to her forehead.

Third, your bones would ache and you would itch.

Katya in our dormitory saying: "I can't sleep. My ankles and knees are hurting."

Katya at the dance class saying: "My eyes are itchy."

Fourth, you would feel sad and tired most of the time. Fifth, you would never laugh again.

Katya gazing at the window.

And sixth, you might die.

Out the front of the room, Dot Pecorino had just finished her speech. "Does anyone have any questions?" she murmured.

"I do," I said, standing up.

But I was not looking at Dot Pecorino.

"Katya," I said. "Did the Sterling Silver Foxes steal your laughter?"

Katya tipped forward, burying her face in her arms.

CHAPTER 51

MRS. POLLOCK WHOOPED WITH
laughter.

That made me jump.

"Theatrics in the classroom!" she hooted.

Katya's head remained in her arms. Her shoulders shook.

Mrs. Pollock sighed. "Esther, you'd better take Katya to the nurse to see why she's so upset. Can you two manage that or must we have more . . ." Here, she leapt to her feet, jumped up and down, and shouted in a babyish voice, *"Katya! Are you a Sterling Silver Fox? And more of this?"* Mrs. Pollock wrapped her arms around the back of a chair and pretended to sob loudly.

I *had* not jumped like that, my voice is *not* babyish, and I had *not* asked Katya if she was a Sterling Silver Fox. Plus, Katya had not sobbed aloud.

Still. Everybody laughed.

I wondered how I was going to take Katya to the nurse if she remained sitting with her head in her arms. But she slowly stood and followed me out, shoulders hunched, head bowed.

"Just go straight to the nurse's office, since it's nothing serious," Mrs. Pollock called behind us. "Don't worry about a pass."

Katya shuffled along. I touched her shoulder, and she glanced at me, trying to smile through her tears.

It made me want to give her a hug, that little smile.

In the corridor light, her face was still pale, but I could not see any blue. I'd probably imagined it! She was probably just *sad*:

her laughter was still there, deep inside her, waiting for happiness to return.

We climbed the stairs, one slow thud at a time.

At the nurse's office, I knocked and there was an irritated sound. "I'm *eating*!" called the nurse's muffled voice. "You'd better have a pass!"

I opened the door and put my head in. Nurse Sydelle was holding a sandwich. Bits of lettuce and cheese spilled from it. A half-slice of tomato had got pasted to the side of her mouth.

"So, *have* you?" she demanded. "Got a pass?" The tomato began to slide toward her chin, and she caught it with her tongue and ate it. "I'll be cross if you don't. I'm cross even if you do, as I've *told* Ms. Ubud I like to eat at this time of the day." She glared, the sandwich hovering.

"No," I said. "We haven't got a—"

"Right then! Out! Don't let me see you here again until you *have* one! Good gracious, I mean to—"

"But Mrs. Pollock said not to worry about getting a pass," I explained. "She said to bring Katya right here."

"Oh she did, did she? Well, Mrs. Pollock doesn't make the rules. *Very* clear, the rules are. Students are to get a pass from the secretary before they knock on my door. How am I supposed to run this office if you all just dash in here at the drop of—"

Katya pushed past me, into the room.

"Nurse Sydelle," she said in a clear, strong voice. "The Sterling Silver Foxes stole my laughter."

Nurse Sydelle dropped her sandwich.

CHAPTER 52

IT DIDN'T TAKE Nurse Sydelle long to recover her cranky mood.

For a moment, she stared at Katya, wide-eyed. Then she opened a drawer and rummaged around in it.

"What makes you think your laughter's been stolen?" she grumbled as she rummaged. "Feeling blue, are we? Esther, give Katya a tickle and see if you can't get a giggle out of her. Probably nothing the matter with you."

She gave up on that drawer, slammed it closed, and opened the next one down.

I glanced uncertainly at Katya, wondering if I was really supposed to tickle her, but Katya shook her head at me and stepped further into the office.

"I just know," she said. "I've known for a while."

"Headaches?" Nurse Sydelle asked—rummage, rummage, *slam!* Next drawer—rummage, rummage. "Itchiness? Blue facial mark—aha! Here it is!"

She held up a silver cylinder, the length of a fountain pen but a little thicker.

"Faery lamp," she told us, clicking a button on the end and shining a pale light at Katya.

As soon as she did this, blue squiggles like bright little worms seemed to jump onto Katya's face.

All over her face. Just beneath the skin, crossing her nose, crowding her cheeks, lined up above her eyebrows, blue squiggles everywhere.

Nurse Sydelle clicked the light off instantly. Her hand jumped away from Katya.

"Blue markings," she murmured. "I'll say there are. Right—" And once again she was rummaging crankily. This time she opened the door of a cabinet and riffled around on each shelf. "You say you've known this for a while, Katya? Whyever would you not come and see me sooner then? You do know how serious this can be if untreated? When I say serious, I mean very, well, I mean . . . Here it is!"

Her hand pounced onto a tiny glass bottle. "Drink this, Katya. All of it. It will make you feel dreadful, I'm afraid, but that's the way with stolen-laughter treatment. Need help with the lid?"

Katya shook her head, unscrewing the lid and holding the bottle to her mouth. She paused.

Nurse Sydelle snapped: "Drink it! Now! Or honestly, based on those facial markings, you'll be dead by"—she glanced at the clock on her office wall—"dinner. I've only ever seen cases this advanced in textbooks. Drink!"

Katya tipped the bottle back, and Nurse Sydelle turned to me. "She'll need to go straight to bed," she said. "She's going to feel really ill for a bit, then she'll fall into a deep sleep. Katya, when you wake up, you'll be far from here. I'm running down to the office to make arrangements." Nurse Sydelle stood, gathering papers.

"Arrangements?" I asked.

"Yes, that's an emergency dose she just took—won't last long—she needs to get to a Faery treatment center. The closest one that could deal with this is two Kingdoms away. I wonder if they can get an automobile to collect her, but—"

Katya made a small screeching sound and began scratching at her own chest with both hands.

"Hurting already, is it?" Nurse Sydelle sounded a little kinder. "Yes, it's horrible—the medicine goes to battle with the shadow magic, see. Is that why you didn't tell us sooner? Were you afraid of the treatment?"

A pause, then Katya whispered, "I suppose so."

"Go on, then." Nurse Sydelle clapped her hands at me. "Put her to bed! I'll be back!"

She ducked around behind us and ran from her office. Her footsteps pattered quickly along the corridor and down the stairs.

Katya was gazing at the office doorway.

"Can you walk?" I asked.

"Of course," Katya murmured, and then she stumbled forward, clutching her stomach. "No," she whimpered. "No, I can't. Please. Help me."

CHAPTER 53

WE STAGGERED TO our dormitory.

Katya was like a blanket that has gotten drenched and muddy in a thunderstorm, making it limp and heavy. She kept slipping from my arms toward the floor. I let her slump onto her bed and reached under her pillow for her pajamas.

She was shivering violently now.

Next I had to help her out of her school uniform and into her pajamas.

"Let's begin with your shoes," I decided. I tried using the voice my father uses when one of us is ill. "Oh, darling," I said. "It's all right, it's going to be all right."

It wasn't though. Even if she lived, she'd never laugh again.

I spoke quickly over that thought. "The nurse said you'd fall asleep soon, and that will stop the hurting. I can see why you didn't go to her sooner—the treatment does seem *awful*, darling."

I pulled off one of her lace-up shoes. Actually, I could *not* see why she hadn't told somebody sooner. It's true that the treatment was making her miserable now but surely dying would be miserable-er?

Strange, too, because Katya had always been a brave, bold sort. Look at how she'd run around to try to help her little chess team girls. I pulled off her second shoe and checked her face—she was biting her lip so hard it was bleeding. Trying not to cry out loud. See? Brave.

"If only Matron had been here," I said.

I peeled off one of Katya's socks.

"As she's got Faery in her, I bet she would have noticed sooner," I continued, peeling off the second sock. "I feel terrible because *I* noticed you were sad, but I didn't even think of— Well, anyway, now, darling, let's get this uniform—"

Wait.

Had I seen that?

I looked back down.

Katya's bare feet. Her toenails—

"Katya," I murmured.

Her toenails were blue.

Katya had wound her arms around her stomach and was rocking back and forth on the bed. I could still see her toenails. Still blue.

Stolen laughter causes blue markings on your face.

Did it also cause blue markings on toenails?

I hadn't read that anywhere.

"Katya," I said again. "Darling, your toenails—" As I looked, the toenails faded back to their regular color.

Katya had stilled. She was sitting cross-legged on the bed at this point, still clutching her stomach. But there was a strange, sudden stillness to her.

I looked at her face, and she looked back steadily.

I knew what it meant to have blue toenails.

I've spent enough time staring at my own toenails, checking, longing—

"Katya," I whispered, checking the open doorway, making sure nobody was about. "Katya, are you a *Spellbinder*?"

Katya carried on looking at me steadily.

"Are you *the* Spellbinder?" I asked, in wonder. "The one who . . ."

Slowly, she tucked her bare feet under the covers, out of sight.

CHAPTER 54

"YOU *ARE*," I said, suddenly certain. I thought fast as I continued helping her to change. "You're the one who's put a Spellbinding around our school." I checked over my shoulder again. "And you've been reinforcing it."

"How do *you* know about that?" Katya murmured. Between us, we managed to get her into her pajamas. She slid under the covers. "Esther," she said, looking up from her pillow. "Nobody's meant to know. How . . . ?"

"Oh." I waved my hand dismissively.

She smiled. "Eavesdropping . . ."—then her smile twisted into a terrible grimace. "It really hurts," she admitted, breathlessly.

"Poor darling." I stroked her hair. It was too bumpy to stroke. The little coiled buns she'd been wearing since Mrs. Pollock came to class in a pink wig. How uncomfortable they must be! I pulled out the pins and untangled the buns so that Katya's curls sprang out again. I stroked the curls instead. This seemed to calm her a little.

"And *that's* why you ran around the pool that day," I realized. "Not just to help your chess team. You were meaning to spellbind the Sterling Silver Foxes!"

"Stupid of me," Katya muttered. "I couldn't spellbind even *one* Sterling Silver Fox, let alone a bunch. It takes all my strength reinforcing the Spellbinding here each night."

"And lately you've been doing that with your laughter stolen!" I shook my head slowly. "You must be *so* worn out. Wait! Is that why you haven't told anybody about the stolen laughter? Because you thought you should stay to reinforce the

Spellbinding and couldn't go away for treatment? But there aren't *really* many Shadow Mages in the mountains, Katya! The Sterling Silver Foxes were a one-off!"

She shook her head at me. "It's so dangerous, Esther," she said, yawning. I'd forgotten she was going to fall asleep soon. "In the mountains, there are so many, so, so . . ."

Her eyes closed, but then her lids fluttered, and she opened them again.

"I couldn't leave," she rasped. "The school needed me. I was trying to wait until—I was going to tell the nurse about my stolen laughter once they . . . they arrived—"

"Who?"

She winced and pressed a palm to her forehead. "Spellbinders. They're coming to the Old Schoolhouse for a secret convention. Four weeks from today. I thought if I could hold out until then, I'd be all right. I thought . . ."

"But, Katya, you're so ill already! You wouldn't have *lasted* another—"

"Shhh," Katya said. "Esther, stop talking. I'm falling asleep and this is important. I think . . ."

Once again, her eyes closed, and she sank deep into the pillow. Once again, she opened them. She patted her own cheeks, trying to rouse herself.

"Somebody needs to know that I'm leaving," she muttered.

"Well . . . ," I said, thinking aloud. "The school will tell your family about your stolen laughter and that you've been sent away. And if your family know about your Spellbinding, and what you're doing, then they can tell—whoever's in charge. Is anybody else in your family a Spellbinder?" I knew it ran in families. "Stefan? Is he one too?"

Katya was shaking her head. "None of them are," she whispered, "and they don't know about me. Please don't tell them. No, it will have to be . . . Esther, will you take a message to the Orange Blossom Tea Shop in town? Talk to the tall, thin waitress, the one who wears a necklace with a little . . . a silver apple pendant . . . tell her . . ."

She was fading again.

"To send another Spellbinder?" I checked.

"Don't say that out loud," Katya murmured, her eyelids half-closed. "I'm not supposed to contact her. They're very strict . . . that's why I haven't been to see her . . . why I've tried to stay . . . but now that I'm going . . . this is . . ."

She was shivering again. I put my arm around her shoulders and she sort of cuddled into me.

"Thank you," she said hoarsely. "I'm so cold, Esther. And I've failed . . . I've failed . . ."

Tears filled her eyes.

"You have *not* failed!" I cried. "Katya! You've been so brave! You've—"

Katya interrupted me. "It's an emergency," she said. "So I have to break the rules . . . the tall waitress . . . the one with the necklace . . . Did I already say that? It's against the rules. But . . . emergency. The school really, really needs . . . Just say this. Say: *The bell is rusty. Please send another.* Can you say that?"

"Of course."

"I mean, *say* it. Now."

I cleared my throat and tried a solemn, significant voice, like a bell ringing myself. *"The bell is rusty. Please send another."*

Katya nodded. "Say that, then leave. Just use your normal voice."

"I'll go tomorrow," I agreed, a bit embarrassed.

"Today," Katya whispered. "My Spellbinding around the school will wear out by tonight. And don't tell *anybody* about this. Esther, promise me. Nobody must know."

"But Principal Hortense?" I suggested.

Katya shook her head. "Nobody."

"What about your family? Stefan?"

Again Katya was shaking her head.

"I could tell my sist—"

"Not your sisters."

"What about Mrs. Pollock?" I tried.

"Mrs. Pollock," Katya repeated, her voice distant. She shook her head again. "Tell *nobody. Promise* me."

I promised.

Her eyes closed and she began to breathe slowly and deeply.

I myself was panicking.

"Are you sure we really need protection?" I asked. "And are you sure there are no *other* Spellbinders at the school? What about Pelagia? Isn't *she* a Spellb—"

Katya shook her head, eyes still closed, hair scratching against the pillow. "Pelagia's not a Spellbinder," she told me. "She's . . . well, I don't know. But there's something about her that I can't . . . Esther, be careful of Pelagia. I'm falling asleep now, Esther. I think . . ."

And she was quiet.

I sat beside her, watching her sleep, until Nurse Sydelle bustled into the room. Behind her were two men carrying a stretcher.

CHAPTER 55

AT LUNCHTIME, I didn't listen to Principal Hortense's speech.

I mean, I knew basically what she was saying. She was telling everyone that Katya's laughter had been stolen by the Sterling Silver Foxes, and that Katya had been whisked away to a treatment center.

Many people gasped. Some smaller children, especially the ones in Katya's chess team, burst into tears.

Some girls giggled. *All* the teachers scolded those girls— but I didn't blame them. Giggles sort of jump out of you sometimes, when you hear something surprising and terrible. Maybe a part of you is hoping it's not real, and is thinking: *if I laugh, it might turn out to be a joke.*

Principal Hortense was also telling us we must make get well cards for Katya and was suggesting we draw flowers and hearts. (Which showed how much she knew about Katya: nothing.)

I might have raised my hand and said, "No, Katya would prefer pictures of the human skeleton," but I wasn't really listening, as I mentioned. I was figuring.

I was figuring out the best way to get into town.

I would go in Free Time, which was between 3:30 P.M. and 4:30 P.M. First, I'd have to ask the school secretary, Ms. Ubud, for a leave pass. You're not allowed into town without one, and you need a "valid reason" and a person to accompany you.

I needed a reason and a person. My reason would be that I had to . . . buy a birthday gift for my mother? Her birthday *was* coming up. In seven months . . .

My person would be . . . not my sisters, they'd be too inquisitive. "Why are you going to the Orange Blossom Tea Shop?" they'd ask. "What do you mean, I can't come in with you? I love their sticky toffee pudding. I'm coming in."

And they'd frown when I tried to get the attention of the tall, thin waitress.

They'd demand to know: "What are you doing? What are you telling her?" in loud voices that gave everything away.

Maybe I'd ask Autumn? She was calm and self-contained.

Now, one problem, of course, was that Ms. Ubud usually—

"Ms. Ubud will *not* be giving out any leave passes," Principal Hortense announced.

Ms. Ubud usually asked several questions before she gave you a leave pass was what I'd been about to think.

This was a much bigger problem.

"No more leave passes?" I cried. I was accidentally talking aloud. Why do I always do that?

"Esther?" Principal Hortense said, reprovingly. "Did you just speak?"

Well, yes, of course I did.

I nodded.

"And without raising your hand?"

Again, she was being obvious.

I raised my hand.

"Yes, Esther?"

"No more leave passes?" I asked.

"That's better. Yes, Esther. No more leave passes. It seems it's a teeny bit dangerous to be outside the school grounds."

Principal Hortense's voice became hushed: "Remember that Shadow Mages have been sighted in the mountains? Displaced from the coastal regions by rising floodwaters? Only a few. Only a handful. You really must *not* worry. They hate our mountains! But"—she paused, shuddered—"even a single Shadow Mage is *deathly, deathly dangerous.* Even a single Shadow Mage could *crush your skull like an egg.*"

Some of the younger children began to cry again.

Tatty Rattlestone raised her hand. "Esther talked about

Shadow Mages in her speech today," she said. "It scared us *so* much. Now I'm *terrified* to leave the school."

"Esther should not have scared you in that way," Principal Hortense said sternly.

"Well," I began, before I remembered myself and raised my hand. "Well, but, Principal Hortense, *you* just talked about Shadow Mages crushing skulls."

Principal Hortense raised her eyebrows. "So I did!" she said. "Life is so strange. So twisty-turny! Anyhow, no more leave passes. No exceptions."

Tatty then raised her hand again and got into an argument with Principal Hortense about whether she could get an exception. She absolutely, positively needed to go into town that afternoon, she said, to buy a copy of a glossy magazine called *Stars and Their Pets.*

"I thought you were terrified to leave the school," Imogen called from her table.

Tatty ignored her. "Our second cousin is going to be in the magazine," she explained. "Her name is Princess Almond-Milk-Honey Chocolate." (That wasn't actually the name, I made that up.)

"And she is being featured in this magazine?" Principal Hortense inquired. "With her pet, I assume?"

"Yes, with her pet cauliflower," Tatty agreed.

"Oh dear," said Principal Hortense.

"Hetty and I have been *so* looking forward to getting a copy," Tatty grumbled.

Everyone looked from Principal Hortense to Tatty and back. Principal Hortense bit her lip. "It *is* a dilemma," she said. "I can see why you'd want to run to town and get a copy. Although, Tatty, is a *cauliflower* really a pet?"

"It is if you love it," Hetty put in stoutly, "and take it for walks each day."

"And your second cousin does this?"

"Yes," Hetty and Tatty declared in unison.

Principal Hortense nodded. "Then the cauliflower is a pet. It may not last long, of course, as it will rot in the end."

"Or somebody will eat it," I said.

"Hand, Esther," Principal Hortense muttered. "Let me think. No, I don't see that I *can* make an exception, Tetty and Hatty. Hotty and Tutty. Tarry and Barry. I'm sure those aren't your names. I'm getting so muddled, what with the dilemma. Look. Perhaps just this once—"

At this point, Mr. Dar-Healey cleared his throat loudly, and several of the other teachers murmured, "No exceptions, Hortense."

Principal Hortense straightened. "*No more leave passes! No exceptions whatsoever! I'm very sorry, Tweety and Hooty. Nobody* is going into town! It's *far* too dangerous!"

She gazed around the hall.

"No need to look so pale, everyone," she said. "We're perfectly safe inside our school grounds."

I blinked.

No, we were not.

Our Spellbinder was gone.

She was meant to be reinforcing her ring of protection each night. Tonight, that would not happen.

I was going to have to break the new rule.

CHAPTER 56

IN FREE TIME that afternoon, I got down on my tummy and crawled to the school gate.

Didn't know how else to get there.

The sprinklers had been watering the lawn, so I was curious about what the mud and wet grass would do to my uniform.

I reached out and pushed at the gate from the ground, but it was locked. So I popped my head up and swiveled it about. Like one of those little furry animals that live in holes in the ground. The first time I did this, I was just happy to imagine myself as a little furry animal. The second time, I concentrated. Nobody around. Just the school driveway, the hedges, rose garden, school sign.

I jumped up and climbed over the fence. Tore my uniform on a spiky bit and landed on the other side.

Then I ran.

Down the path to town I ran, around this curve, around the next. Very bendy road it is, and steep. When you run fast, you feel like the road is flinging you forward. Also like you're about to fall. There is forest either side, thick with dark green pine needles and towering trunks. On the left, the forest climbs up the side of a mountain and begins to thin out until it reaches a great white snowcap. On the right, it is thick with shadows.

Shadows.

Shadow Mages are everywhere.

Faster and faster I ran, tripping almost, stumbling, slowing, and speeding up again.

Another curve and there was the town laid out before me. Breathless, I paused to watch the main street.

Plenty of locals strolling about, shopping baskets on arms. A father pushed a baby in a pram, and the baby leaned back eating a banana. Two women squabbled about ribbons for their hats.

I straightened up and pretended to be busy and important, striding down the slope and along the cobblestoned main street, past the fruit and flower stalls. Opposite the shops, on the banks of the lake, two men were dragging rowboats out of the water. They tipped them upside down with sloshing, sliding sounds and lined them in a colorful row—lime green, powder blue, apricot—like a collection of seashells.

Past the news agency I walked, past the confectioner, the bookshop, the nail salon.

Here at last was the Orange Blossom Tea Shop.

I pretended to study the menu in their front window, but actually I was gazing into the café.

Most tables were full, people eating scones with jam and cream. Clinking spoons, chattering, scraping chairs. I'd been to this café often before—it's my father's favorite when he visits—and I thought I knew the waitress Katya meant. It took me a moment to spot her.

Tall, thin. Gray hair cut short and straight. Stern face.

I stared hard.

Yes, there was a glint—she was wearing a necklace.

Was there a silver apple pendant?

I pushed open the café door and walked in.

I had to hop sideways quickly when a large man pushed his chair back. Almost got my toe.

Waitresses bustled around me. I sidled between tables, around chairs, until I reached the tall, thin waitress.

She was taking somebody's order.

"Lavender tea, I think, and a cherry tart," a young woman with an elegant hairdo was saying. Truly, her hair swooped and swerved like the road from our school into town. "Hm, no. I'm reconsidering."

The woman's companion, a gentleman in a silk shirt, patted her hand. "Take all the time you need," he told her, and then to the waitress he said: "Come back in a moment or two?"

The waitress raised an eyebrow ever so slightly, turned to leave the table, and noticed me beside her.

"Yes?" she said. "May I help you?"

I remembered now that she had an unexpected voice—a musical accent that didn't match her stern face. Now that she was facing me, I could see her necklace clearly.

A silver apple pendant.

"Yes please," I said boldly. "I just—"

I paused.

Could I say it?

The café was noisy with clatter and cutlery.

"I just have to tell you . . . ," I murmured.

The waitress leaned close to me to hear.

"The bell is rusty," I whispered. *"Please send another."*

Her face remained calm.

She straightened up. "Five o'clock," she told me, her voice rising so that people at nearby tables could hear her. "We close at five o'clock. So you've plenty of time to come back with your family."

"Thank you," I replied and walked out of the café.

CHAPTER 57

MY HEART FELT like a packet of marbles that has spilled and is clattering down a flight of steps.

Very noisy, I mean, and sort of rushing along.

I had done it. I had passed on a message to a tall, thin waitress with a silver apple pendant.

The bell is rusty, I had said. (As you know.) *Please send another.*

Just as Katya had asked.

And the waitress had pretended I was asking what time they closed!

(Or did she actually mishear me and think I *was* asking that? No. That was her cover.)

"Thank you," I had replied, like a spy.

Another Spellbinder would be sent to our school now. Its students, teachers, cooks, gardeners, cleaners—everyone would be safe.

I had *saved* our school.

Well, I could be proud of myself later—for now, I'd better get back.

I crossed the street to walk on the path above the lake but paused. Should I buy myself some sweets? To eat while I felt proud later?

I glanced back toward the shops, wondering whether I had enough money in my pocket—

and I saw her.

Stepping out of the news agency, carrying a magazine, adjusting her glasses.

Mrs. Pollock.

CHAPTER 58

SO THEN I was marbles spilling down a flight of steps.

By that I mean I ran down some steps. The stone steps to the lakeshore.

Once I reached the water, I crouched down, hands over my head.

But if Mrs. Pollock walked by the lake, she would look down and see a girl in a Katherine Valley Girls' uniform! (Me.) My hands being over my head would not disguise me!

In fact, they would probably attract attention.

I looked around frantically. Where to hide?

Those colorful rowboats, upside down like shells.

I grabbed the edge of one, scuttled underneath, and let it thud back down.

Then I waited.

Breathing hard.

Crouched and curled into the dark, dank, damp.

And there I stayed.

And stayed.

With only the sound of my own breathing—quick, panicked breaths. In, out, in, out.

Darkness.

Quiet.

The lake splashing softly against the shore. Birds. Sounds from up on the road—horses' hooves, a driver shouting, "Get along with you! Scoot!"—somebody must have walked into his path. A woman's voice shouting, "Going home yet, Scotty? Or here awhile still?" Then a sudden dragging sound—a table being moved—and laughter.

How long should I wait?

Mrs. Pollock could have strolled across to the low stone wall. She might be leaning there now, gazing down at the banks of the lake.

Gazing at this very upturned boat. Admiring its pretty apricot color.

Imagine if the boat she was admiring suddenly tipped up and a girl crawled out!

Esther Mettlestone-Staranise, to be exact.

I would have to stay here.

Until it was dark?

What if Mrs. Pollock liked the moonlight? She might. What if she was going to lean against the wall up there, gazing down at the upturned boat *all night*!

Already I was feeling strange and cramped, and a sharp stone was pressing into my knee.

Mrs. Pollock would not stand up there all night. It made no sense.

I decided to wait a little longer and then take a chance and—

Footsteps down the stone steps.

It was Mrs. Pollock!

She knew I was here!

Crunch-crunch, crunch-crunch went the footsteps on the grass.

A pause.

Somebody was standing right by my boat. I tried to slow my breathing and quieten it.

Then another set of footsteps approached, a bit quicker and heavier this time—*crunchcrunch, crunchcrunch*.

"All right?" said a voice.

Not Mrs. Pollock's but a woman's voice. Low and gentle. Familiar.

"Yes, I'm all right," agreed a man's voice, gruff. "What's this about?"

A sort of shuffling quiet.

"It's fine," the man said, a bit impatiently. "Nobody can hear us."

Hmm, I thought.

"The girl at the school up the road—Katherine Valley Boarding School—she's sent the bell message."

I recognized that voice! It was the tall, thin waitress with the apple pendant!

"Oh, for crying out loud," complained the man. "That means she's had to leave, doesn't it? So they've got no protection there now?"

There was no answer, but perhaps the woman nodded.

"I knew it was a mistake trusting children with this," the man grumbled. "The child probably wanted to go to the seaside with her family."

I had to press my nails into my palms to stop myself screaming: "NOT FAIR! KATYA DIDN'T GO TO THE *SEASIDE*! SHE ALMOST *DIED* TRYING TO STAY AT THE SCHOOL PROTECTING US!"

"We *had* to use a child," the woman's voice said calmly. "Nobody else available. It's the new policy. The girl asks for a new bell. Means she wants us to send somebody else up there to replace her."

"Oh, she does, does she? Twelve-year-olds telling us our business." An irritated snuffling. "Hang about, haven't they got a whole *conference* of Spellbinders coming to the grounds of that school soon?"

The woman *tch*-ed. "That's not for another month!"

"Well, a month isn't so bad," the man's voice decided. "There haven't been any reports of Shadow Mages close to the school, have there?"

"No," the woman replied.

"So, we leave them to it for now."

"But the school *was* attacked," the woman's voice objected. "The Sterling Silver Foxes, remember?"

"They were here in town then," the man replied in a shrugging sort of voice. "At the swimming pool."

Another pause. A rustling of paper. A slurping, sucking.

"I'll have one of those too," the woman's voice said.

More rustling. More slurping, sucking. I think they were eating some kind of boiled sweet.

Moments passed.

"Do you really think it's safe leaving the school unprotected?" the woman asked eventually, her voice a bit garbled by sweet-sucking.

"No," replied the man, "but it's a risk we have to take." He slurped. "Nobody available."

A sigh from the woman.

"I suppose you're right," she said. "Let's hope they make it. Anyway, I'd best get back to the café. Oh, go on, you've forced me, I'll take another sweet."

"I wasn't offering!"

Chuckles. Rustling paper.

Slurp, slurp.

Crunch-crunch, tramp-tramp, crunchcrunch.

The footsteps faded up the stairs and away.

I waited.

Waited.

Waited.

Then I lifted the boat and crawled out.

Mrs. Pollock was nowhere to be seen, but Mrs. Pollock had vanished from my mind.

They were *not* going to send another Spellbinder.

I had *not* saved the school at all.

I tipped sideways and caught myself on the boat.

Let's hope they make it, the woman had said.

CHAPTER 59

I CAN'T REMEMBER getting back to the school.

Well, actually, I can remember, I just thought that would be a dramatic line.

Nothing happened worth describing anyway. Nobody at the front of the school. I clambered over the gate, dropped to my stomach again, and crawled along at high speed. Slipped into a side door, tidied my hair, and walked along the corridor.

I had made it.

And it had all been for nothing.

I'd have to change my uniform now, of course—I pelted up the stairs, and almost bumped straight into Mrs. Pollock coming *down*. She had a windswept, tousled look about her and pinkish cheeks, so she must have only just got back from town herself.

"Hello, Esther." She smiled.

"Hello, Mrs. Pollock."

I carried on up the stairs. She carried on down.

But on the bottom step, she stopped and turned back. "Esther?"

"Yes, Mrs. Pollock?"

My heart: *thud-thud-thud.*

"What have you done to your uniform?"

I looked down at it, breathing out in relief. Streaks of mud and grass, torn and crumpled.

"Well," I said. "I was playing in the gardens, and I fell. I'm going upstairs now—to change."

She nodded slowly, then a grin lit up her face. "It's like a piece of art, your uniform! All those greens and browns!"

"It is!" I agreed, and we both laughed loudly.

Then Mrs. Pollock carried on, and so did I.

I had a bath, dressed in my other uniform, placed the ruined one in the laundry hamper, and went to the small recreation room.

I felt calmer now—baths always soothe me and, after all the suspense, laughing with Mrs. Pollock on the stairs had been strangely beautiful.

In the recreation room, a small crowd of girls was gathered around the Rattlestone twins.

"Oh, she's *beautiful!*" Zoe Fawnwell was crowing. "You're so lucky to have her as a cousin. I mean, you can *see* how royal she is, it shines out of her *ears*. And that cauliflower! What a cutie. I love how she's put a bow on its head."

It was a magazine. *Stars and Their Pets.* The twins were turning pages slowly, pointing out photos of a young woman with a cauliflower cuddled in her arms.

Autumn, who was sitting alongside the twins, was nodding politely, but a *teeny* dimple kept jumping into her cheek. I could tell she was working hard to hide it.

"Did you have cauliflowers in the Whispering Kingdom, Autumn?" Tatty asked her suddenly, using a loving sort of voice.

"Yes," Autumn replied.

"What about pets? Did you have pets in the Whispering Kingdom?"

"Yes."

"Did you have—"

"How did you get that magazine?" I interrupted. "Did you get a leave pass after all?" I hadn't seen the twins in town.

Hetty and Tatty shook their heads, looking up from the glossy pages.

"Mrs. Pollock got it! She just came up here to give it to us! She went into town especially for us! She is the *nicest* teacher we *ever* had!"

"She *is!*" all the Grade 6 girls agreed. "And so funny!"

I nodded.

Mrs. Pollock *was* thoughtful, to buy the magazine for the twins.

If she *hadn't* done it, of course, I would not have seen her in town, and I would not have run down by the lake and hidden beneath the boat, and I would never have overheard that conversation.

Right now, I would happily believe I had saved the school.

That was annoying of Mrs. Pollock, although not really her fault. She couldn't have known the unexpected consequences of her jaunt.

Mrs. Pollock was thoughtful and funny. We were always laughing in class. She and I had just laughed on the staircase. Another teacher would have scolded me for the state of my uniform, but she had said it was a piece of art!

I took a deep breath and decided to be cheerful, like Mrs. Pollock.

I'd done what Katya had asked. I'd delivered the message.

If I hadn't heard that conversation, I wouldn't *know* the message hadn't worked.

I would pretend I hadn't heard.

CHAPTER 60

ON THE WAY to dinner that night, I glanced into the mailroom, toward my own pigeonhole, as usual, and turned away, as usual—never anything there—

And then I stopped.

A glow of white.

An envelope.

There was an *envelope* in my mailbox!

I ducked into the room, tried to slow myself down, partly so that I would not seem overexcited, and partly so I wouldn't slam into all the other girls who were moving toward their own mailboxes—and reached it.

Yes, a white envelope.

Georgia or Hsiang had finally replied to me!

Or maybe Father was able to contact us again!

Could it even be *Mother*? She rarely sent us things at boarding school, but you never knew!

I pulled out the envelope.

ESTHER, it said on the front.

Oh.

Not addressed to Katherine Valley Boarding School.

No stamp.

It was from somebody *in* the school.

I opened the envelope and took out a piece of paper. Here is what it said:

Esther,

I was very disappointed to see the state of your uniform today. You need to learn to respect your property. DEMERIT.

Please note that this is your second demerit. If you get a third, it will mean a Friday night detention.

Mrs. Pollock

CHAPTER 61

THAT NIGHT, I had the dream five times.

Lying on a blanket, it starts to rain.

Wake up with a thundering heart.

Sit up in bed.

Look around wildly. Calm myself.

Go back to sleep.

Lying on a blanket, it starts to rain.

Wake up feeling that my chest had been trampled.

Sit up in bed.

And so on.

New rule, I thought after the fifth time. *No more sleep.*

I walked down the corridor to the window overlooking the back gardens.

Down at the Old Schoolhouse, lights flitted behind the windows, as usual.

I was worn out by my confusion.

I did not understand the dream, or why it kept recurring.

I did not understand why Mrs. Pollock kept giving me C– and threatening me with detentions. She was lovely, kind, and wise, so she must have a good reason, but what was it? Could she see something cracked and broken inside me?

And finally, most important, I did not understand about the Shadow Mages.

On the one hand, the authorities had sent an undercover Spellbinder to protect us, Sterling Silver Foxes had attacked us at the swimming pool, and Katya had seemed very worried about abandoning us. *Let's hope they make it*, the waitress had said. All that made the situation seem very serious.

On the other hand, everybody, including Principal Hortense, believed that Shadow Mages *would not* come around the mountains, and that if there were any, it was only a few, a sprinkling, a handful. *Let's hope they make it,* the waitress had said, but she and her friend had been eating sweets, relaxed and happy.

Surely there was no danger, was there?

My mind turned circles, faster and faster, until it whirled me into a dreamless sleep.

CHAPTER 62

I WOKE IN the corridor, blinked a moment, and leapt to my feet.

I threw on my clothes and ran to the library. It was very early on a Saturday morning, but Carlos was there, twirling in his seat, looking at the ceiling—he does that when he's contemplating life. Clean-shaven today, which made him look boyish.

"Carlos," I said. "Do you have newspapers in the library?"

"Right over there." He twirled away from me and pointed over his shoulder at the stack by the library door.

"Those are just the *Katherine Valley Times*," I said. "Do you have others? From the other valleys and mountain villages around us?"

Carlos spun once more. "Am I the greatest librarian in all the Kingdoms and Empires?" he demanded.

"Probably."

"So of *course* I keep newspapers from the surrounding areas." Spin, spin. He must have been getting dizzy. But his face was serene each time it spun by me. "The lower drawers over in D row. Most recent at the front. Help yourself."

I pulled out all the copies of the *Nicholas Valley News*, the *Darling Mountain Sideshow*, the *Chrysanthemum Village Herald*, and the *Big Valley Daily* from the last year, rustled them over to my table, and began turning pages.

My hands were soon smudged black from the ink.

As I turned the pages, I took notes in an exercise book.

Half an hour later, I stopped.

I looked at my notes.

Feb 3—Darling Mtn—attack by
Radish Gnomes at roadside fruit & veg
store—three people injured

Feb 17—Chrys. Village—sighting of
Witch coven, midnight, by town lake

Feb 28—Nicholas Valley—reports
of Siren calls during school lunch hour
three days in a row; children forced to
eat indoors (very restless)

And that was just February.

My list went on for page after page.

All over the mountains, Shadow Mages were either attacking or lurking. Every article claimed that this was "rare" or "freakish" or "most unusual."

But it was none of those things. Not anymore.

It was *not* just a handful. Not a one-off.

There were Shadow Mages all around the mountains.

And our school was not protected. . . .

I was the only one who knew this, and I could not pretend I didn't know.

CHAPTER 63

I HAD PROMISED Katya I wouldn't tell anybody, but this was too important.

I ran down the steps to breakfast, skidding to a stop at the dining hall door. I decided I would wave wildly at Imogen and Astrid until they saw, then beckon them out into the corridor.

My sisters always know what to do.

But Imogen was not at her table.

Of course not. She and Pelagia had left early that morning for the swimming tournament. Mr. Dar-Healey's class was going to be taught by Principal Hortense while they were away.

I searched the Grade 4 table for Astrid instead—and couldn't see her either.

Well, of course not. She'd gone away early that morning with the mayor and his team.

Slowly, I walked into the dining hall. Slowly, I buttered my toast.

Right.

Here was the problem.

Shadow Mages could attack our school at any moment.

Principal Hortense believed that a student in Grade 6 was protecting us with a Spellbinding, and that there weren't many Shadow Mages around anyway.

Neither thing was true.

It always bothers me in books when a character has a problem, or a secret, and they don't tell anybody.

Sometimes I actually shout at the book: *Just TELL some-body! Who CARES that you promised? This is MORE IMPORTANT!*

You might be doing the same thing to me right now.

All right, fine.

Who do you think I should tell?

The principal, obviously! (You are bellowing—or maybe you're *sighing* out the words.) Or a different teacher! Mustafa, the gardener!

Anybody.

Okay, now imagine the conversation with Principal Hortense.

"Hello, just letting you know that there is no longer a Spell-binder protecting our school."

"How do you know this, Esther?" Principal Hortense would inquire. (Eventually. I mean, first she would blather or sing, cry, or water a plant and ask me to repeat myself seventeen times.)

"I just know."

"And why is our Spellbinder no longer protecting our school?"

"She isn't here anymore."

Tick, tock, tick, tock.

That is the sound of a clock ticking while Principal Hortense thinks for a minute.

"But the only Grade Six girl who has left the school is Katya!" Principal Hortense realizes. "So *Katya* is the Spellbinder? How marvelous! I'd never have guessed!"

The fact is, I couldn't tell anybody the problem without giving away Katya's identity.

Everybody knows that you don't give away Spellbinders' identities. Mrs. Pollock had reminded me of that when I wrote my introduction letter to her.

She'd been right to scold me. I knew that now. I'd been trying to impress her, as I wanted her to like me.

But you just don't do it.

Never.

Not to anybody.

The more people who know, the greater the danger of Shadow Mages discovering the truth. When the Spellbinder was sleeping, or sick, or weak in any way—as Katya was now—the Shadow Mages would attack them. Or they would capture a member of the Spellbinder's family and hold them to ransom.

Even Katya's brother, Stefan, didn't know her secret! How could I tell *Principal Hortense*? She'd probably accidentally tell Imogen's class as soon as she walked in today!

If I told another student, they'd only tell a teacher, and if I told a teacher, they'd have to tell Principal Hortense.

So, you see?

There was nobody to tell.

I hope you understand and have stopped shouting at me.

CHAPTER 64

THERE WAS ONLY one solution.

For the next four weeks, I would protect the school myself.

For the rest of that Saturday, I read
through the notes I'd taken when I did my
speech on Shadow Mages. I returned to
the library and read more. I wrote lists and lists of ideas in
notebooks.

On Sunday, I stole a burlap sack from the storage room
and filled it with supplies. Some I took from the kitchen, some
from the gardening shed, some from the stationery cupboard,
the greenhouse, the music room, and so on. I nearly got caught
about seven times.

Monday morning, I woke at 5:00 A.M.

Day One, I thought. *Let it begin.*

CHAPTER 65

DAY I—MONDAY

I crept downstairs, *creaked* open the front door of the school, and climbed over the gate.

Then I walked around the brick wall that encircles the school grounds, my sack over my shoulder, skirting the edges of the forest behind it, and all the way back to the front gate.

Our school includes the main school building, the teachers' residence, the principal's cottage, the gardener's cottage, the gardening shed, the greenhouse, the vegetable gardens, the Old Schoolhouse, the gardens, the hedges, the tennis court, the pond, and the community of Elves.

What I mean to say is: it's big. A very big school.

It took about forty-five minutes to walk around the outside of the wall.

I scattered cinnamon and nutmeg as I walked. (Spellbinders use it in their spells. I thought it might suggest to any approaching Shadow Mages that we had some at the school.)

I saw nothing suspicious. No sign of Shadow Mages.

I came back inside.

In class that morning, we finished our speeches.

Autumn's speech was on chocolate.

She spoke much more clearly than she had when she'd introduced herself. "How is chocolate made?" she asked, an interesting question, and then she outlined the method, and told stories about the most popular chocolates in the Kingdoms and Empires. She also asked us to call out our favorites, which we enjoyed.

After she'd finished, we all smiled. It's good to spend a few minutes thinking about chocolate. Some people asked her questions and then Mrs. Pollock herself raised her hand.

Everyone giggled.

"Autumn," she said. "Why chocolate?"

"Well," Autumn replied. "I feel passionate about chocolate."

"No, no." Mrs. Pollock shook her head. "I mean, why did you *not* do a speech about the Whispering Kingdom? Now *that* would have been fascinating!"

Autumn scratched her eyebrow. "I don't know. I suppose . . . Well, I'm not *just* . . ."

"Not just?" Mrs. Pollock prompted.

"Not just a Whisperer?"

"Autumn, be *proud* of your heritage! Be proud of who you are!"

Autumn nodded uncertainly. "All right."

She sat in her place, and everyone looked at her, remembering that she was a Whisperer.

At lunchtime, I walked around the school perimeter with my sack again. This was more difficult. (Partly because I was hungry. I was skipping lunch.)

But the main difficulty was that Mustafa was relaxing on a lounge chair in the front garden, eating flatbread with various dips. I couldn't climb the front gate. Instead, I sprinted down to the back of the school, then slowly, slowly slipped further and further back, past the pond, around behind the Old Schoolhouse—and scrambled over the wall.

The wall is high and slippery, but there are crevices between some of the bricks where you can dig in your fingers, and crumbly bits between others, where you can press the toe of your shoe to lever yourself up.

I scattered more cinnamon and nutmeg.

Once again, no sign of any suspicious activity.

At midnight that night, I set out to check again.

Then I crept back to bed.

Day 2—Tuesday

Same perimeter check at 5:00 A.M. No signs of suspicious activity.

During my lunchtime check of the forest behind the school, a bird landed on a branch. I gasped. A mouse scuttled through the undergrowth. I yelped.

That's all.

I felt embarrassed by the gasp and yelp, and scolded myself. I was going to have to work on being braver.

After lunch, I was feeling a bit dim from hunger.

Mrs. Pollock held up a stack of papers.

"These are the grades I've given you for your speeches," she explained. "I won't hand them around yet, as I don't want to influence your voting."

That seemed fair. We all nodded.

Mrs. Pollock told us to get ready to write down the name of the person we thought had given the best speech.

I was trembling.

I *really* wanted to be chosen again.

It's so much fun getting a day off school and going for milk shakes with Katya's brother, Stefan—he *always* gets chosen, and often gets a Special Commendation from the judges. I especially wanted to spend time with Stefan so we could talk about Katya and her treatment.

People were murmuring my name.

I wasn't imagining that.

"Esther," people said, clearly. "Esther's was the best."

Esther. Esther. It'll be Esther. I'm voting for Esther.

I'm trying to be modest but that is what I could hear. I *was* pretty sure the class had laughed more at my speech than any other. And almost everybody had told me that the speech was "so interesting" or "really dramatic!"

"Wait until everybody is ready," Mrs. Pollock called. "All right, pens up, and . . . oh, wait, I need to tell you this."

She shuffled papers on her desk. "Yes, here it is."

She looked up again.

"Now, there are new rules this year. At the district level, certain topics are forbidden. Therefore, if your speech was on one of these topics, nobody may vote for you. All right?"

There was a lengthy silence.

"Righto, let's start voting!" Mrs. Pollock cried.

"Um . . . ," Durba said. "Which topics are forbidden?"

"Oh! Of course!" Mrs. Pollock dove toward her papers again. Everybody laughed. She really was a character. "Right. Ants," she read out.

Ants!

Why would they be forbidden?

Everybody laughed. Nobody had done a speech on ants.

"Orange seeds," Mrs. Pollock said next, running her finger down a list. "Pomegranate seeds. Pumpkin seeds."

Again, we giggled. Nobody had talked about seeds of any kind.

"Toenail clippings."

By now, we were laughing loudly.

Toenail clippings!

"And . . . where is it? Yes. Here. Magic. No speeches may refer to magic of any kind. Right then?"

She looked up.

The class had stopped laughing.

The light hit Mrs. Pollock's glasses so I could not see where she was looking. Her face was expressionless.

Tatty raised her hand. "We can't vote for somebody who did a speech about magic?" she asked.

"No speeches may refer to magic of any kind." Mrs. Pollock nodded.

Faces turned to look at me. Sympathetic faces. Sad shrugs.

"Sorry, Esther," somebody whispered. "I was definitely going to vote for you."

My face felt like it was burning from the inside.

No magic of any kind?

But why?

Why would they have banned speeches on that topic? Ants, seeds, toenail clippings, and magic? Why had the judges chosen that strange list?

Why had Mrs. Pollock approved my speech topic?

By now, everybody was writing.

I wrote down Autumn's name. I'd enjoyed her speech on chocolate.

We handed in the cards.

Mrs. Pollock read them and divided them into little stacks. The stacks all seemed similar in height to me. She studied these stacks, testing them against one another.

Meanwhile, we all sat silently.

People carried on glancing at me. I could feel it.

"Right," Mrs. Pollock said at last, swooping up one of the stacks. "This person had the most votes, so *this* person gets to represent the school at the speech competition! Ready?"

Nobody spoke.

"It's Hetty Rattlestone! With her *marvelous* speech on her family tree!"

"What!" Hetty exclaimed, leaping up from her desk, bright pink spots on her cheeks.

"Congratulations!" Tatty cried.

Zoe Fawnwell hugged them both, and the three girls bounced up and down on the spot together.

Around me were many quiet sighs.

After that, Mrs. Pollock handed out her own score sheets for our speeches. I heard both Hetty and Tatty shriek, "A plus! Could this day get any better?"

Here's what mine said:

Esther, your speech made the important subject of shadow magic much too frivolous. Your cartwheel was also very clumsy: you are no gymnast and only embarrassed yourself.

Don't try so hard to impress your audience.

C—

CHAPTER 66

DAY 3—WEDNESDAY

By the third day, I was starting to wonder if the school actually *needed* my protection.

As far as I could tell, there were no Shadow Mages around. Or if there were, the Spellbinding Katya had created was still keeping them away, even though she was gone. It would probably last for the next four weeks! She's very clever at schoolwork, Katya, so she was probably a better Spellbinder than she realized too. It's very common for smart people to say, "Oh, I failed that exam" and then get 100 percent.

I was tramping around the forest behind the school wall at lunchtime thinking all this and decided that I should eliminate lunchtime checks from now on. I was so tired and hungry. And I wasn't a Spellbinder. Katya was. This was—

That's when I heard voices.

"I tell you," said one, a growly, gruff voice. "Spellbinding ring is *well* gone. This is the time."

I stopped still.

Slid back into shadows and crouched at the base of a tree.

"Agree," said another voice. "Claw attack?"

So it was Radish Gnomes.

To attack, they release their claws. The claws fly at ankle height and slice open your skin, often cracking the bone. The Radish Gnomes carry away the injured and extract their teeth. These are ground down to enhance their shadow spells.

"Let's have a look then," a third voice grunted.

A small figure, stocky, shaggy hair, approached the school wall. He pressed his large hands flat, the claws clattering into place. Then he scrambled almost to the top.

Peered over.

Slid back down.

He returned into the shadows of the woods.

"Plenty of girls outside having their lunch break," he said. "Perfect."

Slowly, slowly, I reached into my burlap sack. I fumbled around until I found what I needed.

Green apples. I gathered as many of these as I could hold. Pulled them to my chest.

What if the book was wrong?

My heart thudded, as if somebody with strong, fast fists was using it as a punching bag.

I took in a deep, silent breath, held it—and rolled the apples straight toward the voices.

"Oi!"

"It's not!"

"It is! Watch your feet! Watch your feet!"

"Yech! One just touched my toe!"

"Where are they coming from?"

"There must be apple trees around here! They're falling on us!"

I drew out another handful.

This time, I flung them strong and straight.

"There's more! There's more! Nasty!"

"That's it. I'm outta here. Not worth it."

"Let's go!"

Thud-thud, thud-thud, and seven or eight Radish Gnomes trotted right by the tree where I was hiding, vanishing into the forest.

I held the last apple in my hand.

It's a phobia, apparently. I'd read about it in *Astonishing Truth.* Radish Gnomes are terrified of small green apples.

Nobody knows why. Some think it's because a Radish Gnome king once grew ill after eating too many and spread the word that they were dangerous.

I waited until I was sure they were far away, then I climbed over the wall again and returned to school.

CHAPTER 67

THAT AFTERNOON, I was so tired that I danced very badly at our class with the boys from Nicholas Valley.

I kept bumping into people. My dance partner, Arlo, thought I was doing this on purpose to be funny, and he laughed his head off. He kept getting into trouble with Ms. Potty for laughing—she was taking the class while Mr. Dar-Healey was away at the swimming tournament—but this never affected Arlo for long. So at least somebody was having a good time.

At the end of the class, I found Stefan and asked for news of Katya. He was grim and serious.

"It's not good," he said. "She'll *live*, but she'll always be weak. And always sad."

I found that irritating. I wanted *good* news about Katya.

I know this was unfair, as it was not Stefan's fault. I just really wanted Katya to be okay.

Stefan asked if I'd been chosen for the speech competition.

I shook my head.

He looked sorrowful again and I had to stop myself stamping my foot. Stop looking so sad about everything!

"How about you?"

He nodded—still sad. "I'll miss seeing you on the day."

"What's your topic?" I asked. His speeches are usually about ancient battles with dragons or trolls. He likes old stories: his eyes brighten when he discusses them.

"*Fiends.*" He turned slightly as he spoke—Ms. Potty was bellowing for the boys to *get moving,* and he was keeping an eye on her.

"Oh, those stories from classical history? From the time before magic? I thought about doing something about them too!"

Stefan checked on Ms. Potty again. She was distracted by students wrestling on the floor, so he continued. "In my speech, I compare the powers of some famous Fiends from the stories with the power of today's Shadow Mages. At first, I was going to just do my usual topic—you know my usual topic?"

I nodded. "Ancient battles with swords."

"Right. So I was in the archives of the town museum looking through boxes of old books of military history. And this classical history book was stuck between the pages of one. I found myself getting absorbed in the stories of these Fiends. Professor Lillian Joyce Armstrong would sit up in a tree, tilt her head, and crush passersby—exactly as if they'd been crushed by falling logs. Jonathan J. Lanyard clicked his fingers and drowned a thousand people instantly. Anyone came near him? Dead. Caleb Vincenza, a Desert Fiend, suffocated people—they felt like they were choking on sand. Marjery—"

"Boys! Line up at the door!" Ms. Potty called.

Stefan glanced toward her then back at me. "The intriguing part? In the preface of the book it said the classical stories were true."

"The book said that Fiends were *real*?"

"More real than my hand." He held up his hand, and I checked that it was real. It was. "It also said that today's shadow magic is literally just a shadow of the true original evil of the Fiends."

A shiver zigzagged down my spine.

"Anyway, probably not true." Stefan shrugged at the same time as Ms. Potty bellowed: "NICHOLAS VALLEY BOYS, WE ARE LEAVING *THIS INSTANT!*"

He raised an eyebrow at me and loped off toward the door.

"Bye," I called. "Congratulations on your speech."

Stefan turned. "Thanks!" he said and smiled.

At least that was *one* smile from Stefan, although Ms. Potty thwacked the back of his head as he passed—"Get a move on!"—and the smile vanished again.

Later that night, after I'd completed midnight check of the school perimeter, I had the dream.

I woke up with my usual postdream rapidly beating heart and just-trampled chest.

Then a word jumped into my head: *magic.*

Stefan had said his speech mentioned magic. It compared the Fiends of before-magic to the magic of Shadow Mages today.

And magic was a forbidden topic.

CHAPTER 68

DAY 4—THURSDAY

After the encounter with Radish Gnomes, I decided I'd better increase my checks, rather than cutting out the lunchtime one.

Throughout the day, whenever I could, I pretended I needed to go to the bathroom, or to fetch a cardigan. I ran, ran, ran, all the way to the top floor of the school, creeping past the teachers' lounge and peering through each of the windows up there. I scanned the road, the forest, the mountains as far as I could see. Then I ran back to class.

We were all working hard preparing for the fundraising weekend by now. It was in just over a week. Our class had finished our weather paintings and Mrs. Pollock had promised to glue them to—"What was it? A balloon? A cat?" Everyone laughed and reminded her to glue them to corkboard.

But we still had to make decorations: paper chains and streamers. These were strewn, half-made, across every classroom.

Every grade also had to perform a song at the twilight picnic and, whenever I ran up the stairs for my checks, I'd hear classes breaking into song.

Then I'd hear teachers shouting, "No! *Together!*"

Day 5—Friday

Around dawn, as I was heading out for my morning check, I glanced through an upstairs window and saw a crew of Fire Sirens gliding up the road toward the school.

I could tell they were Fire Sirens because they were tall, elegant women, and trees kept bursting into flames as they passed.

For a moment, I considered pounding on doors, waking teachers, shouting: "Look! Fire Sirens!" But I'd read about Fire Sirens attacking shopping malls and police stations, and nobody had been able to stop them. The malls and stations had burned to the ground.

I crept out, splashed ink all over the front gate, then hid and watched while the Fire Sirens pushed on the gate. Almost at once, they began to shriek: "It's ink! I'm coming out in hives!" and hurried away to get ointment.

Sirens are extremely allergic to wet ink. I'd read that in *Astonishing Truth* too.

CHAPTER 69

DAYS 6 AND 7—SATURDAY AND SUNDAY

On Saturday morning, I came up with the idea of hanging my black coat over the back wall. I thought it might look like a Spellbinder's cloak—they wear these when they're working in public, to hide their identity—and make Shadow Mages hesitate. (I was very sleepy by now, and not thinking clearly.)

Between my perimeter checks, I did homework. On Friday, Mrs. Pollock had asked us to write a narrative account of a true event.

"It can be something that happened to *you*," she had told us. "Or something you read about in the news! Bring it to life for your readers!"

The narrative account that I wrote for this assignment is Part 1 of this book. Which means you've already *read* my narrative account. (Unless you skipped Part 1? But why would you do that?)

Don't worry about flicking back. I'll remind you.

The Stolen Prince of Cloudburst.

I have a cousin, Bronte, who is an adventurer. Her best friend is named Alejandro, and Bronte met him after he'd escaped from a pirate ship. Recently, Bronte and Alejandro discovered that Alejandro is, in fact, the Stolen Prince of the Kingdom of Storms.

It had all been in the news, so I decided it was the perfect topic for my narrative account. I would make it suspenseful, exciting, and descriptive.

Should I mention that I had met Alejandro myself? I wondered. And that Bronte is my cousin?

Yes, I decided. *I should.*

When Hetty did her speech about her family tree, Mrs. Pollock had said: "You made your project so much more interesting by bringing *yourself* into it! You shared your remarkable connections to such important people!"

Sunday night, after my perimeter check, I stayed up until 2:00 A.M. finishing the narrative account.

This time, I thought, I'd get an A+ for sure.

Day 8—Monday

No suspicious activity. I handed in the narrative account.

Day 9—Tuesday

During my midnight check, I stumbled on a coven of Witches.

There was a bright silver moon, a strong, chilly wind, and fifteen or twenty Witches, both women and men, in a clearing. They were having a singalong around a fire.

I knew they were Witches because they wore strings of beads and socks with sandals. Many of them were stroking their black cats and singing softly. Harmonizing.

I crept backward, bumped into a tree, bit my lip to stop myself gasping.

I decided to climb the tree.

Tricky to climb quietly. Leaves rustle, twigs snap. But it was a blustery night, as I mentioned, and the Witches were singing.

Once I'd reached a high branch, I straddled it and, shivering, looked down on the clearing.

The song had finished. One Witch, a man in a woolen beanie with a pom-pom, carried on humming softly. The Witch beside him nudged him. "Hush."

"Sorry," he said.

A Witch leaned forward and stoked up the fire, shifting it

about with a stick. Another coughed and rubbed her eyes—the smoke was blowing directly toward her.

"After this," said the Witch with the stick, "we'll Spell the school. They'll all be sleeping now. Let's rock the building so they tumble out of their beds."

"*Really* rock them hard, though, so their bones break when they fall."

"Yes, and then we'll have wardrobes and things fall on them."

They all chuckled and murmured agreement.

Witches find pranks like this hilarious. Their victims are usually less amused.

What else did I know about Witches?

Come on, come on! *Think!*

Their favorite food is sticky jam buns?

That was not much help.

I didn't have any sticky jam buns, did I?

Think, think.

Of course, I knew that more than any of the Shadow Mages, they were—

And I *could* . . .

Should I?

Risky.

I reached into my burlap sack again, and this time I drew out a paper bag.

Crackle, crackle went the paper.

A Witch glanced up. "What was that?"

"Wind in the leaves."

At that moment, a gust of wind rushed by me. I opened the paper bag, shook it—

Rose petals soared into the night sky.

Come on, come on, I coaxed the petals.

"Oh!" One of the Witches brushed her shoulder. "Something hit me! What *is* that?"

I reached into the sack again and drew out the xylophone. Had to rummage around for a while to find the mallet, and I could hear Witches saying, "It *is* a rose petal—there's another one."

I raised the mallet and hit the xylophone as gently as I could.

Ding!

I hit a few more keys. *Ding. Ding! Ding.*

"Xylophone!" a Witch blazed.

"Rose petals and xylophones! Those Crystal Faeries! They're *everywhere.*"

"Let's get out of here."

"But the school! I so wanted to inflict some fractures tonight!"

"Not worth it. I'm retching just *thinking* about Crystals."

"All right. Stamp out that fire, would you?"

And the Witches gathered their things and set off through the forest, grumbling.

Crystal Faeries are always scattering rose petals and playing xylophones.

And Shadow Mages, especially Witches, find Crystal Faeries tooth-achingly irritating.

CHAPTER 70

DAY 10—WEDNESDAY

At lunchtime, a fifth grader named Carla found my jacket and brought it to me.

"*Esther,* look what I found!" she said, handing it over importantly. "Your coat! It was hanging over the back wall of the school! Aren't you the silliest?"

She expected me to be grateful too. This was as irritating as Crystal Faeries.

Before dance class began, I told Stefan about the new rules in the speech competition.

He frowned. "What are you talking about? New rules?"

"Certain topics are forbidden," I explained. "Ants, orange seeds, pomegranate seeds, pumpkin seeds, toenail clippings, and magic."

Stefan grinned.

It *did* sound like a joke.

"Maybe edit your speech?" I suggested. "Instead of comparing the stories of Fiends with today's shadow magic, just make it all about the Fiends?"

Stefan was still grinning. It was good to see him smiling, but this was important. I didn't want him getting disqualified.

"Right, everybody!" Ms. Potty called from the stage. "Line up in positions! Find your partners!" She sounded snuffly. I think she had a cold.

I was shaking my head at Stefan. "It's not a joke," I scolded. "My class couldn't vote for me because my speech was on magic."

Stefan raised a single eyebrow. He's quite good at that—I think he practices. "Wait here," he told me, and away he wove, through the crowds of boys and girls. A few were lined up ready to dance, but most were chatting. The girls were excitable because the fundraising weekend would take place in just two days, and the boys were always excitable.

Stefan climbed up onto the stage and approached Ms. Potty, who was rummaging in her handbag. She pulled out a handkerchief, then turned to him. They spoke earnestly. Stefan looked over at me. He waved.

What did he mean by that? Annoying.

"What?" I mouthed.

"There are no new rules," he shouted. "No topic is banned!"

"EVERYBODY LINE UP IN POSITIONS AND *DANCE!*" Ms. Potty shrieked.

Stefan winced, covered his ears, and grinned over at me.

I did not grin back.

* * *

During my midnight check, I dealt with an attack from a couple of drunken Sirens. I pretended to be a wolf in the undergrowth. Sirens love wolves for some reason. These two chased me through the forest for over an hour, calling and singing, begging me to slow down so they could pet me. Eventually, they slipped on a slick of mud, landed on their backs, laughed hysterically, and decided that, now they were down, they might as well have a sleep.

Back at school, I washed myself of mud and grass as quietly as I could, changed my nightgown, went to bed, and had the dream five times in a row.

After that, I lay awake for a while.

The speech competition crept into my head and stayed there. If Stefan was right, and there *were* no rules about topics, then the class might have voted for me.

It was too late now of course: they had voted for Hetty, and she'd been dragging dresses out of her wardrobe each evening, holding them up and saying, "This one? Should I wear *this* in the contest? Will my speech sound its best in *turquoise* or *aqua*?"

"That's actually *my* dress you've got there," Dot Pecorino had whispered at one point. Hetty pretended not to hear her, dropping Dot's dress to the floor and turning back to the wardrobe.

So I couldn't ask for the class to vote again. Should I let Mrs. Pollock know she'd made a mistake? Maybe I could be a back-up speaker, in case Hetty got sick?

In the morning, I decided, I would do that.

CHAPTER 71

DAY 11—THURSDAY

However, the next morning, Mrs. Pollock was in a giddy mood. She performed our greetings three times each, having us march out of the classroom and back in again for this purpose.

"Tomorrow night!" she reminded us. "*Tomorrow* night is the twilight picnic! The fundraising weekend is . . . about . . . to . . . begin!"

She galloped around the classroom, whinnying like a horse.

Everyone laughed and shouted, "Hooray!"

I myself had a headache.

As well as galloping, Mrs. Pollock was neighing, rearing into the air, pretending to munch on carrots, and shaking her hair about as if it was a mane. I didn't see how I could interrupt her to tell her she'd made a mistake about the speech competition rules. I tried to laugh along so I wouldn't look like a bad sport, but to be honest, it wasn't very funny. And my head felt like someone was smashing it with tambourines.

When Mrs. Pollock finally settled down, she said, "All right! Let's rehearse our song again! Everyone ready? And—oh, wait, before we do that, I have your narrative accounts to hand back. Great work on these, everyone! I *loved* them!"

Oh, good! I thought, smiling. *She loved them! I'm going to get an A+!*

That would help to make up for the speech contest.

She handed back our narrative accounts.

If you have a good memory, you already know what she wrote on mine. If not, here it is again:

Esther, yes, I have read much of this story, or its basic facts anyway, in the newspapers. You have not made them more interesting here. Worse, you have tried to put yourself in the story. You might be related to some of these interesting people, but that does not make YOU interesting. Do not put yourself in stories where you do not belong.

Do not tell fibs. You are very far indeed from Cloudburst, and highly unlikely ever to so much as glimpse the Stolen Prince.

Also, do not begin sentences with the words "And" or "But." Do not break your sentences and paragraphs into pieces; it makes your tale very disjointed. Do not boast by saying that your asides are "helpful"—that is not becoming.

I see that you stayed up past midnight doing your homework. Dreadful behavior. DEMERIT. As this is your third demerit, please attend detention on Friday evening as punishment.

Finally, you began this story with the words "Long ago, far away, on a damp and sniffly day." Please write out the following, 100 times:

A DAY CANNOT BE "SNIFFLY."

C–

Here is the strange thing.

When I read this, I didn't feel anything.

Not angry, not upset, not shocked.

Even though a moment before I'd been imagining an A+, well, I think I'd only been *pretending* to myself.

A deeper part of me had known it would be like this.

I still wasn't sure what a "detention" was, but nothing mattered anyway.

Nothing except sleep.

All I wanted was to sleep.

I gazed around the classroom at the other girls, many of them exclaiming, "I got an *A!*" or "Oh, B plus! Nice!" and my eyes accidentally landed on Mrs. Pollock.

She was studying me. And she was smiling a quiet, thoughtful smile.

I blinked.

CHAPTER 72

AT THE END of lunch, after I'd sprinted through my perimeter check, I found another envelope in my mailbox.

This time I didn't leap to it, imagining a letter from Georgia or Hsiang, or my father or mother.

I wandered sleepily over and took it out.

Once again, there was only my name on the envelope, no address or stamps.

I opened it.

Esther,

Re: Your Detention

As you know, you have three demerits and now have a Detention on Friday night.

Please report to the upper teachers' lounge this Friday, and remain there from 6:00 until 9:00 P.M. I will leave mathematics worksheets on the table for you to complete.

Mrs. Pollock

I frowned and put the letter in my pocket.

When the bell rang for afternoon tea that day, I paused on my way out of the classroom. I was blocking the doorway and girls had to push their way around me, but I was too tired to step aside. Eventually, I turned back and stood at Mrs. Pollock's desk. She was busy scribbling.

"Esther," she said, looking up and smiling kindly. "How can I help?"

"The note about the detention—" I began.

Mrs. Pollock smiled more broadly. "Yes?"

"You mean *next* Friday night, I suppose? Not tomorrow night?"

"Why would I mean *next Friday night*?" She imitated my voice when she repeated the words, making it sound high-pitched and babyish.

"Well, you can't mean tomorrow night?"

"Indeed?" Mrs. Pollock pulled one of her clown faces. "And why can I *not* mean that?"

"The twilight picnic," I explained, smiling at her funny face. It was all right. She was joking.

"And?"

Or perhaps she was not joking.

"But I would miss—"

"You *will* miss the twilight picnic." Mrs. Pollock nodded. "Yes, dear. You will miss the songs, the cakes, the Elves, the games. You will miss it all. This is called a *punishment*, Esther. Do you know what a punishment is?"

I stared at her.

"Well, do you?"

I nodded slowly.

"Right then, dear. Personalized greeting, and off you go! Afternoon tea time! Enjoy!" She smiled warmly and turned back to her papers.

Day 12—Friday

Once, long ago, when my sisters and I were playing at home, we took turns rolling each other up in the living room carpet.

It was very fun and mildly scary, being tightly wrapped in the soft-yet-prickly darkness and then standing up and being shoved around the room. What happens is, you bump into furniture and tip over but you're (mostly) protected by the carpet, and your sisters make sure you don't smash through a window. You become confused and disoriented and then your mother comes in and roars at you to stop.

That's a bit how I felt. As if I'd been rolled up in a carpet. Only this time I had to carry it around myself, rather than be shoved about by my sisters, and there were no giggles, and no mother angrily unrolling me.

Everything was blurred and heavy, I mean.

I did my checks and perimeter walks. I brushed my teeth and braided my hair. I joined in rehearsals for the song I wouldn't be singing, and helped tidy our classroom and hang samples of our schoolwork and crafts around the walls, ready for other girls' parents. I watched as other girls' parents began to arrive.

Many parents were coming for the fundraising weekend. They would attend the twilight picnic, then stay at the inn in town, returning for the art show, classroom visits, and evening auction the next day.

My sisters had both arrived back from their trips at breakfast time. I waved, and they waved back, but they were surrounded by friends who wanted to hear their stories. Both Imogen and Pelagia had won medals in the swimming tournament, and Astrid had "impressed international leaders with her astute powers of observation." (I knew this because Principal Hortense had told us all, very emotionally, while we ate our eggs.)

At the Grade 6 table, we had all smiled at Pelagia and congratulated her. Her skin was darkly suntanned and her eyes were bloodshot. From chlorine, I guessed.

"Was it fun?" I asked.

Pelagia shrugged. "It was fun spending time with Imogen and Mr. Dar-Healey," she replied.

"Tell us all about it!" Hetty demanded, and everyone grinned, ready for Pelagia's stories.

But Pelagia shook her head. "What's been happening here?" she asked instead.

* * *

After breakfast, I was busy with my regular checks, and my sisters were busy rehearsing and preparing for the twilight picnic with their own grades. There was no chance to tell them about my detention. And although the carpet wrapped around me was heavy, I also felt safe and warm inside it. Telling my sisters might have been like unwrapping a little of the carpet, letting in the cold.

(You understand that the carpet was imaginary, I hope.)

I'm not sure *I* understood this completely that Friday. I could *see* it so clearly—navy blue with rows of tiny yellow flowers stitched around its borders—and I could feel its tickly texture and solid weight.

At 6:00 P.M., I walked upstairs to the teachers' lounge and knocked. Nobody answered, of course, as all the teachers were outside setting up for the twilight picnic. I pushed open the door, looked around the empty room, and saw a stack of mathematics worksheets on the coffee table. *For Esther,* said a note on top of these papers. A pencil and eraser sat alongside.

Over the next three hours, as I worked through the questions, hopping up now and then to stare through the window at the distant lanterns; the busy crowds of girls, teachers, and parents; the tables of cakes, pastries, and fruits; the tiny stages where Elves were performing their comedy shows—I could hear the distant, muffled sounds of people laughing at the Elves, the faint melody of each grade performing its song, the loud applause that followed the songs, and then, for the longest time, the gentler sound of a string quartet playing, while teaspoons clinked against plates, conversation and laughter floating wistfully on the breeze—

—as all that happened, I told myself that my carpet was

actually magic, a flying carpet, and that, if I flung open the window, unrolled my carpet, and sat on it, it would fly me far from here, far into the star-filled sky.

* * *

At 9:00 P.M., the door opened and Mrs. Pollock put her head in.

"Hello, Esther," she said, beaming. "I'm sure you've learned your lesson now. Go on to bed. Sweet dreams!"

CHAPTER 73

DAY 13—SATURDAY

No suspicious activity during my dawn perimeter check.

At breakfast, Principal Hortense gave a speech about what a marvelous night it had been, how *scrumptious* the cakes were, how hilarious the Elves, how *beautifully* we had sung, and so on. We all gave rounds of applause for the cook, the Elves, and ourselves.

After breakfast, we were going directly to the gymnasium to meet with parents and look at artworks, and then parents would visit the classrooms.

"Those who don't have parents here may read a book or catch up with homework," Principal Hortense suggested.

I still had the carpet wrapped around me.

As we headed out of the dining hall, I wondered if I was going to be able to read a book through the carpet. Could I see the pages? (Again, I was forgetting that it was imaginary.)

I was almost at the gymnasium when Imogen skidded up beside me.

"Esther!" she said. "I was calling you! Didn't you hear?"

Sounds were very muffled behind the carpet. I shook my head. "Sorry."

"Where were you last night?" she asked. "I couldn't see you anywhere at the twilight picnic. Are you all right? You don't look well."

I shrugged. "Well . . . ," I began. But where to start?

Some of Imogen's friends were calling her anyway. "Come on, Imogen! We're supposed to be in the gymnasium!"

"Coming!" she called back and then to me: "Listen, you won't believe it! I got a telegram this morning—guess who's coming to school today?"

I waited patiently.

"*Mother!*" Imogen cried. "Can you believe it? Me neither. She *never* visits!"

And she skidded away to join her friends.

I stopped perfectly still in the middle of the corridor and only moved again when somebody slammed into my back.

A thin ray of light shone into my carpet and began to tap quick and soft against my heart.

CHAPTER 74

IN THE GYMNASIUM, we were allowed to wander around looking at the different grades' artworks, and then we had to gather in front of our own grade's piece to wait for our parents.

Our Grade 6 artwork was called: *SUNSHINE.*

Other girls from my grade were already huddled around it saying, "Oh, that's mine! Ha ha, my sun's crooked!" and "Yours looks great, Maria!"

Our paintings were glued in rows.

A golden circle against a blue background, a golden circle against a blue background, a golden circle against a blue background—

And so on.

Some of the circles were pale, some buttery, some a fierce yellow, almost orange. Some were a bit wobbly and many had lines radiating out from the circle like spider legs.

Parents began to pour into the room, and girls called, "Father! Over here!" or "Mother! This way!"

"Autumn," said a voice. "Are *your* parents coming?"

I spun around. Zoe Fawnwell had asked the question, a worried smile on her face. Others looked away from the influx of parents and toward Autumn, many blinking. Once again, we'd forgotten that Autumn was a Whisperer.

Which meant her parents were Whisperers too.

"Only," Zoe added, "we should *prepare* ourselves if adult Whisperers are about to arrive. They could *literally Whisper* us!"

"Zoe!" Tatty cried, placing an arm around Autumn's shoulder. "It's not *Autumn's* fault she's a Whisperer!"

"I'm *sure* they wouldn't let *actual* adult Whisperers in," Hetty added, giving Autumn's arm a squeeze. "Don't be silly, Zoe."

"They're not coming," Autumn replied, gazing up at the artwork.

There was a ripple of relief mixed with disappointment, but then, suddenly, parents were amongst us. Girls embraced their own and pointed to the artwork: "See that one? It's mine! No, not that one, the second from the right."

Various parents exclaimed: "Oh, what a lovely artwork!" or "Gracious, isn't it beautiful?"

A golden circle against a blue background, a golden circle against a blue background, a golden circle—

I turned and there was my mother. Sunlight caught at a pattern of dust in the air and lit up her hair. She hesitated in the doorway to the gymnasium, her head darting around, not sure what to do. Her satchel was clutched beneath her arm, as usual. Her hair was neatly combed and she wore her best blue suit with silver buttons.

The shaft of light tapped against my heart once more: tap-tap-tap-tap.

"Mother!" I called, but at that moment, Mother marched across to where Astrid was waving. She stopped to admire the Grade 4 picture of a school of rainbow fish.

Well, she would come to me next.

Or perhaps to Imogen and the Grade 7 artwork, I supposed. But *then* to me.

I turned back to our artwork.

Golden circle against a blue background—

A golden circle against—

I stopped.

You might be thinking it was taking a while for me to catch on, but remember my imaginary carpet? Everything was hazy through woven fibers.

So this was the first moment I wondered.

More slowly, I ran my eyes along the pictures—golden circle, golden circle—

I ducked around girls and parents—golden circle, golden circle—and that was it.

I had seen the whole painting.

"Mrs. Pollock?" I asked.

She was standing to the side, arms behind her back, accepting compliments from parents.

"Yes, Esther dear?" Mrs. Pollock crouched to hear. Some of the parents saw this and smiled lovingly.

"I can't see my painting."

"Oh, Esther dear." Mrs. Pollock's face became sorrowful. She spoke in a soft, confiding murmur. "Your painting was gray and rainy, remember? I couldn't include it in an artwork called *SUNSHINE,* could I?"

That made sense. I nodded.

Mrs. Pollock straightened and began chatting with Zoe Fawnwell's mother. After a moment, I realized that Autumn and Pelagia were either side of me. They were the only girls in our class whose parents had not come.

"Your painting would have looked perfect in the center," Autumn commented quietly. "Rain with lots of sunshine radiating out from it."

Pelagia spoke even more softly. "She didn't *have* to name the artwork *SUNSHINE.*"

I hadn't thought of that.

The three of us stood in a row staring at the sunshine.

I glanced across the gymnasium and caught sight of my mother in a crowd of Grade 7 parents. Imogen was standing on tiptoe, pointing out the crepe paper flowers she had added to her class's "Garden" artwork. Mother looked pleased.

Any moment, Mother would approach and say, "Hello, Esther. And which one of these is *your* painting?"

I walked out of the gymnasium and back to my classroom.

CHAPTER 75

NOBODY ELSE WAS there yet.

Our classroom looked festive: streamers and paper chains, sample exercises and drawings tacked all over the wall, self-portraits hanging from strings across the ceiling.

My painting was sitting on my desk.

I smiled at it. The colorful umbrellas were very bright against the rainy background. Maybe not as neat as I'd remembered, but still—

It was a beautiful painting.

I knew what I'd do. I'd give it to my mother as a gift.

It was *lucky* it hadn't been included in the artwork! As soon as Mother came in for the classroom visit I'd hand it over.

Girls and parents began to file into our classroom then, and there was more exclaiming from the parents. "Oh, what a lovely classroom!" and "Show me your desk?"

I sat waiting for Mother. I supposed she might go to Astrid's classroom first, and then to Imogen's. Or perhaps she'd come straight to mine after not finding me in the gymnasium?

I watched the doorway.

More girls came in, leading their parents. The room began to fill with people studying the walls and decorations and making humorous little comments to their daughters and to each other.

I picked up my painting. The edges really were a bit smudged, but never mind.

I turned it over to see if I'd splashed any paint on the back. I often do that, I don't know how.

Mrs. Pollock's handwriting was on the back of the painting. In large, black ink, she'd written:

Very messy, and much too gray. Do you want to depress people??? Next time, try sunshine.

C–

I slid out from behind my desk, crossed the room, and dropped the painting in the wastepaper bin. Then I returned to my seat and carried on watching the door.

CHAPTER 76

MOTHER TOOK A seat at a corner table in the Orange Blossom Tea Shop.

"Imogen, you take that chair by the window," she instructed. "Astrid, come by me. Sit down, Esther, you funny thing, don't hover!"

There was nowhere for me to sit. Only three chairs at the table.

"Well, grab one from another table then! Use that clever brain of yours!"

We had just walked into town together. Imogen had found me in my classroom alone and called from the door, "Mother's taking us into town for afternoon tea! Come on!"

So here we were. It took me a while to find a spare chair. The café was crowded with girls from Katherine Valley having afternoon tea with their visiting parents.

"What will you all have? Choose whatever you like," Mother told us.

We ordered from the waitress—not the tall, thin one; she was across the café and hadn't even glanced at me—but a short waitress with a droopy face. She cheered up when my sisters and I ordered chocolate-strawberry pies, and Mother ordered the scones, and she gathered our menus and walked away. After a few moments, during which Mother checked that none of us had grown out of our shoes, by crouching at our feet and pressing at the toes, the waitress returned with our orders.

Imogen turned to Mother. "It's a shame you missed the twilight picnic last night," she said.

"Twilight picnic?" Mother took a large bite of her scone, grimaced, chewed, swallowed, took another bite, and swallowed again. She shuddered. "This scone is *very* dry. I can't think why they're famous for their scones. What picnic is this?"

"Last night," Imogen explained. "Most parents came."

Mother chuckled. "No, dear, parents were invited to see *artworks* and do *classroom visits*. No picnic. Funny thing."

"Actually, there *was* a—" Imogen began, but she decided not to bother. "What did you think of the art? And the classrooms?" she asked instead.

Mother's eyes widened. "Just wonderful!" she said. "Really excellent classrooms you all have!" She took another bite of her scone.

I raised my eyebrows. "We *all* have?"

Mother nodded. "Lucky things!"

"But you didn't *see* my classroom."

Imogen and Astrid looked at me in surprise.

"Of course I saw your classroom, Esther! Yours had the—the decorations. A really magnificent room."

"No." I shook my head. "You didn't visit my classroom."

"I most certainly did. I went the moment I'd finished looking at the artworks. You were probably still in the gymnasium chatting with your friends."

At that point, the waitress arrived to check if we were enjoying our food. I think she wanted us to say, "Delicious!" but Mother said, "A little dry," and my sisters and I, being distracted, only said, "Yes, thank you."

"I left the gymnasium *early*," I told Mother—and the waitress, disappointed, slid away. "I was the first one at my classroom."

Imogen piped up. "You didn't go to Esther's class first, Mother. Remember, you and I left the gymnasium together and walked to my classroom?"

"And then you came to mine," Astrid put in, "as it's only two doors down from Imogen's. She showed you the way."

"Well, honestly, I'm not sure why it's important to *pinpoint* the time I saw your classroom, Esther! I suppose it was *after*

Astrid's then." Mother reached her fork out to my chocolate-strawberry pie. "You don't mind if I try a little, do you? I'm so disappointed with my scones."

"I waited in my classroom," I told her steadily, "until all the parents had gone. That was where Imogen found me and we walked into town."

Mother nodded seriously. "I hope you girls never walk into town unsupervised."

"We're not allowed in town anymore," Astrid explained, through a mouthful. "Because of—"

"Shadow Mages." Mother took a forkful of Astrid's pie. "May I have a little? Don't talk with your mouth full, sweetheart. Yes, there are Shadow Mages in the mountains." She glanced at me. "You are being careful, Esther? I expect this is the first you've even *heard* about the Shadow Mages around here!"

I stared at her.

Imogen and Astrid both protested: "Of course she's heard about the Shadow Mages in the mountains! Principal Hortense made an announcement! And we were *all* at the pool when the Sterling Silver Foxes attacked! Esther's friend Katya had her laughter stolen! *Esther's* the one who realized about that! She saved Katya's—"

Mother laughed. "Don't make such a fuss, girls!" she said. "I'm only teasing Esther. She's absentminded, that's all I mean. You lucky girls, ordering this pie. It's *much* better than the scones."

We all glanced at Mother's scone plate, which was perfectly empty, except for a few crumbs. As we watched, Mother picked these crumbs up with her fingertips and ate them.

"Why don't you order yourself a slice of pie then?" Astrid suggested.

Mother laughed. "Pie *and* scones! Oh, to be a child!" She beckoned the waitress.

"Did she really not come to your classroom at all?" Astrid asked me, while Mother was distracted.

"Did she see your artwork in the gymnasium?" Imogen asked.

I shrugged.

I was all right.

I only had to pull the carpet more tightly around me. Safe and soft here.

Mother was ordering herself another pot of tea.

"Right," she said, turning back and scooping up a piece of Imogen's pie. "Where were we?"

I pushed back my chair.

"Excuse me," I said, and I walked out of the café.

CHAPTER 77

THERE WAS A crisp breeze outside.

I let it tousle my hair and flick my cheeks. I didn't do anything else. I just stood there.

The sky was blue and the flowers bright in their buckets at the stalls. More girls from school wandered the streets with their parents. Everyone was shiny-eyed and chatty. The parents listened closely to their daughters' words and then laughed or said, "Oh, really?"

In my pocket, I had a few coins and a pebble. I don't know why the pebble was there. It was not pretty or smooth, it was just a pebble.

Soon, Mother would pick up her satchel and return us to school. There, she would kiss us each on the cheek and set off to catch the coach back home.

Once again, I would begin my checks of the school's perimeters. Running up to the top floor and looking through the windows. Climbing over the wall. Sneaking into the kitchen to replenish my supplies. Searching the library for ideas on how to defeat Shadow Mages.

Studying my toenails for hours, longing for them to turn blue, as it would be *so much simpler if only I was a Spellbinder.*

It was only for two more weeks, I reminded myself. In two weeks, the Spellbinders would arrive. *They* would take care of the school!

Only two more weeks.

Two weeks.

Fourteen days.

I leaned against the glass of the café window.
Fourteen days.
I counted them.
One,

two,

three,

four.
The numbers seemed to go forever.

Five,

six.
They moved so slowly! Each was a giant, slimy slug.

Seven.
I couldn't do it.
I couldn't even count that high.
Schoolwork, homework, dance lessons, running up the stairs,
clambering over the wall.

Eight.

Nine.
But I had to do it.

Ten.

Eleven.

A man was walking down the street in the direction of the café. He wore a striped jacket and an interested expression, glancing around at everything he passed. He was quite bald. He ducked around families, smiling and calling, "Hello there!" to some and "Nice to see you again!" to people at the stalls.

Twelve.

The man looked toward the café.

Thirteen—

The man saw me. His face lit up. He raised a hand to wave. "Esther!" he called.

The carpet unfolded itself and fell with a thud to the ground. Air and brightness flooded me.

I ran into my father's arms.

CHAPTER 78

I TOLD HIM everything.

Well, first I burst into tears. I didn't plan that. I was laughing with happiness, actually, as I ran into his arms, but a strange thing about laughter is this: it can fall into crying. Sometimes laughing is like running along the edge of a pond of tears.

Father's voice changed at once from "Esther! It's you!" to "*Esther!* Oh, darling! Esther?" He held on to me very tightly, patting my back, and then he set me down and said, "Wait here." He ducked into the café and I watched through the glass as he strode across to my mother and sisters' table. He hugged each of them quickly, spoke a few words, and came back out to me. Imogen's and Astrid's faces were quite bewildered, I saw, but Mother's back was to me. So I cannot describe her face.

"I said I had to duck out for new shoelaces," he explained. "Now, let's go sit by the lake."

That's where I told him everything. As we sat on a bench by the lake, watching boats slide by, and ducks, I told him about the conversation I'd overheard, hiding in the mailroom, and how I'd thought the secret Spellbinder must be one of the two new girls. I told him about the Sterling Silver Fox attack, and my research for my speech, and Katya's laughter being stolen.

I told him how I'd seen Katya's blue toenails. Katya asking me to pass on the message, and my promise not to tell a soul. The tall, thin waitress. Hiding by the lake. I pointed to the boat under which I'd hidden, still lying upside down just along the bank from us. Seeing the boat brought my tale to vivid life for him (my father said).

I told him about the people I'd heard eating toffees and saying they wouldn't send protection for my school. How I'd decided it was my job to protect the school, and how I'd gathered items from the kitchens and garden shed and so on, and how I'd been patrolling the walls, watching from the windows. How Imogen and Astrid had been away swimming and helping the mayor.

How I'd been alone.

I talked very quickly, my words spilling over each other. I told him all about my encounters with Witches, Sterling Silver Foxes, Radish Gnomes, and Sirens.

Father went quite pale at several parts of my story. He didn't speak, just nodded as I talked, shaking his head at some bits, widening his eyes, and muttering, "*What?*"

When I described chasing Shadow Mages away, he was absolutely still, his face whiter than paper.

"And I've been so tired," I said, trying not to cry, "and it's hard to get my homework done, and there are still two weeks before the Spellbinders come, and"—it was tricky saying all this without crying again—"and now I've betrayed Katya because I've broken my promise not to tell."

I finished by telling him about the three demerits, the detention, and missing the twilight picnic. For some reason, this *did* make me cry again, properly—sobbing, really.

Father hugged me fiercely. "So unfair! All the work you'd done protecting the school and you're rewarded with detention? And *missing out on the twilight picnic*! Ridiculous!"

A few moments later, he murmured, "Still, what with breaking into kitchens and garden sheds, stealing school property, and running around the forest in the middle of the night, you could *technically* have been expelled about fifty times over."

He chuckled a little, and I did too. He couldn't really stop chuckling for a while, and I accidentally joined in because, it turned out, you could also fall from crying into laughter.

CHAPTER 79

AFTER WE'D LAUGHED for a while, Father became serious again.

"A tall, thin waitress, you say? At the Orange Blossom Tea Shop?"

"Yes. With a silver apple pendant."

"Back soon," he promised.

He ran up the stairs and onto the street. I waited on the bench. A few parents and students from Katherine Valley strolled by, some smiling at me.

Not long after this, Father came down the steps again, the waitress beside him. Following them was a square-shouldered man with an important nose. I mean that his nose seemed to be proud of itself, and to take up a lot of room in the world. I knew who it was. Carson Brody. Local mayor. Astrid's employer.

The three of them turned right and stopped on the far side of the upturned boats. They waited until there were no passersby about, and then Father began talking.

I couldn't hear what he was saying, but I could hear his tone. Grim and angry. Now and then, both the waitress and the mayor interjected. The mayor, I realized with surprise, was the owner of the other voice I'd heard from underneath the boat.

Now and then, Father's words became a kind of roar, and both the mayor and the waitress touched his arm, trying to quieten him.

Once, I heard Father half-shout, "Carabella-the-Great!" and then something-something-something.

Eventually, all three voices lowered to murmurs, then the

waitress and the mayor shook Father's hand and hurried up the stairs and away.

Father stood with his back to me for a moment, then strolled toward the bench, whistling. He sat beside me.

"Right then, Esther," he said. "All sorted."

"All sorted?"

"An experienced Spellbinder will be at your school within the next hour. He or she will set up a solid Spellbinding around the perimeters. It will keep the school safe at least until the Spellbinding conference begins in two weeks, and you, my child, can go back to being a schoolgirl."

I stared at him. I'm sure my eyes were shining.

"Another thing," he continued. "Katya asked you not to tell anybody about this, yes?"

I nodded, miserable again. He was going to remind me not to break promises.

But Father held up his hand: "You can always tell me any-thing. Understand?"

"Well," I began, doubtfully, but he interrupted.

"Esther," he said. "A promise not to tell never applies to your parents."

"It doesn't?"

"In fact, if somebody makes you promise not to tell your parents something? That actually means you probably should tell them. If you have excellent parents, I mean. Which you do."

He was so serious that I nodded. "All right."

"Good girl. Come on then." Father brushed down his trou-sers. "I've been dreaming of those scones."

"Mother didn't like them," I told him.

Father laughed. "Of course she didn't. Let's go join them—Oh, wait a moment, mind if we pick up some shoelaces? Need them for my cover story."

CHAPTER 80

BACK AT THE tea shop, Father ordered scones.

"Oh, I wouldn't do that," Mother advised.

"Wouldn't you?" he replied and asked for double scones, adding a strong coffee to his order. Then he turned to Imogen and Astrid.

"Tell me," he said, "every single thing that has happened so far this term at Katherine Valley Boarding School, and every single thing that happened during your swimming tournament, Imogen, and during your tour with the mayor, Astrid."

"But wait, how did you *get* here?" Imogen asked. "I thought you were out of reach!"

"I was," Father agreed. "But I needed to travel back to this region for a meeting. And I wanted to see you and your mother."

"Hmph," said Mother.

"What?" Father asked, turning to her curiously. "Why *hmph*?"

"Oh, I don't know. I suppose it's good to see you."

"Of course it is. You're delighted. *Hmph* is just automatic with you even when you're over the moon."

Mother allowed a small smile, then rolled her eyes.

"I'd hoped to get here by yesterday afternoon," Father continued, addressing my sisters and me. "But the meeting that was meant to end at noon yesterday carried on until well past noon *today*. Such a shame. I wanted to come to your art show and classroom visits today. Not to mention your twilight picnic last night, of course."

All three of us girls glanced over at Mother, but she was squinting fiercely at the tea leaves in her pot.

Father's scones arrived then. He took a mouthful and said these were the most delicious, mouth-melting, light-as-air delights he had ever eaten and ordered extra for my sisters and me. My sisters chatted with Father, Mother drank her tea and ate a piece of each of our scones, and I leaned back in my seat.

I felt wrung out. Light-headed with relief. Zingy with joy.

No more getting up in the night to climb over the school wall. No more zipping up the stairs at morning tea and lunch. No more figuring out how to scare off Shadow Mages.

I could not believe it.

I was so dreamy, I closed my eyes, and I might have been drifting off to sleep when Mother suddenly exclaimed.

"Oh gosh!" (That's what she exclaimed.) "Almost forgot!"

She reached into her satchel and drew out a gold-embossed card.

"You know the Stolen Prince of Cloudburst?" she asked us.

"You mean Alejandro?" Imogen said.

"Bronte's friend?" Astrid put in.

"That delightful boy from the pirate ship? The one who later turned out to be the lost prince from the Kingdom of Storms?" Father put in.

"Yes, yes," Mother said impatiently. "The Stolen Prince of Cloudburst. Well, you know how they're having a big party to celebrate his return?"

We all nodded.

"They've only gone and invited our whole family," Mother said.

CHAPTER 81

THAT WAS SUCH exciting news it needed a new chapter.

We all gasped.

"Why would they invite us?" Imogen breathed. "*We* don't know the King and Queen of the Kingdom of Storms."

"But we know the prince," Astrid pointed out. "Remember? We met him at the Whispering Kingdom when Bronte was a hero! And he's been living with Bronte since then so he's practically our cousin too! He must have asked for us!"

Mother laughed. "Oh, you only met him for an afternoon! And we've not had any visits since, so he wouldn't remember you girls. But Bronte will be going, of course, and she must have been allowed to invite you. You probably won't even get a glimpse of the prince himself at the party as he'll be so busy. I can't possibly attend, as I'm so busy—but I think your father is heading to Vanquishing Cove, which isn't far from the Kingdom of Storms, and so it *might* work out that he could take you girls along?"

Father was nodding vigorously as he studied the invitation. "You're right! I have a conference there, right around the time of the party. I *could* go. And bring the girls!"

My sisters and I prepared to gasp again, but Mother was talking. "I've looked into transport," she said. "And you'd have to leave tomorrow morning. You'd miss the next two weeks of school. And Imogen and Astrid have already missed the last two weeks! And after *that*, it's not long before your poker jaunt! Can you miss that much education? Will you be able to do schoolwork while you travel, do you think?"

We all assured her, very earnestly, that we could.

Father spooned more cream onto his scones. "Wait a moment, I'm remembering something," he said. "It's on the tip of my . . ." He made a sudden swipe at his elbow. "Got it! It was on the tip of my elbow. Your *father* is a history professor!"

"*Is* he?" we exclaimed.

We were joking, of course. We know he's a history professor. I mean, he's been our father all our lives.

"I *am*." Father nodded. "And therefore I can *tutor* my daughters! Missing school won't matter! Let's do it!"

Mother nodded. "All right," she said. "We'd better get you back to school so you can pack—and maybe spend this afternoon doing as much homework as you can in advance? We'll talk to your principal. What's her name again?"

"Principal Hortense," we all replied at once—including Father.

Mother called for the bill.

PART

3

CHAPTER 82

MY SISTERS AND I were in our pajamas. So was my father. His pajamas are blue-and-white striped. Imogen's are spotted with rosebuds, Astrid's with balls of yarn and kittens, and mine have a friendly-snowman print.

That's in case you want to know what our pajamas are like.

We had plates of cinnamon toast and mugs of hot milk. Moonlight shone through the window—wait, what do you call a window on a ship? A pothole? No, that's in the road.

A *porthole.*

It was the third day of our journey, and Father had been spooning honey into our hot milk when he remembered his promise to tutor us.

"Righto!" he said, excited. "Let's get to it!"

He becomes very enthusiastic about schoolwork. This can be pretty irritating, to be honest. Otherwise, I like him.

We took out our workbooks. Right away, Astrid got buttery fingerprints on one of her books, and Imogen spilled milk on hers.

Meanwhile, Father had opened my composition book and was reading my narrative account: *The Stolen Prince of Cloudburst.*

When he's concentrating, his lips purse as if he's whistling. Now and then he stopped pursing his lips and chuckled.

At one point, he looked up at me.

"How old are you again, Esther?"

"Twelve," I replied.

"Twelve."

Then he carried on reading.

When he finished, he read Mrs. Pollock's comment and now his mouth flew wide open. It no longer appeared that he was whistling, it was more as if he was stuck in a yawn.

Next, he took out a red pen and set to work editing Mrs. Pollock's comment.

He handed my composition book back to me.

Esther, yes, ~~I have read much of~~ this story, ~~or its basic facts, anyway, in the newspapers. You have not made them more interesting here. Worse, you have tried to put yourself in the story. You might be related to some of these interesting people, but that does not make~~ YOU ~~interesting. Do not~~ put yourself in stories ~~where you do not belong.~~ — more often! *is the best I've ever read.* *are so*

~~Do not tell fibs. You are very far indeed from Cloudburst, and highly unlikely ever to so much as glimpse the Stolen Prince.~~

~~Also, do not begin sentences with the words "And" or "But." Do not break your sentences and paragraphs into pieces; it makes your tale is very disjointed. Do not boast by saying that~~ your asides are "helpful" ~~—that is not becoming.~~ VERY

and I love how you break up your sentences in such funny, unexpected ways! Like syncopated rhythm! So fun!

I see that you stayed up past midnight to do your homework. ~~Dreadful behaviour. DEMERIT. As this is your third demerit,~~ please ~~attend detention on Friday evening as punishment.~~ *accept my congratulations!*

Wow! That's so dedicated of you! Well done!

Finally, you began this story with the words "Long ago, far away, on a damp and sniffly day." ~~*Please write out the following, 100 times:*~~

A DAY CAN~~NOT~~ BE "SNIFFLY."?

ABSOLUTELY

✗

GREAT OPENING WORDS! LOVE IT! GENIUS!

A +++

Imogen read all this over my shoulder, scrambled for her history test, thrust it at Father, and told him to please change her D+ grade to an A+++.

"Of course," Father agreed, but then he studied Imogen's test and said: "Imogen, your answers *are* all wrong. Even this one that's been marked correct is wrong actually. Mr. Dar-Healey's made a mistake there, or maybe felt a bit sorry for you and said to himself, *Oh, close enough.* I'm afraid I can't change this grade. I *am* a historian, remember, so this is more or less my area of expertise. I'd have given it an F, to be honest. I could change it to an F if you like? Yes, actually, hand me that pen, and I'll—"

Imogen grew very loud and passionate, shouting: *"DON'T YOU DARE!"* and snatching her book away, but then, when she realized he was only joking about the F, she went back to trying for an A+++.

"You must treat *all* your daughters equally," she reasoned. "If you change Esther's grade to an A+++ then you must change mine. Otherwise, I will forever believe that you love Esther more than me. Is that what you want? Is it?"

And so on.

I mean, she was joking herself, but she got caught up in the splendor and sense of her argument (as she put it) and became so thunderous that the person in the next stateroom thumped on the wall.

Father laughed loudly, congratulated Imogen on her debating skills, and said, "Great lesson, girls, well done. Let's call it a night."

And we climbed into our bunks and fell asleep.

CHAPTER 83

THE NEXT MORNING at breakfast, Father frowned at the coffeepot.

There was nothing wrong with the coffeepot. It was shiny silver with an elegant lid. That's just what Father does when he's thinking deeply: chooses an innocent object and glares at it.

After a while, he reached out a finger, flicked the coffeepot, turned to me, and said, "This Mrs. Pollock."

There was a pause.

"Yes?" I prompted. "My teacher?"

"You say you like her?"

I nodded. I'd already told him about Mrs. Pollock, and how much fun she is. "She's funny!" I reminded him. "At first, everyone was frightened, because we thought she was an Ogre."

"An Ogre." Father nodded. "Well, you would be frightened."

"Yes," I agreed. "But she's not. She's tiny. And she does silly faces and voices! We never stop laughing."

Astrid, I noticed, was frowning intently at me, as if I was a coffeepot.

Father himself shifted his frown to the chandelier. It was swaying gently above us.

"I mean," I said, "it's true that she's sometimes stricter than other teachers, and tougher at marking. But that means she's a *good* teacher. She's helping us improve."

"Hmm." Father's frown reached the pastry basket. "So you think your work is improving because of Mrs. Pollock?"

At this point, I should say, we were in the ship's dining room.

Through the windows, the day was calm, islands passing now and then, like creatures rising from the ocean surface before sinking down again. The ship rocked softly.

The ship, by the way, was the *Riddle and Popcorn* cruise ship. My Aunts Maya and Lisbeth are captains, and talented sailors. As we are related, we always sat at the captains' table.

Mostly, though, the aunts did not dine with us. We hardly saw them for the entire voyage, actually. Aunt Lisbeth apologized for this, saying, "The ocean currents are acting up! Running in the loopiest directions—no time to scratch our rear ends!"

And Aunt Maya added, "Sea creatures popping up in the entirely wrong part of the ocean! It's the cat's pajamas! A real hoot!"

Still, they both looked more lined, puffy under the eyes, and *old* than I remembered them.

("You mean they look *tired*," Father corrected me, when I mentioned this.)

They were not at the captains' table this morning either, which was a shame as I was beginning to feel itchy.

"Yes, of course my work is improving!" I said—or maybe snapped. I didn't know why I felt cranky suddenly, I just did. "Why don't you ask Astrid more about working for the mayor? Ask Imogen more about her swimming tournament!"

Astrid and Imogen both straightened in surprise.

"Well," Astrid said, after a beat. "I could tell you about the day when the mayor fired me."

"He *what*?"

We all swung to look at her.

Astrid reminded us that her job had been to listen behind glass as the adults took turns speaking.

"There was a button to push to talk into the mayor's earpiece," she said, "and tell him who was lying. Well, one day the mayor himself was talking, and *he* started lying. I pressed a different button and told the whole room."

"You *what*?"

"It was only fair." Astrid shrugged. "He knew when the others were lying."

"He must have been cross," Father said admiringly.

"Furious," Astrid agreed. "He unfired me the next day though, as he found it too confusing going to meetings without me. I said I'd keep telling the others if he lied again, and he sighed like this . . ." She demonstrated: a deep, slow sigh. "Then agreed. He's only lied three or four times since."

After we'd laughed for a while, Imogen told us that the most fun part of the swimming tournament had been train and coach rides, and lunches and dinners, with Pelagia and Mr. Dar-Healey.

"Pelagia acts out her stories so dramatically. Like, she'll huff and puff as if she'd just run a big race if she's describing a chase scene. Or she'll wave her hands around to demonstrate flames if fire is part of her story. Mr. Dar-Healey and I were transfixed. Although . . ." Imogen paused and sipped from her orange juice. "She changed as the trip went on. She was winning everything so she ought to have been happy, but her stories got shorter, and less theatrical, and then she stopped telling stories altogether. Mr. Dar-Healey and I tried to cheer her up, and to ask what was wrong. She never answered.

"Plus, a few times she wandered away from the hotel when we got to a new town, even though we were supposed to stay together. Mr. Dar-Healey got a bit stern with her about that, and she cried, and then he felt bad and explained that we were his responsibility, and he cared about us, and she only cried more, and he looked over at me, like: *help!*" Imogen demonstrated Mr. Dar-Healey's helpless face. "I didn't know what to do, and then Mr. Dar-Healey suggested a game of Scrabble, which, surprisingly, cheered her up. But she was never the same. It was str—"

I think she was going to say *strange*, although I can't say for sure because there was a mighty *creak* and everything slid off the table.

CHAPTER 84

COFFEEPOT, NAPKINS, PLATES, cutlery, milk jug, fried eggs, salt and pepper shakers. Everything.

It was happening all around the dining room. People shrieked, grabbing at things, or tipped over in their chairs. The chandeliers swung wildly, and breakfast food continued crashing and splattering to the carpet.

Another *cre-e-e-a-k,* a *boom!* and the ship righted itself again. Then, just as we began to pick up chairs and plates, a voice from out on deck shouted, "Aquatic Elves!"

Everyone dropped the items they'd gathered and rushed out onto the deck. Aquatic Elves are extremely rare. There are only a handful of colonies, all of these in the far north waters of the Northern Climes.

"It won't be Aquatic Elves," Father warned us. "We're too far south."

But it was.

A colony, riding their net along the ocean surface. Aunts Maya and Lisbeth must have had to tack sharply to avoid them.

Their net looked like the white pith inside orange peel. It blended with the foam of waves, so you had to squint before you understood what you were seeing.

The Elves, each the size of a teaspoon, and each with a spray of white hair like a dandelion puff, paid us no attention. Some were curled up asleep, but most scurried about, straightening the edges of the net, gathering sea krill, jumping into the ocean to splash about, plucking baby Elves from the water so they wouldn't be left behind. It was mesmerizing to watch.

They moved so quickly! Very different to land Elves, who tend to be leisurely except when playing music or sport.

The ship's deck was crowded now. There were people like us from the dining room, passengers who'd run upstairs in their nightgowns, and early risers who'd already been playing shuffleboard or reading on the deck.

Everyone exclaimed and pointed, running from port to starboard, bow to stern, trying to keep up with the Aquatic Elves as their net skimmed this way and that in the water.

Soon, though, the net began to drift steadily away from the ship. We peered into the distance for as long as we could, but it vanished, merging with sea spray.

"Aquatic Elves! I can't believe we saw Aquatic Elves!" everyone chattered, shiny-eyed.

"What are the chances?" a passenger breathed.

"Minuscule," said a man in a straw hat.

"Vanishingly small," added a woman in a bathing suit.

After a moment, my father spoke in a thoughtful voice. "Nonexistent," he said and glanced at us. "There's *no* chance of seeing Aquatic Elves here."

We told him that that made no sense as we'd *seen* the Aquatic Elves so there had to be *some* chance, but he was strolling back into the dining room, taking no notice at all.

CHAPTER 85

THE NEXT IMPORTANT thing to happen on our voyage to Spindrift was that we stopped in Cloudburst for a night.

Cloudburst is the capital of the Kingdom of Storms and is right in the middle of that kingdom. (Spindrift is on the coast, but it's quicker to travel there overland than to sail around. That's a helpful aside, in case you're puzzled—or a geographer.)

While we were in Cloudburst—

—I broke my ankle.

How did I do that?

Well, first you should know that Cloudburst is crowded, hilly, and rainy. The Royal Palace stands at the top of the steepest hill like a worried parent frowning down on its children as they scurry about in the rain. Cobblestone roads are pockmarked with puddles and lined with fancy shops, in and out of which people bustle, raincoats flapping. "Excuse me!" they sing to each other. "Oops! Got our brollies tangled."

Honestly, the place is an accident waiting to happen. *Anybody* could slip and break an ankle.

You can't blame the person who breaks the ankle. You have to blame the town.

We arrived in Cloudburst in the morning, checked into the hotel, and set off to see the Cloudburst Museum. I was pretty bored by the museum, if I'm honest. Don't tell Father I said that. He was so proud of himself. "Educational!" he said, as we waited in line. "Fascinating! You'll *love* it!"

He's a historian. It's his job to love it, not mine. I can't even remember a single thing we saw. A vase, maybe? No flowers in it.

Next, we had lunch in our hotel dining room. Father was called away during the pumpkin soup to take a telephone call. My sisters got out their detective novels to read at the table, but I'd already finished mine. So, after a bit of staring around at other diners (one man curled his arm around his plate, as if I was *hurting* his food by looking at it), I pushed back my chair.

"Be right back," I told my sisters, who only carried on reading, and I slipped out of the hotel.

I ran all the way up the steepest hill in Cloudburst until I reached the palace.

Why did I do that?

I had the strange idea that I might see Alejandro, the Stolen Prince of Cloudburst, through a palace window. As I've mentioned, my sisters and I had met him once, two years earlier. Mother had been sure he wouldn't remember us and I was anxious to prove her wrong, as soon as possible.

I didn't have an umbrella or coat, but that was all right, I love the rain. (Teachers never seem to think that's important. They're always carrying on: "What were you doing outside in that downpour!" And when I reply, soothingly, "It's all right, I love the rain"—they brush that aside as irrelevant. It's all about "catching a chill" with them, and "have I lost my mind?")

Anyhow, once I reached the palace, I walked around it three times, the rain pattering pleasantly on my head and shoulders. The golden red sandstone walls were made richer and redder by the rain, the elegant balconies and balustrades shone, and the royal flags drooped and dripped. Each time I passed a guard, I waved, but the guards stood grimly, rain streaming down their faces, and took no notice.

Other people were staring up at the palace too. They had umbrellas. One woman kept twirling her umbrella, which was a bit careless as she was sharing it with a friend. The friend had to prance about like a goat to stay sheltered. Anyway, the twirling one said to her friend: "Can you believe the young prince is in there? Never thought I'd see the day when he'd be back!"

The friend sprang sideways and ducked under the twirling umbrella. "I know," she agreed. "I hear they're traveling to Spindrift early in the morning, for the party. Wish *I'd* been invited."

"They couldn't invite the entire Kingdom, I suppose."

"Suppose not."

After that, the two women clipped back down the hill.

High-heeled boots they wore. Dangerous on slippery roads. Could so easily break an ankle.

CHAPTER 86

I CIRCLED THE palace one more time. This time I peered hard at the windows, hoping to spot Alejandro. Or even glimpse King Jakob and Queen Anita hugging Alejandro? The queen would kneel before her son, holding his face in her hands. Tears sprang to my eyes just imagining it.

Each time I passed a guard, I almost called out: "You know Prince Alejandro? Guess what? He's a friend of my cousin Bronte! I'm Esther!"

But I was never quite brave enough. I imagined the guards might not believe me. They'd think, *How could such an ordinary child have anything to do with our* prince? They might sniff at me.

Or what if they hollered into the palace: "Prince Alejandro? Your friend Esther is out here!"

And next came the sound of Alejandro's voice: "Esther? Who's Esther? Never heard of her."

Because really, it had been a very busy afternoon when we met Alejandro, one that featured many cousins. Alejandro could *easily* have missed me altogether.

That would be embarrassing. Also the guards might arrest me, thinking I was a spy.

Not worth the risk, so I didn't call out.

I was about to return to the hotel when I happened to notice that three grand houses stood opposite the palace. One of these, the grandest, had a high, peaked roof. If you were doing repairs on that roof, I thought, you'd be able to see directly into the palace windows.

Next thing I knew, I was climbing onto the roof.

It really was like that. I didn't make a *decision* to climb—that would have been a silly decision—I just found myself doing it.

(Later, when I tried to explain this, nobody really got the distinction. Father said, "Well, you *did* make a decision, Esther," in a serious voice. "It's not as if you were *Whispered* to climb. You just wanted to." This was true, and Father is never serious generally, so I nearly cried.)

It was easy to climb. There was a drainpipe running up the side of the house, and you could sidestep onto window ledges for rests. It was almost as if it was *designed* for a passing child to climb.

Up on the roof, the slope of tiles was steeper than it had looked from the road. So that's not my fault. That was a bit misleading.

I scrambled up, sliding down now and then, until I reached the peak. This, I straddled.

It was very windy up there, and my hair swirled around, splashing against my face. Again, how could I have known that would happen?

I peered across at the palace.

You couldn't see a thing. The windows over there ran with rain and were fogged and misty. Also, there were curtains.

Oh well, I thought. *This was a waste of time.* And I swung my leg back over, ready to climb back down.

I was being very careful, I promise.

I glanced back toward the palace just one more time as I swung my leg, and, right at that moment, a curtain was whisked aside.

I saw a face.

Somebody was pressing their forehead to the glass to look outside.

A woman's face.

Queen Anita!

I recognized her from newspaper pictures!

Right there, across the way! The queen!

And her expression—the expression on her face—there was something about it that I could not quite—

Then I was skidding down that roof at an alarming speed, bump-bump-bump, grabbing wildly, but finding nothing to hold on to (they should have handles or something up there) and then, oh, it's the edge—I'll have to catch on—

I was skidding too fast.

No chance to catch on to anything.

Crashed over, tumbled down the side of the house, grabbing at window ledges all the way —

The ground slammed into me like something furious. *Snap* went my ankle.

CHAPTER 87

THE DOCTOR AT the hospital was an enormous man with a ferocious scowl.

(A palace guard saw me fall and called an ambulance, if you're wondering how I got to the hospital.) The doctor asked what had happened, stared at my ankle, checked it against the other one, and had me move and twist my foot. Although his expression was fierce, his hands were gentle, as if they knew just how much the ankle hurt.

Eventually he straightened and said he was sending me for an x-ray, but that he was pretty sure it was fractured.

"You say this happened while you were climbing onto the roof of a house?" he asked. "One of those big houses opposite the palace?"

"Well, I mean, it happened when I *fell*," I said, "rather than when I was climbing."

His frown deepened and it seemed like he was about to scold me for climbing in the first place. So I quickly pointed out that the people who own the house should place a sign outside saying the roof was steeper than it looked. And warning children about how windy it was up there. A sign like that might have saved me a lot of trouble. I also mentioned how slippery the roof tiles had been from the rain, so in a way it was the fault of the rain, and of Cloudburst itself. Cloudburst is an accident waiting to happen, I said.

He listened to this with the same fierce frown, but then a woman dressed in a blue uniform came in, and the frowning doctor asked her to "please take Esther to x-ray for me."

And when he swung around to leave the room, I caught a glimpse of his face and he was grinning.

Not long after the x-rays, my father and sisters arrived.

Father said, "Oh, Esther! You're white as a ghost! Esther! What have you done, Esther darling?" and gave me a big hug. He had actual tears in his eyes and kept stroking my hair. (It was the next day that he became serious about making sensible decisions in relation to roof climbing.)

Imogen and Astrid were just hugely jealous and wished they could fracture their ankles too. They were so impressed by how my ankle had swollen up and turned purple and gray. I told them about how much it hurt but they didn't see that as important.

CHAPTER 88

LATER ON, THE same doctor returned and told me I didn't need surgery. I hadn't known that surgery was possible and was a bit disappointed. I mean, I wasn't completely sure what surgery was, but it sounded important.

Next, the doctor wrapped my ankle in plaster. Two nurses helped, dipping bandages in a basin of water and winding the white cloth around and around my foot and leg. It was like a craft project. The nurses snipped the edges to tidy them up and dabbed away any spilled bits from my skin.

My sisters stared and stared at the doctor as he worked, and the doctor glanced over at them, as if curious to know why all the staring.

Once he was done, the doctor said the plaster would "dissolve" when the ankle was healed. A nurse would come by with a pair of crutches for me in the morning, he explained next, and would demonstrate how to use them.

At this point, Astrid became agitated because she's always wanted crutches. She begged for an extra pair for herself, "to keep Esther company." The doctor seemed bewildered.

But Father had a question. "Will Esther be okay to travel to Spindrift tomorrow? With that plaster? We're going to that big party, the one to welcome the Stolen Prince home."

"Of *course* I will!" I cried before the doctor could speak. "If it's not okay to travel with plaster, I'll just take it off! Hand me those scissors!"

I lunged for a pair I could see on a shelf. The doctor did not take much notice of me, except that he picked up the scissors just before my fingertips reached them and slipped them into the pocket of his white coat. He turned to my father.

"She should be fine," he said. "I'll give her something for the pain. I'm heading to Spindrift myself for the party. Might see you there."

Then Father and the doctor had one of those boring conversations about life—the doctor said he'd grown up in Spindrift, in the orphanage, and that he'd known Queen Anita back then and had worked with her in hospitals. That's why he was going to the party.

I'd forgotten that Queen Anita was a doctor herself, and I'd forgotten she also grew up in an orphanage.

I listened to all this over the sound of my heart beating loud and fast at the idea that I might have had to miss the party.

The next day, a nurse came around early, before breakfast even, with crutches for me to try. He also brought a cupcake with pink icing, and he told me that I'd been very lucky to get Dr. Eli.

That was the frowning doctor's name, apparently.

"He's Faery," the nurse said. "He's also famous for another reason, but I'm not supposed to talk about that. We're very proud to have a Faery here at Cloudburst General, because they're rare in the Kingdom of Storms. They don't like the Wicked and Nefarious Kingdoms nearby."

I told him that we didn't have that problem in my area. There are Elves, Faeries, and Crystal Faeries scattered all over Katherine Valley, I told him, and we even have a part-Faery matron at our school. Or we used to, anyway, before she went traveling.

"Well, then you'll know," he said. "You'll know how clever they are with healing, the Faeries. Eat your cupcake, won't you?"

"No thanks," I replied. "I'll give it to my sister Imogen. I don't really like pink icing, but it's her favorite."

The nurse shook his head. "It's not for your sister Imogen," he said. "It's for you. It's a Faery healing cake—Dr. Eli made it especially, to help with the pain."

So I ate the cake. It was delicious, even with pink icing.

"There," the nurse said. "Good work. Dr. Eli will have added Faery healing to the plaster yesterday too. Any other doctor and you'd have been stuck here a week. The x-ray shows that it's a very nasty break. Actually, if a different doctor does the rounds this morning, they'll be wanting to keep you in another few days, I expect, just to be sure."

Which is why, the moment the nurse handed over the crutches, I flew down the corridor toward the exit as fast as I could. The nurse had to chase me, shouting, "You have to wait for your father to collect you! You've not had your breakfast yet! You're still in your hospital gown!"

CHAPTER 89

IN THE END, I was able to leave the hospital in the proper way, in my day clothes, having eaten breakfast. A Dr. Luellen came around to see me and said: "Oh, lucky you! Dr. Eli! Well, you'll be fine to go in that case! It'll heal super-fast too! Go on then, skedaddle!"

So off we skedaddled.

We took a coach directly to the train station.

While we waited for the train, Father stayed with the luggage and I practiced swinging up and down the platform using the crutches. Imogen and Astrid walked alongside, giving advice and suggestions (mainly: "Okay, now go faster"). All the other people waiting for trains stared at me. I think my sisters were proud.

The crutches were the kind that you prop underneath your arms, and you put the points on the ground and swing yourself forward. You probably already know how crutches work. It had stopped raining but the platform had a few puddles, and sometimes I splashed through these. Grown-ups said, "Oh!" whenever this happened.

That's all they said: "Oh!"

I got so quick that my sisters began racing me, until Father told us to cut that out please.

Then the train arrived and off we went to Spindrift.

Father took the opportunity of the journey to ask what I had been thinking, climbing onto the roof of a mansion. But after a while of me trying to explain, without really *having* an explanation, Imogen said, "Oh, let's forget about that, Father, and think about the party instead."

Father sighed and said, "Well, as long as you promise not to climb onto any more mansions for the purpose of seeing into palace windows, Esther. Or for any other purpose," he added quickly, seeing a potential loophole for me there. So I agreed.

*   *   *

The party!

It was held on a beach called the Beach with the Yellow Sand. Guess what color sand it has?

Ha ha. Yes, yellow.

But we could hardly see the color of the sand because it was covered by party. If Dr. Eli *was* here (I thought), there was no chance we'd spot him in the noisy, happy crowds: everyone in sundresses and sandals, or linen trousers and rolled-up shirtsleeves, all playing games, eating toffee apples, or waving little *Welcome Home, Alejandro!* flags.

Remember the Spindrift children? From Durba's speech? Well, that's one reason that Spindrift is famous.

It's also famous for another reason and that reason—

—is this.

Shadow Mages from nearby Kingdoms and Empires often move to Spindrift. To make a fresh start as good people. They promise to set aside their shadowy ways. Also, pirates occasionally abandon their pirating and move into Spindrift, for the same reason.

What this meant—

—was this.

There were Shadow Mages and pirates at the party.

I will begin a new chapter in case you need a moment for the shock.

CHAPTER 90

MY SISTERS AND I did.

Need a moment, I mean.

But life is not divided into chapters, so we didn't get one. We just had to be agog. (That means stare in astonishment.)

Imogen and Astrid had almost no experience of Shadow Mages, just those Sterling Silver Foxes at the swimming pool, really. But lately, as you know, I'd been chasing Shadow Mages away from my school.

Father must have remembered this, because he placed a hand on my shoulder. "It's all right, Esther," he murmured. "These Shadow Mages have chosen not to use shadow magic, remember?" He spoke softly. "In her doctoral thesis, your mother challenged the fundamental premise of the Kingdoms and Empires that all True Mages are inherently *good* and all Shadow Mages inherently *evil*. She came to Spindrift on a research trip into the issue when you girls were very young—she still works on a number of ethics committees that draft regulations around the issue."

I realized I'd been trembling, my heart racing—I'd even been fumbling for my burlap sack—but Father's soft, steady words calmed me, even though I couldn't quite follow them.

Meanwhile, my sisters were hissing:

"Look! That's a Witch!"

"Oh my goodness, you're right! There's another one! Cat around his shoulders! No, that's a scarf, not a cat. Still, I *swear* he's a Witch!"

"Over there! Don't look now. *Don't look!* Wait. Okay—now!

That *must* be a Radish Gnome! Those *can't* be regular finger-nails! They must be *claws!*"

"Esther, is that a *pirate*? At the soda fountain! IT IS! IT'S A PIRATE! RIGHT THERE! JUST *LOOK* AT HIS MUSCLES! HIS MUSCLES ARE *ENORMOUS!*"

"Right!" Father blurted. "Come on, girls, let's try the banquet tables." And he hustled us away.

The banquet tables were incredible! It took a while to reach them—crutches are tricky in sand—so we didn't know they were incredible straightaway. But there was plenty to see on the way.

The party covered the beach and extended up over the boardwalk to the terraces of a row of hotels. Entertainers played music on stages. Dancers and acrobats twirled and spun on rugs. Fire breathers and jugglers strolled amongst the crowd, but it was the sort of stroll where you stop now and then to spit out a gust of flames or to throw seven daggers into the air. You know, that sort of stroll.

Everywhere we turned, banners waved in the breeze, proclaiming:

WELCOME HOME, PRINCE ALEJANDRO!

But where *was* Prince Alejandro? And where were King Jakob and Queen Anita?

Imogen spotted them first.

They were at the opposite end of the beach on a fancy stage, strung about with silk ribbons. The king, queen, and prince sat in a row of chairs. A long line waited at the foot of the stage, and one by one, people walked up the steps, shook Alejandro's hand, and spoke to him.

I suppose they were saying, "Welcome back! So glad to see you home again!" It was tricky to tell from that far, but I did see one woman fling her arms wide as she approached, as if to hug Alejandro. A guard quickly intercepted and gestured for the woman to *shake Alejandro's hand*. You could tell she was trying to turn the handshake into a hug. The guard led her back down from the stage, and the next person came up.

Poor Alejandro, I thought. *How boring.*

As I watched, he turned away from the line of people and seemed to look straight at me. I waved, but he only turned to the next person in line.

The ocean was calm with occasional plashes, as Water Sprites, floating on their backs, kicked their feet. Often the Water Sprites dove under to refresh themselves. Several divisions had been invited to the party, Father told us, "to demonstrate that the Royal Family forgave the Water Sprites for taking Alejandro in the first place."

By the way, it was *not* raining in Spindrift. The sun shone golden warm and the sky was a bright curve of blue.

And *in* that sky? Dragons.

Swooping about, sending brilliant shocks of flame into the blue. "There's a fascinating history with the dragons here," Father said excitedly. "Shall I tell you?"

But Astrid changed the subject smoothly: "Oh, look, they have puff pastry pinwheels."

For at last we had reached the banquet tables.

As well as puff pastry pinwheels, they had caramelized onion and beef sausage rolls, persimmon bruschetta, spiced chicken wings, baked potatoes with sour cream and chives, giant maywish chocolate coins, lemon meringue cloud cakes, and rosewater pistachio cupcakes.

Everything was labeled, which is how I knew their correct names.

After we had tried a sample of almost everything, we wandered around the party. We were very cheerful. Very full too. A bit queasy, even.

I can't remember everything we did, but I know we stopped at crafts tables and made hats and jewelry, *with the guidance of a Sterling Silver Fox.* We also went on a tour of the Radish Gnome caves led by an *actual Radish Gnome.* He glanced over at me just before the entry. "Leave the crutches here," he suggested. "There are rails in here. Sing out if you need a break."

"Thank you," I replied.

It was very strange: a polite conversation with a Radish Gnome.

My sisters and I widened our eyes at each other.

We also tried to dunk a Fire Siren by throwing a coconut at a target, won yo-yos by spinning a prize wheel, admired sand sculptures (there were castles taller than Father!), and got our faces painted.

We kept an eye out for people we might know—apart from Dr. Eli, we knew that our cousin Bronte was here somewhere with her parents, and also our Aunt Franny. (Remember that my mother has ten sisters, so there's always a chance you'll run into an aunt wherever you go in the Kingdoms and Empires.)

We considered joining the line to say "Welcome home" to Alejandro—we'd bring him a plate of treats, we decided—but it seemed like a waste of a party to spend it standing in a queue.

Not long after we'd made this decision, a catastrophe happened.

CHAPTER 91

THE CATASTROPHE UNFOLDED—

—like this:

We had just run into our Aunt Franny.
She was on the terrace of one of the
fancy hotels, dancing a quick step with
a short, stout woman. The quick step
has a lot of prancing, skip-jumps, and twirls. Other couples
were also prancing and skipping, often bumping into each
other, but friendly and joyful about the bumping.

Aunt Franny is one of my favorite aunts. She has a very definite personality, a hoarse voice, and she always chews on
carrots.

Say a queen approached her and said, "I am Queen!" Aunt
Franny would munch on her carrot and demand, through a
mouthful of chewed orangey bits: "And?"

Although Aunt Franny lives in Nina Bay now, she once lived
in Spindrift and was its mayor. That's why she was at the party.

Father is also fond of Aunt Franny and only a teeny bit
afraid of her.

Anyhow, we waved from the edge of the terrace until she
noticed us. She did not say "Excuse me" to her partner and
cross over to us, as we'd expected. She beckoned us to join her
on the dance floor. If somebody else did this, you might smile
and say, "No thanks!" but when Aunt Franny beckons, you slip
right in and join the dance. Well, Father and my sisters did that,
anyway. I raised my crutches so Franny could see my dilemma,
and her eyes skipped from the crutches to my plastered ankle.
She beckoned again anyway. That's the sort of person she is.

So I leaned my crutches against the hotel wall and hopped over to her.

Father was already dancing with both Imogen and Astrid at once, confusing for a quick step, but they managed. Aunt Franny spoke over her shoulder: "Broken a bone, have you?"

Before I could answer, she and her partner had pranced away—the dance made them. I swayed to the music as much as I could on one foot and tried not to get in anybody's way.

Whenever Aunt Franny danced close to me, or to Father and my sisters, we all talked at once, about our journey, the party, and how I'd broken my ankle falling from a roof. (Franny nodded seriously, as if it made perfect sense: *Yes, you could easily break an ankle falling from a roof.*)

It was around now that Father happened to glance at the ocean. "Is the tide coming in?" he asked, frowning. His dancing slowed, although Astrid and Imogen dragged on his hands trying to speed him up again.

Aunt Franny spun her partner in a sudden circle, making the woman stagger a little. (I'm still not sure what her partner's name was. Franny's not the type for introductions.)

"No," she said. "Tide's not due to come in until late."

"Are you sure?" Father asked. He had stopped dancing altogether, which meant that Imogen and Astrid had also been forced to stop, and he gestured across the boardwalk and down to the sea.

As we watched, three things happened, one after the other.

Two little children building a sandcastle at the water's edge squealed as a wave crashed over their castle.

A group of adults picnicking on a blanket hopped up and dragged their blanket further up the sand, just avoiding the splash of a second wave.

A man called, "Oi! Somebody catch that for me!" and waded into the ocean, reaching for a hat that had been carried out to sea by a third wave.

Separately, these things might not have seemed important. The small children began building a new sandcastle at once. The adults with the picnic blanket set to eating again. And a

Water Sprite plucked the man's hat from the sea and tossed it over to him. "Cheers, mate," said the man, wringing out his hat.

But from up here it seemed very much as if the tide was coming in.

"Freak waves?" Imogen wondered.

We all stood at the edge of the terrace, watching the beach. Everybody down there remained happy and lively. A long line still waited to greet the Royal Family and to shake Alejandro's hand. At the other stages, people gathered to watch performances, many patiently nibbling corn on the cob. Quite close to the water's edge, a group of small children—four- or five-year-olds—were marching up onto a stage. Wooden levels formed a kind of staircase, and the children lined themselves up, each new row of heads popping up above the one before. It must be a choir, I decided.

Meanwhile, waves crept further and further up the sand, each one inching closer to frolicking children and adults. Scarcely noticing that they were doing this, more and more people reached for bags or shoes and shifted them away from the water, then carried on chatting or eating.

"Strange," Aunt Franny muttered to herself, then she looked up, blinked sharply, and raised a hand.

"Out there," she said.

CHAPTER 92

EVEN AS SHE pointed, Aunt Franny was swiveling.

"*SOUND THE ALARM!*" she shouted. "*CUT THE MUSIC! SOUND THE ALARM!*"

The music stopped almost at once and the other dancers paused midswing, confused, before turning toward the ocean.

Way out near the horizon, a wave the size of a building was thundering toward the shore.

All at the same time, the Water Sprites seemed to become conscious of it. There was a strange, silent choreography of Water Sprites diving in perfect arches and disappearing out to sea.

Then the alarms rang out: *CLANG! CLANG!* And there was a surge of movement on the beach as everyone turned toward the water.

You will be imagining a terrible panic next: Shrieks! Wails! People being crushed and shoved!

That's what I imagined.

But instead of panic, a great calm seemed to settle on the beach, a strange stillness. Honestly, you could almost see them all weighing up the situation. The eyes of adults, and children too, calculated the size and distance of the wave, its likely reach, number of people on the beach, amount of space on the boardwalk above the beach—and then, in concert, they moved.

Royal Guards whisked the king, queen, and Alejandro from their stage and rushed them toward the highest nearby point: the lighthouse. A small group of adults—mostly constables,

I discovered later, but they wore party clothes, so I couldn't tell— bellowed commands. These were obeyed instantly. The tiniest children were gathered up, fanciest instruments grabbed, and people swarmed like patterns of insects up the sand toward the boardwalk.

On the boardwalk, meanwhile, people were being steered into the hotels, clearing the way for those on the beach.

My sisters, my father, and I found ourselves hurrying into the hotel behind us: the Elegant Seahorse it was called, very fancy, with thick, plush carpet that made me want to push off my sandal and feel it on my toes. No time, though. Once in the lobby, we were instructed to go directly to the roof. We joined a parade marching up the stairs: a challenge with my ankle. Imogen carried my crutches and I used the railing to help, hopping from step to step.

"Is the wave going to flood the hotel?" Astrid asked.

A woman behind her replied. "No," she said. "It'll stop just short of the boardwalk. It'll cover the beach and wash away the party, but it's not going to hit the hotels."

"This is just precautionary," an elderly gentleman agreed. "And to ensure there's space for all those on the sand to come to safety." He stopped to wheeze into his handkerchief but quickly hurried on.

They seemed very calm and knowledgeable. It was soothing.

Just as we reached the roof and joined the crowd up there, the wave hit.

The sound! It was a slow, crackling, majestic

CRAAAAAAAAAAASH!!!!

I don't know if I've ever held my breath for so long. Everyone on that roof did, I think. Everyone on the row of hotel roofs. Everyone down there squished on the boardwalk.

Well, not the last few people who were scrambling up onto the boardwalk, of course. And not the people grabbing the hands of those last few, hauling them up. They were busy and had no time to hold their breath.

But for the rest of us the suspense was like someone drawing a bow across a high note on a violin.

Where was the wave going to stop?

I should have stretched the word. It was more like this:

CRA-A—A-A-A-A-A-A-A-A-A-A-A-A-A-A-
A-A-A-A-A-A-A-A-A—A-A—ASH!!!!

It reached, reached, reached up and up and up the beach in a storm of froth, up, up, up—

And it stopped.

Right at the edge of the boardwalk.

It seemed so *proud,* the wave! It was like a great creature that smashes itself down into a flower bed and instantly, gleefully sets to work tearing apart any flowers that survived the smash.

"DID EVERYBODY GET CLEAR? IS ANYBODY IN THE WATER?" That was Aunt Franny shouting into a megaphone. She was right at the edge of the roof, hanging over the railing. Her head was turning back and forth rapidly as she scanned the beach—awash with foaming seawater—and she was bending her neck at an awkward angle, trying see straight down to the boardwalk below.

"EVERYBODY CLEAR? EVERYBODY CLEAR?" came the same call from the other hotel roofs, one after the other.

"CLEAR!" came a reply.

"CLEAR!"

"CLEAR!"

It was the same call from down there, moving along the boardwalk.

"How do they *know* it's all clear?" Imogen demanded beside me. "You can't *see* what's happening in the water!"

She was right. The wave was still tearing all over the sand, tossing plates, blankets, food, paint pots in every direction, washing right over the platforms of the stages, swirling around the beach huts—their roofs just poked out.

It was as if the wave was thinking to itself: *This is fun up here! I should come more often!*

"CLEAR!"

"CLEAR!"

The voices continued.

Somehow everybody had got off the sand *just* before the wave hit.

A cheer rose up, from the roofs of the hotels and inside the hotels and all along the boardwalk.

"What about those children?" Astrid asked me. She was squinting and pointing into the distance.

It was the stage I'd noticed with the built-up staircase, the one I had decided must be for a children's choir. The wave had encircled the platform itself, but the staircases rose above the water.

Fifteen or so tiny children still stood there, lined up in rows, as if for a photograph.

CHAPTER 93

EVERYONE SEEMED TO notice the children at the same time.

Shouts from everywhere: "THE PRE-SCHOOL CHOIR! THE PRESCHOOL CHOIR!"

There was a brief swirl of fury and disbelief that the children had been forgotten.

"Don't blame," muttered the elderly man I'd followed up the stairs. "Find a solution!"

That seemed sensible, but I did wonder why the children's parents hadn't noticed they were missing.

Everyone shouted about getting boats out to rescue the preschoolers, until Aunt Franny yelled: "WAIT!" into her megaphone.

She was peering into the water. The wave still dashed and thrashed across the beach, white and foamy, agitated and angry.

She studied the distant preschoolers. They seemed very tiny and still, standing in their rows. Some held hands or linked arms.

"Will that platform hold?" Aunt Franny murmured. She raised the megaphone, "WHO BUILT THAT PLATFORM?"

From the next roof along, two young men raised their hands. "We did!"

"WILL IT HOLD?" Aunt Franny called.

All along the roofs and boardwalk, people were silent, listening to this exchange, craning to hear.

The two men squinted at Franny.

"WILL IT HOLD?" she shouted again. "IT'S TOO ROUGH! BOATS WILL CAPSIZE! BUT THE WATER IS NOT RISING!

EVENTUALLY, THE WAVE WILL RECEDE!" Franny lowered her megaphone and peered out to sea again. "The question is," she muttered to herself, then she raised the megaphone again: "THE QUESTION IS: WILL THAT PLATFORM HOLD?"

The men turned to each other. There was a pause.

"DID YOU BUILD IT PROPERLY?" another voice demanded. That was a police constable down on the boardwalk. Several voices called the same question.

"All the other platforms are holding," somebody pointed out. This was true. The other platforms emerged solidly each time the water thrashed against them.

"Exactly." Franny nodded. "DID YOU BUILD IT PROPERLY?"

At this, the two men nodded firmly.

"Of course!" one shouted through cupped hands.

Aunt Franny squinted at them. They stared back, gazes steady.

"Right then." Aunt Franny raised her megaphone again and blared into it: "CHILDREN! STAY WHERE YOU ARE! WE WILL COME FOR YOU SOON! STAY WHERE YOU ARE!"

Other voices shouted the same instructions. The tiny children remained still. It was not clear if they could hear. A crowd of adults gathered around Aunt Franny, all of them talking urgently.

"They're lying," Astrid said.

Imogen and I both swung around. Astrid was still staring across at the two men who had built the platform.

"You can tell from this distance?" Imogen asked.

Astrid nodded. "They didn't build it properly. There's something wrong about the platform."

"You don't think it *will* hold?" I asked.

Astrid shrugged. "I don't know. But I know those men are lying."

"Aunt Franny!" I called, and I used my crutches to push the adults aside. They seemed irritated by this. "The platform wasn't built properly!"

Aunt Franny frowned at me. I pointed to Astrid, who repeated what she'd just told us.

The other adults scowled.

"She always knows," I promised. "She can tell if people are lying."

Father, who had been pressed against the railing, watching the preschoolers, joined us. "It's true," he told Franny. "Astrid knows."

Aunt Franny raised her megaphone and once again shouted at the next roof. "LAST CHANCE!" she bellowed. "DID YOU BUILD THAT PLATFORM PROPERLY?"

The young men hesitated.

"Well . . . ," one began.

That was enough for Aunt Franny.

"GET THE BOATS OUT!" she shouted into the megaphone. "GET THE BOATS!"

Below us, the water churned and sizzled, waves leaping sideways as if surging to catch a ball.

"Is that somebody *swimming*?" a voice beside me asked in wonder.

And there, in the chaos of white water, a dark head moved steadily through the water.

"Who would do that?" voices clamored. "She'll drown! The currents are too strong!"

Strange coldness gusted up from the bottom of my stomach.

"Imogen?" I whispered, searching around me. "Imogen?"

CHAPTER 94

IMOGEN WAS SWIMMING.

"Imogen!" Father roared. His face twisted like the roots of ancient trees.

Four boats had been dragged into the water, but three capsized at once, and one spun in helpless circles, motor shrieking.

Several men and women stripped down to their bathing suits and struck out toward the platform, swimming hard. Most were swept into whirlpools, or dragged to sea.

Imogen alone inched toward the platform. Her hands slapped the water, arms rotated—slower and slower.

She was tiring.

She stopped altogether.

Her head reared up, and she trod water. The current dragged her sideways and water hammered her head. Her face splashed down again and she swam.

"Imogen," Father breathed.

Astrid was crying. "It's my fault," she said. "The platform probably *is* going to hold. The platform is—"

That's when the platform collapsed.

Clatter! Clatter! Clatter!

A sound like crockery spilling.

Whoosh!

The screams of tiny children sailed to us on the wind.

CHAPTER 95

IMOGEN GRABBED FOR a broken piece of platform—a length of timber. She held it steady on the surface, treading water, and she reached out one at a time, plucking children from the waves. She urged them to cling onto the floating timber. One child, two children, three, four, five. Even from the rooftop we could hear her calm, strong instructions.

She let go of the wood and dove for the sixth child, the seventh.

She struck out after the eighth.

The children were like scraps of wet rag draped over that length of wood, and the wood rocked and tossed in the white water, drenched now and then by great splashes of white.

Imogen wrenched more and more children from beneath the waves.

"RIGHT THEN! EVERYBODY HOLD TIGHT!" she bellowed. Took a mouthful of water, spat it out.

By this time, another swimmer—an immense man, shiny with muscles—had almost caught up. At last one of the boats seemed to be tossing its way in the right direction.

A woman, also muscular, reached them too.

Between them—the people in the boat, the swimmers, Imogen—they towed the children slowly, steadily, back to the boardwalk.

Back to safety. Into the weeping, grateful, hysterical arms of their parents.

CHAPTER 96

SOME OF THE preschool children had been injured when the stage collapsed. Many had cuts and bruises, and one had a broken wrist.

A group of doctors took care of these children on the boardwalk.

One was Queen Anita. I respected her for setting aside her queenliness to step in. Another was Dr. Eli, who'd set my broken ankle in Cloudburst. Alongside him was a third doctor, a woman, who looked *exactly* like Dr. Eli.

"Twins," the elderly man on the roof told me. He was leaning on the railing, watching along with me.

"Yes, they must be," I agreed.

"Not *must* be." The man was annoyed. "*Are.* That's Eli and Taya."

A breeze of realization blew through me and I half-gasped: "Eli and Taya? The Children of Spindrift?"

"Exactly." The man was less irritated now. "Don't tell anybody, though. Attention makes them snappy."

I was giddy. A Child of Spindrift had plastered my ankle for me. I touched the plaster and felt a *zing* from the past, from Spindrift, from the Whispering Wars! But that could have been Dr. Eli's Faery magic. Or my imagination.

Imogen was whisked away to a hotel room to bathe while Astrid was encircled by people who wanted to know *how* she'd known the young men were lying.

They hadn't meant any harm, those young men, by the way. It turned out they'd built five or six stages before they reached that one, and were tired: melting under a hot sun. When they ran out of nails, they'd decided to take a break for a beer in the town square. They'd got caught up in a drinking game and had forgotten to return.

They should have admitted this straightaway, of course, but they'd panicked—Aunt Franny can be frightening—and had been trying to recall just how important the missing nails might be, when Astrid had seen through them.

Astrid was suddenly too shy to explain how she'd read their faces, so I explained about her talent at poker. At once, some friendly local pirates challenged all three of us to a poker game—Imogen was back by now. Astrid won three treasure chests—empty of treasure but with plenty of sentimental value, the pirates promised.

Father suggested Astrid return the treasure chests, as the pirates were teary, but the pirates refused, saying she'd won them fair and square. We arranged to have them shipped home, and Astrid planned to keep toys and books in them in her room.

By now, the party had splintered, with people either going home to get dry and warm or tidying up the mess. Father was marveling about how calm everyone had been in the crisis, and Aunt Franny reminded him that Spindrift is a seaside town, and the people of Spindrift had lived through wars, cyclones, and hurricanes. "It *is* in the Kingdom of Storms," she pointed out. Also, she said, local Shadow Mages and pirates come from lives of great danger and conflict. Spindriftians are not easily frightened.

We realized we hadn't yet seen our cousin Bronte, but Aunt Franny told us she hadn't come to the party at all. She'd been called away on some kind of secret, urgent mission. (She's an adventurer, as I've mentioned.) It was true that we were going to see her when we went to Gainsleigh for the poker competition, of course, but we were disappointed. We love our cousin Bronte.

We also hadn't seen Alejandro, the Stolen Prince of Cloudburst. The guards had hustled him away when the wave came, and he never emerged again.

Altogether it was very strange. We'd been invited to a party yet had never even spoken to the guest of honor. It was as if we'd been to *half* a party. This, we agreed, during dinner that night, was peculiar.

"It's like I've swum half a lap of a pool," Imogen said. "And hopped out."

"It's like I've walked away from a poker game halfway through a hand," Astrid said.

"I've walked out of a lecture midway through," Father contributed, wanting to join in. "Although, to be honest, I often do that if I get a new idea."

I almost said, "It's like I've stopped a story in the middle," but it didn't seem to fit the pattern. My stories are not my talent, the way swimming, poker, and history lectures are my sisters' and Father's talents. They can't be. They always get C–.

CHAPTER 97

EARLY THE NEXT morning, we set off to the Kingdom of Vanquishing Cove so Father could attend his conference.

The train compartment was small— two double-facing seats, Father and Astrid in one, Imogen and I in the other. Velvet drapes hung in the windows but these had been pushed open and looped into place.

Sunshine was free to shine through, warming the leather seats. It seemed to glide through my veins and light up my heart. That's how proud I was of my sisters.

As the train chugged out of Spindrift Station, we were still chattering about the catastrophic events at the party the day before. That rogue wave! The forgotten little children!

And most important, how Astrid had recognized that the young men were lying, and how Imogen had swum in the violent sea.

My sisters were being modest and shrugging—"Oh, it was nothing"—but Father and I were praising them. Father's praise of Imogen was more complicated than mine, because he wanted her to know she'd been brave, but he *also* wanted her to know she ought not jump into a ferocious ocean where she could easily drown.

"You were *heroes*," I told my sisters and then, reflecting, "All I did was stand on the rooftop watching."

My family reminded me that I had a broken ankle and was therefore exempt from being heroic, and then the door to our compartment opened and a waiter wheeled in a breakfast trolley. With a flourish, he invited us to help ourselves.

CHAPTER 98

NOBODY WOULD EVER enter the region of Wicked and Nefarious Kingdoms.

Nobody who was not a Shadow Mage, I mean. Not if they wanted to live.

But a single train line runs through this shadow realm. It connects the Kingdom of Storms, where we had attended the party, and the Kingdom of Vanquishing Cove, where we were headed.

Which meant our train would soon enter the most dangerous shadow realm of them all.

The train has a regularly updated Spellbinding ring around it and strict treaties require the locals to refrain from attacking it.

So it is perfectly safe.

But as the train whooshed through the Kingdom of Storms, ever closer to the border of the shadow realm, my sisters and I found ourselves staring at the signs affixed to our compartment walls. In large red lettering, the signs said:

<u>WARNING</u>
NO DISEMBARKING FROM THE TRAIN.
IF THE TRAIN STOPS, LOCK YOUR COMPARTMENT
DOOR, DOUBLE-LOCK YOUR WINDOWS, AND
REMAIN SEATED.
THE WINDOWS <u>MUST</u> REMAIN CLOSED AT
ALL TIMES.

<u>WARNING</u>
IF GHOULS ARE ACTIVE, YOU MUST CLOSE THE

DRAPES TIGHT AND LIGHT THE ADDITIONAL
LANTERNS.
IF ANY SHADOW MAGE OF ANY SIZE ATTEMPTS
TO BOARD THE TRAIN, <u>SOUND THE ALARM
IMMEDIATELY AND CONCEAL YOURSELF
BENEATH THE SEATS.</u>

WARNING
IN THE CASE OF EMERGENCY, REMAIN IN YOUR
COMPARTMENT WITH THE DOOR LOCKED.
IN THE CASE OF THE TRAIN BREAKING DOWN,
REMAIN IN YOUR COMPARTMENT WITH THE
DOOR LOCKED. <u>DO NOT ATTEMPT TO GET
OFF THE TRAIN.</u>

WARNING
AT NO POINT SHOULD A PASSENGER ATTEMPT
TO GET OFF THE TRAIN BUT <u>ESPECIALLY NOT
AT NIGHT.</u>

NOTICE
THE SHADOW TRAIN CORPORATION SHALL NOT
BE LIABLE FOR THE DEATH, INJURY, ILLNESS,
LOSS, SUFFERING, OR GENERALIZED ANXIETY
OF ANY PASSENGER.
PASSENGERS TRAVEL AT THEIR OWN RISK.
PLEASE RELAX AND ENJOY YOUR TRIP!

"Why especially not at night?" I asked.

Father looked up. He'd taken out a stack of folders and papers from his case and was preparing for his conference.

"Especially what at night?"

I pointed to the sign: *AT NO POINT SHOULD A PASSENGER ATTEMPT TO GET OFF THE TRAIN BUT <u>ESPECIALLY NOT AT NIGHT</u>.*

"Oh, don't worry about the rules," Father said, his eyes roaming from notice to notice. "That's just lawyers getting carried away. It's perfectly safe, this train ride."

"But what do they mean: *especially not at night*?"

Father scratched his chin. "Well, it's not at *all* safe at night," he admitted. "Not remotely. Night is when the rules collapse. Night is when Shadow Battles take place. Night is also when wolves, bears, Wild Radish Gnomes, and outcast Witches emerge. The ponds turn to swamps; the mud boils; and the Ghouls rise, multiply, and look for human spirits to consume."

"Oh, is that all?" Imogen asked a bit acidly.

"Well, that's enough, isn't it?" Father seemed cheerful. "You'd never survive the shadow realms at night. Certainly not if you got out of the train. No chance! I doubt the Spellbinding around the train would even hold if we ended up stuck here at night!"

Father looked back down at his papers, and then, realizing that all three of us were staring at him, he straightened up again. "Don't worry, though," he said. "We arrive in Vanquishing Cove long before nightfall. It's not that far, really; you could walk there from Spindrift in a couple of days."

"But if we break—" I began.

"If the train breaks down, they'll fix it before night," Father promised. "If they can't fix it, they'll *tow* the train out of the region."

Imogen pointed at another of the signs. "What do they mean by 'Shadow Mage *of any size*'—how big do Shadow Mages get?"

Father glanced through the window. Fields rushed by, and occasional run-down farmhouses. "We're coming to the border now," he told us. "I think you're going to love it, girls. It's so special to see this region. Very educational."

A pause.

"As to how big Shadow Mages get," he continued, clearing his throat. "Well, you know the regular Shadow Mages—the type that look most like us and sometimes roam about in our regions?"

"Witches, Sterling Silver Foxes, Radish Gnomes, and Sirens?" Astrid counted them off on her fingers.

"Right," Father agreed. "But there are hundreds—thousands—of other types. Pillboxes, Cantalops, Sandweeds, Seafloss,

Backpedalers, Pocketdwellers, Chimney Reds. Some are tall and thin like beanstalks, some as heavy and large as a house! Then there are tiny little critters that get into your fingernails or live in the seams of your pockets. They pierce your fingertips if you happen to put a hand in there. The Kwilligus takes the form of lukewarm water—looks like weak tea—and swims in a poisonous stream down gutters. If you happen to step into that water it'll burn through your shoes and your feet right to the bone. Spit-Lolly Vacancies are the size of snails. They leave a trail of poisonous stripes wherever they go—if your dog tastes the stripe, it will die. So many different ways of being evil, you see, even while appearing tiny and harmless. The sign means we should sound the alarm if a Shadow Mage breaks in, even if it seems harmless. Even if it fits into your palm. All right?"

We all nodded.

"But nothing will get in," Father concluded. "Spellbinding ring around the train, remember? Here, share these crisps."

And he handed out packets of crisps and bowed his head over his papers again.

Shortly after that, a bell rang, *Brrrrring! Brrrring!* And a train guard knocked on our compartment door and half-sang: "Bell means we're coming into the shadow realm! Enjoy!"

Father flipped to the next page in his notes and my sisters and I turned to the windows to watch.

CHAPTER 99

IF YOU EVER get a chance to ride the train through a shadow realm, take it.

It's astonishing.

We flew by villages, towns, cities, through parks, woods, gardens, past mountains, fields, and plains, through an Empire of Witchcraft, a Colony of Radish Gnomes, the Cailleach Kingdom of Sirens and Sterling Silver Foxes, and countless other kingdoms, empires, and principalities—and there was always something to see, to make you gasp, or grab your sister's arm and point.

It was the strangest mixture of ordinary and unexpected. I saw ladders leaning up against buildings, and goats walking along paths. I saw a field covered in cauldrons, at least twenty Radish Gnomes lie down and roll across a tennis court, and a group of Sirens singing shrilly as they thatched the roof of a cottage.

We plunged into a rainforest, saw shimmering waterfalls, and then watched in amazement as tiny children plucked at the waterfalls, gathering strands of silver into their arms.

"Not a *water*fall," Imogen breathed. "A *silver*fall. Those are Sterling Silver Fox children."

We saw cities encased in walls of water; cities made from ice or glass; and the tallest, slenderest trees, reaching up, up, up into the clouds, where they braided themselves together and plunged back down to the ground.

We saw a field covered in pods, exactly the color and shape of pea pods, only each the size of a large carriage. As we hurtled by, one pod slowly opened, revealing a row of baby cradles.

In the Empire of Witchcraft, town after town was painted in oranges, beiges, and taupes: the Witches' favorite colors. I glimpsed a Witch with a toddler sitting astride his shoulders, beckoning for another child, who had crouched to tie his shoelace, to hurry.

A group of Sirens leapt from rock to rock in a stream.

Further along the same stream, a gang of Radish Gnomes were doing target practice: their claws spun and whirled through the air, piercing and shattering rocks.

We saw automobiles open to the wind that sped along cobblestone streets, and carts being pulled by lions. I can't remember all the animals we saw, both inside city walls and on the plains, but I know I saw camels, tigers, antelopes, horses, monkeys, and wolves.

We passed three or four Sterling Silver Fox cities and had to shelter our eyes from the glare. Buildings, trees, lampposts—everything was draped, studded, decorated with jewelry: silver, rose gold, white gold, chains and beads, heavy with diamonds, emeralds, amethysts, and rubies.

In one town, a straggling group of teenagers used spray cans to paint huge numbers along a wall. The train slowed as we followed this wall, and Astrid began to read the numbers aloud.

"Seventy-two . . . Sixty-four . . . Twelve . . . Sixteen . . . Four hundred and—"

Father suddenly dropped his notes and placed a hand over her mouth.

"Stop!" he exclaimed. "Astrid! Hush! Stop reading the numbers!"

He pulled his hand away, and Astrid blinked up at him.

"I'm so sorry, girls," Father said, a little breathless. "I should be paying closer attention. Those teenagers were Cantalops. They *want* train passengers to read the numbers aloud—it's part of a shadow spell. Just a moment—"

Father rang the alarm bell, and a moment later, the guard arrived, very apologetic.

"Yes, several other passengers have complained about those

Cantalops," he said. "We've already sent word to the authorities." He checked that none of us had read the numbers aloud.

Astrid gave a little yelp.

"Oh, that's all right," the guard said soothingly. "Five or six of them, you say? That's nothing. Won't have caused any harm—you'll all feel a bit hungry is all. Which is perfect timing, as we're about to serve lunch. I'll be sure you get extra."

He did too.

He returned a few moments later with a banquet.

CHAPTER 100

AFTER THAT, FATHER packed his papers back into his case and watched the windows with us.

He became quite educational, but it was more interesting than usual. When we passed a series of towns with huge open fields in the center, ringed by squat houses, Father explained that the spaces were designed for spell battles. The most beautiful reds and golds lit up the distance like a sunset, and Father said that was a Fire Siren victory celebration.

"See that?" he said, pointing.

A crowd of people were throwing their hats into the sky and watching with upturned faces as the hats came spinning back down.

"And *there*." He pointed again.

A group of people stood in rows, each holding a teapot. At exactly the same moment, they all tipped the teapots and liquid streamed from the spouts onto the grass. We craned our necks to watch as the train swept by.

"Anytime you see groups acting in concert like that, they're practicing spell enhancements. Witches are quite mesmerizing when they— Oh, there you go! Witches! It's all right to look, they're just practicing."

Men and women were lined up by the track, each wearing corduroy trousers and cardigan, each holding a broomstick high and turning it in slow, synchronized circles.

There was something very sinister about these quiet scenes blowing by the train. They sent pleasing chills down my spine.

At one point, the train entered a tunnel in the side of a mountain and everything went black. We wondered if it was Ghouls and if we should light the extra lanterns, but then we whooshed back out into the light again. We were in countryside now, no people about, just fields of golden crops.

"Shall we order lemon ices?" Father suggested, and that was when the train slowed, slowed, slowed—

—and stopped.

Tick, tick, tick, said the engine. A gust of smoke drifted by the window. On distant trees, leaves fluttered.

CHAPTER 101

THE GUARD KNOCKED on our door.

"No need to panic," he said, poking his head in. "Engine often stalls here. Old shadow mine deep underground, often messes with the engine. It'll be sorted out in no time, you'll see."

We watched the stillness outside, silent, waiting for the train to start again.

It was strange because it was as if our silence was growing quieter and quieter. We were sinking deep into it. The stillness outside seemed to be creeping into the compartment with us. A faint breath of wind. Father sighed suddenly and I jumped. Imogen whispered, "It's okay. It'll start."

Father pulled out his work again and began to read.

Each page he turned made a sound like a *slap*.

Time sat very quietly with us, waiting.

Waiting.

And then the train gave a shudder, a *clang*, and set off again.

My sisters and I breathed out all at once, in a *whoosh*. Father chuckled. "There was nothing to worry about, girls." But I noticed him smoothing his trousers down, once, twice, three times.

I smiled and looked back to the window—

And that's when I saw it.

Flashing by—

—a dense thicket of trees, and a huge rock—

—shaped exactly like a turtle—

—a turtle standing on its side, and poking its head from its shell—

The rock formation from my dream.

CHAPTER 102

"THERE!" I SHOUTED.

Father and my sisters, still jumpy from the train's breakdown, all leapt to their feet in fright.

Which probably explained why, when I told them that we'd just passed a scene from my dream, they became a bit snappy with me.

"Your *dream*," Imogen said, getting her breath back as she sat back down. "Where?"

But it had gone.

"What was it?" Astrid asked.

"A rock shaped like a turtle. I've dreamed about it *so* many times! I dream I'm lying on a picnic blanket and looking up at the trees. I must have *been* here before! I've had a picnic here! There's strawberry jam on the rug."

Even Father, who is usually interested by our dreams, was a bit short with me. "Esther," he said. "I can one hundred percent guarantee that you have never once had a picnic in this or any other shadow realm. With or without strawberry jam."

"It was just a dream," Imogen muttered.

"But why am I dreaming about a landscape from *here*?" I persisted.

"Perhaps you saw a picture in a book," Father suggested. "You've never been in this region before, Esther." His voice became kind again. "Rocks come in all sorts of shapes. I've seen plenty shaped like turtles. It's just a . . ."

"A coincidence," Astrid filled in. "Oh, look, we're coming

into a town again—this one's *made* of rocks! Perhaps there'll be another turtle-shaped one for you, Esther?"

Everyone was distracted by the views again.

But I leaned back in my seat, a peculiar wash of cold and heat running rivulets through my heart.

CHAPTER 103

WE ARRIVED IN the Kingdom of Vanquishing Cove in the late afternoon. The Kingdom is actually just a quaint seaside town, and our hotel overlooked the ocean.

The next day, Father went to his conference and my sisters and I played on the beach. It was too chilly to swim but that was lucky because my ankle was in plaster. I would have been jealous of my sisters. Mostly I sat with my foot propped on a sandcastle while Imogen and Astrid ran and collected shells and seaweed.

We were sunburnt and sandy when Father scuffed down the beach to collect us that evening, and all three of us had different suggestions about dinner.

"It's *very* important that we eat at the finest dining establishment in this Kingdom," Imogen reasoned.

But Astrid wanted fish and chips, and I was in the mood for room service in the hotel.

Father simply slumped onto the sand beside me and stared out to sea. He was still wearing his suit. Gradually we all stopped arguing and looked at him. His shoulders were hunched, his eyes narrowed, his mouth twisted into a scowl.

He was in a mood.

He's almost never in a mood.

"What is it?" Astrid asked, worried. "Are you sorry you missed a day playing on the beach? I could bury your feet now, if you like? Here, let me take off your shoes."

"Oh." Father shook himself, tried to smile, but the smile vanished almost at once. "Thank you, Astrid. Sounds lovely.

It's just the conference. Didn't go as I'd hoped. Those pompous, patronizing . . ." He cleared his throat.

"What was the conference about?" I asked.

Father sighed. He adjusted his position, then apologized for spilling the sand that Astrid had already begun pouring onto his feet. "Well," he said at last. "Have you noticed that the oceans are peculiar lately?"

We considered and then nodded. The giant wave in Spindrift, obviously. The strange currents on the cruise ship that had kept our aunts so busy. The Aquatic Elves. ("*Impossible*," Father had said.)

"That fishing town," Imogen remembered. "Bobsleigh. The one that ran out of fish so we had the fundraiser. Is that the ocean being peculiar?"

Father nodded. "It is."

"And there are Shadow Mages wandering in our mountains because their homes have been flooded by rising tide waters?" I remembered.

"Quite." I think Father was pleased to be talking. He finds it soothing to be educational. "Ocean changes are causing Shadow Mages to leave their kingdoms and drift to higher regions— Spellbinders have been stretched to the limit trying to protect everyone. Now, have you all heard of Tilla Tarpaulin?"

Of course we had. Tilla Tarpaulin is often in the papers. She's a stern-looking woman who dresses in black trouser suits and wears strings of white pearls. She reminds me of a domino. She's also the director of the K&E Alliance, the organization that tries to patch up quarrels between Kingdoms and Empires and to solve big problems like hunger, disease—and, I suppose, peculiar ocean conduct.

"Well, Tilla directed experts from all over the Kingdoms and Empires to hold a conference, talk about the issue, and report back to her. Oceanographers, marine biologists, aquatic scientists, meteorologists, geologists, Magical-Sea-Creature specialists . . ."

He carried on listing experts for quite a while, and both

Imogen and Astrid lost interest. Imogen began to help Astrid in her work burying Father's feet.

Father didn't seem to notice he'd lost most of his audience. "The experts *all* had different theories," he said.

Imogen and Astrid glanced up at that, but then Imogen suggested they needed to dampen the sand on Father's feet, to hold it in place. They both ran down to the shore with buckets to collect water.

"But why did they need you at the conference?" I asked, confused.

"Oh, well, I suggested it," Father said, his face growing gloomy again. "They didn't pay a bit of attention to me. Two Whisperers I know came along too and they spoke beautifully—they agree with me—but *that* didn't help. Nobody trusts Whisperers, which is ridiculous. They shut the three of us down. Told me I was ridiculous; that I'd cause a Kingdom-wide panic. I had to swear not to repeat it! It was as if I knew *nothing*!"

I was confused. I didn't want to offend him but I was pretty sure he *did* know nothing about the ocean. "You're a *historian*," I reminded him gently.

"Yes." Father nodded firmly. He didn't seem to take my point. "I mainly do modern history, of course, but my doctorate was in classical."

My sisters were back with their buckets of seawater.

"One, two, three, go," Imogen ordered, and they both began to tip water—slowly, slowly, a fine trickle—onto the sandcastle covering Father's feet.

I watched the water falling—slowly, slowly—and as it fell, so did the word *classical* that Father had just spoken.

Classical—

It fell, with a *thunk* into my memories, where it hit:

> —the classical history books I'd considered when I was
> writing my speech, with classical stories of Fiends
> chosen by nature for evil powers—
> —Stefan listing the names of Fiends—

—The intriguing part? Stefan had said. *In the preface of the book it said the classical stories were true.—*

—Professor Lillian Joyce Armstrong would sit up in a tree, Stefan had said, *. . . Jonathan J. Lanyard clicked his fingers . . . Caleb Vincenza . . .—*

—Last summer, me beneath the kitchen table, drinking lemonade, Father on the telephone.

"Well, that sounds like Jonathan J. Lanyard, of course," he'd said and asked another question, about the temperature of *water,* and then—

—Father's face had turned the grayish white of a late winter storm.

I looked up.

"Father," I said. "You think the stories from classical history are real. You think there's a classical Fiend causing the problems with the ocean. Someone like the Fiend named Jonathan J. Lanyard. *That's* why you went to the conference."

At this, Father's legs jerked back, the sandcastle crumbled, and my sisters wailed.

He looked at me hard. "Not *like* Jonathan J. Lanyard, Esther," he said, speaking quickly. "But somehow—impossibly—Jonathan J. Lanyard himself."

Then he scrambled to his feet: "Right! Dinner! Fish and chips, was it?"

And while Imogen argued and Astrid cheered, Father murmured to me, "Please don't repeat that to another living soul."

PART

4

CHAPTER 104

WHEN WE ARRIVED back at school, my feet were springy and I smiled at everybody.

I had just had an adventure. I'd voyaged across the Kingdoms and Empires, climbed a mansion, glimpsed a queen through a palace window, fractured my ankle, had it plastered by a grown-up Child of Spindrift, attended a grand party, watched a wave tear the party apart, seen my sisters save the day, traveled by train through the Wicked and Nefarious Kingdoms, and had a pleasant day by the sea.

I was a different person now: braver and stronger and with many more emotions.

For part of our journey home, I'd worried about Father's theory that a Fiend had returned from the past to play with the oceans, but then my worry had faded. The actual ocean experts would solve the ocean's issues. Fiends were nothing but stories from long ago.

Also, school was going to be great! No more defending against Shadow Mages—a Spellbinding encircled us and Spellbinders were now staying in the Old Schoolhouse. (Father had told me they were planning to be there for months!) (Principal Hortense told us they were filing clerks! Ha!)

What could be safer? Nothing!

Georgia and Hsiang were gone, of course, but I was used to that by now, and I had two new friends: Autumn and Pelagia.

On Saturday, my sisters and I would take another journey, this time for the Junior Poker Competition; we would see our cousin Bronte and hopefully win another trophy. And then holidays would begin!

And finally, I'd done so much extra homework the afternoon before we left that I was now two weeks *ahead*.

I was so happy I slid down the banister. Mr. Dar-Healey, who was passing by, said, "Esther!" But then he winked at me.

* * *

Sixteen days later I was lying in the mud in the gardens behind the school, rain hammering my face, sobbing.

CHAPTER 105

MY FIRST FULL day back, the classroom had changed.

Instead of rows of desks, they had been pushed together to form four separate tables with chairs around them. Hetty and Tatty Rattlestone explained this to me as we walked in.

"Each table is named after a Kingdom or Empire," Hetty said. "Rowan is that one there. That's the top group—the smartest people."

"Kate-Bazaar is second-smartest, Ricochet is third, and Endiva is the *bottom* group." Tatty lowered her voice and stage-whispered, "The people who *just aren't smart.*"

"Mrs. Pollock moves us around between tables," Hetty explained, "after each test. So you can go up or down. It's ingenious because you have motivation to work hard."

"Oh, and look, everyone except the Rowan table—the *top* table—has chores. See that list at the front of the room?" Tatty pointed. "Looks like you've got . . . cleaning the chalkboard dusters, Esther. You do your chores each morning right after breakfast."

That was good. I liked banging chalkboard dusters together.

"Welcome back, Esther!" Mrs. Pollock cried from the front of the room. "You must tell us all about your trip this afternoon!"

She beamed at me. I beamed back.

"Oh, Esther, have the twins explained our new table system to you? Good for them! You'll find your desk over at the Endiva table, all right? The right-hand corner there?"

"The Endiva table?"

"Yes."

Tatty gave me a sympathetic pout.

I decided not to mind.

It must be because I'd been away when she set up the new system. She would move me to a higher table after the next test, surely. Also at my table were quiet little Dot Pecorino, tall Durba, and Pelagia.

Hetty and Tatty Rattlestone, I noticed, were at the top table, Rowan, sitting either side of Autumn Hillside.

"Homework booklets first!" Mrs. Pollock said, handing these out. "You all did very well! A pleasure to mark! Now, don't leave this week's homework until the last minute, will you? Do a little each night."

My homework booklet landed on my desk.

I smiled and flicked through it.

Mrs. Pollock had graded the homework I'd done for the weeks I was away. There were no ticks or crosses, just a letter at the bottom of each page.

C–

C–

C–

Confusing.

Our homework each week is just a few pages of spelling and mathematics exercises. They're always simple—just for practice. I was sure mine had been correct. How had I gotten C– for everything?

Well, I must have made mistakes, rushing to get it done before we left. Or maybe it was my messy handwriting.

I turned the page to the next few weeks of homework, thinking I would check my answers before I handed the booklet in next week. We do our homework in pencil, rather than ink, so it would be easy to—

I turned the page.

Turned it back again.

No answers. Blank spaces.

No answers. Blank spaces.

I stared.

Turned the pages back and forth, forth and back.

Had I *imagined* working ahead with my homework?

No! I was *sure* I'd done it.

I peered closely at a page—held it to the light—and caught glimpses of my own handwriting. Little pieces of letters. Indentations from where I'd pressed hard.

And specks of eraser.

My homework had been erased.

Who would erase my homework?

I looked at the girls around me. Who would be so spiteful?

"Oh Esther," Mrs. Pollock called. "Are you wondering why your homework has gone?"

I blinked, clutching the booklet so tight the pages crumpled.

"I had to get rid of it. You cannot do homework in advance like that! Homework is meant to be done on a schedule! Now. This morning, we have a fun activity, we're going to . . ."

I don't remember what she said, or what fun activity we did.

My teacher had erased my homework.

* * *

That afternoon, Mrs. Pollock invited me to tell the class about my journey.

I'd been looking forward to this.

I started by describing how I'd fractured my ankle.

Hetty raised her hand.

"Wait, you fractured your ankle in the last two weeks?" she asked, frowning. "But where's the plaster?"

"And why aren't you limping?" Zoe Fawnwell put in from the Kate-Bazaar table. She tilted her chair back so she was almost touching Hetty. "You're walking normally, Esther!"

"The plaster dissolved while I was sleeping," I explained, "on our journey home."

Mrs. Pollock giggled. "The plaster *dissolved*," she repeated. She giggled again and put her hand over her mouth. "Sorry,

Esther, it's just—I've never . . ." She collapsed into laughter again.

The class all began to laugh too.

"Oh," I said, trying to make them hear me. "You see, it was a *Faery* doctor who treated my ankle, and he gave me a healing cupcake. So it recovered very quickly. He used Faery dissolving plaster. He was a Child of Spindrift, by the way."

As I said all this, Mrs. Pollock kept repeating my words and shrieking. "A *Faery* doctor! . . . *Shriek!* . . . A healing cupcake! . . . *Shriek!* . . . *Dissolving plaster! Shriek!* A *Child of Spindrift! SHRIEK! SHRIEK!*" By this point she was howling with laughter. So was the class.

"Esther!" Mrs. Pollock cried, wiping her eyes. "I'm sorry, but you are *hilarious*! There would *not* be a Faery doctor in the Kingdom of Storms, my dear. The place is surrounded by Wicked and Nefarious Kingdoms! Faeries never go there! There's no such thing as dissolving plaster! What an idea! As for a *Child of Spindrift* treating you? Your imagination really *has* got you carried away! Do go on. Tell us more."

I tried.

I tried to explain about Dr. Eli, how he was one of the only Faeries in that region, having grown up in the Spindrift Orphanage, and about the party and the wave, and how we had taken a train through the Wicked and—

I had to stop there, though.

Nobody could hear me. The class were in fits of laughter. Mrs. Pollock was pounding the table and bellowing. She kept shouting interruptions, and the class got into the spirit of the game and began shouting themselves.

"Wait, so you're telling us you never actually *met* the Stolen Prince of Cloudburst?"

"Well, I've actually met him already, a couple of years ago, but at the party—"

"She doesn't know the Stolen Prince at all! I don't believe she even *went* to the party!"

"And you're saying there was a *giant* wave so you *ran* up a flight of stairs in a hotel? *With a fractured foot!*"

"Not ran. I sort of limped, and—"

"And you never even got *near* the King or Queen of the Kingdom of Storms!"

"No, because—"

"Oh, Esther!" Mrs. Pollock said, waving her hands at the class to quiet down. "What a great laugh you've given us. I must say, I should give you a demerit for lying like that—so many lies! I cannot believe you suggested your father took you on a train trip through a shadow realm. The worst one! No father would do that. That region is much too dangerous. You owe him an apology for suggesting it! Still, I haven't laughed that hard in an age. Come here and let's do a personalized greeting for your comedy. All right, sit down, dear, and do make an effort to be better."

* * *

A curious thing happened that afternoon.

I was walking by the front windows of the school, admiring the gardens. Deep red autumn roses were blooming, swaying gently in the breeze. A figure darted by the front gate and my heart jumped—Shadow Mage? But it wasn't. The figure hurried on up the road. A girl.

A girl in a yellow dress with a red coat.

A girl with long dark hair.

A brisk step, a straight back.

A *very familiar*—

I threw open the door of the school, tripped down the stairs, and ran along the path, shouting: "BRONTE! BRONTE!"

It was my cousin!

My cousin, Bronte Mettlestone!

Walking right by my school!

She had not paused, although she must have heard me calling. In fact, she had picked up her pace.

"*BRONTE METTLESTONE!*" I shouted again, reaching the gate and peering through.

But the girl hurried on into the distance and rounded a curve in the road.

I must have been mistaken.

It was not Bronte at all. Why would it be anyway? She lived far away in Gainsleigh! I would see her soon when we went to the poker competition. My imagination had picked me up and flown away with me.

* * *

One final thing happened that first day back.

I found a large package in my mailbox. It had arrived in the afternoon post.

Hsiang! I thought. *Or Georgia? They're sending me a gift to apologize for ignoring me for so long!*

Hmm, perhaps I *wasn't* used to being without my best friends, I realized, as I drew out the package.

But it was not from Georgia or Hsiang.

It was from my Aunt Emma. A small stack of paintings, and a note.

Darling Esther,

So sorry! I only just got your request for paintings for your school auction! Had a spot of bother with the law again and your cousin Bronte was NOT here this time to spring me from the local jail as she did once before! It was just a misunderstanding. My darling friends Sugar Rixel and the Water Sprites sorted it all out in the end, and I'm free as a bird again.

Here are some paintings for your school
to auction.

Hope I'm not too late!

Love, love, love,
Aunt Emma

Just a *little* too late, Aunt Emma.

I flicked through the stack. Aunt Emma lives on Lantern Island, and most of the paintings depicted her cottage there. (I recognized it because I've visited her with my sisters, and because she's always sending us paintings of her cottage. Her art was in a "cottage phase" for years.) There were also some landscapes I did not recognize—fields of flowers and mountains with sun rising majestically between them. Another field, grassy, with a picnic blanket and a little group of women and children, bushy trees behind them, a rock shaped like—

I stopped.

Stared at the painting.

A rock shaped like a turtle poking its head from its shell.

It was the landscape from my dream again.

The same one I had seen from the train in the shadow realm.

CHAPTER 106

LATER THAT NIGHT, I gazed at the painting.

It was twilight in the painting: streaks of orange in the sky, and the trees and the turtle rock were deeply shadowed. The picnicking people were only silhouettes—dark shapes in the dim light. Two women, two small children, and a baby in a pram.

The picnic blanket was blue. When I peered more closely, I found a smudge of red on the blanket—

Strawberry jam?

I wrote to Aunt Emma.

Dear Aunt Emma,

I'm very sorry to hear you've had a spot of bother with the law. What a shame my cousin Bronte wasn't there to help you this time. Bronte is a proper hero, isn't she? So are my sisters, by the way. But I'm just Esther.

Thank you for the paintings! I'm afraid they're too late—we've already had the auction. Shall I post them back to you?

Can I ask a question? One of your paintings is of a picnic. There are bushy trees and a rock shaped like a turtle. Do you remember where that landscape is? And who the picnicking people are?

Love, love, love,

your niece, Esther

I had the dream seven or eight times that night. Each time I woke more breathless and panicked than the time before.

CHAPTER 107

ON MY FOURTH day back at school, I was cheerful because—

—the very next day I would be traveling to the poker competition with my sisters!

A newspaper headline caught my eye as I walked into the dining hall for breakfast.

DEEPEST DARKEST OCEAN

I stopped to read the article. The first paragraph was about the strange behavior of the ocean lately. Currents awry, tides upside down, fish dressing up in suits and ties and taking the train to work. (Ha ha. No. It just said that fish were vanishing.)

The article continued:

Alfreda Reinozovski, leading oceanographer, explains, "To be honest, odd things have been happening in the ocean for the last thirty years or more—but lately it's been getting out of hand. Whales migrating in the wrong direction. Ships sinking. Oysters floating on the surface. Surfing competitions canceled because no waves. It's so intriguing! My team and I are pretty sure the issues are coming from the deepest, darkest part of the ocean, not far from the Candle Islands."

The next step, Alfreda says, is a trip in a newly constructed submarine. "It's the first submarine ever built that can withstand the water pressure way down there," Alfreda gushes. "Once I'm down, I'll see if I can figure out just what the problem is."

I looked at the picture of Alfreda. She had a friendly, smiley face and very curly hair.

If my father was right, and the problem in the deepest, darkest ocean was actually an evil Fiend from a thousand years ago—well, Alfreda's friendly, smiley face could be in serious danger.

That was a strange moment for me.

Ordinarily my father *is* right. That's my experience of him, anyway.

Which meant I should send an urgent telegraph to this Alfreda, saying:

DON'T DO IT. DANGEROUS!

But the experts at the conference had laughed at Father. They'd found his idea so silly, they'd made him swear not to repeat it.

Fathers, even *my* father, must make mistakes sometimes.

Alfreda and her curly hair would be fine.

* * *

Later that morning, just before morning tea, a terrible thing happened.

I suppose "terrible" might be an exaggeration, but that's the word I've typed, and I don't want to go back now and change it.

Mrs. Pollock called me over to her desk and whispered, "My dear Esther."

At last! I thought. *We are going to have our private chat!*

"Look at your hands," she said.

I looked.

My hands were covered in fine white powder.

"It's all over your face too," she murmured. "Didn't you say you traveled by train though the Wicked and Nefarious Kingdoms on your trip?"

I nodded.

"All right, you've picked up a serious shadow illness while there. I've read about this. It's called Lire syndrome—that's L-i-r-e—sounds like *liar*, but not how it's spelled. We are going to have to keep a *very* close eye on you. No poker competition,

I'm afraid. Your father should never have taken you on that train trip!"

My head went into a tumble.

"But *before,* you said . . ." I began—then stopped. She hadn't believed me when I said we'd been on the train. She'd laughed at me.

But that was missing the point.

"The poker competition?" I said. "But I *have* to go!" Why did I have to go? It was—I just really wanted— well, actually, I *did* have to go! "My sisters need me! We need a team of three to compete!"

"Shhhhh!" Mrs. Pollock lowered both her hands, trying to quiet me. "I don't want to alarm the class. You could die from this disease, you know. That's why you *must* stay at school, to be sure you don't die. Your sisters will understand."

"I feel fine!" I argued. "I'm perfectly healthy! Why don't I go and see the nurse? I'm sure she'll say—"

"That I'm wrong?" Mrs. Pollock interrupted, little dimples in her cheeks. "You're not suggesting that I'm *wrong*, are you, Esther?"

"Well, no . . . I mean . . ."

"I'm certainly *not* wrong. Quick greeting to cheer you up."

That was brave of her, I thought—she could catch the illness?

"Right, better now? Back to your seat. I'll pop around to Principal Hortense to let her know."

Her chair squealed as she pushed it back, and she hurried from the room. "Back soon!" she hissed to the class from the doorway. "Try not to miss me too much!"

Everyone giggled.

I looked at my hands.

There *was* white dust sprinkled all over them.

Maybe I *was* sick?

But there was something familiar about—

"Mrs. Pollock!" I shouted.

I ran out of the room and chased her down the corridor. I caught her outside the closed door to Principal Hortense's office.

"*Esther!*" she exclaimed. "What are you doing here?"

"It's chalk dust!" I clapped my hands together. Dust flew into the air between us, swirling in the light. "I'm not sick! It's chalk dust! I was cleaning the dusters this morning! Remember? That's my job now!"

Mrs. Pollock nodded, smiling gently. "Yes, that's what it looks like," she agreed. "But it's Lire syndrome. Return to the classroom, Esther. Try to breathe slowly, dear, don't pant like that. You'll speed up the progress of the disease."

"I'll go and wash it off right now!" I said. "It will all just wash away! I promise you, it's chalk dust!"

"Esther, sometimes teachers have difficult tasks. This is one. I am giving you uncomfortable news and this is harder for me than for you. The news is this: you have Lire syndrome. Yes, the dust *may* wash off. But that means nothing. The syndrome imitates chalk dust. Now please return to the classroom and allow me to speak to Principal Hortense. Another word—" I had begun to argue again, and she had raised a finger. "Another word out of you, my dear, and you'll get three demerits."

* * *

At morning teatime, I washed my hands and face, and of course, the dust disappeared.

I bumped into my sisters just by the entrance to the dining hall.

"You won't believe it!" I said.

They both nodded sorrowfully. "We already know," Imogen said.

"Principal Hortense called us into her office earlier," Astrid added. "She told us you can't go to the poker competition tomorrow because they think you've got some strange disease."

"I don't!" I said. "It was just *chalk dust*! Look, it's gone!"

They both sighed. "It does seem ridiculous," they said. "You seem *fine*. What's up with Mrs. Pollock? She seems like—"

"Oh, it's not her fault," I said quickly. "She's just made a mistake. She's really lovely."

Imogen and Astrid both frowned at me. "Anyway," Imogen continued, "now that they *think* you have it, they're not letting you go. Principal Hortense says she's already contacted the competition organizers to tell them."

"It's not *fair!*" I cried, and then, remembering again, "It's not fair to you two! Now you can't go either!"

"Well . . . ," Imogen began.

"Um . . . ," Astrid winced.

A peculiar feeling, a twist, turned in my stomach.

"We're still going," Imogen said. "Sorry, Esther, but Principal Hortense asked if there was anyone at school who could replace you."

"And we suggested Autumn," Astrid said apologetically. "She practiced with us a couple of times and she was really good. I think Principal Hortense is asking her now."

She pointed to the other end of the dining hall, where Principal Hortense was crouching to speak to Autumn. I saw Autumn nodding.

All right, here are some of the things I should have said:

"Great! I'm glad you don't have to miss out."

Or: "Excellent idea! Yes, Autumn *was* good! Good luck!"

Anything similar to that.

Instead, I said: "You are *not serious.*"

They both blinked. *Blink. Blink.*

"YOU CANNOT TAKE AUTUMN INSTEAD OF ME!" I blazed. (It really was a blaze—fire seemed to pour from my chest and out of my mouth.) "THAT'S NOT FAIR!"

Here, they both frowned. They have identical frowns, my sisters. Straight lines across their foreheads and tweaks at the corners of their mouths.

"Esther," Imogen said. "I know it's hard, but come on."

"NO, *YOU* COME ON!" I blazed again. "YOU ARE BOTH BEING RIDICULOUS AND CRUEL AND *UNFAIR!*"

I stomped out of the dining hall and missed my morning tea. Everyone was staring.

* * *

That afternoon, Mrs. Pollock told the class that we should all congratulate Autumn Hillside.

"She has been selected to join Imogen and Astrid Mettlestone-Staranise in the poker competition! They leave tomorrow!"

Everyone—including Autumn herself—glanced over at me, looking worried.

I scowled at her.

"Don't worry about Esther! She'll be fine!" Mrs. Pollock promised. "Look at Autumn instead! Hasn't she come far? A girl from the Whispering Kingdom is now representing our school!"

After that, Mrs. Pollock babbled for a bit. Something about how we all had to help Autumn to be *one* of us. (*What?* I thought. *But she's* not *one of my* SISTERS.) And how you could see that Autumn was a Whisperer just by looking at her *very* long hair (*Could you?* I wondered. *We never noticed before she told us,*) but that hopefully people would not stare at her at the competition. And hmmm, would the long hair give Autumn an *advantage* at the poker competition, by allowing her to *Whisper* her opponents?

"Oh." Autumn smiled. "No, I'm not old enough to Whisper yet."

But Mrs. Pollock kept talking. She truly hoped Autumn would fit in. She knew Autumn's friends—nodding encouragingly at Hetty and Tatty—would think of *ways* to help Autumn fit in. It was *so* kind of Hetty and Tatty to have welcomed Autumn, even though she was an *outsider*, a *stranger*, and how *truly good friends* help their new friends to *fit in*—think of *clever* ways, *brave* ways to do that, that they—

I don't know.

It was boring and repetitive.

It didn't make sense.

I stopped listening.

My heart was just a fire burning fiercely.

CHAPTER 108

ON MY FIFTH day back at school, I woke in the morning to a scream.

A scream like scalding water.

It was Autumn. She was sitting up in her bed alongside mine, clutching her head.

Her long hair was gone.

All that was left was a ragged, short cut.

"*Who?*" she shrieked. "*WHO DID THIS?*"

She looked directly at me.

"No, no!" I said frantically. "I would *never*—"

But I could see why she might think it. The way I'd scowled at her yesterday. I'd known it was unfair of me, but my face had done it anyway.

"Um," said a voice.

Hetty Rattlestone.

She and Tatty were in their nightdresses, standing by the door.

"We did it," Hetty said.

"In the night," Tatty agreed.

"We cut it off with scissors."

A shock of silence.

"But why?" Autumn whispered.

"Well, to help you—fit in . . . at the poker competition."

"So you would't look like a Whisperer."

"We were being . . . good friends."

The twins glanced at each other. A flash of uncertainty.

Autumn stared at them.

"We still have the hair," Tatty offered. "In a bag. In our wardrobe. If you . . . need it." She coughed.

"I suppose it's not much use anymore," Hetty admitted.

There was a long, terrible quiet.

After a moment, Autumn got out of bed.

She glanced at me. "Sorry," she said. "Sorry to accuse you. Sorry to replace you in the competition too."

"No, no," I said. "*I'm* sorry I was mad. It's not your fault that I can't go. It's not my sisters' fault, either—" I stopped. "Are you all right?"

Autumn tried to smile. She was making her bed. "My hair doesn't help me Whisper or anything yet, but it's . . . well, a Whisperer's hair is *part* of who they are. It grows along with us, it's like the essence of us. So it *hurts*. It *hurts* not to—"

She couldn't speak. She was crying too much. She dropped the pillow she'd been straightening and ran from the room.

I wrote a note to my sisters and, when Autumn returned, asked her to give it to them:

Imogen and Astrid,

Sorry I was angry. Say hi to Bronte
for me.

Have fun & win,

E xxx.

Then I watched from an upstairs window as Autumn and my sisters climbed into the carriage. Mustafa was driving them to the port.

Autumn glanced up toward me and even from this distance I could see that her eyes were puffy. Her fingertips kept reaching around, touching her own bare neck.

Into my head sprang a thought: *Mrs. Pollock is awful.*

I shook myself quickly—*No, she's not! She's funny!*—and the thought fell away.

CHAPTER 109

ON THE NINTH day back at school, another newspaper headline caught my eye as I walked into the dining hall for breakfast.

FAMOUS OCEANOGRAPHER DEAD

The same smiling photograph of Alfreda Reinozovski.

> *In a tragedy that has rocked the oceanography community, Alfreda Reinozovski has been found dead in her submarine. Professor Reinozovski trialed her new, state-of-the-art submarine yesterday at 6:00 A.M., diving with it to the deepest, darkest part of the ocean. The submarine returned four hours later, but the professor was found to be dead. Doctors have so far not been able to ascertain the cause of her death.*

I turned around and walked straight back out of the dining hall.

I wanted my father, but he was traveling again.

I wanted my sisters, but they were at the poker competition.

Mrs. Pollock had not said another word about my "Lire syndrome." When I asked her about it, she chuckled and waved me away.

I was having trouble catching my breath; it kept jumping away from me.

I realized I was muttering: *Alfreda, Alfreda, Alfreda.*

I walked out of the back door of the school, into the gardens, telling myself, over and over: *She would not have listened anyway.*

Even if I *had* telegrammed her and warned her about the Ocean Fiend, she would have smiled her friendly newspaper smile. I was just a twelve-year-old girl.

But still: *Alfred, Alfreda, Alfreda.*

I needed to go to the pond. To put my feet in the water.

As I approached, I saw that Pelagia was sitting on the edge, leaning forward, head tilted.

I breathed more slowly. Pelagia. She was my friend. More Imogen's friend after the swimming tournament, of course, but she could be mine too.

My *only* friend now.

I would tell her—not the whole story, but part of it.

Just as I reached the pond, there was a flash of light. It dazzled me. I blinked.

"What was that?" I asked.

Pelagia jumped.

She swung around to look at me.

"Nothing," she said quickly. "It was nothing."

Strange reply. I pulled off my shoes, peeled off my stockings, and sat down beside her.

Pelagia shifted a little to make room.

"You didn't see that flash of light?" I tried.

"No. What flash of light?"

I frowned.

A moment ago, she had said, "Nothing. It was nothing."

But there *had* been a flash of light.

"It sort of zipped across the water lilies on the pond," I said. "It was so bright!"

"You imagined it," Pelagia assured me. "Or . . ." She paused and pointed to the windows of the Old Schoolhouse. "Or maybe it came from there. Actually, yes, now I think about it, it *was* from there. It's the people having a convention now. Filing clerks, isn't it? They must be shining lights from their windows for some reason."

I looked at her closely. She was biting her lower lip and staring fixedly at a water lily.

"Are you all right, Pelagia? Has your laughter been stolen?"

She chuckled, so I knew it hadn't been.

I remembered again how Pelagia had started the school year with boxes of chocolates and stories of adventures. Where had that Pelagia gone?

"Can you tell me one of your adventures?" I asked. Maybe that would cheer her up? Bring her back.

Pelagia was silent.

"I remember once overhearing you tell a story to Hetty Rattlestone," I said. "It was while we were walking to our first swimming lesson. Something about hiding from Whisperers in a bowling alley?"

Pelagia nodded. "Yes. That's right. There were twelve Whisperers. I hid in a cupboard."

She sounded listless.

Also, the story had changed.

When she was telling Hetty that day, there'd been seven Whisperers and she'd hidden in a shoe rack.

* * *

We had a dance class that day.

Arlo had stopped picking his nose, luckily, but he never spoke to me. Now and then he grinned—usually when I made a mistake with a dance step, which I did quite often. He was pretty good at the steps himself by now and sometimes reminded me what to do by gesturing.

I had an idea.

The day we'd found out we'd be dancing with boys from Nicholas Valley, Pelagia had mentioned a boy from her hometown. I would speak to that boy. Ask him about Pelagia and her adventures. Did she make them up? Or get her memories mixed up when she was sad? Maybe I could even ask *him* to cheer her up?

His name was . . . Charlie? Oliver?

No.

I closed my eyes, trying to remember.

"Hello?" said Arlo.

I opened my eyes. "Sorry."

Arlo nodded once, and we started dancing again.

Clive.

That was it.

"Which one of the boys here is named Clive?" I asked. "Do you know?"

Arlo stepped forward, stepped back, side, side, and swing, swing.

"I don't know," he said eventually, looking worried. "I don't know *anybody* named Clive." He spun me in a twirl.

"Never mind," I said.

He burped. Nearby, boys guffawed. Arlo grinned at them and at me.

I found Arlo very confusing.

Later, I saw Stefan.

"How's Katya?" I asked. "Is she getting any laughter back?"

"Not good," Stefan said gloomily, as usual. "Nothing's working. She'll never laugh again."

I scratched behind my ear, cranky.

"Do you know somebody at your school named Clive?" I asked. "Is he here? Can you point him out to me?"

Stefan shook his head firmly. "There's nobody at my school named Clive."

"How can you be sure?"

"I know everyone. I know all the names."

Hmmm.

Why would Pelagia invent a friend named Clive?

Later that night, just as I was falling asleep, Katya's voice spoke in my head: "Pelagia's not a Spellbinder," she had said. "But there's something about her that I can't . . . Esther, be careful of Pelagia."

I had completely forgotten. Or I'd set it aside. Katya's illness was making her babble, I'd thought at the time.

Now it was back again, chiming and clear: *Esther, be careful of Pelagia.*

CHAPTER 110

THE FIFTEENTH DAY back at school was my birthday.

"Happy birthday!" everyone chorused the moment I woke up. We always do that on birthdays, but it was a lackluster chorus that morning.

For one thing, "everyone" was only three people. There were two empty beds in our dormitory: Katya was still at the treatment center for stolen laughter, and Autumn (along with my sisters) was still at the poker competition.

Dot Pecorino was there, only she is so quiet I wonder if she truly feels herself to *be* anywhere, if you see what I mean. And the twins had been subdued ever since they'd cut off Autumn's hair.

Both Mrs. Pollock and Principal Hortense had scolded them about that, and, when they tried to explain, Mrs. Pollock had cried, "I certainly did *not* mean for you to do this! I told you to be a *friend* to Autumn, not *cut off her hair*! The *idea*!"

The twins had also been shocked by Autumn's distress. I think they'd assumed she would be quietly grateful, as usual, and say something like "Oh, thank you for cutting my hair. *Now* I can fit in." Everyone else in the class was angry with them too—even Zoe Fawnwell—and the twins had become quite snappy with each other. It didn't help that Hetty had scored lower than any other competitor ever at the speech competition. (Zoe had told me this in a hissing whisper that Hetty must have been able to hear.)

There was a birthday card from my father in my mailbox, a few from various aunts, and one from my sisters.

Father's card said:

So sorry I can't take you out for a birthday tea, as usual. Enclosing money—buy yourself a treat. We'll celebrate when my work quietens down. Much love.

I'd never seen such a short note from Father. He likes to take any opportunity to talk, whether aloud or on paper. He must have been very busy.

My sisters' card said:

We are smashing the competition.
Wish you were here.

Happy Birthday,
Imogen and Astrid

P.S. Autumn says happy birthday, too.

P.P.S. Bronte not here either—we think she's on some secret adventure? But we're sure she'd also say happy birthday if she WAS here. Lots of love.

So at least my sisters had forgiven me.

There was nothing from my mother.

In class, Mrs. Pollock had everyone sing a birthday song for me but then she handed back a stack of tests. Every one of mine had a big red C–.

One was an arithmetic quiz. It had been very easy. Here it is.

$$7 + 8 = 15$$
$$3/5 + 2/5 = 5/5 = 1$$
$$20 - 12 = 8$$
$$15 + 15 + 15 = 45$$
$$300 \times 2 = 600$$
$$4 \times 20 = 80$$
$$5 + 7 \times 3 = 26$$
$$4 \times 6 = 24$$
$$5 \times 3 = 15$$
$$10 \times 10 = 100$$
$$12 + 8 = 20$$

Check your work more carefully, Esther

C−

Again, I don't want you to have to do extra arithmetic, but I'm pretty sure all my answers were actually correct.

I didn't bother telling Mrs. Pollock. She was busy anyway, having her quiet conversations with individual girls at her desk— as usual, they returned to their own desks, looking solemn.

And then she got busy playing a game where she makes everyone stand at the front of the room, reads out each of our names along with the name of our new table, and you have to run to it. If you get there before she's finished speaking, you get a sweet. Most people had shifted tables, but Dot Pecorino and I were still on the Endiva table. I didn't run to it, I *sighed* to it, so no sweet.

That afternoon, Principal Hortense took me and three other birthday girls to afternoon tea in town. Visits to town were allowed again at this point, although only with teachers. Principal Hortense said she'd been told that the area was "perfectly, mysteriously safe from Shadow Mages at the moment." (Not a mystery to me. An Old Schoolhouse filled with Spellbinders was the reason.)

"You must all tell me an amusing anecdote!" Principal Hortense instructed as we walked into the Orange Blossom Tea Shop.

"Oh, brother," said the Grade 8 girl beside me.

We pulled back our chairs, ready to sit down, and that's when I saw them.

They were pushing open the café door, chatting to each other. They paused, looking around for a free table—and their eyes landed on me.

"Georgia!" I shouted. "Hsiang!" To the others at the table, I cried: "It's my lost best friends!"

At which, Georgia and Hsiang spun around and ran from the café.

CHAPTER 111

I CHASED THEM.

But by the time I'd woven between the crowded tables to the door, pushed it open, ducked around other customers trying to get in, and burst out into the street, they were gone.

I searched the street, the shops, the open-air stalls, and the lakeshore, sprinting in every direction, calling their names.

Principal Hortense caught up with me in the bookstore. She was fairly cross.

"It *can't* have been Georgia and Hsiang," she scolded. "They left the school, remember? And you must *not* be running around town on your own!"

But it *was* them. I was absolutely sure.

Or anyway, I thought I was.

Back at school, I checked the mailroom and the afternoon delivery had arrived. More birthday cards from different aunts. Nothing from my mother.

I went around to Ms. Ubud and checked whether any telegrams or telephone calls had come for me.

"If they had, we'd have notified you." Ms. Ubud frowned. "You know the system, Esther."

* * *

A peculiar thing happened at dinner that night.

It was raining outside and the dining hall was warmly lit with lanterns. I was eating my roast chicken with carrots and peas, and as I reached for the gravy jug, I happened to glance at the teachers' table. Mrs. Pollock was pulling one of her curious faces. She was pushing her top teeth over her lower lip and going cross-eyed. She was making fun of Dr. Lanwish. He makes that face when he's rummaging around in his briefcase or picking bits of crisp from between his teeth. The teachers on either side of Mrs. Pollock were laughing, and Dr. Lanwish himself, further along the table, was chuckling too. I was just about giggle when—

—*Mrs. Pollock is awful.*

I stopped.

Where had that thought come from?

It was a memory, I realized. I had thought that the morning when the twins cut Autumn's hair.

No, she's not! I argued, strangely panicked. *She's funny! Dr. Lanwish doesn't mind! Look, he's laughing!*

But when I studied Dr. Lanwish more closely, I caught flashes of teeny creases, like claw prints, appearing and disappearing around his cheeks and eyes. He was uncomfortable and was trying to hide this—even, I realized with surprise, from *himself.*

I put down my fork, although I'd just pierced three peas.

"Mrs. Pollock is *awful,*" I announced.

The girls around me gasped and turned disapproving looks on me. "She is certainly *not,*" they protested. "She's wonderful!"

"She teases people," I said.

"People don't *mind,*" Tatty declared.

"I think maybe they *do,*" I began, but Tatty held up a palm.

"Not if they have a sense of humor they don't," she said.

"Where's your sense of humor, Esther?" Zoe Fawnwell demanded.

"Esther is only saying that because she's getting bad marks," Hetty informed the others. "She's at the Endiva table. It's not Mrs. Pollock's fault that you're not as smart as you used to be, Esther."

"Just because it's your birthday, doesn't mean you're allowed to be unkind," Tatty lectured.

"Look at how nice she was to Tatty and me when we cut off Autumn's hair!" Hetty added. "Principal Hortense thought we should get a detention, but Mrs. Pollock only scolded us a little and said we hadn't meant any harm. We'd only overthought things, she said, which is a sign of our high intelligence."

"But," I argued, "it was *because* of Mrs. Pollock that you did it! She—" How to explain this? She had *manipulated* them into cutting off Autumn's hair. "She *made* you!"

"What are you *talking* about?" Hetty and Tatty demanded. "That's *ridiculous!*"

They shifted their chairs away from me, turning their shoulders, and the others did the same. I looked across at the teachers' table again. Mrs. Pollock was holding up her knife, studying her reflection in the silver.

She's awful, I thought once again, but more softly.

The thought faded and dissolved. She wasn't awful. She was funny and clever. *I* was the one whose schoolwork was dismal, and I was trying to blame my teacher.

I felt ashamed.

* * *

The last thing that happened on my birthday was this.

I was in bed in the dormitory. It was "quiet chat" time. Nobody was chatting with me. The twins were still furious with me, and Dot is as quiet as moonlight.

I was arranging my cards on my bedside table, but they kept tipping sideways. One slid to the floor, and I reached down for it. It was from Aunt Emma, a handmade card decorated with Emma's own sketches of little frogs. When I'd opened it earlier I'd admired the frogs and not taken much notice of her message. It was just

Darling Esther! Happiest of birthdays! Love, love, love, Aunt Emma.

(She is the most enthusiastic of my aunts.)

I read it again, finding the *love, love, love* soothing, and that's when I realized there was a *P.S.* on the other side I hadn't seen before.

Here is what it said:

P.S. Esther! Darling child, just got your letter! SO sorry my paintings didn't arrive in time! Don't send them back; keep them!

Oh, the picnic painting? Funny you should ask—you are IN that painting! It's in the region of Wicked and Nefarious Kingdoms. Back when they'd just started running the train. Your mother and I were visiting your Aunt Franny in Spindrift and you and your sisters were tiny. Your mother was doing research work, and your father was away on a research trip of his own...We read about this exciting new train in the paper and decided to take a ride on it! Just for a lark. We didn't tell Franny, she'd have forbidden it as too dangerous...but the paper said it was safe! We believed it!

Anyhow, the train broke down and we had a picnic. I painted the scene afterward from memory.

Your mother was not planning to tell your father about our adventure, as he'd have got into a state about the dangers.

Actually, he'd have been right, too! It's safe NOW but it was VERY dangerous back then. How did we survive? Anyway, we did, and I'm sure she must have told your father all about it by now so it's all right for me to tell you!

Much Love,
Aunt Emma

I dropped Aunt Emma's card, took the stack of paintings from the back of my closet space, found the picnic painting, and brought it back to my bed.

I studied it.

Imogen must be the little girl pointing toward the sky, I decided, and Astrid was the baby in the pram. The woman gazing at the trees was probably Aunt Emma, and the other woman, standing by the pram, resembled my mother.

So I was the small child lying on the rug.

Actually, Aunt Emma, I thought suddenly, *I don't think my mother* has *told my father all about this picnic by now.*

Eventually, I fell asleep. I only had the dream once, but I woke with a more powerful pain in my chest than I ever had before, and with the single, searing question: *Where was everyone else?*

In the painting, my mother is there, and Aunt Emma, and my sisters.

In the dream, there is nobody but me.

CHAPTER 112

THERE IS A telephone in Principal Hortense's office.

No student or teacher is allowed to use it. In an emergency we may request to send a telegram, but Principal Hortense is the only person in the school permitted to use that telephone.

On my sixteenth day back at school, a Wednesday, I woke up very early, crept down the stairs and into the principal's office, and telephoned my mother.

CHAPTER 113

MOTHER'S VOICE SOUNDED muffled. I had woken her.

"*Esther!*" she cried, sharpening up. "Whatever is the matter?"

"Did we take a train through the Wicked and Nefarious Kingdoms when I was little?" I asked.

"What on—?" Mother laughed. "What a suggestion! Of course not! That imagination of yours!"

I heard water running then. Our telephone is in the kitchen, and its cord stretches as far as the sink. She must have been getting herself a glass of water.

"Aunt Emma told me we did," I said.

The water stopped running.

"Oh, *Emma*," she said. "Her imagination is almost as wild as yours."

"Aunt Emma sent me a painting," I continued, "of us all having a picnic. The train broke down, she said, and we had a picnic. I saw the exact spot on the train with Father."

There was a pause. The sound of Mother drinking her water, and then a *clink* as she set the glass down.

"Oh, well, that sounds *vaguely* familiar," Mother said. "I'm not at all sure why you had to telephone at this hour to tell me though: that was *years* ago. Funny thing that you are. All right then, off to class now, goodbye, dear—"

"Mother," I said.

A thumping noise. I think Mother was tossing wood into the fireplace.

"Yes?"

"Was I left alone? At that picnic? Did you all . . . go for a walk or something and leave me on a blanket?"

A pause. Then Mother shouted with laughter.

"Of *course* not! The idea! You were two years old! Do you believe I would leave you alone? In a shadow realm? The *idea!*"

"It's just—I've been having these dreams—and—"

"DREAMS!" I had to hold the telephone away from my ear. "Oh, this is the limit. I really must get ready for work, Esther, I—"

"It was my birthday yesterday," I said.

"Of course it was," she agreed at once. "Happy birthday."

"Did you forget?"

"Forget! Of course not! What an idea! I sent you a gift *and* I left a message for you. All right? I *must* get on! Goodbye!"

"I didn't *get* a gift or a message," I began, but there was a *click* and Mother had gone.

I crept upstairs to the dormitory, washed and dressed, and was at the reception desk waiting when Ms. Ubud arrived.

"Are you *sure* there were no messages for me yesterday?" I asked.

"As I said yesterday, Esther," Ms. Ubud snapped, "if there *had* been, we'd have let you know!"

CHAPTER 114

LATER THAT MORNING, Mrs. Pollock said we were going to write stories.

I straightened up.

Something good at last. I love writing stories. It was raining outside again, and our classroom glowed in the dim light. Perfect.

"Use your imagination!" Mrs. Pollock said. "It's free choice! Entertain me!"

Around me people grumbled: "*I don't know what to write about.*"

It always confuses me, people saying that. My head brims with stories waiting to be told.

I picked up my pen and smiled to myself.

Put my pen to the paper.

A Story, I wrote, by *Esther Mettlestone-Staranise.*

Smiled again.

Tapped the pen against my forehead, ready for the idea.

Smiled.

Tapped my pen. Tapped the paper.

Around me, people were writing busily.

I put my pen down.

Use your imagination! Mrs. Pollock had said. *Entertain me!*

But I wouldn't entertain Mrs. Pollock. She would write:

This is very disjointed.

Or

Please try to use common sense.

Or

Please try to use logic and reason.

Or

Don't try so hard to impress.

And then she would write:

C–

I sighed so deeply that Dot, beside me, glanced over.

Then I coughed to clear away my thoughts.

Picked up my pen again.

Waited for an idea.

That imagination of yours!

I stared at the paper, and stared.

Nothing happened.

I looked up in surprise.

Mrs. Pollock was watching me. A tiny smile. She held my gaze. Lowered her eyelids slowly, and opened them again.

I shuffled about in my chair.

Picked up my pen—

My hand was shaking.

I wrote:

There was once—

And stopped.

For the longest time, I stared at the words.

There was once . . .

There was once—

What was there once?

That's when I stood up, ran from the room, along the corridor, through the back door, and out into the grounds, where I threw myself into a muddy garden bed, and the rain hammered my face, and I sobbed.

CHAPTER 115

I SOBBED BECAUSE I had no stories left to tell.

And because my mother had forgotten my birthday, my sisters were away, my best friends gone, my new friend Autumn was playing poker instead of me, my new friend Pelagia was not to be trusted, an oceanographer with curly hair had died, I dreamed about a picnic blanket each night—

And so on.

I found plenty of reasons.

The rain crashed against my face, bounced off my nose, slid down my neck, clattered against my arms and legs.

I don't know how much time passed.

Actually, that's not true. I'm just trying to be dramatic again. I know exactly how much time passed because I heard the bell ring for morning tea, for the end of morning tea, for lunch, for the end of lunch, for the end of class, and for afternoon tea.

Eventually, I stopped sobbing. You can't keep that up for five hours and thirty-seven minutes. Now and then the rain paused, as if it also needed a break, but then it started again. Meanwhile, I lay in the mud and stared at the low gray sky through the splash and blur.

The rain slowed to a faint drizzle. I closed my eyes.

"*Esther!*" came a voice.

A boy's voice.

I opened my eyes.

Stefan stood holding an umbrella and staring down at me. His shoes and socks were mud-splattered.

Dot Pecorino and Arlo hovered behind Stefan. Neither of them held an umbrella. They also stared, rain sliding down their cheeks.

I sat up in the mud.

"What are you staring at?" I asked. I was a bit annoyed. I knew I was muddy and bedraggled, but honestly. Their eyes were the size of giant squids.

"We were in dance class," Stefan explained quickly. "Dot asked me to help her find you. She was worried. Said you ran out earlier today and never came back inside."

I looked at Dot in surprise, but she was busy goggling.

"Arlo wanted to help," Stefan continued steadily, "as he's your partner. Said he can't dance without a partner. So we slipped out of the auditorium into the grounds—and here you are—but, Esther . . ." Deep lines ran across Stefan's forehead.

"What?"

"You've gone peculiar," Arlo announced.

"Mm-hmm," Dot murmured.

"What?" I looked down at myself, opened my palms. "Oh!"

It was as if a colorful spider had spun a web and imprinted it on my skin. Silver, blue, gold, and green lines intersecting. My palms, my hands, my wrists.

"Esther," Stefan said. "I've *read* about this. If the book is right, it means—"

"It means what?" I pushed myself up to my knees.

"It means nature has chosen *you* to—well, to become a Fiend."

Arlo and Dot both swung to look at him.

"What's a Fiend?" Dot asked.

"Like from those stories in classical history?" Arlo said at the same time. "That you talked about in your speech, Stefan? The evil monsters? That's what that pattern means? But it's—"

"It's all over her," Stefan agreed.

CHAPTER 116

I STUMBLED TO my feet, smacked my hands together, rubbed at my arms and face.

"Go away! Get off me! Go away!" I shouted.

Unexpectedly, the fine lines on my hands began to fade.

Stefan was solemn. "Look, the book might be wrong. Remember that it's generally believed that those were just *stories*, not real. But if it *is* real, and you *have* been chosen, you're going to turn into an evil monster, Esther. We need a Spellbinder or a Faery to help you. Can your school nurse find one?" His forehead creases deepened. "Oh, but the pattern's completely gone now."

"Nurse'll just laugh at us," Arlo pointed out.

I looked at their faces.

And into my mind came my father's face as he spoke to his research assistant on the telephone: his startled eyes, the color draining.

Fear, like a jagged lightning strike, tore through my body.

Classical history is real.

And I was about to be a Fiend.

I wobbled. Almost tipped sideways. Straightened up.

Think, Esther.

Who could help me?

Not Mrs. Pollock. Not Nurse Sydelle. Not Principal Hortense.

Stefan was right, I needed a—

I spun around and marched through the squelchy grass, around the pond, and up the stairs of the Old Schoolhouse. I waited while the others caught up, then I reached for the knocker.

CHAPTER 117

THE DOOR OPENED almost immediately.

"Come in!" exclaimed a large woman, ushering us into the lobby.

Scratched and dented floorboards. An umbrella stand crowded with umbrellas. A coat stand heavy with overcoats. A telephone sitting on a little round table. High ceilings. Staircase running up to the next floor.

The large woman's hair was swept into a butterfly clip.

She was smiling at me.

I smiled back, astonished.

I knew who she was.

Carabella-the-Great, the most powerful Spellbinder in all the Kingdoms and Empires.

You know how I mentioned earlier that I know a secret about Carabella-the-Great?

I will now tell you the secret.

She is one of my mother's sisters.

"Aunt Carrie!"

"Hello, Esther," Aunt Carrie said. "What's up?"

CHAPTER 118

"OH, YOUR _AUNT_ is here," Stefan said, relieved. "I thought you'd lost your mind, Esther. I knew there were filing clerks having a convention here so I _couldn't_ understand why you were—I mean, what possible use—no offense, Mrs.—er. I'm sure filing clerks are _very_. . . . It's just— Anyhow, good afternoon!"

Stefan reached out and shook Aunt Carrie's hand vigorously.

"Call me Carrie," she suggested.

"Pleased to meet you, Carrie. I'm Stefan, Esther's friend from Nicholas Valley Boys, and this is Dot, my dance partner. Here is Arlo, also from Nicholas Valley."

He was well brought up, Stefan, and had apparently just remembered this.

But he was also worried and his voice hurried on, speaking over Aunt Carrie's invitation to come into the— She didn't finish.

"This is a bit hard to explain," Stefan said. "But I recently read a book about classical Fiends, and, well, I'm worried that they were _real_ . . . and that your niece has been . . . chosen. Now, I realize that—" Stefan took a deep breath, ready to explain, but Aunt Carrie's smile had vanished.

"Yes, I know about classical Fiends," she interrupted. "What makes you think Esther's been chosen?"

Stefan became even graver. "Just now, her skin was covered in a web pattern."

Dot and Arlo nodded.

"It's gone now," Stefan admitted. "But it was all over her. The book I read said that people chosen—"

"Yes," Aunt Carrie interrupted again. "I know." She was looking hard at me in a way that made ropes of fear loop around my knees, as if keen to topple me.

Stefan continued, clearing his throat: "If Fiends are real, they're pure evil. So, if you know a Spellbinder or Faery who might help your niece, I think that could be . . . her only hope."

Arlo whistled through his teeth and leaned up against the coat stand. It wobbled. He jumped away from it muttering, "Sorry."

Aunt Carrie's face was gray and stony. "How have you been feeling lately, Esther?"

I considered. "Strange. Angry. And I keep imagining I see people—like Bronte, and my old friends, Georgia and Hsiang, even though I know they're far away."

In the quiet that followed my words, there was a steady *drip . . . drip . . . drip.*

Rainwater was dripping from my clothes and hair to the floor. A puddle had formed around my feet.

"Oh," I said. "Sorry."

Aunt Carrie blinked. She gazed at the puddle and then at me.

"Esther," she said softly. "You're drenched. Have you been out in the rain?"

I nodded.

"For how long?"

"All day," I replied. "Since I ran out of class."

"And tell me, Esther," she said. "Do you often run out into the rain? Do you *like* the rain?"

Dot, surprisingly, answered for me. "She loves it." Her voice was so soft that Aunt Carrie crouched to hear. "She gets in trouble for running out in the rain all the time. She collects rainwater. When everyone else painted a picture of the sun, Esther painted rain."

Something peculiar was happening to Aunt Carrie. Ripples crossed her stony face as if a statue was coming to life.

"What *color* was the web pattern?" she demanded suddenly.

"Different colors," Stefan said. "Silvers, blues? I think also greens and golds?"

Dot and Arlo nodded.

"Right." Aunt Carrie clapped once. "You lot go back to school and don't breathe a word of this to anyone. I'll see to Esther."

At the door, Stefan hesitated. "Good luck, Esther," he said solemnly, and Arlo added: "Yeah, try not to turn into a hideous, evil, wicked, monstrous—"

Dot coughed.

"All right, Arlo," Stefan said. "Let's go."

CHAPTER 119

ONCE THE DOOR had closed on them, Aunt Carrie held up a finger, meaning I should wait, and she telephoned Principal Hortense. She told the principal that she was my aunt, a filing clerk in the Old Schoolhouse, that I was ill, and that she was keeping me here for a while.

Principal Hortense's high voice chittered in the background, wanting a full-fledged conversation, but Aunt Carrie cut her off.

"Now," she said eventually, hanging up the phone. "First thing is to get you warm."

Surprising. I would have thought the first thing would be to cure me of Fiendishness.

I dripped all the way up the stairs behind her. At the top she glanced back down at the trail of water and said, "Slipping hazard. I'll see to that. Bathroom is third door on the left. Everything you need is in there. Pajamas in your size in the closet."

She was right.

In the bathroom was a stack of towels, a claw-foot tub, bubble bath, and a cupboard piled with folded pajamas.

Why did a convention of filing—Spellbinders, I mean—why did they have pajamas in children's sizes?

When I emerged from the bathroom in a cloud of steam, I felt embarrassed to be wearing pajamas. Daylight still shone through the window.

"You'll be very tired," Aunt Carrie said, as if reading my mind. "Hungry and tired. Supper and bed. But first. Follow me." Like Aunt Franny, she can be a forceful person, my Aunt Carrie.

Obediently, I followed her along a corridor of closed doors until she paused at one. A square window was set high in it.

"Here," she said. "Have a squiz," and, surprisingly, she whooshed me into the air and held me close enough to the glass to bump my nose.

An ordinary classroom, lined with desks at which were seated boys and girls around my age. At the front, a woman in a gray skirt appeared to be teaching. The children were writing.

"What are—" I began, confused, but then my eyes landed on one of the girls.

In the far corner. Black hair curled below the ears.

Hsiang. I was sure of it.

Automatically, my eyes swung to the left—and yes, that was Georgia. Dark skin, bright eyes.

"Keep looking," Aunt Carrie instructed me. She seemed to be having no trouble holding my weight.

My eyes ran along the rows, and—

Middle desk. Raising her hand to ask a question.

My cousin.

Bronte Mettlestone.

"So," Aunt Carrie said, setting me down and bustling along the corridor again. I followed. "You aren't losing your mind. You *did* see Hsiang, Georgia, and Bronte. Nobody's supposed to know they're here. Top secret. That's why the girls ran when you spotted them."

"What are they *doing* here?" I called, but Aunt Carrie was already racing up another flight of stairs, and along another corridor of doors. She threw one open.

"Perfect," she said. "Hop into bed, Esther. Supper soon, a chat first."

It was a small room, curtained windows, a single bed with a blue spread, and a wooden desk with chair.

Obediently, I slid under the covers and sat up, leaning against the headboard. Aunt Carrie dragged out the desk chair and sat down.

"Right," she said, briskly. "If you have been chosen by an element of nature—rain, I assume—to become a Fiend, well, there's not a thing that I or any Spellbinder, Faery, doctor, or anybody alive today can do about it."

I stared at her.

"Nothing?" I whispered.

"That's not meant to scare you. That's meant to say, let's not even think about it for now. I've telegrammed your father to come here urgently. Maybe he'll know more—he's the expert. Meantime, keep in mind that most people think Fiends were never even real. And the pattern on your skin has gone now, so that's something."

My head was spinning. "If I *am* going to turn into an evil monster, is it even *safe* for me to be here? Will *you*—and everyone else here—be all right?"

"Of course it's not safe," Aunt Carrie declared. "You'd no doubt want to kill us all."

My voice trembled. "I promise not to do that."

"You can't promise that. Won't be able to keep the promise. If you became a Fiend, there'd be nothing good left of you at all."

I knew this was the wrong question but I couldn't help asking: "Will I be *very ugly*?"

Aunt Carrie considered, eyes to the ceiling. "Don't remember seeing a picture of a Rain Fiend in any of the books, but I would think your appearance would change in some peculiar ways."

I started to cry then. Embarrassing. I was about to turn into a monster and kill my best friends, my cousin, my aunt, and all the other various strangers here, and I was bothered about becoming ugly.

Aunt Carrie patted my head. "Let's talk about something else," she said. "Put it out of your mind. You'll be wondering why Hsiang, Georgia, and Bronte are here." That was true. "Right, I suspect you already know that I'm not a filing clerk."

"Well . . . ," I began.

"You know a lot, Esther. You listen, don't you?" She smiled as if this was a compliment. Surprising. I'm usually being scolded for eavesdropping.

"You know I'm actually a Spellbinder?" she checked.

I nodded. "Carabella-the-Great," I whispered.

She chuckled. "Grand title. And you know this is a convention of Spellbinders?"

"Well, my friend Katya told me *that*," I said defensively.

"And you know there've been issues with the oceans?"

"*Everybody* knows that."

Aunt Carrie laughed. "You're not in trouble, Esther," she said. "Nothing wrong with knowing things. For several years—decades actually—Spellbinders have been worried about the oceans. We sense an evil force there but it's not regular shadow magic. Tides have changed directions. Berg Trolls have let loose their quills. People have died. Your father's theory is that it's a Fiend from classical times. *Nobody* believes him—not Spellbinders, not anybody else. But I like and respect your father, so I've listened to him. I've read the material he's given me. And I think he *might* be right."

I must have looked worried because she added quickly, and gently: "But maybe not. It's more likely just environmental change and some twist on shadow magic in the ocean."

A knock on the door.

Aunt Carrie opened it and a whiskery man in a cardigan entered carrying a tray.

Carrot soup, a bread roll, sausage pasta, and a bowl of ice cream.

The man set this before me and withdrew.

Gesturing for me to begin eating, Aunt Carrie resumed talking: "Ocean changes have displaced many populations. Shadow Mages have been moving to new, unprotected regions—such as these mountains—and wreaking havoc. You know Dahlia in the Orange Blossom Tea Shop? Wears an apple pendant? She and the local mayor, Carson Brody"—she grimaced—"they've been coordinating protection around these parts. We've needed more Spellbinders lately so we've started training children." She sighed. "I don't know if I agree. It's too young. I *said* that your friend Katya wasn't ready to maintain a Spellbinding

ring around your school, but that Carson"—another scowl—
"disobeyed me. And then he didn't get anybody to replace her!
Not until your father put his foot down and mentioned he knew
me! However." She breathed deeply, calming herself. "If your
father is right and there's a Fiend in the ocean, we will need a
team of the strongest Spellbinders to bind his evil. Young Spellbinders are capable of nimble, imaginative spellbinding. I'm
putting together a team of the new Spellbinders along with
older, experienced ones. Which brings me to your cousin Bronte
and your friends Hsiang and Georgia. As you've probably
guessed by now, they're all Spellbinders."

I *should* have guessed. I mean I'd just seen them in the classroom. Still:

"Hsiang and Georgia?" I dropped my soup spoon with a clatter. "No! Hsiang got a cricket scholarship to a sports academy
and Georgia got invited to a conservatory to play her flute!"

Aunt Carrie shook her head. "Those are their cover stories.
They were recruited to training centers early this year. I've
invited them here with the most talented Spellbinders for specialized training. Of course, they *are* very talented at sport and
music—Spellbinders often have some other specialized skill."

"Of course they do," I said flatly.

Aunt Carrie blinked.

"I already knew Bronte was a Spellbinder," I admitted. "And
she's a great swimmer. That's another skill of hers. My sister
Imogen can also swim. Astrid can read people. Whereas I'm
just Esther. And about to be a Fiend."

There was a long quiet from Aunt Carrie. She squinted,
studying my face.

I wished she would hurry and leave because I wanted to cry
again.

She was silent a long time, and then she spoke slowly. "Your
friend Stefan, in his reading about classical history, he only
read one book, yes?"

"I think so."

"And it sounds like the book was all about Fiends?"

"Yes."

"I don't blame him," Aunt Carrie continued. "Exciting. Esther, you know how the early mages used to mine for thread for their spells? Whereas now they just imagine the thread?"

That seemed an odd switch of subjects, but I nodded.

"What color thread did Shadow Mages use?" she asked.

I knew this one. "Red and black."

"Spellbinders?"

"Green and gold."

"Right. And what about True Mages?"

"Silvery blue."

Aunt Carrie smoothed a rumple in my covers. "There's both evil *and* good in nature," she said. "If Stefan had read any more, he'd know that in classical myth a colorful pattern appeared on the skin of people chosen by nature to be *Weavers* too. Not just Fiends."

I stared. I'd forgotten about Weavers.

"Fiends were evil, Weavers were good. There's always balance."

I nodded, interested.

Aunt Carrie placed her hands on my shoulders and looked into my eyes. "Esther, I don't know what color the patterns were in the ancient stories. But if those stories were true, I think that Fiends and Weavers were the predecessors to today's magic. And the web pattern on your skin. Think about what color it was."

Something fluttered in my chest. Green, gold, silver, blue.

The colors of Spellbinders and True Mages.

"It's *possible*," Aunt Carrie said, speaking very gently. "I'm not at all certain, but it's *possible* the rain did choose you. Not to be a Fiend, Esther. To be a Weaver. A Rain Weaver."

CHAPTER 120

ONE MORE THING happened as Aunt Carrie left the room.

She paused at the door.

Rain Weaver, I was thinking, *Rain Weaver, Rain Weaver.* The words like swinging lanterns in my heart.

"I'm probably wrong," she said. "Likely you've not been chosen for *anything.*"

Oh. The lantern light snuffed out.

"But I know I'm right about this," she continued. "You are brave, strong, and very bright. Your father told me how you protected your school after Katya left. I was so astonished I dropped my coffee! Stained my favorite trousers!"

"Sorry," I said automatically.

Aunt Carrie rolled her eyes. "My point, Esther, is that I forbid you to say even *one* more time—" She paused and echoed my words angrily: *"I'm just Esther."*

"Just Esther," she muttered, marching out of the room.

I stared at the closed door, my heart stumbling about like somebody lost in a dark forest—then, and this was almost at once, I fell asleep.

CHAPTER 121

THE NEXT MORNING I woke to a *tick—tick—tick.*

The clock on the wall.

5:00 A.M., it said, but I was wide awake. Outside the window the rain fell steadily.

Rain Weaver, I thought, and my heart joined the *tick—tick—tick.*

It was a wild guess, I reminded myself. Aunt Carrie had said she was probably wrong. Also: wouldn't I *know* if I was a Weaver? And wouldn't I know how to . . . *be* a Weaver? I had no clue.

Still.

Tickticktick.

I opened the door, slid along the quiet corridor, down a flight of stairs, and stopped on the landing.

Below me, Aunt Carrie, in a robe, was opening the front door.

"Carrie!" cried a low voice, and into the lobby burst my father.

I was about to run down the stairs to him, but Father was already talking.

"Is it true?" he said in a quick, hoarse voice. He was closing an umbrella and pushing it into the stand. "You think you've found a *Rain* Weaver? Seriously?"

I crouched down, watching through the banisters. Father's eyes were bright and excited.

"Maybe," Aunt Carrie said cautiously. "I'm not at all sure—I just—"

"But if it's true!" Father shrugged out of his coat. "This could *save* the Kingdoms and Empires, Carrie! You have the person here, you say? Is it a man or a woman?"

"Neither." Aunt Carrie's voice was low and hesitant. "It's a child."

Father, who had been reaching to hang his coat on the rack, paused. He turned slowly and looked at her.

"Oh," he said gravely. "Well, now. I suppose—"

"Nigel, there's more." Aunt Carrie placed a hand on his shoulder. "It's Esther. It's your Esther."

Father's face was as white as plasterboard. His coat fell slowly to the floor. "It's not," he whispered. "It's not."

CHAPTER 122

NOW, I DON'T know about you, but confusion annoys me.

And I was *completely* confused at this point.

Was classical history real? Had *I* been chosen? To be good or bad? Was I a Fiend or a *Rain Weaver*? And if I was a Rain Weaver, wasn't that a good thing? Why did it make my father drop his coat?

I had other questions too but those were key.

Ordinarily I might have crept back to my room so that Father and Aunt Carrie wouldn't know I'd eavesdropped, but I'd had enough.

I ran downstairs, skidded to a stop before the pair of them, and demanded: "*What* is going on?"

Aunt Carrie led us into a room just off the entryway. She called it "the drawing room." It had once been a classroom and still had a blackboard on the wall, with a tin of chalk. For a moment, I thought we were all going to "draw" in the "drawing room." There was a ring of armchairs where the desks should have been though, and we sat in these. Tea, warm muffins, and orange wedges (for vitamin C, Aunt Carrie said) were brought in for us by the whiskery man.

First, Aunt Carrie explained to Father why she thought I might be a Rain Weaver. "Of course," she finished, "the only thing I know about classical history is the material you've sent me, Nigel."

Father leaned back in his armchair. He said the muffins were very good and remarked on the good luck of Stefan having read about the markings on the skin. He seemed much calmer now, and this relaxed me. I even ate a wedge of orange.

"All right, Esther," Father said, steepling his fingers. "I'm going to be honest with you. You might have read about the oceanographer named Alfreda who traveled to the deepest, darkest ocean and was dead when she returned?"

I nodded.

"As I told you in Vanquishing Cove, I'm almost certain there's an Ocean Fiend down there—Jonathan J. Lanyard—and he killed her." Father studied me gravely. "Yet I still can't convince the authorities that the classical stories were even *real*, let alone that one of the Fiends has somehow returned." He sipped from his tea. "Hand me another of those muffins, will you? What are they? Apple and cinnamon? So good!" He was being very matter-of-fact considering how serious he sounded.

"If I'm right," he continued, brushing away the muffin crumbs, "I believe that Jonathan is planning something big. Now, the Fiends and Weavers in the stories used to be drawn to the element or landscape that had chosen them. They would spend more and more time in that element. In one story, a Fiend did not leave his forest for fifty years and then, when he *wanted* to leave, it was impossible. So I would think that, if this *is* Jonathan, he is now fully entwined with the ocean, so to speak. That would explain why he hasn't emerged from the deep. That's something at least—he can only affect life in the ocean and along its coasts. If he could move about on land, nothing could stop him."

"Not even Spellbinders?" I breathed.

Aunt Carrie and Father glanced at each other, and then Father placed his cup back into its saucer. "Fiends are a thousand times more powerful than today's Shadow Mages, Esther," he said gently. "If it really is a Fiend, even if we got every Spellbinder working together to bind his power—the binding would last an afternoon.

"Only a classical Weaver could defeat him."

Tick, tick, tick. (The clock from my room seemed to be trapped in my heart.)

"You don't think *I* might—" I felt embarrassed even to say it.

Father sighed. "I'll tell you a true story. Around a year ago, a couple named Soren and Livia Hillside, both Whisperers, happened to hear a Whisper from the future. The Whisper told them that a classical Fiend would turn out to be living in deep water near the Candle Islands. They didn't understand what they were hearing. They knew the classical stories but had assumed, like everyone else, that they were merely stories. So they contacted the universities with classical history departments. Nobody took any notice, of course. Apart from everyone seeing the stories as merely mythology, Whisperers are not yet respected as they should be, I'm afraid. However, when I got the Hillsides' letter, I asked a research assistant, Gordon, to get in touch.

"Gordon met with the Whisperers last summer. They took a boat out to the Candle Islands together. That's when Gordon called me. When he described what he'd seen, I knew it was a Fiend. And most likely Jonathan J. Lanyard."

"I was under the table," I reminded him.

Father nodded. "With the lemonade. The stories of Jonathan J. Lanyard describe him as having been in his late twenties when he was chosen. Short, broad, red hair, freckles, and enormously charming. *A dash of bright light in his blue eyes* is how the stories put it. *A smile like golden sunshine after a blizzard.* He was a fisherman living in a coastal village, but he had sailed to the nearest coastal city and used his charm to cheat the local hospital there out of a sack of gold that had been a charitable gift to them. Sailing back home with his stolen gold, Jonathan saw the weblike pattern on his skin—

"Back then, everyone knew what the pattern meant. He'd been chosen by the ocean to become a Fiend. He accepted. After that, his power was immense, his heart truly rotten. He traveled about, building himself castles on the coast of every kingdom. Befriended and partied with the Fiends of lakes, rivers, and streams. Purely for his own pleasure, he sank ships, washed away harvests, drowned thousands. He spent more and more time in the ocean, and eventually grew gills along his jawline. They say his blood turned cold, his bones softened, nerve system altered. Went about town dressed only in his swimming trunks, skin covered in a luminous layer of pearl-blue fish scales.

"With most Fiends in classical stories, there is eventually a tale of the Weaver who defeats the Fiend. With Jonathan, the story is that, over time, he had all the luxuries of his castles shifted to sea caves, spending ever more time beneath the waves. He battled and *defeated* an Ocean Weaver, then subsided deep into the ocean. For a while, he still emerged on occasion—to capsize passing boats, send immense waves across beaches and into villages beyond. Each of Jonathan's attacks, it was said, was preceded by strange discolorations and temperature variations in the water. The water would appear patterned in layers of black and red—eventually a murky orange color—and it would turn ice cold, boiling hot, ice cold again.

"Other Weavers hunted Jonathan, but land Weavers could not compete with him in the ocean, and water Weavers—of lakes, rivers, and so on—were never going to be as strong as the Fiend of the Ocean.

"Eventually, there were no more sightings or attacks, and it was assumed he had died. Fiends and Weavers were not immortal—they could die of illness, accident, old age.

"A thousand years went by. And then Soren and Livia Hillside, as I mentioned, heard the Whispers. Gordon traveled with them to the islands and studied the water. On their return boat trip, the Hillsides both heard a *second* Whisper from the future. This one said that a classical Weaver was going to emerge amongst the Grade Six class at Katherine Valley Boarding School."

Tick, tick, tick, tick, tick.

"But *I'm* . . ." I began.

Father smiled. "Yes, you're in the Grade Six class at Katherine Valley. However, I believed the Weaver must be the parent, or other adult relative, of a child in your grade. In all the stories,

Fiends and Weavers have *always* been adults." He gave me a rueful glance. "This is why I've been so busy all year. The Hillsides and I have been traveling across Kingdoms and Empires, visiting the parents and relatives of every girl in your grade. Trying to locate the Weaver amongst them."

There was a knock on the door, and the whiskery man came in and took our plates away.

"Incidentally," Father said to me, "the Hillsides needed a boarding school for their own daughter while they traveled. I recommended this one—she's in your grade."

"Autumn Hillside!"

"Exactly." Father nodded. "Now, Esther, what with the Whisper the Hillsides heard, the patterns that appeared on your skin, and the fact that you've got a connection to rain—it seems *possible* that the rain might have chosen you. But—"

He stopped. Brushed the muffin crumbs from his trousers again. Stood and picked up a piece of chalk from the pot by the board. "In classical times," he said, "if a person was chosen to become a Fiend, it was because he or she had experienced some great pleasure at another's cost. Jonathan was delighted to have tricked the nearby hospital into giving him their charitable gold."

He wrote a word on the board:

Pleasure.

"This would catch the attention of the evil in nature. It would offer the person the chance to become a Fiend. The web pattern on the skin indicated the offer had been made. To accept, the person needed only speak the traditional words. In those days, everyone knew the words. Jonathan would have known what the pattern meant when it appeared. He would have chosen to speak the words."

"Wait, so they wouldn't *have* to accept?"

I'd been worrying for nothing! If I'd been chosen to become a Fiend, I could have just said: "No thanks!" Or just *not* said the traditional words.

I'd have to tell Stefan to read more than one book on a topic in the future.

"Why would anyone accept?" I asked.

Father pressed the chalk against his palm. "Some people love power. And this is *immense* evil power. There's also this. When a Fiend speaks the words of acceptance, he or she experiences again the great pleasure that caught nature's attention in the first place. Now, on the other hand, when a person was chosen to become a Weaver, it was because—"

He glanced at Aunt Carrie before continuing: "It was because the person had endured great—"

And he wrote a different word on the board:

Suffering.

"So *much* of this," he said, tapping the word, "that the *good* in nature would notice, take pity, and save the person." Father's voice softened. "This makes me doubt that you have been chosen, Esther. As your father, I would surely know if you'd ever suffered that much, wouldn't I? But I travel often, so perhaps I missed it? Can you think? Can you remember a time of immense suffering?"

I thought hard. "I've had ear infections," I said. "And tonsillitis. Grazed my elbows and knees a lot."

"I don't think those would've been enough," Father said apologetically. "Although they do hurt, I agree."

"Oh!" I cried. "My broken ankle! It was agony! And it was raining that day!"

Father tilted his head. "Perhaps," he said doubtfully. "It could have happened at any time in your life—the rain would have chosen to save you and would have made the formal offer of Weaver-ship at that time. You may not have noticed it then. But it would find ways to remind you of the offer—such as through the pattern on your skin you saw today. Nature has profound knowledge of itself and would know that an Ocean Fiend is growing in power. So it would have been *urging* you to accept the offer lately. Frantic for your attention. But here's what you need to know. To accept the offer to become a Weaver, the person must speak the traditional words." He stopped, took a breath, and added: "At which point, the person suffers the exact same pain again."

I blinked. "That seems a silly system," I ventured.

"Yes." He turned to the board, raised the chalk as if to write something, then turned back. "Which is why—apart from the fact that you'd have to battle with an Ocean Fiend—I hope it's not you."

"Well, but if it's important," I said bravely. "I'm sure I can manage that broken ankle again."

Once again, Father and Aunt Carrie exchanged glances.

"If I *have* been chosen, and I *do* accept by . . . saying the words . . . then what will happen to me?" Would I grow tall and strong, and suddenly have a sword in my hand? Would I know how to *use* the sword?

"Nothing," Father replied. "You would simply have immense power—to defeat evil and do good. Rain Weavers were amongst the strongest Weavers, I believe."

Father wiped his hands on a napkin. "Can I use the telephone, Carrie?" he asked. "I'll call Nancy." He looked at me. "Perhaps your mother will remember something else that might have brought this on."

CHAPTER 123

MOTHER COULD NOT recall a single incidence of my having suffered enormously in the rain. I could hear her speaking earnestly through the telephone speaker.

Eventually, Father hunched his shoulders, turned away, and lowered his voice. Then he hung up.

"She's taking the morning coach here," he told me. "We can talk through memories together and see if we can solve this. We should also get your sisters across from the school to ask them."

"They're away at the poker competition," I said. "Due back tomorrow."

Father startled. "Why aren't you with them?"

"Mrs. Pollock said I had Lire syndrome and couldn't go."

"*What* syndrome?" Father muttered, but he didn't wait for an answer: "We'll ask your sisters tomorrow. I'll check in with Principal Hortense too."

Once again, I was confused. Why did it matter what "suffering" might have caused me to be chosen? I either had been or had not. If someone would just tell me the "traditional words," I could speak them and find out! Either nothing would happen or I'd "suffer"—the broken ankle hadn't been *that* bad—and be done with it.

Then somehow I could defeat the Fiend? That part seemed vague.

But I didn't get a chance to ask any of this, as the whiskery man approached, cleared his throat, and said: "Excuse me? Today's newspapers?"

And handed over a stack to Father.

The front page of each bore a huge headline.

COASTAL TOWNS DRENCHED BY KING TIDES, said one.

DARK TIDES SWEEP OCEANS, said the next.

The third simply said: TIDAL WAVE!

Father and I read the articles together. In the last two days, it turned out, several coastal villages had been swept away. Coastal cities were reporting seaweed flung about their streets, fish in puddles, turtles and stingrays in gutters. Ships' captains were sending urgent, panicked messages, then falling silent.

Father made several phone calls. They all ended with him slamming down the phone.

Eventually, he and Aunt Carrie had a serious discussion.

"They won't believe me," he told her. "Nobody will believe it. In fact, the authorities want to send *another* submarine down to deepest ocean—a team this time—to see if they can find out what *aquatic phenomenon* is causing these ocean issues. They think Alfreda Reinozovski died because of the pressure in her submarine not being properly equalized. They think the idea that it's a *person* down there is preposterous. Everyone in that submarine will die, Carrie."

Carrie gazed at him carefully.

"We'll deal with it," she decided. "My Spellbinders and I will bind him for as long as we can. For enough time to keep the people in that submarine alive, anyway. We'll go to the Candle Islands. We'll set out this afternoon."

"It'll take a few days to get there," Father pointed out.

But Aunt Carrie said she'd been holding meetings with Crystal Faeries in the area. They'd created a helium-filled balloon for her, as a form of transport. It could carry passengers through the sky at rapid speeds.

They'd take several of these balloons and arrive the next day.

Gravely, Father agreed.

* * *

Half an hour later, I stood against the wall in the entryway while over a hundred Spellbinders—men, women, and children—poured down the stairs toward the front door. They wore Spellbinder capes and appeared agitated and excited.

Two of these figures tore sideways and threw themselves at me.

Georgia and Hsiang.

My best friends. Their beautiful, beaming faces under hoods. I almost burst into tears.

"Esther! We miss you so, so much!"

"We're *so* sorry we had to run away when we saw you in town!"

"Also we're really, really sorry we haven't answered your letters this year. We weren't allowed."

"How come you're here, Esther? Are you training too? Are you a Spell—"

"GIRLS! COME ALONG!"

Aunt Carrie beckoned my friends away, and they hugged me again, waved, and disappeared into the crowd of capes.

A moment later, another hand touched my shoulder and lifted back her cape to reveal her face. It was Bronte, the adventurer. She was smiling broadly. "Hello, Esther."

I hugged her. "Darling Bronte!" Once again, I was a bit overcome.

"Sorry I had to run away when you saw me passing the gate."

Everyone was apologizing. They were heading out into severe danger, apologizing as they left.

"LET'S KEEP GOING, EVERYONE!"

Bronte shrugged, nodded at me, and rejoined the others.

"Good luck," I called to her.

She turned back and grinned.

Now, I might not be as talented as my sister Astrid at reading faces, but I *am* pretty good at it. I've had plenty of practice. In Bronte's smile, and in Georgia's and Hsiang's waves—in the gestures and movement of all these hurrying Spellbinders—there was a single, powerful emotion.

Terror.

They were as frightened as a poker player who's bet his entire fortune on nothing but a pair of twos.

Not surprising.

They were about to take on the greatest evil ever known.

CHAPTER 124

BY THE TIME Mother arrived, the Old Schoolhouse was quiet.

Father ushered Mother into the drawing room while she was still trying to close her umbrella.

"Shall I take my bag—" she began, but Father said, "Put your bag down. We'll find you a room later."

It was a strange conversation then. We ate afternoon tea and we listed every illness and injury I'd ever had.

Father kept saying, "Oh yes, the bronchitis, that was nasty but no," or "Hmm, didn't she tear her foot open on a nail that time—no, that was Astrid."

Mother kept shaking her head saying: "Honestly, she *can't* have this rain thing, Nigel. She can't."

And I kept trying to prove that I *had* suffered, by listing splinters, paper cuts, and particularly unpleasant head colds.

Eventually, Father tapped on his own head and reached for his briefcase.

"Look," he said. "Principal Hortense says there's nothing in their records about Esther getting particularly sick or injured. They'd have contacted us anyway. Maybe it *was* just the ankle?"

"Is there a room here where I can do some work?" Mother asked, reaching for her satchel.

"Hold up." Father was leafing through papers quickly. "Here's something. Listen to this. It's my own translation, but I think I got it right. *One knows that one has received the offer when one sees the pattern on the skin.* Hold up, Nancy, there's more. Sit down. *But the Weaver may also speak of strange visions, dreams, and glancing memories, especially if the call for a Weaver is an urgent one.* Have you had any recurring dreams or visions lately, Esther?"

"Oh, *dreams*," Mother said, standing abruptly.

The fluttering had started up again. It was in my stomach, and around my temples.

"I *told* you about my dream," I said to Father. "All year, I've been dreaming about lying on a picnic blanket. Remember, I recognized the landscape from the train?"

Father nodded seriously. "So you did. But, of course, you'd never been to that region, so—"

I cleared my throat and looked at Mother. She sighed and shrugged.

"I *had* been there," I said. "Mother and Aunt Emma took us on that train when we were little. And we *did* have a picnic by the rock shaped like a turtle."

Father flung himself back in his armchair, dropping his papers. "Nancy! You didn't! On that visit you took to Spindrift years ago? The train was brand new then! So dangerous! And with the *girls*?"

"Oh, hush," Mother said. "It worked out. Nothing went wrong! The train did break down and everyone got off to have picnics. They couldn't fix the engine but they sent a convoy of carriages to rescue us and we all got out fine!"

Tickticktickticktick. The clock was inside my head now, and running much too fast.

"But, Mother," I said. "Something *did* go wrong. In the dream, I'm alone! And in the dream—" I realized this with a rush and turned to Father: "In the dream, it *starts to rain and I always wake with a terrible pain in my chest.*"

Father was holding his palm across his face, as if to protect himself. "Nancy," he said softly. "Did you leave her alone? Just for a few moments? To go and—I don't know, pick a flower or something?"

"No!" Mother cried. "Of course not! Why would I leave a two-year-old alone on a picnic blanket! Esther, honestly, as if I'd ever *forget* you!"

A rush of cold flooded me from the top of my head to my toenails. "Mother," I said. "You *do* forget me."

"Nonsense! I—"

"You forgot to come and see my artwork."

"Oh, for goodness—"

"You forgot to visit my classroom."

"Now, I *know* that's not—"

"You *forgot my birthday this year.*"

Father's head had been swinging back and forth between us, and here he exclaimed, "Nancy! Did you?"

"Of course not! Esther, goodness, what a lot of fuss. Did you have breakfast this morning? Because you *always* get cranky when—"

I stood up. I looked her in the eye.

And I shouted:

"YOU DO FORGET ME! STOP MAKING EXCUSES!"

"Esther," Mother scolded. "Now honestly—"

I took a deep breath, and screamed.

A scream without words, a real scream, a scream that burned my throat. Both my parents reeled back, shocked, and then surged toward me. I batted their hands away, took a deep breath, and screamed again and again and again—

Until I saw something—

My mother's face had been filled with frowns, but suddenly, in an instant, all the frowns, the concern, the color, the expressions, seemed to sweep *up* toward her hairline, and then to plunge away.

I stopped screaming.

Mother made a peculiar wheezing sound. She shook her head slowly and staggered sideways. Father caught hold of her, helping her back into her armchair.

"I remember," she whispered.

Then she curled up her legs, and—slowly, slowly—she spoke.

CHAPTER 125

HER VOICE WAS very strange. It was as if she was reaching deep into the motor of a machine and wrenching out its pieces, one at a time. Shaking her head in disbelief at each piece. Reaching in once more for the next.

So the story emerged like this:

We'd been waiting for the train to be repaired . . .

For hours . . .

It was getting dark . . .

Lots of people having picnics around us . . .

But Emma and I knew how dangerous the setting sun was . . .

We were growing . . . anxious . . .

Shouts came . . .

. . . carriages were coming to rescue us. They were rolling up on the other side of the train . . .

There might not be enough for everyone, people were saying. *Run across the fields,* they said . . .

. . .

. . .

I told Emma to take Imogen. The pair of them took off at a sprint. Emma held Imogen's little hand. Her little legs zooming, keeping up . . .

Later, I heard, they got onto the first carriage . . .

I got into a panic . . .

Two small children . . .

How to take them fastest?

Should I push baby Astrid in her pram and carry Esther? . . .

Esther was asleep on the rug . . .

Should I put Esther in the pram too? . . .

But the field was muddy and bumpy. Pram could slow us down . . .

I picked up baby Astrid . . .

I would carry them both . . .

Leave the pram. Or was that a mistake? Faster with the pram? . . .

More shouting—louder . . .

"Hurry!" "The carriages can't wait!" "Anyone who doesn't go now will be left behind!"

A man running by turned and hollered at me: "WHAT ARE YOU DOING? *RUN! . . .*"

The word snapped through my daze . . .

I *ran* . . .

Baby Astrid in my arms . . .

Just squeezed into the last carriage—and we galloped out of there, the carriage rattled and swung from side to side . . .

Shadow Mages were chasing us, hurling spells, jeering . . .

It was all I could do to hold on to the baby, not fall out the back . . .

Just got to the border of the realm . . .

And away, reached an inn . . .

I was told that Emma was at a different inn.

. . . I knew she was with Imogen and I got it into my head that she had Esther too . . .

I don't know why. I just got it into my head . . .

The others are at the other inn, I thought . . .

So baby Astrid and I were both shaking, trembling, Astrid crying . . .

It was all I could do to find her some milk—settle her . . .

Then I collapsed into deepest sleep . . .

Next morning . . .

Very early . . .

Woke suddenly . . .

A pitchfork through my heart . . .

Emma had taken *Imogen* . . .

Just Imogen . . .

Not Esther . . .

I'd seen them running, Imogen's little legs . . .

Esther was still on the blanket.

The worst—the worst moment of my life . . .

I left Astrid sleeping in the cot . . .

Stole a horse from the inn's stables . . .

Rode back—rode that poor horse so hard—

The sweat was . . .

I remember I couldn't see from the sweat rolling down my forehead . . .

I stank of my own fear—

And, oh the relief—

She was there! You were there, Esther! Sitting on that picnic blanket. Babbling happily. Soaked through from the rain. But you were all right . . .

You were all right, weren't you, Esther?

And I said to you: *Let's pretend that never happened.*

And I took you back to the inn.

Astrid was still asleep in the cot.

See? I said. *It never happened.*

Mother stopped speaking at last, and looked up at me, her eyes crimson with tears.

"I'd forgotten," she said. "I made myself forget. But I did leave you there, Esther."

"All *night*," I whispered. "I was there *all* night?"

I hadn't expected that.

Father stood slowly. He placed a hand on my shoulder, paused for a moment, and walked out of the room.

He didn't look at Mother once.

CHAPTER 126

I WENT UPSTAIRS to my room and fell asleep.

That might sound odd but I couldn't think what else to do. I was suddenly overcome by tiredness, and fell into a deep, deep sleep.

The next morning, Father knocked on my door.

I blinked in the bright sunlight—it had finally stopped raining—and he walked in carrying a breakfast tray. It was strange, as if I was ill.

"A child left outside in a shadow realm for an entire night," Father began, pulling up a chair by my bed, "would almost certainly have been attacked by Ghouls. They would have tried to extract the essence—the light, I mean—of the child. The suffering would have been immense. Enough to kill a two-year-old, certainly. If the child did survive, it would only have been because of some extraordinary intervention. For example, an ancient power taking pity on the child."

This was even stranger. Father must be talking about *me*, but he kept saying "a child" or "the child." Also, Father is *always* funny—or trying to be funny, anyway. Even when he is angry with us, he can't resist tossing in a joke.

But I studied his face and all of his humor had fled.

"If the rain protected the child," Father continued, still in his peculiar, flat voice, "it might offer to make the child a Weaver. That offer would have been available to the child all its life. To accept the offer, the child would only need to speak the traditional words. Each line spoken would immerse the child in the suffering again—the suffering of Ghouls . . . of Ghouls extracting your light, Esther."

I nodded, trying to match his seriousness.

"Still, if I did that—and became a Weaver—I'd have a chance of stopping Jonathan J. Lanyard?" I asked.

Father nodded.

"All right," I said. "I'll try now."

Before more coastal towns got washed away. Before Bronte, Hsiang, and Georgia—and Aunt Carrie—and all the other Spellbinders—were in danger. Before the new submarines dove close to the Fiend.

"You need to think about it," Father urged. "The suffering will be—"

I interrupted. "What do I have to do?"

Father took a paper from his pocket, unfolded it, and straightened it out. There were four lines written in a language I didn't recognize.

"That's classical language," Father said. "Roughly translated, it means:

I thank you, oh great nature, oh mighty nature,

Marvelous rain

for this gift beyond gifts, beyond compare

I thank you, lo, what an honor!

I accept.

"I've written it out phonetically—you pronounce it just as it appears. As soon as you speak the first few words, you'll begin to feel the effects. It will get worse as you go along, only stopping when you reach the end. Give it some thought and try when you're ready."

"I'm going to try now," I announced.

Father flinched. "Have breakfast first," he suggested. "You would need all your strength for this. *All* your spirit."

I shook my head.

"I don't want to wait. Who cares if it hurts?"

It was very simple to me.

I snatched the paper out of his hand, looked down, and—

I don't like to tell this part of my story.

But here it is.

I read the first three words aloud and started screaming.

For the second time in two days, I screamed and screamed and screamed.

Dropped the paper.

"I *can't*," I sobbed. "I *can't*."

Impossible.

CHAPTER 127

 **IT WAS LIKE** lying on the ground with a huge boulder beside you and somebody decides to roll this boulder, very slowly and steadily, over your body.

Your skin, muscles, and bones crunch, splinter, and flatten.

Actually, that's not just what it was *like*.

That's what it was.

"I can't do it," I whispered, through my tears.

Father stroked my hair. He took the paper gently from my hand, crumpled it, and tossed it in the bin.

"You don't have to," he said. "Carrie and her Spellbinders will stop the Ocean Fiend. It's only one person. One freckly man. Eat your breakfast and don't even think about it. It's too much to ask—I shouldn't have let you try. I mean, you already went through it *once*, back—"

He stopped. A choking sound.

He left the room.

Later, I overheard him talking on the telephone in the entryway.

"She can't do it," he was saying. "It's not surprising. It's too much to ask of anyone, let alone a child."

Slowly, I walked back up the stairs, took the paper from the bin, studied the words, memorized them, looked up, opened my mouth to speak, and—

Before I'd even said a word, I shook violently, like a tree in a hurricane, dropped the paper, and ran back down the stairs, fleeing the very idea.

CHAPTER 128

FATHER FOUND ME sitting in the drawing room later that morning.

"Right then!" he said, clapping his hands.

He was going to send me back to school. I was useless to anyone, just Esther, a schoolgirl.

But he shook his head. "No, no. It's the last day of term. You may as well miss it. You need time with your sisters. They've returned from their competition and they're walking over here. We're all going out for lunch. We'll go into town as I'm meeting some people there."

"With Mother?" I asked.

"Your mother's in her room," Father said briskly.

Cluck, clack, clack went the door knocker.

I threw open the door, and there were Imogen and Astrid grinning at me.

As we walked down the hill to town, my sisters chatted, skipped a few steps, slowed down, skipped again. They leapt like goats between topics—

(Imogen would object to being described as goatlike, but I'm not changing it, sorry, Imogen.)

Topics of conversation included suspenseful moments in poker games, bedspreads in their hotel rooms, and the fact that a classical Fiend was sending the oceans and tides into chaos.

"We'll all drown," Astrid said, in such a matter-of-fact, resigned way that we laughed.

"We're very far from the coast here," Father told her, "and very high in the mountains. We'll be fine. And anyway, I'm sure the Spellbinders will succeed!"

We took a curve in the road, and there was Pillar Box Town laid out neatly before us. The main street and its flower stalls, shops, and cafés. Rows of houses and gardens. The games field. The swimming complex, freshly rebuilt, glass refracting the sunlight into sparkles. The silvery lake, reflecting the blue sky. Sounds of the lake lapping gently against its shores, birds querying this and that. *Everything,* I thought, smiling, *is going to be okay.*

That's the exact moment when thumping footsteps and panting breath sounded behind us. We all spun around.

CHAPTER 129

IT WAS PELAGIA.

Puffing, bending forward, hands on her knees. Her Katherine Valley tunic was crumpled.

"Hello!" said Father, very friendly. He strained to look behind her for a companion. He knows students aren't allowed to walk to town alone.

"It's just me," Pelagia panted. "I need to . . . Please help! I've got to . . ."

Imogen reached out and patted her shoulders: "What is it, Pel?"

At last, Pelagia straightened. Her cheeks were dark pink. She took another deep breath, stilled herself, and spoke loudly and clearly: "I am the child of Jonathan J. Lanyard."

CHAPTER 130

"EH?" SAID FATHER.

"My father's name is Jonathan J. Lanyard," Pelagia told him. "We live in a cavern in deepest, darkest ocean. We can breathe underwater and on land. This is why I swim so well."

"Oh *pffft*," I said. The others blinked at me.

"She's making it up," I said. "She must have been eavesdropping at the Old Schoolhouse somehow, and heard us talking about Jonathan J. Lanyard. Those stories she tells? They're lies."

"ESTHER!" Imogen cried.

Be careful of Pelagia, Katya had said.

"Sorry, Imogen," I said steadily. "I know you and Pelagia are friends. But you can't trust her."

Pelagia's face crumpled like old bark. Sudden tears rushed down her cheeks.

"You're right!" she sobbed. "I do make up stories! You *can't* trust me! But if you *don't* trust me"—she heaved a huge breath—*"people are going to die."* Then she spoke quickly, snuffling back tears, looking at her feet. "I truly am the child of the Fiend. He has sent me here on a mission."

Father seemed enthralled, like a professor who has uncovered an exciting new direction in his research. "Jonathan had a *child*?" he enthused. "I haven't seen that in any of the stories. Are they lost stories? You haven't inherited his red hair, I see. So it really *is* him back after all this time! And you're on a mission, you say?"

Pelagia glanced at Imogen. "I'm sorry, I wasn't allowed to tell the truth. That's why I had to invent stories about my past." Then she spoke to Father: "Yes, my mission was to wake the ten sleeping Fiends of rivers and lakes."

At this, Father stumbled sideways, as if someone had given him a shove. He stopped being a professor and became a person. His voice was hoarse: "*Ten* sleeping Fiends? There are *more* than just Jonathan?"

Pelagia wiped away her tears, her chin snapped up and she recited: "Many thousands of years ago, Fiends roamed the lands and the waters. But the evil Weavers destroyed too many of them, too easily! Almost all the Fiends of the land were crushed. My father realized that he and his Water Fiend friends would also be crushed. He persuaded his closest friends to conceal themselves deep within their water territories and to use their powers to place themselves in a form of hibernation. *In one thousand years,* they agreed, *we will wake and—*"

"Did they set an alarm for a thousand years?" Astrid checked.

Pelagia's brow crinkled slightly. "Not an alarm, exactly. More a thousand-year spell. However, only Father had the power to cast such a spell. As Ocean Fiend, he is the most powerful of all Water Fiends." Her voice returned to its strange tone, as if she was reciting a school text. "*In one thousand years, they agreed, we will wake. By then, the Weavers will no longer guard the lands and oceans!* Anyway, when Father woke, the plan was that he'd wake his friends. Together they would rule the Kingdoms and Empires. Together, they would swamp as much of the Kingdoms and Empires as possible with the waters that they commanded, so that they could live in a world of water. Five decades ago, my—"

"Hold up," Father said. "They'd *what*?"

But Pelagia only sped up her recital. "Five decades ago, my father woke as planned. He found he could no longer leave the ocean. Since then, he has been building his powers anew—playing with currents and coastal floods. He raised me to live upon land and in water, so that I might travel the Kingdoms and Empires, diving deep to wake his friends."

Pelagia's chin returned to its regular position. "I've done it. They're awake. Now they want to cover as much land as they can with water."

"We'll drown!" Astrid cried.

"Land dwellers have structures that float on the water," Pelagia replied. "Boats and ships, they're called. If they put their minds to it—my father told me—they could also learn to live *under*water."

"Well, I don't know about that," Imogen said sternly.

Pelagia nodded at her. Her voice was becoming more and more her own again. "That's what I've been realizing, you know. Even if some people survive on boats, so many will drown! But the Fiends are awake! I woke the Fiend in Turquoise Lake first. I sneaked into town before breakfast, dove until I found her, woke her, and told her to wait for the signal to begin the flood. I woke the others during the swimming tournament. We traveled close to the nine other Fiends, Imogen—that's why I kept sneaking away. But the more time I've spent here, the more I've grown to like land-dwelling people! It's not your fault you can't live in the water! And now I don't *want* everyone to drown!"

"Of course not," Astrid murmured, patting her arm sympathetically.

Father was making peculiar sounds in the back of his throat.

"Today, my father has signaled for the flood to begin," Pelagia continued. "The Fiends will have received the message. And Turquoise Lake is huge. We need to warn the people! I don't know how much—"

At that moment, a ripple ran right across the lake as if it was being unzipped.

"Oh!" cried Pelagia—and my father began to run.

So did my sisters.

"GET TO HIGHER GROUND!" my father shouted in the direction of the streets below, his arms waving wildly. The people there turned slowly, gazing back at him.

Pelagia set off too, but I grabbed her by the sleeve and dragged her back.

CHAPTER 131

SHE WAS TELLING the truth.

I knew it now.

I remembered a flash of light, Pelagia slipping through the school's front door, hair wet, a towel over her shoulder.

Sitting by the pond, murmuring, "There's too much . . . responsibility."

Wistful and sad: another flash of light.

"He will use the ocean to flood all the coastal regions," she told me now, speaking firmly. "And the ten lakes and rivers across the Kingdoms and Empires will swamp inland regions."

"Too much for the Spellbinders," I breathed.

"Come on!" Pelagia urged. "We need to warn the town!"

But saving one town was not enough.

"How do you communicate?" I asked. "With your father?"

"Bioluminescence."

I nodded—then stopped. "Bio-what?"

"Bioluminescence. It means light. Living light. Like glow-worms and fireflies. It's how sea creatures communicate in deepest, darkest ocean. Since we've been on land, Father has been sending light messages to me and to the newly woken Fiends in their lake and rivers."

As she spoke, I was watching the main street—my father and sisters were still shouting, but people were either smiling at them, frowning at them, or taking no notice. The lake, a huge expanse of blue, was perfectly still again, shining in the sun.

On its shore, people threw crusts of bread to ducks. On its surface, they relaxed in paddleboats.

My mind began racing so fast I could hardly catch up with it.

"What if *you* sent a message?" I asked. "Pretend it's from your father? Tell all the Fiends that the flooding has been canceled!"

Pelagia's face startled. "I mean I *could,* but . . ."

But what? Why would she not? Then I realized: "You'd get in trouble?"

We held each other's gaze, Pelagia's face animated by emotion.

"You're frightened?" I whispered.

That's when the lake attacked.

CHAPTER 132

HAVE YOU EVER been lying down in a bathtub and slid yourself forward, and then quickly back, then forward, and quickly back, forward, back, forward, back—

—faster and faster

—until the bathwater surges *right over the edge of the tub and lands with a SPLASH!* on the floor? (Bath mat, clothes, tiles get drenched—*big* trouble from your mother.)

Well, at first the lake appeared to be playing that game. Water seemed to *lean* in one direction, then back, *lean,* and then back, lapping at the distant banks then careening toward the closest, back and forth, back and forth—

Until a great *surge* of water threw itself with a sound—not a splash, but a sound like the *CLASH* of giant cymbals, onto the banks—

—drenching the people standing there—

Back into the lake, washing first one way, then the other, back and forth, back and forth,

A bigger, mightier wave forming—

And then, with a ferocious howl, a thunderous roar, it flung itself at the town.

CHAPTER 133

"TRY!" I SHOUTED. "Pelagia! *Please!*"

Water was climbing the hill rapidly toward us. Pelagia and I sprinted away from it, splashes dashing at our ankles and backs.

We scrambled up a tree, branch after branch, scratched by bark and spiky leaves, and stopped when we could climb no further.

The water stretched toward us, then slid away, back down the hill, back into the town, and there it joined the huge body of water that had once been the lake but that now frothed and surged, swerving around corners and up laneways, pounding against brick walls, thwacking windows.

Again and again, water reared up and *smashed* down, *boom, boom, boom.*

For a moment all I could see was swell and foam—and then amidst the chaos, I caught glimpses of objects—a rubbish bin rolling across the water's surface, books flying along, pages flapping wildly, doormats, tables, chairs. A carriage, half-submerged, was tossed about, fruit stalls broke into splinters, umbrellas, napkins, cushions, panes of glass—

Another *boom* and the newly constructed swimming pool wall exploded. Shattered glass scattered onto the water's surface, gleaming in sunlight—

A dog paddled madly—

—People.

People clambering onto roofs, dragging others up behind them; wrapping arms around lampposts, legs flailing in the rush of water; clutching at upturned pots to keep themselves afloat—

People slipping under the surface, bursting out, spluttering, slipping under again, and under again, and under, each time for longer—

Men, women, children—*my father, my sisters*—all of them drowning.

CHAPTER 134

THE WEIGHT OF all that water was crushing my family, crushing my heart—

And I could not speak the words.

I could hear the words. Their strange shapes. Poised in my mind, ready to pounce, but my mouth was closed tight against them.

Come on, I urged. *Speak.*

But how?

I wasn't strong enough, good enough, bright enough.

C–

C–

C–

Go and sit at the Endiva table.

The light glancing off Mrs. Pollock's glasses.

Just Esther.

Of course, I cannot do it.

But you must, I begged myself. *Or everyone will drown.*

My lips parted ever so slightly—

Water splashed at my ankles. Shattering glass. Crashes and screams. The frightened yelps of dogs, yowls of cats.

And I clamped them shut again. My hand slapped against my mouth, pressing it closed.

Esther, you can do it, said a voice in my head, so clear, so bold, so certain that—

At last I spoke the words.

CHAPTER 135

I DON'T WANT to think about, or talk about, or even *touch* the memory of speaking the words—

And I don't want you to say that I was *brave* or *courageous* or *strong*— because I was not.

I shrieked, writhed, and wailed on the branch of that tree, scratched by bark, tearing at leaves.

The only thing I will say—

—something I noticed as I spoke the words—

—was this.

The greatest pain was not the Ghouls, the Ghouls slowly, steadily crushing tendons and bones—

—It wasn't that at all.

I was a small child again on a blanket in the rain, Ghouls slowly, steadily crushing me as they reached for the essence of me—and the greatest pain, the heart of the anguish, was that I knew that my mother had left me there.

Over and over, I cried out for her while the moon rose slowly over the turtle-shaped rock.

CHAPTER 136

BUT THEN I spoke the final word, and silver rainfall ran through my body.

As soothing as honey, or pillows, as warm tea in winter, a walk in a forest, a leap from a jetty in summer, Father chuckling, Imogen diving, Astrid fanning out her cards, cake.

It was exactly like those bubbles in a swimming pool when your palm slaps the surface of the water, so you twist about to feel it on your skin.

An odd thing happened then, difficult to explain. Say a balloon or a parachute catches a *whoosh* of wind and soars upward? That was me.

I was whooshing into the sky.

Only not.

I was not in the actual sky, I was still on the tree branch. I could still feel the leaves against my face, the texture of bark beneath my palms, but somehow I was also above.

Above place, above people, above time—above the story.

I could see the Kingdoms and Empires, all of them, both Northern and Southern Climes. Coastlines, rivers, islands, like pages in an atlas. I could also see the finest details, a man's wrist, a colored pencil rolling down a desk.

And I could see this:

Monstrous waves were slamming against coastal towns; ten lakes and rivers were frothing and surging down roads, through villages, towns, fields.

A small group of Spellbinders, both adults and children, stood on a distant beach, hands moving briskly in the air. Peering more closely, I found my cousin Bronte, her hair blowing sideways in the wind; Aunt Carrie, her movements smooth and powerful; Hsiang and Georgia, faces fierce in concentration.

A wave was poised midair, ready to devour them all—

Elsewhere, I saw pirates and fisherfolk tossing out nets and life rings, reaching out hands to drag drowning people aboard.

Water Sprites swarming to help—

In cities and on mountains, Crystal Faeries worked with Faeries and Elves, even with some *Shadow* Mages—Fire Sirens, Sirens, Sterling Silver Foxes, Radish Gnomes, Witches—together casting spells to raise ladders and construct boats and rafts, to lift babies from the sea and breathe air into their lungs—

Scanning the Kingdoms and Empires, I found my other aunts—Aunts Maya and Lisbeth scooping people out of the sea as they sailed their cruise ship; Aunt Isabelle and the Butler, Uncle Patrick and Aunt Lida, swimming steadily along a flooded street in Gainsleigh toward a stranded family; Aunt Sue, shouting at her boys to climb higher in the orange trees; Aunt Emma, thrusting the paddle of her rowboat to collect an elderly woman; Aunt Alys, directing the people of her Kingdom in a coordinated climb onto her palace roof; Aunt Franny, wading shoulder-deep through muddy water, guiding a herd of horses; Aunt Sophy flying a dragon low over the water, swooping now and then to rescue a child or a cat.

I even glimpsed *myself*, clinging to the upper branches of a tree, and just below me, Pelagia, amongst leaves and branches, one hand curled around the trunk, while, with the other, she sent flashes of light from her fingertips. The light leapt from point to point, cascading through Kingdoms and Empires.

Go back to sleep, Pelagia's message commanded. *This is not the time. Go back to sleep.*

For a moment I thought: *It's all right.*

Between the Spellbinders, the Mages, the brave and the strong, the Kingdoms and Empires will win.

But when I looked again, I knew that they would not.

Ships were capsizing. Cliffs were crumbling.

Water was surging, shoving at buildings, and spreading like fire.

Here, a flood stretched itself out and out to touch the edge of another; there, bodies of water leaked at the edges, thin strands of water, rushing like blood, joining forces, rivers to ocean, oceans to rivers, sending waves of blue-black to devour the greens and golds of land.

People flailed, screamed, sprinted, clambered—and drowned.

Steadily, the ocean encroached. The Mages were tiring, fading, slowing—

I looked into the ocean.

Sea horses, jellyfish, plankton, and Berg Trolls.

Deeper and darker I looked—

Deeper, deeper,

blindingly dark

and then the faintest light.

A wall of sandstone.

A roughly constructed underwater house. Its walls curved and pale. Lit with an eerie underwater glow.

I saw a master bedroom and, across the hall, a smaller bedroom decorated with shells and seaweed.

Pelagia's room.

Along the corridor to a living room.

—and there he was.

Jonathan J. Lanyard.

An ordinary man, thinning orange hair, orange freckles on a pale face, curling hair on a bare chest, dark swim shorts, solid calves and muscular forearms.

He was reclining in an armchair, legs crossed at the ankles.

As I drew closer, I saw that his skin was covered in fine, translucent scales, and there were gills cut neatly into his neck, just above his collarbones.

I found myself standing in his living room.

He glanced up, saw me, and smiled.

A shot of panic darted through me.

I might have officially become a Weaver, but I felt exactly

the same as I had before. I was a child, and this was a grown-up, a man, comfortable in his own home.

Also, he was a Fiend.

A Fiend was a thousand times stronger than today's Shadow Mages. This man was the strongest Water Fiend of them all. A Fiend of the ocean. I felt the weight of water again, the weight of an immensity of water. What was a sprinkling of rain compared to the ocean?

I was only a Rain Weaver, a child who knew nothing, and this was an Ocean Fiend.

What happened next was strange and dreamy. I'm still not sure if it was my imagination.

It was like this: Jonathan J. Lanyard stood and held out his hands. I saw that he was holding the edges of a cloth. Somehow I realized that he'd been holding this cloth the whole time.

The cloth was the size of a bath towel, but a silky, wavy bath towel, a towel much too beautiful for a regular bathroom. It shimmered with colors: reds, blacks, golds, greens, silvers, and blues. Jonathan indicated that I should take the other end of this towel-shaped cloth. So now we were facing each other, like two people about to fold laundry together. He still had a wry, friendly smile, as if he was indulging me in a little game: a friendly uncle agreeing to play with a child.

He began to fold the cloth in half, and my hands automatically followed the movement. As this happened, the red and black threads rippled across its surface. I felt their power tendril through my fingertips and palms, burning through my bloodstream. The turn of the cloth was also, I realized, a surge of water, waves, a rush of cruelty on the surface.

And I was helping him.

Jonathan smiled more broadly. The muscles in his forearms twitched.

I would just have to fold the cloth in the other direction, I decided uneasily. But the cloth was already moving, and my hands were once again moving with it—

And then suddenly, a peculiar memory came to me.

Our class was doing speeches.

Katya was speaking about "the cycle of life," in that flat, sad voice of hers.

"All water was once gas," she had said. "When temperatures dropped, it condensed into rain. Rain fell into the great basins and troughs . . . and formed oceans and lakes."

I laughed aloud.

Jonathan raised his eyebrows at me, making ready to turn the cloth again.

But it was clear now.

The oceans, the lakes, the rivers—they had all started as rain.

And I was a Rain Weaver.

"Good defeats bad," I told Jonathan J. Lanyard. "Rain defeats ocean."

He smirked at me, as an adult might to a girl chanting a skipping rhyme.

"Rain defeats ocean," I repeated, and ever so gently, I tugged at the cloth between us—

It sprang out of Jonathan's hands.

His brow crumpled in surprise, and he grabbed at it, but now it was sailing out from *my* hands like a flag. As I watched, it began to grow. Steadily, it grew to the size of a blanket, a sheet, a tarpaulin—the golds, the greens, the silvers, the blues dazzled and shone now. They darted back and forth across the surface, blending with the texture of the ocean, and the cloth grew and grew, extending beyond the ocean, rising into the sky—

—and everywhere, waves and water calmed.

I glanced at Jonathan again.

He had stumbled back, hitting his armchair. He fell into it.

"So much power," he whispered.

"Go back to sleep," I suggested, and, at once, his eyes closed and he was perfectly still.

"Go back to sleep," I murmured over and over, and I could see them all, the other Fiends of lakes and rivers, also slipping back into their deep, deep sleep.

And all over the Kingdoms and Empires, the wild water of the ocean, of the seas, rivers, and lakes, slid neatly and rapidly, like water down a drain, back into place.

PART

5

CHAPTER 137

"FATHER SAYS YOU'RE invited to the meeting," Imogen said.

"And we're allowed to miss the first day of term and come too," Astrid added, "to be loving and supportive of you. Like we've been for the last two weeks."

Two weeks had gone by since the flood, and my sisters had just come into the room and woken me.

After the Fiends were defeated, I collapsed into the branches of the tree and rescuers had to scramble up and carry me down, and all the way back to the Old Schoolhouse. I stayed there, resting, for the next two weeks, and my sisters—who were staying in the room next door—brought me news each day. It was a curious way to spend a school holiday.

Everybody in Pillar Box Town, including my sisters and father, had survived the lake flooding—although there were broken ribs, bloody noses, scratches, concussions, and bruises.

Across the Kingdoms and Empires, there were similar injuries, many more severe and, sadly, some lives were lost.

"But imagine how many *more* would have been lost if not for you," Astrid told me when we heard this. "You're a hero, Esther."

"Don't let it go to your head," Imogen advised.

That was my sisters' job, apparently: to stop me from growing conceited.

In the days after it happened, the school closed for the holiday, students went home, and everybody else—including my parents, most teachers, and Mustafa—got to work in town setting things right-side up again. Wringing out soggy rugs.

Straightening fences and chimney pots. Rebuilding houses. Placing tiles back on roofs and doors back into frames. Raking and sweeping.

This, of course, was happening all over the Kingdoms and Empires.

The Fiends remained in deep sleep, and there was a lot of talk about the dangers of their waking again.

"They won't," I said, "and if they do, they are no longer Fiends. I've washed away their evil powers."

That surprised even me. I hadn't known I'd done that. But I knew it now, somewhere deep inside me.

The displaced sea creatures returned to their homes, and so did the wandering populations of Shadow Mages, and so did the Spellbinders—including Bronte, Aunt Carrie, Hsiang, and Georgia. They were exhausted and needed to rest with their families.

Now I sat up in bed. I was hungry. As if he'd been waiting right outside the door for me to have that exact thought, the whiskery man swept in with a breakfast tray: bacon, sausages, eggs, toast, beans, fried potatoes, pancakes, waffles, juice, hot chocolate, and a flower in a vase.

"I thank you," the whiskery man said solemnly—he'd been saying this each day. "My family thanks you. The Kingdoms and Empires thank you. You are a hero." He blinked away tears and left.

"It's true but don't let it go to your head," Astrid reminded me.

That's when my sisters told me that Tilla Tarpaulin, the director of the K&E Alliance, had called a meeting to discuss just how a Fiend and his daughter, Pelagia, had managed to nearly end us all.

And that Father had given us permission to attend.

"It's happening right here in the Old Schoolhouse," Imogen said, "since you're here. And you're so important."

"But don't let it go to your head," Astrid repeated.

CHAPTER 138

TILLA TARPAULIN LOOKED like a domino with furious eyes.

Her eyes might not always be furious, I suppose, but that day, at the secret meeting, they were like flash fires.

"What *I* want to know," she demanded, "is why nobody believed Professor Staranise here? He *knew* it was a Fiend all along! He even knew *which* Fiend it was!"

We were in the drawing room off the entryway of the Old Schoolhouse. As well as Tilla, there were ten or twelve adults, mostly wearing suits and serious expressions, and various security guards. One of the adults was Carson Brody, local mayor with important nose. Two of the adults were Whisperers—I knew this because their hair fell to their ankles and because other adults shifted their chairs as far from them as possible. They must be Autumn's parents, I realized; they had exactly the same calm, quietly humorous expressions.

My sisters and I were seated against the far wall. We had promised Father we would be "absolutely silent," but when Tilla arrived, she marched over to me, gripped my hand, and said, "You are truly a hero."

"Thank you," I replied (breaking Father's rule).

"No," Tilla said, solemnly. "Thank *you*."

Imogen and Astrid both shot me meaningful looks, so I didn't let it go to my head.

Father started the meeting by giving a little classical history lesson about Fiends and Weavers. He pointed out the two Whisperers—Soren and Livia Hillside—and said that, as well as having been part of the resistance during the Whispering

Wars (which made them heroes), they had heard future Whispers about the Fiend and the Weaver.

"And you said all this at the Vanquishing Cove conference?" Tilla checked, glancing at the people nearest her. "You heard him say this?"

People pretended interest in their notepads.

That's when Tilla Tarpaulin demanded to know why nobody had believed Father.

The other adults cleared their throats and defended themselves, muttering things like "We thought it was all myth!"

"We thought he was *bananas*!"

"I mean to say—they were *Whisperers*."

Tilla interrupted with a loud sigh. "More on that later. I want to know about this *child* who helped the Fiend."

Father explained that the Ocean Fiend would have adapted so thoroughly to the ocean that he could not leave it, which is why he had needed his daughter to wake the other Water Fiends.

"And where is she now? Who's taking care of her?" Tilla asked.

A woman rose, said, "That'd be me," and turned into Matron from school! She'd obviously been Matron all along but I hadn't recognized her with her hair so neatly brushed.

Astrid whispered to me: "We forgot to tell you. Matron's back from the Northern Climes. Got back just after the flood."

Tilla, shuffling her papers, asked: "You're Faery?"

"Part Faery," Matron agreed proudly.

"And I take it the child is a young Fiend?"

"Oh *no*!" Matron almost chuckled but stopped herself. "The little dear. No, she's a regular child. She had the scent of Fiendish evil on her, certainly—I assume that's what the scent was anyway—a lot like shadow magic, only stronger. Enough bubble baths and Faery cake and it's gone now. She's certainly not the biological child of Jonathan J. Lanyard."

Heads swung toward her.

"No, she *believes* he's her father, but it seems to me she was taken into the sea when she was very young, perhaps an infant, and raised by him."

A silence.

"He stole the child?" somebody breathed.

"She must have been young enough to adapt to ocean life," Matron continued, "he's given her bioluminescence and the power to breathe underwater—and to forget her life before. He told her tales of how evil Weavers destroyed his friends, so of course she believed him. It's a marvel she found the courage to defy him near the end."

Tilla nodded thoughtfully. "I wonder how the Fiend managed to capture a little—"

That's when I broke my promise a second time.

I jumped to my feet and shouted: "The Stolen Prince of Cloudburst!"

CHAPTER 139

EVERYONE STARED AT me, of course.

"Prince Alejandro of the Kingdom of Storms! He was paddling on a beach at Spindrift when he was taken by a Water Sprite! That's in the region where the Fiend lived! Maybe the Fiend put the Water Sprite in a trance and made him steal Alejandro, meaning *Alejandro* to be his child? Only he never got to collect Alejandro from the ocean lily because pirates picked him up! So he stole Pelagia instead!"

There was a short silence. Then:

"Well, *perhaps*" went flitting around the room. Everyone looked at me, admiringly.

Father said, "Hmm," and people swiveled to look at him instead. They were very respectful to Father generally, I noticed, feeling guilty for having been so disrespectful before.

"Yes," Father said. "It makes sense. But listen, Pelagia had clothes and stories and was enrolled in a school. Somebody else must have helped the Fiend."

Matron was nodding as he spoke. "They did," she said. "Pelagia told me there *was* somebody else. Jonathan would take the child to see this person on the shore, and she'd have lessons in ordinary life. Pelagia says she loves this person and she *refuses* to give their identity away. She simply *can't*, she says. It's curious because there is definite love for the person— but also there is fear."

Tilla gazed at the ceiling. She was thinking.

But then a gruff voice spoke up. It was Carson Brody. "All right, let's think about who this *person* is. Who do we know who, *one,* lives fairly close to where the Fiend was living; *two,* has a habit of stealing children; and *three,* can control minds?"

To which several voices chorused, *"Whisperers!"*

"Now, hold up there," Autumn's parents protested in unison.

"Let's not jump to blame the Whisperers!" Father joined in. "Ten years ago they were still behind the Spellbinding! They can't have been running errands for an Ocean Fiend back then!"

"Who knows what powers the Fiend had?" Tilla pointed out. "He could have infiltrated the Spellbinding. And it *was* broken a couple of years ago."

"The Whisperers *Whispered* Water Sprites to steal the children—first Alejandro, then Pelagia," Carson Brody declared. "They *Whispered* the Water Sprites to forget why they'd done it. They prepared Pelagia for life on land and *Whispered* Pelagia to love them and fear them! *THE WHISPERING KINGDOM HAS BEEN WORKING WITH THE OCEAN FIEND!*"

After that, I don't know what happened.

All the adults were shouting at once.

Father was ranting about prejudices against Whisperers and trying to give a history lesson; the Hillsides were protesting that Whisperers would have no reason to help a Fiend cover the Kingdoms and Empires in water; Matron was advising everyone to take a breath; Tilla was commanding silence; and everybody else was screaming for the Whispering Kingdom to be placed under a Spellbinding again.

When a chair got thrown against a wall, Imogen stood up quickly and said, "Let's get out of here."

CHAPTER 140

WE CLOSED THE door behind us, and there was Pelagia.

She was standing by the coat rack in the entryway, eating a sticky bun.

"Want some?" she asked, with her mouth full. She tore the bun into pieces and handed them around before we'd answered.

Her eyes darted between us, nervously.

"Sorry," she said. "Sorry I'm the daughter of a Fiend."

Imogen, Astrid, and I all exclaimed that it was *not* her fault, and that she'd actually been stolen away to be his daughter and brought up to believe his stories, and she'd been so brave sending those light signals out the day of the flood.

"You're a true hero," I said. And then automatically: "But don't let it go to your head."

"Oh, she can if she wants," Imogen allowed generously.

Pelagia pointed at the drawing room door—the shouts carried on in there, but muffled by the closed door—and asked, "Do they need me to come in yet? I was supposed to answer questions."

We said we didn't really recommend that and told her about the argument.

"*Was* it a Whisperer helping your father?" I asked.

Pelagia shook her head. "I can't really tell you anything about the person."

"Can you *try*?" Astrid suggested. "Just give us some clues?"

Miserably, Pelagia murmured: "Please don't ask me."

We sat on the floor, leaning up against the wall, eating the sticky bun.

"What's it been like, pretending to be a regular person?" Imogen asked her. "You're good at it. Fooled me."

"Well, at *first*, it was exciting," Pelagia answered. "An adventure. I had a whole invented personality and a suitcase full of chocolate boxes to share."

We stretched our legs out on the entryway floorboards and listened to the *thumps*! and *crashes*! from inside the drawing room.

"Should we be worried about Father?" Astrid wondered.

"They're just tossing things around for emphasis," Imogen said. "If an actual fistfight breaks out, the guards will stop it. Keep going, Pelagia. It was exciting at first and then—"

"I started to feel homesick," Pelagia admitted. "I missed water so much it was like toothache. I was so happy about the swimming tournament because it meant I could do swimming training, but even that wasn't enough. I spent as much time as I could with my feet in the pond here. My father would send me messages while I was there."

I nodded, remembering the flashes of light.

"And then I started to make friends," she finished. "And to *like* people—like you, Imogen. And Esther. Sorry, Astrid, I never really got to know you. And the responsibility of helping to cause a flood! Of drowning people! It was too much!"

Astrid patted her shoulder. "Don't blame yourself," she said. "It was the Fiends. Not you."

Again, we were quiet, licking treacle sauce from our fingers, listening to *roars*! and angry *ha ha has*! from the drawing room.

"Are you sure you can't tell us who packed your suitcase for you?" Astrid checked. "And gave you the chocolate? And brought you here?"

Pelagia's voice trembled. "I can't let that person get into trouble," she said. "I really care about that person. I promise: that person is a *good* person."

"I wish I hadn't shouted about the Stolen Prince of Cloudburst," I said. "That seemed to lead to them blaming the Whisperers."

"Someone would have thought of it anyway," Astrid said comfortingly.

"Yes, the Whispering Kingdom is so close to where the Fiend was," Imogen agreed. "So there's—"

But I don't know the rest of what Imogen said because that's when I stood up, mumbling that I had to go, and ran out the front door of the Schoolhouse.

CHAPTER 141

I RAN THROUGH the gardens.

It was strange to be outside again, strange to be running under a warm sun. I took deep breaths of fresh air.

I reached the school and flung open the door.

Inside, I ran along empty corridors—everyone was in class for the first day of term—and clattered up the stairs to the library.

"Esther!" Carlos, his beard at its bushiest, leapt up from his spinning chair with such speed the chair began to topple backward. He swung around to catch it before it crashed.

"Hi, Carlos," I said once he'd straightened up again. "I need information on Horseshoe Ogres, please."

"Of course, but first, can I say congratulations on being a Rain Weaver and saving all the Kingdoms and Empires?"

"All right," I agreed.

"Congratulations!"

"Thank you," I said, nodding seriously.

Carlos saw the urgency of my quest.

"Let me help," he said. And he emerged from behind his desk, hurried to a shelf, and began picking and choosing volumes until he'd gathered a stack. He handed this to me.

He rarely does that. He usually requires us to do our own research, only calling out the section of the library we should search.

It almost made me cry.

"We don't have any books that are just on Horseshoe Ogres,"

he apologized. "But if you check the indexes of these ones, there'll be a few paragraphs in each."

I thanked him again, sat at a table, and read what I could about Horseshoe Ogres.

Hours went by.

I turned page after page.

Nothing seemed helpful.

And then I read a line that, for a moment, made my heart scramble to its feet, spin in place, and then sit back down again and carry on as before.

That's how it felt, anyway. It was odd.

CHAPTER 142

PRINCIPAL HORTENSE BUMPED
into me as I was emerging, slowly, from
the library.

She was striding by, dressed in a
beaded evening dress with a feathered
headband.

"Oh my lucky stars!" she cried. "Esther! Here you are!"

"Yes," I agreed.

"What a *relief*! You did give me a scare! I was *crossing fingers and toes* we'd find you in time! The dining hall is decorated! People have been arriving all afternoon! I do worry about you, Esther, as you always forget to raise your hand when you speak and now you've disappeared for the afternoon. But what a good girl you are! Bumping into me just in time! Lucky I didn't cancel!"

"Thank you," I said faintly. "Cancel what?"

"We've all been looking. Your sisters say I forgot to invite you three girls, which is funny, as *you* are— Anyway, what are you going to wear? No time to change, actually! It's starting now! Come along."

And she led me firmly into the dining hall.

The hall glowed with candlelight and gleamed with silver cutlery, crystal glassware, and white linen napkins. It had been completely rearranged, crammed with extra tables, and it swarmed with elegant waiters, trays held high. They moved about between men, women, and children, all got up in suits, gowns, tizz, and silk.

Amongst the chatting strangers, I began to see familiar faces. Girls from my school, and boys from Nicholas Valley

Boarding School. What were *they* doing here? Many of the adults from today's meeting were also there—Carson Brody, Tilla Tarpaulin, some of the other officials. Only a few hours earlier, they'd been shouting and throwing things at each other. Now, they were reaching for champagne, chuckling gently as they tapped each other's elbows. It was very strange.

"Just a moment, dear," Principal Hortense said to me, and she disappeared into the crowd.

I felt both shy and confused. For one thing, I was wearing my blue sailor dress, which was not nearly shimmery or flouncy enough. I hid in the back corner and watched, hoping to understand what was happening.

Eventually, I realized that a cluster of girls from my own grade were standing quite near me. I hadn't recognized them with their shiny frills. They were circled around Mrs. Pollock—herself in a pink drop-waist dress with two strings of pearls—and were concentrating fiercely as she performed their greetings, one at time, at rapid speed. There was a brief pause as Autumn approached the group, leading the Whispering couple from the meeting.

"Excuse me, Mrs. Pollock," Autumn said politely. She looked very elegant, her short hair tucked beneath a beret, her dress spangled and knee-length. "I'd like to introduce you to my parents: Soren and Livia Hillside. From the Whispering Kingdom."

Autumn's parents had wound their long, long hair into tidy loops, but the group hushed and some girls stared openly at these loops, retreating slightly.

"It's all right," Autumn's mother said to them calmly. "See? We're not wearing wristbands. We can only Whisper in the old way. You are safe." She held out bare arms, and the girls nodded, embarrassed. Then she turned to Mrs. Pollock.

"It's a pleasure to meet you," she said, in her soft, polite voice. "Thank you for taking such fine care of our daughter this last year." There was the faintest twitch in the corner of her right eye as she said this. *Curious*, I thought.

Autumn's father nodded. "Yes, we have heard much of you from Autumn. But surely we have met before, Mrs. Pollock?"

"Yes." Livia Hillside nodded. "I was thinking the same thing. You are very familiar, Mrs. Pollock. Perhaps we have crossed paths?"

Mrs. Pollock pulled one of her hilarious clown faces. "I think not!" she said. "But let me show you what your daughter chose for *her* personalized greeting!"

Then she and Autumn carried out their greeting, and the game began again, with Mrs. Pollock moving around the circle, greeting everyone, faster and faster. Other girls from my grade, and then from other grades, and boys from Nicholas Valley, various teachers and adults moved closer to watch, and Mrs. Pollock, not pausing, called to them to join the circle and invent their *own* greetings. Soon, she was spinning in place, greeting everyone who approached, the circle growing ever larger, roars of laughter filling the room. She began to spring about the room slapping every hand she saw! Girls ran after her, laughing.

Two flashes made me blink, and I turned to see people taking photographs.

"Smile!" one told me, still clicking. "Thanks!"

Mysterious.

But then Principal Hortense was speaking into a microphone: "Excuse me! Attention, everyone! Take your places, please!"

And the event began.

It turned out that the school was holding a banquet and dance in my honor. I was to receive a school merit award for having saved the Kingdoms and Empires. Embarrassing. The local press had been invited, as had various officials, parents, and the Nicholas Valley boys: we needed them for dance partners.

I was taken to the high table, where the teachers smiled, and my father jumped up and pulled out the seat alongside him.

He looked tired and harried. His bow tie was crooked.

"Hello, Esther," said a low voice, and I realized Mother was on the other side of Father.

I had not seen her for the last two weeks. She'd been traveling around, coordinating the cleanup.

Principal Hortense gave a speech, which I think was about what a hero I'd been, but I didn't hear it. I was buttering a bread roll and watching my parents. Mother murmured to Father to pass her the water please, and Father reached for it and poured her a glass with such icy politeness it was as if he was pouring it over her head.

"What happened at the meeting?" I murmured to Father, to distract him.

"Still blaming the Whisperers," he whispered back. "Tilla's already ordered the Spellbinding back around the Whispering Kingdom."

"I would now like to invite Esther to accept her merit award and to say a few words," Principal Hortense declared, and I dropped my bread roll.

I was supposed to make a speech?

Reporters gathered closer, holding their pencils ready.

My heart zipped about like a puppy dog.

Then I looked back at my father and knew exactly what to say.

CHAPTER 143

I SHOOK PRINCIPAL Hortense's hand, accepted the merit award, held it up for the cameras—*Flash! Flash!*—and took the microphone.

"Thank you," I said. "I am very happy that the Kingdoms and Empires are not underwater. Sometimes though, I think that happiness is made of sadness. Or that they run side by side, intertwined, like laughter and tears."

"Ooh, *fancy*," murmured a voice, followed by chuckles. I blinked and looked back at the teachers' table. Mrs. Pollock. She winked. I cleared my throat and carried on.

"I am happy that so many people survived, but sad that many were injured—and especially sad that some people drowned. I'm happy that the Fiends are now asleep, but sad that one caused so much suffering these last years. Because of him, people have been killed. Fishing villages have starved without—"

"Fish!" Mrs. Pollock interjected, as if this was a guessing competition. "Yes, that was a shame. Fish! Fry it up in a little flour and butter!"

Laughter. A few teachers said, "Hush!" to Mrs. Pollock, but in good-natured voices.

"Changes in tides meant that Shadow Mages moved around causing trouble," I continued. "I was happy that Autumn saved us from the Sterling Silver Foxes, but I'm sad that Katya, who is still at the treatment center, will never laugh again."

"Happy, sad, happy, sad," Mrs. Pollock called. "It's a seesaw! A teeter-totter!" She grinned and the crowd laughed.

She's awful, said a voice in my head. I shook the thought away.

"I'm happy that Pelagia is free now, and will hopefully be able to find the family that lost her, but sad that—"

"Make up your mind!" called Mrs. Pollock.

Giggles.

"Sad that—" What had I been going to say? "Sad that her family must have *lost* her around ten years ago. When I was visiting Cloudburst not long ago, I climbed onto a roof and looked across—"

"Trespassing, were you?" Mrs. Pollock chipped in.

Bursts of laughter.

She's AWFUL.

The thought was larger.

For some reason, I glanced across at the Grade 6 girls again. Autumn Hillside was gazing at me. She blinked once.

"Quite the dramatic pause!" Mrs. Pollock commented.

MRS. POLLOCK IS AWFUL.

My eyes swept back toward Autumn.

I needed to concentrate. I'd been going to say that I'd glimpsed Queen Anita and her expression had puzzled me, but that now I realized it was a mixture of joy and heartbreak. Her son, Alejandro, was back. But she'd missed so much of his childhood.

There was no point saying this. Mrs. Pollock would only joke about me spying on a queen.

I decided to get to my point.

"It wasn't just *me* who saved the Kingdoms and Empires," I said. "It was many brave people. Pelagia herself. Spellbinders. True Mages and Shadow Mages. Sailors, pirates, police, soldiers. Whisperers. Brave people who flew on dragons or reached out their hands. They *all* deserve merit awards. When I rose into the sky and saw so many working together to—"

"Eh? You *rose*? Climbing buildings again, Esther?" Mrs. Pollock wheezed with laughter. Others joined in.

I pressed my mouth closer to the microphone. "Two years ago, my cousin Bronte helped to free the Whispering Kingdom from a Spellbinding."

"Name-dropper," Mrs. Pollock giggled.

I ignored her. "Right now, there are people who believe, without *any* evidence, that a Whisperer helped the Ocean Fiend. They have imprisoned the Whispering Kingdom behind a Spellbinding again. They are—"

"Ooh, she's sounding very la-di-da lawyerly!" Mrs. Pollock observed.

"They are—" I tried again.

But there was too much laughter. The room heaved with it.

I fell silent.

Mrs. Pollock gave a cute little shrug.

I waited until the laughter had quietened, then I raised the microphone to my mouth.

"Mrs. Pollock," I said. "You are awful."

CHAPTER 144

GASPS AROUND THE room like steam trains setting off.

"Esther!" Principal Hortense scolded.

Several girls in my grade half-rose, their faces furious.

"She's *not* awful!" they clamored. "She's *wonderful!*"

The audience muttered. Several teachers frowned at me.

Mrs. Pollock shot me a sly smile. "I think Esther might have lost her sense of humor," she crowed. "Perhaps she dropped it climbing a building!"

A burst of laughter from the audience.

Embarrassing. Confusing. I must be wrong.

"Sorry," I whispered. "Sorry, Mrs. Pollock. Anyway—" I'd lost my train of thought.

Then a voice cried: "Oh, for goodness' sake!"

Mother was on her feet. "Don't *apologize* to that dreadful woman, Esther!" she commanded. "You've been making a very sensible speech and she keeps interrupting! She's *rude* and *nasty!*" She looked out at the audience. "You're all ridiculous. Mrs. Pollock *is* awful, and Esther *is a hero.*"

With a sobbing sound, Mother slumped back down.

Father blinked.

CHAPTER 145

THERE WAS A long, startled quiet.

Mrs. Pollock is awful, Mrs. Pollock is awful was drumming in my head again. All around the room, faces were bewildered—although Autumn, I noticed, was peering at me fiercely and nodding along with the beat in my head.

I spoke into the microphone. "Mrs. Pollock *is* awful," I insisted. "She only *pretends* to be kind. But she stopped me from going to the twilight picnic and erased my homework. She invented rules about a speech contest to prevent me from competing and invented a disease to stop me from playing in the poker competition. Worst of all, Mrs. Pollock . . ." I turned and faced her. "Your jokes are always at the expense of other people."

The audience fell silent.

Mrs. Pollock chuckled. "I think you'll find," she said, "that your friends in Grade Six disagree—"

Autumn was no longer looking at me, I realized. She was gazing at Dot Pecorino, beside her—and Dot Pecorino suddenly leapt to her feet.

"Esther is right!" she said—the room hushed to hear her soft voice. "Mrs. Pollock makes fun of people! Of me for being shy. Of Durba for being tall! Of Katya, for her hair being curly and for being smart! Of Lee Kim, for her laugh! But Lee has a wonderful laugh!"

Autumn had pushed back her chair and was gazing at the other girls in my grade in turn. They twisted shoulders and stretched arms like people waking up. One by one, their eyes widened, and they began to stand.

Every girl in Grade 6 spoke up. Rhadi said that Mrs. Pollock had told her she ought to stop sewing—that her stitches were clumsy. But Rhadi makes beautiful clothes! Sulin had been told she shouldn't sing, Cora that her gymnastics was embarrassing, and Ildiko that her parents were only pretending to love her.

This was what Mrs. Pollock had been doing in her private chats with girls: gently and kindly crushing the things they valued the most.

Mrs. Pollock was still babbling, trying to make jokes of what the girls were saying, yet the dining hall took no notice.

"You are *horrible!*" Zoe Fawnwell cried. "Mrs. Pollock, you made me feel that I was worthless unless I was friends with the Rattlestone twins, which is exactly what I've always secretly wondered myself! But at the same time you made the twins think they had to be friends with Autumn instead of me! And, as for the twins, you *made them into the worst version of themselves!*"

"Well, I don't know about that," Hetty and Tatty complained—but even they were scowling at Mrs. Pollock.

"But she *is* nasty," Hetty added. "She made us think we were the most special people in the class—top of the class, selected for the speech contest—but deep inside we knew we weren't. We couldn't even do the work. I got the lowest results ever recorded in the speech contest. She made us think we had to cut Autumn's hair, and then we really hated ourselves! Sorry, Autumn."

Autumn's eyes were flitting around the room.

Dawning expressions rippled across the teachers' table. One by one, they shook their heads or rubbed their eyes. It was as if they'd all been hypnotized.

Pelagia was the only one who hadn't spoken. She was blinking rapidly and staring, openmouthed, at Mrs. Pollock.

And that's when, like an upturned jigsaw puzzle that spills onto a table fully formed, everything fell into place.

CHAPTER 146

I SPOKE INTO the microphone again.

"Everyone," I began—and paused. I decided to hold up the puzzle pieces one by one. "This afternoon, I was in the library reading about Horseshoe Ogres," I said. "And there was a line that made my heart scramble to its feet."

Puzzled faces.

"It's a metaphor," I scolded them. "I mean the line shocked me. This is what it said: *The Ogres of Horseshoe Island are just as huge as all Ogres. However, they are curious in this way: the older they get, the more they shrink. Very old Ogres can shrink to the size of ordinary children.*"

The audience carried on frowning, but I moved on to the second piece of the puzzle.

"Horseshoe Island is close to where Jonathan J. Lanyard, the Ocean Fiend, lived deep underwater. So any Ogres living in the sea caves there could have come into contact with him.

"*Mrs. Pollock* is from Horseshoe Island," I said.

That was a small puzzle piece, and so was the next.

"Autumn's parents—Soren and Livia Hillside—met Mrs. Pollock tonight, and they both felt like she was familiar."

A twisty piece.

"Ogres have a history of helping Shadow Mages," I said. "That's why I was reading about them in the library today— wondering if *they* might have helped the Fiend rather than the Whisperers."

People were staring at me, transfixed by their own confusion over all the little pieces. "*What's her point?*" somebody hissed.

"That history," I continued, "means that Ogres have come into contact with shadow magic frequently. It has given them powerful handshakes. I know this because—"

Well, there was no need to say I knew it because I'd eavesdropped on the teachers from the attic.

"I just know it," I continued. "At first, I thought it meant that Ogres have very *strong* handshakes. Of course, most Ogres aren't friendly, hand-shaking types, they're more the kick-you-into-a-lake type."

A few chuckles.

But I stayed serious: "I think the power of their handshake means something different. I think the touch of an Ogre's hand makes people fall under the Ogre's spell. I think it makes them love the Ogre, even if they have no reason to love them."

Now people were frowning in a different, thoughtful way.

It was time to put the pieces together.

"Mrs. Pollock," I said, turning to her and speaking clearly so everyone could hear. "I believe you are an Ogre. You are tiny because you are elderly. I believe that you've been helping the Ocean Fiend, Jonathan J. Lanyard. I believe you've helped to raise Pelagia, that you brought her here, that you made sure she woke the other Fiends—it was *you* who gave Mr. Dar-Healey the information about the swimming tournament that took her near those places. I believe you made Pelagia love you by using the powerful shadow magic in your handshake. And told Pelagia that she must not tell anybody."

I took a deep breath. I'd been talking very fast and needed some air. Around me, the hall was silent.

"On the first day of class," I continued, "you told us your job had been ferrying tourists across to Horseshoe Island. I believe you ferried Autumn's parents—the Hillsides—and that's why you were familiar to them—"

At this, the Hillsides both murmured, "Oh yes! Of course!"—which was a relief.

"It was on the trip back from the island that the Hillsides heard the Whisper from the future about a Weaver in Grade Six at this school. You overheard this Whisper. You told the

Fiend. That's why he sent you to this school, along with Pelagia. You were to crush the spirit of every child in the class. He knew that becoming a Weaver requires strength and belief in oneself.

"And all the while, you played your greeting game with us and shook the teachers' hands, and so, without any good reason, we loved you."

CHAPTER 147

MY FATHER WAS rising to his feet.

"You're right!" he cried. "Esther, that all makes sense! It wasn't *Whisperers* who helped the Fiend. It was Mrs. Pollock!"

He seemed alarmingly happy. He jiggled about, peering across the tables until he caught sight of Pelagia.

"Is it true, Pelagia?" he called.

Pelagia nodded slowly. "She's the person who brought me here. She's the one who taught me all about life on the surface. But I . . . I *loved* her. And she's . . ."

"She's awful," several voices agreed.

"What did Jonathan J. Lanyard promise you, Mrs. Pollock?" Father called. "Why'd you help him? I suppose you just wanted more shadow power? I mean, imagine how much power a *Fiend* could bestow on you. And Ogres like the ocean, so you wouldn't mind if most of the place was underwater. And—"

But the dining hall was alight with astonishment, and Mrs. Pollock was gaping like a fish.

"This is *utter nonsense*," she babbled. "The most *ridiculous* pile of *rotting, stinking garbage* I ever heard!"

Astrid stood up at her table and called: "I *knew* something was wrong with Mrs. Pollock the first time I saw her." Then to the room: "Everything Esther said is true. Mrs. Pollock's face admitted it all."

Cameras clicked. Reporters scribbled.

"Ridiculous!" Mrs. Pollock huffed.

"She's still lying." Astrid grinned.

Principal Hortense, who had been watching all this with a

dazed expression, rose. "Good gracious, Mrs. Pollock!" she cried. "You're an *Ogre*! Why ever did I employ you? You're fired!"

Beside her, Mr. Dar-Healey was grim. "Hortense, if Esther is right, I think we need more than dismissal."

Already, Tilla Tarpaulin had clicked her fingers at security guards, and they were marching toward Mrs. Pollock.

She shoved back her own chair with a squeal, flung herself sideways, and sprinted down the passage between tables.

Hands reached out to stop her, but she shoved them aside.

Her mistake was running by the Grade 6 girls. Several legs stuck out, tripping her and sending her flying.

While Mrs. Pollock was flat on her back, Ms. Potty from Nicholas Valley strode over and got her in a headlock. She held her there, easily, ignoring Mrs. Pollock's struggles and squawks, every now and then shouting over to the boys' table, "Cut that out, Ryan!" or "Adam, so help me!"—until the guards told her it was all right, they had it.

CHAPTER 148

LATER, AFTER THE guards had taken Mrs. Pollock away, and the press had taken enough photos and quotes, and we had eaten our turkey and roast potatoes, and our ice cream and chocolate pudding—

—we all marched from the dining hall to the gymnasium for the dance.

I found myself walking beside Autumn.

"Funny," I said, "that we've all been under Mrs. Pollock's greeting spells all year, but we snapped out of it tonight."

"Hmm," she agreed.

Our footsteps continued, side by side.

"I wonder how," I said softly.

Autumn was silent. Her eyes darted sideways and caught mine. "Don't tell anybody," she murmured. "I know I'm not supposed to Whisper."

"How did you do it? Aren't you too young?"

Autumn nodded. "Remember the morning the twins cut off my hair, when I was leaving for the poker competition? I saw you watching from the window, and I just *really* wished you knew about Mrs. Pollock. I was thinking: *She's awful!* And I felt that thought jump into your head. It was an accident. But that's when I knew I could do it."

"But how did *you* know Mrs. Pollock was awful?"

"I didn't. Not until that morning. Before that, I kept sensing something strange about her. Then, when my hair was cut off, it was like—well, instead of ruining my Whispering, it shocked it into me. Then the trance fell away." She half-smiled.

"The funny thing is that Mrs. Pollock thought she'd crush my spirit by getting the twins to cut my hair."

"Like when she made me so sad I ran out into the rain," I realized, "and rain made the Weaver pattern show up."

We both laughed, then fell silent, reflecting on Mrs. Pollock's backfiring plans.

"So what made you decide to Whisper everyone tonight?" I asked.

She sighed. "I tried before but I couldn't get through to anyone. Tonight, I just *had* to try again. But it wasn't until your mother's outburst that it worked. She was so sure of herself that it opened a crack in people's minds for me to Whisper through. Of course, my Whispers are faint. You could all have shaken them away."

"But we didn't."

We'd reached the entry to the gymnasium, and Autumn smiled. "That's because it was the truth. Truth is powerful."

CHAPTER 149

BEFORE THE MUSIC and dancing began, while we were all still pouring into the gymnasium, everyone babbling about the exciting events of dinner, Autumn and I joined a group of girls.

My sisters were part of the group, and a few Grade 6 girls, all surrounding Pelagia, asking if she was all right.

She was very grim.

"It's like this," she was saying. "Jonathan J. Lanyard was my father, and now it turns out he's an evil being from a thousand years ago who stole me away. Mrs. Pollock was like my mother. She was never kind, but I adored her anyway. And now I've discovered that she's an Ogre who only made me *think* I loved her."

We all tried to comfort her, but most of this was outside our realm of experience. Nobody could say, "Oh, I know *just* how you feel."

The twins tried saying that anyway, which made Pelagia smile, wipe away a tear, and hum softly to herself.

"What's that tune?" Imogen asked her. "It's pretty."

Pelagia laughed, embarrassed. "I don't know. I used to sing it when I was small. My father—Jonathan J. Lanyard, I mean—used to tell me to hush. He didn't like it."

"But where would you have heard it?" Astrid wondered. "Could it be from your life *before* he stole you away?"

"I don't remember anything from then." Pelagia shrugged.

But Imogen was rising up onto her toes, waving at us to shush. "Wait, shush, wait! Sing it again, Pelagia! Hum it again!"

Obediently, Pelagia hummed.

Then Imogen swung in place, grabbed Pelagia's hand, and pulled her away—so fast that Pelagia lost her balance—urging: "Come with me, Pelagia! Come with me *now*!"

Imogen skidded across the gymnasium, dragging Pelagia behind her, darting between people, breaking apart dance partners who'd already joined hands—until she reached the stage. She hurried Pelagia up the stairs and skidded up beside Mr. Dar-Healey. He himself was busy with the gramo-phone player, trying to get the music started.

Astrid and I had followed, so we heard the conversation.

"Hello, Imogen! Hello, Pelagia!" Mr. Dar-Healey said, light-ing up. "How are my swimming champions?"

"We have something important to discuss," Imogen informed him.

"Do we?" Pelagia wondered.

"Well, always happy to discuss things, but can it—"

"No! It cannot wait!" Imogen insisted.

Mr. Dar-Healey shrugged and turned to face her.

"Your little girl was lost while you were on holiday at the Candle Islands, right?" Imogen demanded, breathless.

Creases of pain formed on Mr. Dar-Healey's forehead. "Imo-gen," he said softly.

But Imogen persisted. "About ten years ago? And she was two?"

"Imogen," he repeated.

"Hum your tune, Pelagia. Hum it!"

Pelagia, baffled but obedient, began to hum.

"You see," Imogen cried. "It's *your* tune, Mr. Dar-Healey! It's the one you always sing when it's quiet in class! And the Candle Islands are near where the Fiend was living! And it was ten years ago that the Fiend tried to steal the Prince of Cloudburst—only he was taken by pirates—and Matron said that Pelagia was little when she was stolen, and now she's sing-ing your tune! She could be your baby!"

Hmm, I thought. *That tune could be common.*

"She said she's *always* sung it!" Imogen added. "Mr. Dar-Healey, don't you think . . . ?"

Mr. Dar-Healey was staring at Pelagia, the creases fading from his forehead. "I made it up," he murmured. "It was my lullaby for my baby."

He began to hum along with Pelagia, their tunes lining up side by side.

"Paige?" he whispered.

I looked from one to the other, and that's when I saw what I should have before: Mr. Dar-Healey had the exact same snail-shell nose as Pelagia.

His was bigger though. That's why I hadn't noticed, I suppose.

Pelagia stopped humming. She looked up at him quizzically.

And Mr. Dar-Healey burst into tears.

Imogen took a step back and beamed. She likes to fix things.

* * *

After that, the dance began.

I do remember seeing Father offer his hand to Mother and, when she took it, waltzing with her quietly for a moment.

I remember seeing Pelagia and Mr. Dar-Healey sitting side by side, sometimes talking incessantly, sometimes very quiet.

I remember people gathering around—me and Arlo included—wanting to eavesdrop, and Mr. Dar-Healey told us all how, when his little girl vanished—drowned, he'd believed—he had gone back to the nearby town of Spindrift and spent months there, wandering the streets, lost. He'd met a fortune-teller in the square—an old man named Snatty-Ra-Ra—who had told him that his shattered heart would heal if he found a job as a teacher in a boarding school in a faraway Kingdom. "There are mountains there," the fortune-teller had said. "And these mountains are crowded with Elves and Crystal Faeries."

So Mr. Dar-Healey had decided to apply for a teaching position at Katherine Valley Boarding School, and, over the years, his heart *had* healed in a way. He had learned to be happy again from the pleasure of teaching.

"But now," he said, "I wonder if Snatty-Ra-Ra meant *this*."

"Of course he did!" we all agreed.

Then Pelagia began telling stories, in her old, dramatic way. Only this time, I realized, she was sharing *true* adventures. Stories of deepest, darkest ocean, of soft coral and sponge gardens, giant clams, leaf-shaped baby eels, fish like circles of slimy mud, viperfish, hatchetfish, a fish the length of a football field that trailed a chain of stinging nettles.

Pelagia's eyes shone, and so did the eyes of her listeners: we were all transfixed, none more than Mr. Dar-Healey himself, who kept wiping away tears, laughing as he did. At the end of one particularly harrowing story, he offered to give Pelagia a hug. She accepted.

The dance began again.

Arlo and I were dancing steadily when Stefan and Dot Pecorino swished by us.

"Great speech," Stefan told me.

Dot nodded in agreement.

They danced away.

The next time they passed us, Stefan spoke again: "Great detective work."

Again, Dot nodded, and again they danced away.

"But one thing," he said, the next time.

And danced away.

Finally, he told me something extraordinary. I was so surprised and pleased I flung my hands into the air—

—and Arlo reached out, very seriously, returning my hands to the correct position for the dance.

Arlo, I realized, sleepy with surprise, is a great dancer.

But I suppose I was exhausted because, soon after this, when my eyelids drooped and my feet scraped the floor, Arlo sighed, lifted me up in his arms, and called, "Somebody take Esther to bed?"

CHAPTER 150

I DREAMED AGAIN that night.

The rock shaped like a turtle. Trees. A picnic blanket.

At first, I was annoyed because I was sure this dream was finished now!

Then I realized it was a different dream.

I was seated somewhere high, on a cliff top, looking down at the turtle-rock, the trees, and the blanket.

A woman sat very neatly on the blanket, her satchel lying beside her, hands clasped in her lap. Perfectly still.

She's so tiny, I thought, astonished, and I began to cry.

I cried so much I woke myself up.

I was sleeping back in my dormitory that night, but my sisters had insisted on taking the beds on either side of me. They'd thrown out the twins and shifted Autumn one along. They can be bossy.

Both sisters sat up and whispered, "What's wrong?"

I told them I'd dreamed that our mother was sitting on a picnic blanket.

"From the cliff where I was," I explained, "she looked tiny."

My sisters were quiet in the dark, sleeping room.

After a moment, Imogen said, "You know I don't remember our mother ever once saying sorry about anything?"

Astrid and I both murmured, "I know."

"Everyone makes mistakes," Imogen said slowly. "The important thing is being able to admit it and say sorry. I mean, Father wasn't paying attention when we were on the shadow train, remember? Then he apologized and started paying attention.

That's what parents are supposed to do. You can apologize too, Esther. Remember when you sent us an apology note on the poker tour?"

"You two can too," I pointed out. "I mean, sometimes."

"Thank you," they both whispered.

"So what I'm realizing," Imogen continued, "is that you're more grown-up than Mother. She was *small* in your dream because she *is* much smaller than you." Imogen spoke faster, as her thoughts grew. "She made a huge, terrible mistake when you were little, so huge she couldn't even look at it. But that meant she couldn't really look at *us* anymore—especially not you, Esther—not properly anyway. She can't even see *herself* because it's like she's had to make herself teeny tiny and hide herself away."

Another long quiet.

"No wonder I can't beat her at poker," Astrid said softly.

"And no wonder she didn't fall under Mrs. Pollock's spell," I added.

Imogen sat up suddenly, clutching her pillow, and spoke to me fiercely: "But that doesn't mean you have to feel sorry for her, Esther. You should be angry! Astrid and I are *furious!*"

A curious calm fell over me. I *was* angry with Mother, but knowing my sisters were also angry seemed to lift some of my anger away.

Astrid yawned. "Maybe one day she'll be able to look at what she did properly, and think about it," she said.

"And then she might be able to see us properly," Imogen put in, "and start being our mother."

"It *was* brave of her to ride alone into the shadow realm to collect you," Astrid murmured sleepily. "And to stand up to Mrs. Pollock tonight."

Quiet, sleepy breathing.

"Even though Mrs. Pollock tried to crush my spirit," I whispered, "I think I know why I could still become a Rain Weaver."

"Why?" they both whispered.

"Because I have you two."
I could hear my sisters smiling in the darkness.
"But don't let it go to your head," I added.
And we all fell asleep.

EPILOGUE

SIX WEEKS LATER

During the last six weeks, Mrs. Pollock has been arrested, tried, and found guilty of Aiding and Abetting an Ocean Fiend, Unlawful Shadow Hypnosis, and Conspiracy to Drown the Kingdoms and Empires.

A new teacher named Professor Harvey is teaching Grade 6. He chuckles deep into his bushy gray beard, but his jokes are never at other people's expense. Also, he has rearranged the classroom so we don't have graded tables.

The first time we had a mathematics test, he handed mine back with a large red B+.

I burst into tears of happiness.

Embarrassing.

Nobody took any notice though, as *everybody* has been crying lately. Principal Hortense says it's delayed shock about having been tricked by a nasty Ogre teacher, and "all of that nonsense with the Fiend." She weeps quite openly herself, during most meals.

In my spare time, I've been writing this book, mostly in the school library, and lately in train compartments, ship cabins, and hotel rooms.

Guess why that is?

I am taking a journey around the Kingdoms and Empires! My sisters are accompanying me and so is my cousin Bronte Mettlestone.

Guess where we are staying right now?

You never will.

It's the Royal Palace in Cloudburst in the Kingdom of Storms!

Alejandro ran down the palace steps to meet us when we arrived, exclaiming, "Finally! The Mettlestone-Staranise girls! I invited you to the welcome party but it was washed away before I got to see you!"

So he *had* remembered us! We are very pleased about this.

He has a beautiful smile, Alejandro, and he's very interested that I'm writing this book.

"There is one thing that I do not understand," he said. "You have called it *The Stolen Prince of Cloudburst*, yes?"

"Yes."

"This is wrong. This is *your* story, not mine."

He thinks I should call it *Esther, the Rain Weaver* instead. Which is kind of him.

But I won't change it—or only a very little. His idea would give away the ending.

* * *

You may be wondering why we are on this journey.

Well, remember when Stefan told me something "extraordinary" at the dance, so I flung my hands into the air? This is what it was. He'd been reading more about Weavers, and had learned that a Weaver is actually the original form of both a Spellbinder and a Faery.

"Therefore," Stefan concluded, "you've got the power to heal, as Faeries have, *plus* the power to bind shadow magic, as Spellbinders have. Which means you have a particular kind of healing power. You can heal people of shadow magic spells. Like stolen laughter."

This turned out to be true.

And that is why we have been journeying—we're visiting Faery treatment centers and hospitals all over the Kingdoms and Empires, and I'm curing people.

Father says it's important to be tourists too, and visit galleries and museums, but we've interpreted that to mean we should visit beaches, cinemas, and arcades. That's our kind of tourism, Imogen says.

It's been a lot of fun.

The greatest fun though is this: Katya's face, and the faces of all the other people I've met in the treatment centers when I raise my hands and wash away the shadows. Their faces light up like sunshine, and their laughter—cautious at first, then building into joy and music—is exactly like the summer rain.

* * *

One final thing.

When we arrived here at the Cloudburst Palace, a package from my mother was waiting for me.

This is what the cover note said:

Dear Esther,

I hope you & your sisters are having a lovely time.

Listen, after I left you behind on the picnic blanket that night, I knew I was a terrible, terrible parent. I decided to leave most of the parenting to your father, and concentrate on my work. So I was a terrible parent that one time, and then I just carried on being terrible! I see that now! I thought I was doing the right thing for you, but I owe apologies to all three of you!

I know you may never forgive me—

But, Esther, I'm sorry.

So very sorry.

See you soon, I hope.

Love,
Your Mother

Enclosed in the package was a copy of the new G. A. Thunderstrike book.

I burst into tears. I'm not sure if that was to do with the letter or the book.

"It's not a bad letter," Imogen conceded when she read it.

"Imagine her knowing who your favorite author is," Astrid added.

I will write a reply tomorrow.

In my reply, I'll tell Mother that I realized something important as I fell asleep last night. Here's what it was.

The voice that I heard in my head when everyone was drowning, and I was still too frightened to speak the ancient words?

The voice that made it possible for me to speak those words?

It was the voice that had taught me to play poker, to swim, to kickbox, to tie my shoelaces, to thread a needle, to squeeze the lemons for a jug of lemonade.

Esther, you can do it!

A little impatient and cranky, but perfectly sure that I could.

ACKNOWLEDGMENTS

I am delighted and honoured to be published by Levine Querido. Thank you so much for the extraordinary, wise, warm, patient, and insightful publishing and editorial work of Arthur Levine and Meghan Maria McCullough; Susan Brown's copyediting and Mandi Andrejka's proofreading prowess; to Antonio Cerna and Alex Hernandez for their marketing and publicity masterminding; and to Leslie Cohen and Freesia Blizard for their production exellency. Thank you also to my excellent Australian and UK publishers, Allen & Unwin and Guppy Books respectively; to Jim Tierney for a cover and initial caps that make my heart sing and turn cartwheels and to Paul Kepple for interiors that make me feel just the same; to my brilliant agents, Jill Grinberg and Tara Wynne; to early readers of this manuscript, including Nicola, Steve, Liane, Nigel, Maddie, and Piper; to Maria, Deborah, and Rebecca at Coco Chocolate; to my beautiful sisters and Mum; all my excellent friends (with special mention to Rachel, for the ice cream and pizza, and to Corrie, for parkour, cake, and poetry); and to my very fine boys, Charlie and Nigel. And remembering Dad with love.

Some Notes on This Book's Production

The art for the jacket and the title lettering were hand-drawn by Jim Tierney using a Cintiq tablet and Adobe Photoshop. The text was set by Westchester Publishing Services in Danbury, CT. The body text is set in Gazette, designed in 1977 at D. Stempel AG, a type foundry in Frankfurt founded by David Stempel in 1895. The Gazette font family was designed to with newspaper print in mind, to withstand high-speed presses and coarse newsprint and to guarantee legibility despite long press runs. The display is set in Elan ITC, designed by Albert Boton, characterized by small serifs and even line weights. The initial caps are set in Rough Cut, a sturdy, gothic font designed by Simon Walker, and the illustrated framings for each initial cap were created by Jim Tierney. The book was printed on 78 gsm Yunshidai Ivory uncoated woodfree FSC™-certified paper and bound in China.

Production was supervised by Leslie Cohen and Freesia Blizard

Book jacket, case, and interior initial caps designed
by Jim Tierney

Book interiors designed by Paul Kepple at Headcase Design

Edited by Arthur A. Levine

LQ
LEVINE QUERIDO